Shift

Southern Werewolves
Book One

Heather MacKinnon

Shift

Copyright © 2018 by Heather MacKinnon

Cover: SelfPubBookCovers.com/Ravenborn

All Rights are Reserved. No part of this book may be used or reproduced in any manner whatsoever without written permission, except in the case of brief quotations embodied in critical articles and reviews.

This is a work of fiction. Names, characters, businesses, places, events, and incidents are either the products of the author's imagination or used in a fictitious manner. Any resemblance to actual persons, living or dead, actual events, or organizations is entirely coincidental.

Table of Contents

Chapter 1 5
Chapter 2 12
Chapter 3 19
Chapter 4 27
Chapter 5 36
Chapter 6 44
Chapter 7 53
Chapter 8 60
Chapter 9 68
Chapter 10 75
Chapter 11 83
Chapter 12 92
Chapter 13 100
Chapter 14 107
Chapter 15 116
Chapter 16 122
Chapter 17 129
Chapter 18 136
Chapter 19 143
Chapter 20 151
Chapter 21 159
Chapter 22 166
Chapter 23 173
Chapter 24 180
Chapter 25 187
Chapter 26 194
Chapter 27 202
Chapter 28 209
Chapter 29 217
Chapter 30 225
Chapter 31 233
Chapter 32 241
Chapter 33 249
Chapter 34 257
Chapter 35 265

Chapter 36 272
Chapter 37 279
Chapter 38 286
Chapter 39 293
Chapter 40 300
Chapter 41 307
Chapter 42 314
Chapter 43 322
Chapter 44 330

Chapter 1

"We, the people, find the defendant: not guilty."

Yes.

The courtroom erupted with sound. Some in celebration, some in denial, but I sat there quietly.

This was my first case as lead attorney, and I'd knocked it out of the park. The jury had only deliberated for an hour before they'd returned with their decision. The only decision I'd left them with, after the words I wove, and the evidence I'd pranced before their eyes. Since the first day of this trial, I knew they'd be putty in my hands.

My lips pulled into a small, tight grin as the judge called for order. She dismissed the case with a bang of her gavel, and my lips stretched into a full smile.

I did it.

I packed my things in my brown leather briefcase and stood to face my colleagues.

"Nice work, Montgomery," John Walsh said as he extended a hand for me to shake. The brittle smile on his face belied his sincerity.

"It was a team effort, John," I lied.

He'd been expecting me to fail, like most of the other men I worked with as junior associates at our law firm. I'd had to work harder, stay later, and take on more cases to get exactly where that half-wit was standing.

But it had all paid off.

The other lawyers on the case offered their own brand of insincere platitudes and half-hearted handshakes, and I took them all with a smile. Just like the good southern girl I was.

When I got to the end of the line of lawyers, my defendant was standing there seemingly lost in thought. I cleared my throat, and his dark brown eyes snapped to mine.

"You did it," he said softly.

My smile returned. I wanted to pump my fist, and make a celebratory lap around the courtroom, but instead, simply nodded.

"I did." I was sick of sharing the win with the other attorneys. *I'd* done the research. *I'd* done the interviews and fact checking. *I'd* been putting in the overtime for the past few months, and damn it, *I* would take the credit.

"I don't know how I can ever thank you. You saved my life."

His words hit me hard, but I recovered quickly. That I'd had such a huge positive effect on this man's life humbled me.

"I did my job and made sure you weren't convicted of something you didn't do. It's so tragic that your wife took her own life, but it would have been made worse if you'd gone to prison over it. I'm just glad it all turned out the way we'd hoped." *The way I'd planned all along.*

Without warning, Henry launched his short, pudgy frame at me, and wrapped his stubby arms around my waist. I'd never been comfortable with displays of affection, and this was no different. My face burned with what I'm sure was a fierce blush as I awkwardly patted his back.

"There, there," I muttered, hoping I'd placated him enough to get off me.

Henry pulled back with a sniffle, and I pretended to not see the wetness in his eyes.

"It was nice working with you, Henry. Hopefully, our paths won't cross again professionally." My attempt at dry humor did its job, and Henry's face cracked into a small smile.

"Yeah, no offense lady, but I hope so too."

I gave him another smile and a nod before making my way out of the courtroom, and into the warm North Carolina day.

It was only May, but the air was humid, and the sun was hot. I slipped my suit jacket off my shoulders and folded it over my arm as I made my way to my car.

I zipped across town, making good time in the light midday traffic. When I got to my office building, I rushed inside and over to my cubicle. If I could get out of here in the next thirty minutes, I could make it to my apartment, and be on the road before rush hour.

"Heard about your win, Montgomery. Nice work."

I froze at the voice behind me but didn't turn.

"Thanks, Ben."

"So, are you free Saturday night? There's this new French Bistro that just opened downtown, and I thought you could accompany me."

My eyes squeezed closed, and I took a steadying breath before facing him. "Sorry Ben, but I have plans."

His eyes narrowed, and his lips tightened. "Is that right?"

"Afraid so. I've rented a cabin out in Asheville. I'll be away all weekend."

"Who are you going with?" His voice had a touch of belligerence.

I straightened my spine and sent him a withering look. "Nobody. This is a solo trip. Now if you'll excuse me, I need to get on the road."

Ben was one of those guys that thought since I was single, I was fair game. I was not. I didn't have time to date, and if I did, it wouldn't be with someone who gave me the creeps like Ben did.

I swiped the rest of what I thought I'd need into my briefcase and stood. Ben still hadn't moved from his spot, so I had to walk around him to leave my cubicle.

My brisk pace took me through the office, and as I reached out a finger to call an elevator, I heard my name being bellowed from the corner office on my right. I slowly retracted my pointer finger and curled it into a fist. With a deep breath, I spun around, and made my way to where my name had been called.

Mr. Hildebrandt was a hefty old man with only small tufts of white hair left on his shiny head and liver spots on his hands. He looked up when I walked in, and a rare smile graced his withered face.

"Good work on the Walker case, Montgomery. That's what we like to see around here."

I nodded. "Thanks, Mr. Hildebrandt."

"I know you're heading out for the long weekend, but I expect you in my office Tuesday morning for an important meeting. Eight AM sharp, got it?"

My palms began to sweat, and my stomach erupted in butterflies. This was it, I would finally make senior associate.

I nodded again. "I'll be here."

"Good, good. Now get out of here. Have a good weekend, Ms. Montgomery."

He'd put the "Ms." in front of my name. That was a good sign.

"Thanks Mr. Hildebrandt, you too."

I closed his office door before practically sprinting to the elevators. I needed to get out of here before someone else called my name or needed something from me.

When I finally stepped back into the bright Carolina sunlight, I let my lips stretch into what felt like the first genuine smile all day. With the windows down, and my music blaring, I drove the fifteen minutes to my apartment on the other side of Raleigh.

The dash clock showed I had about half an hour to get changed, take care of Charlie, and get out of the city before hitting rush hour. I was up the stairs, and in the cool darkness of my apartment in record time.

My briefcase was abandoned at the door as I called out, "Where's my handsome man?"

The black and brown striped tabby cat poked his head out of a bright purple flower-shaped cat tree in the corner. He let loose a joyful *meow* before stepping onto a giant furry petal and leaping to the floor. Charlie came barreling toward me, smashing into my shins when he couldn't stop himself in time on the smooth hardwood floor.

I picked him up and scratched his head as I walked toward my bedroom in the back of the apartment. "Boy, I swear, you are the clumsiest cat I've ever met." He responded by rubbing his furry face against my jaw.

"Now while I'm away, I'm countin' on you to watch this place, all right?"

I walked through the multi-colored strings of beads that hung in the hallway, and into my bedroom. He leapt out of my arms, and onto the rainbow zebra-striped bedspread, making himself comfortable in the center of my pillow.

"I'll only be gone three nights, but I have this nice lady comin' by every day to check on you. So, you'll have to get along with her, Charlie."

Turning to my white and turquoise painted dresser, I took off my everyday formal clothes, and traded them for a white polo shirt and khaki colored capris. I tugged on a pair of sneakers and faced Charlie.

"I know how you feel about strangers, boy, but this lady's your meal ticket for the next few days. It would be in your best interest to make friends." With a glance towards the feline, I saw that I was being ignored, and let out a sigh.

"Don't say I didn't warn ya."

My bag was packed, so I shooed Charlie off the bed and out of my room, closing the door behind me. In the kitchen, I made sure he had enough food and water for the day and took a quick look around the apartment. Everything looked neat, and tidy, and colorful, and interesting. Just the way I like it.

"All right Bubba, I'm leavin'."

Charlie rubbed the length of his body against my leg, and I relented by giving him one more head scratch. With my apartment locked up tight, I got back in the car, and pulled up my GPS app. As I typed in the address of the cabin I'd rented, I was interrupted by an incoming phone call. I recognized the area code as being from North Carolina, but not local.

"Hello?"

"Hi, Elizabeth Montgomery? It's Mabel, with the house rental."

"Ah, yes, of course. I was just heading your way now."

"Oh, perfect! I'm fixin' to head over there and drop off the key. It'll be in the box on the doorknob. We could leave the key there all the time, but sometimes we go weeks without a renter, and I just don't like the thought of leavin' the key just sittin' there. I know you need the code to open the box, but they got all kinds of gadgets these days to steal just about anything, don't they? I don't trust it. Besides, I can take a look around while I'm there, and make sure nothin's gone wrong. Most of the folks we get are good people, but there's always a rotten one in the bunch every now and again. Ya' know, one time we had a man leave a bunch of needles in the kitchen trash?" She sounded scandalized.

"Maybe he was a diabetic?" I offered.

"Ya' know what, honey? That could be true. The man *did* look...well fed. Ya' know, I had a girlfriend who had a diabetes spell, and it took her foot! Poor thing's hobblin' around now—"

"Ma'am? What did you say the code was? I want to write it down." I knew she hadn't offered it yet, but I needed to get her to stop talking without being rude. There was no surer way to make an enemy in the south than by forgetting your manners.

"Oh, sure, baby. You ready now?"

I rolled my eyes but smiled. "Sure, ma'am, I'm ready."

"It's 0-8-1-3-8-7. Ya' got that, now?"

"Yes, ma'am. I got it."

"Okay, sweetie. You need anything, you call me, ya' got it?"

"Yes, ma'am, I got it," I repeated. In situations like this, it paid to keep it simple. Taciturn.

"Okay, honey, take care. I'll talk to ya' later."

"All right, thanks, you too," I responded and quickly ended the call.

Dang that woman could talk.

I typed in the address and headed toward the highway while the directions finished loading. I had a three hour and forty-three-minute drive ahead of me. At a red light, I plugged the aux cord into my phone, and selected the new Nicholas Sparks novel I was listening to.

The narration sounded through the speakers, and I dug out my sunglasses with a smile. This long-fought-for weekend away was just what I needed. The pressure to work harder, be smarter, stay longer than all my male counterparts wore on me. I didn't let it show, but I felt what the stress was doing to me.

I'd lost a few unnecessary pounds for that reason. Between working through lunch and being so tired after work I sometimes fall asleep before dinner, it was no wonder my clothes were loose. I'd always relished being a curvy girl, and unlike most women, wasn't happy losing those few pounds. Even my honey blonde hair was looking duller.

This weekend I'd promised myself no work, and I think that's exactly what I needed right now. A few days to read, nap, hike, and take pictures. All the things I used to love doing before work consumed my life.

    Wish I'd known then how much I should have appreciated my blissfully simple life. Wish I could have somehow prepared myself for how this weekend would change everything.

Chapter 2

The steep, unpaved road seemed to go on forever, before I pulled up to the small wooden cabin I'd be spending the weekend in. I lowered the volume on the audiobook as I rolled to a stop, the incessant crunching of the gravel finally silent. With the windows down, I could hear birds chirping, and leaves rustling, and not much else. No highway noises or loud planes overhead. It was heaven.

The cabin's covered front porch had two old rocking chairs, and a set of wind chimes that tinkled with the light breeze. Beyond the porch was a teal colored front door flanked by two large bay windows. The trees surrounding the small home were full of bright green leaves; the ground coated with a thick blanket of old pine needles. The breeze brought the rich scent of the forest with it, and I inhaled with a satisfied smile.

I grabbed my things, and made my way to the front door, finding the lockbox on the door handle as Mabel had promised. With a wry smile, I spun the dials, and removed the key from its depths.

Once inside, I found the downstairs was one large room, with a kitchen area off to the side opposite the living room. A beat up, but comfortable looking sofa sat in front of a fireplace of interlocking river rocks. A polished, wooden staircase led to the loft above.

The bedroom upstairs wasn't large, but plenty big enough for me. A queen-sized bed with crisp white sheets, and a mountain of pillows dominated the center of the space. Behind it was a wall of windows, the view breathtaking. The Blue Ridge Mountains rose in the distance, the navy, cobalt, and cerulean peaks stretching toward the clear sky above.

I was dying for a good hike, so I dug out my camera, looping the strap around my neck, and tucked my phone in my back pocket.

It almost immediately chirped, and I begrudgingly pulled it out. The office was calling.

"Hell no," I muttered.

When the call went to voicemail, I turned it off, and stuffed it back in my pocket.

"Outta' sight, outta' mind," I proclaimed to the dense forest ahead of me.

After just a few minutes of walking, I took a look over my shoulder. The cabin was completely obscured by the thick trees. Thankfully there was only one trail, and it would be easy enough to follow back when I was done.

A bright yellow bird flew overhead and landed on a branch nearby. I quietly picked up my camera and snapped a picture. The lighting was too dim this deep in the woods, and the bird's bright colors weren't showing up like I wanted them to. I turned the flash on, and tried to take another shot, but the bird was gone. In its place was a large black raven. Some think they're bad omens, but I don't believe in superstitions, so I took its picture too.

I lost track of time as I walked along the trail, admiring the flora, and taking pictures of anything I found interesting. It wasn't until I stumbled upon a small blooming meadow at the end of the trail that I realized how late it had gotten. The sun was falling behind the tall trees, and I knew it was time for me to get back before I got stuck out here in the dark.

I turned around to head back the way I'd come, when the unmistakable snapping of a branch sounded from nearby. Whipping back around, I scanned the meadow, and tree line around it, but saw no movement. With a shrug, I took off back down the trail.

A few short minutes later, the sun had fallen faster than I'd anticipated, and with the heavy canopy above, it had become darker than I was comfortable with. Thankfully, I could still make out the trail, and decided to pick up my pace. Soon, I was lightly jogging, narrowly avoiding tree roots, and pointy rocks that threatened to trip me.

A soft thud came from behind, and I once again spun around to scan the dark woods. Something shiny caught my attention, and I bent down to pick up the phone that must have fallen out of my pocket.

"Whew! That woulda' been bad if I'd lost you out here."

I dusted off the phone and stuck it in my front pocket this time, so I'd be able to feel if it fell out again.

Another branch snapped behind me.

Knowing it would be useless to try to find the source of the noise with the encroaching darkness, I ignored it, and took off again toward the cabin.

I'd gone only a few feet before I heard a low rumbling growl from behind me. My feet froze in place, my heart thudding in my chest. Maybe if I stayed really still, and quiet, whatever it was would just walk away? I clenched my fists and did my best to slow my harsh breathing.

After a few moments, I could tell the sound was getting closer, and I inched my way down the trail again. Before long there was more crunching behind me, along with the heavy thump of footsteps. I spun around, but nothing was there. After a few minutes of scanning the area, and finding nothing, I gave up.

"Well, this was stupid, Elizabeth," I chastised myself. "It's probably a harmless deer, and I'm standing here like an idiot," I huffed before turning toward the cabin again.

The snapping twigs seemed to follow me through the woods as I walked as quickly as I dared in the darkness. I didn't think it was common for deer to follow humans, but I wasn't an expert by any means. Pushing those thoughts from my head, I concentrated on putting one foot in front of the other.

When the deep, menacing growl came again, I stopped in my tracks. Adrenaline pumped furiously through my veins, my chest rising and falling with my rapid breaths. Wracking my brain, I tried to identify what was following me. Were there mountain lions in this part of the state? Bears perhaps?

Maybe it was a human? Humans could growl too, right?

"Hello?" I called.

No answer.

Shit.

I listened closely, but heard nothing more, so I turned toward where I remembered the trail being and took off running. Darkness completely obscured the path by now, but I was beyond caring.

Branches scraped along my exposed skin and tugged at my clothing while tree roots made the path treacherous. Finally, one of the roots caught the toe of my sneaker, and I fell forward onto the forest floor, my forehead smashing into something hard.

"Holy friggen' ouch," I panted as I tried to regain my bearings.

A soft tickling sensation made me swipe at something on my forehead.

When I brought my hand close to my face, I could see the crimson staining my fingers.

"Okay, no big deal, Elizabeth. Nothing some bacitracin and a bandage can't fix."

I rolled over on the damp ground and tried to catch my breath. The wound on my head continued to bleed freely, dripping into my eyes, and running down the side of my face, blurring my vision. With a grunt, I pulled myself into a sitting position, and surveyed my surroundings.

Trees. All I could see were trees.

"This is no good," I whispered.

Terror spiked in my veins once more when another deep growl came from close by. I scanned the darkness, but that only made things worse as every shadow became sinister.

Finally, a large, dark mass pulled away from the others, its shape solidifying. My breath caught as it stalked close enough I could make out its features.

Only, I almost wish I hadn't.

It was a wolf.

A humongous wolf.

And there I was, bleeding, on the forest floor as a giant carnivore headed my way.

I was so screwed.

With shaky movements, I climbed to my feet. A surge of inspiration hit me, and I raised my arms high in the air, yelling as loud as I could.

"HEY! GET OUT OF HERE!" I bellowed. I'd read somewhere that if you made yourself appear bigger and meaner, that you could sometimes scare off a predator.

That tactic was *not* working.

The wolf made a coughing noise that almost sounded like a raspy chuckle as it continued to stalk toward me. Its creepy eyes locked onto the blood still streaking down my face. The beast licked its chops, razor sharp teeth dripping with saliva, and I swear, its eyes gleamed with hunger.

Unfortunately, I was the only thing on the menu.

I frantically scanned through all my options and found them bleak. How was I going to get myself out of this? I had no weapons, I could barely see where I was going, and I'd gotten turned around at some point. Things were not looking good for me.

The wolf stopped advancing only a few feet away, and just stood there. My chest heaved as I struggled to calm my breathing. This reminded me I still had my camera around my neck, and a plan formed in my head. Maybe not a good plan, but it was the best I could do under the circumstances.

With slow movements, I grasped the device, letting my pointer finger hover over the shutter button. The wolf bared its teeth, almost as if it was grinning at me, and crouched down, preparing to launch in my direction.

I pressed the button on the camera. The click of the shutter sounded like a gunshot in the quiet woods, and the bright light of the flash momentarily lit up the night. Although the light affected me as well, it seemed to have stunned the wolf for a moment, and I took that opportunity to wheel around, and sprint away.

I ducked and weaved through the trees, hoping to at least make it harder for the wolf to catch me. Maybe it would see me as too much trouble and give up. Or maybe, I just provided it with a fun game of tag.

My breaths were wheezing out of me by now, and my muscles were burning. If I got out of this alive, I promised myself I'd get back into the gym.

With no sounds of pursuit, I figured the wolf had given up, and my only obstacle now would be finding my way back to the cabin in these unfamiliar woods. I slowed my pace to get a look at my surroundings but couldn't see much as blood was still dripping into my eyes, making them sting, and blinding me.

The woods were silent except for the pounding of my frantic heart. I did my best to put one foot in front of the other. My eyes on the ground, watching for anything that might slow me down.

No sound preceded the attack.

Blazing hot pain engulfed my calf, wrenching a scream from deep in my chest. I fell once again to the ground with the wolf's teeth clamped around my leg.

It snarled as it shook its head violently from side to side. Unbelievably, the pain doubled, radiating up my leg, and causing me to cry out again.

"Stop! Stop! Get off me!"

A mixture of tears and blood burned my eyes, and I squeezed them tightly shut. Using what little strength I had left, I tried to jerk my leg out of the beast's impossibly strong jaw but made no progress. When that didn't work, I resorted to beating at the creature's head with my fists and scratching at its eyes with my short nails.

The wolf didn't like that and chomped down harder. I knew it had to be close to the bone at this point. Could it bite my leg off? I wouldn't put it past the giant beast.

Suddenly, the wolf released my leg, and trotted away, its shape melting into the shadows. I didn't wait to find out where it had gone, or if it was gone for good. With a whimper, I rolled onto my stomach, and dragged myself forward, my sorry, mangled leg following limply behind me. The pain seemed to get more severe as time went on. It wouldn't be long before it crippled me completely.

Without warning, two large, strong hands gripped my hips from behind, and dragged me backward. I screamed and flailed against them, but it made no difference.

"There's no use fighting, princess," a deep man's voice whispered from behind me, echoing my fears.

Where the *hell* had this guy come from? Was the wolf his pet or something? They'd pulled the old "bait and switch" on me, and my head was spinning.

I kicked and thrashed, twisting and turning as I struggled to get away. What did he want with me? Why was he in the middle of the woods at night? How had he found me out here?

"Let me go!" I grunted, my energy waning as the adrenaline petered out of my system.

His hands left my hips, and one of his thick, muscled arms wrapped around my neck. He flexed, and I made an involuntary choking sound. A satisfied chuckle danced across the back of my neck, sending a shiver down my spine. This man was evil. I could feel it. Practically taste it in the surrounding air.

It was painfully obvious I wouldn't make it out of these woods alive.

The best I could hope for was a quick death. Would anyone ever find my body? Would anyone figure out what happened? Or would my murder remain a mystery?

And who would lead the search? My loving parents? That was a joke. That would mean my father would have to pry himself from the golf course, and my mother would have to curb her gallon-a-day wine habit.

My body was running dangerously low on oxygen, and black spots, even darker than the night dotted the edges of my vision. My head felt lighter, and my ears rang with a steady white noise. I would lose consciousness soon and knew I wouldn't ever regain it.

A final tear leaked from my eye as a large emptiness settled in my chest. The fear and desolation I felt when I thought about dying out here was like a physical weight pressing on my lungs. Or maybe that was the poor organ screaming for the oxygen it'd been denied for too long now.

The last thought I had before the blackness claimed me, was I was leaving this world the same way I'd spent the past decade of my life–alone.

Chapter 3

A dull pain in my ribs broke through the blackness I'd succumbed to. Whatever was nudging my side was becoming more insistent. With a groan, I tried to bat it away with my hand, but when I felt the coarse fur and wet nose, the events of the night came rushing back.

With a gasp, I jerked back, and tried to wriggle away from the beast that had attacked me. The movement sent fiery agony shooting through my leg, but I refrained from crying out. I realized the pain in my side was the wolf's nose when it nudged me again, harder this time. The shove rolled me onto my back, and I got a look at my attacker.

Through the blood still streaming from my head and into my eyes, I saw the wolf had brilliant blue eyes instead of black.

Was this the same wolf?

It couldn't be. How could he have changed his eye color?

Maybe there was a whole pack of them.

The thought of trying to fight off a whole swarm of murderous wolves knotted my stomach and sent my heart racing.

I couldn't do this anymore.

I had no more fight left in me.

My body went limp on the damp forest floor.

"I give up," I told the wolf. My throat ached, and my voice was barely above a whisper. "I'm so tired and cold. I just want this to be over."

Silently, I said goodbye to all the dreams and goals I'd had. I said goodbye to Charlie–hopefully he'd get adopted by a good family. Angry tears gathered in my eyes as I thought about all the things I'd miss out on. Things I'd always told myself I'd have time for.

This wasn't *fair*!

The anger built like a pressure cooker until it boiled over. I glared at the gray wolf again, and found him sitting there, watching me with his head cocked to the side.

"What are you waiting for?! If you're going to eat me, just get it over with!" I rasped. My throat felt like I'd swallowed a box of razor blades, and I'd had enough.

The blue-eyed wolf continued to stare for another few moments, before he stood, and trotted off into the darkness.

"What? Are you going to retrieve your big human friend again?! Can't finish me off yourself?"

I wasn't sure why I was taunting the murderous carnivore, but I was beyond caring. If I was going to die, I'd do it kicking and screaming. With a cautious look at my mangled leg, I amended that to just screaming.

A loud crack sounded from where the wolf had disappeared to. Next there were a short series of softer snaps before the woods were quiet again. Strangely quiet.

Moments later, a large, naked man emerged from between the trees, his face shrouded in darkness. He walked slowly, and purposefully toward me. With a squeak, I struggled to crawl away from him, my brutalized leg screaming in agony. I don't know why he hadn't killed me the first time, but I wasn't sticking around to give him a second chance.

Like you have a choice, Elizabeth. You can't even stand.

Helplessness threatened to overtake me once again, but I fought it.

"What do you want?!" I screamed at the man, injuring my throat worse.

He was closer now, and I struggled to keep my eyes above his waist. I would *not* check out my attacker's junk. Not that there wasn't a ton to look at from there up because there was. Even in the dark, I could see his tanned, chiseled chest, and thick arms.

Was this Stockholm Syndrome? This wasn't the time or place to be fantasizing about my attacker.

When his deep voice broke the silence, I forced my eyes from his physique to his face.

"I won't hurt you," he said softly.

As he came closer, I could make out his facial features. He had a strong, clean shaven jaw, and thick, dark eyebrows above what looked like light-colored eyes.

Damn, my murderer is beautiful.

"You already did," I reminded him.

His head shook slowly. "I didn't, I promise. I just want to help."

The adrenaline was rapidly leaving my system. My throat felt raw, I had a pounding headache, and my leg was on fire. And I was wet? Had it rained? I smelled horrible.

The man was closer now, and I watched as he cautiously knelt next to me. With my last reserve of energy, I shuffled and squirmed as far away as I could. The movement sent sharp shooting pains up my leg, and I gasped in surprise. How was the pain still getting worse?!

"Shh shh shh," he soothed. "Take it easy, I don't want you to hurt yourself."

"*I* didn't hurt myself, *you* did," I hissed, my voice barely above a whisper.

"I promise, I won't hurt you."

His words sounded good, but how could I trust him? A naked man shows up in the middle of the woods right after I'd been attacked, and I was just supposed to take his word for it?

Not likely.

But what choice did I have?

"Where are your clothes?" I whispered harshly.

He smiled but declined to answer.

Weirdo.

"May I pick you up?"

The decision was coming dangerously close to not being mine to make anymore as my vision narrowed. The man leaned over me, a lock of his dark hair falling onto his forehead. Now that he was closer, I could clearly see the brilliant color of his eyes. His denim blue gaze met mine, and I felt their pull instantly. I watched as his expression changed from concern to surprise. He reached out a hand and gently swept some sticky hair off my face.

His eyes were tender when he asked, "What's your name?"

I searched his face frantically for the assurance I was looking for. Soon I'd be unconscious again, and at the mercy of this stranger. Could I trust him not to harm me? I didn't have much of a choice right now. Besides, there was a kindness in his eyes I couldn't ignore. After working as a criminal lawyer for so many years, I was adept at knowing the good ones from the bad ones.

"Elizabeth," I croaked. "Please, help me."

With that, I closed my eyes, and let my body go limp. It was too much work to stay awake when all I wanted to do was sleep. For a decade.

Gentle hands slid underneath my battered body and cradled me against his warm chest.

"I've got you, Elizabeth. I won't let anything hurt you ever again," he promised.

How he could make such a promise, I didn't know. But at that point, nothing mattered but the cool darkness of oblivion that beckoned.

Wakefulness returned slowly. I stretched my arms above my head with a groan. It felt like I'd slept for years.

I cracked one eye open and looked around the unfamiliar room. This was not my little two-bedroom back in Raleigh. In fact, my whole apartment could fit in this room. The walls were a deep green, and the furniture dark mahogany.

Memories of recent events swam to the front of my brain. I remembered winning my case and leaving work early. I'd driven out to the mountains for the weekend. But this wasn't the cabin I'd rented. That whole cabin could have probably fit in this room too.

So, where the hell am I?

I tried to swallow, but my parched throat ached. With another groan I pulled my sore body into a sitting position. My head spun, and throbbed, and I squeezed my eyes shut until the feeling lessened.

When I opened them again, I saw I was in a large canopy bed that had what looked like thick tree trunks as posts that branched outward to connect with each other. My eyes roved over the strange room until they caught sight of another person.

Familiar blue eyes met mine and widened in surprise. The woman they belonged to looked to be about my age, with elfin features, and lightly tanned skin. She sat up straight and held up one hand in a friendly wave.

"Hello," she said with a big smile.

Why did she look so familiar? I'm sure I'd never met her before.

"Hello?" I said, but it came out more like a question.

"How you feelin'?" she asked, true concern lacing her soft voice.

"Um…" I responded unintelligently. My eyes continued to scan the room I was in, frantically searching for answers.

I turned my attention to my body, and found it clad in a soft, white nightgown unlike anything I've ever owned. Where were my clothes? What was I doing here? Where was *here*?

My internal freak-out was interrupted by a door opening on the opposite side of the room. A cloud of steam billowed out of the room that must have been a bathroom. A tall, shirtless man appeared out of the fog, and stopped short in the doorway when his blue eyes met mine

Those eyes!

The events of the attack came rushing back all at once.

The wolf bite.

The strange man strangling me.

The second wolf finding me.

And this man, right in front of me, promising to keep me safe.

I whipped the covers off my legs. There was a thick bandage taped around much of my calf. I ran my fingers along the soft, white gauze. Who did this? Whoever it was, they clearly knew what they were doing when it came to first aid.

I looked back at the man, and then the woman. My eyes bounced between the two until I made the connection. That's why she looked so familiar. She looked just like the man who'd saved me in the woods.

Wait, was I saved?

Or was I captured?

"Who are you?" I finally voiced one of the thousands of questions running through my head.

The man stayed silent, his gaze fixed on my bare legs. My stomach knotted, and I quickly covered myself again. He seemed to snap out of the daze he'd been in and instead turned his intense eyes to the woman.

"Evey? What are you doing in here?"

The woman fidgeted in her seat and averted her eyes.

"I wanted to check on her," she said with a shrug.

The man sighed and ran a big hand down his face. "I told you to stay away for now." The irritation was evident in his voice, but surprisingly, a note of tenderness was there too. Who *was* this man?

"I *know* what you said Abey, but I was worried about her after the condition you brought her home in."

"I know you're concerned Evey, but I told you–"

"Hello? Could you stop talking about me like I'm not here? Who are you, and where am I?"

Both of their blue eyes locked on me, and I felt like a specimen underneath a microscope. My skin itched with their intense stares, and I worried the sheet between my fingers. No matter what I tried to concentrate on, my eyes were drawn to the man's. *Abey,* she'd called him. His eyes seared through mine and seemed to burrow into my soul. I felt bared before him despite how I'd covered myself.

Why was he getting to me like this?

"My name is Evelyn, but everybody calls me Evey," the woman said, interrupting my staring match with the man. "And that's my brother, Abraham," she added with a nod in the man's direction.

Abraham.

Finally, there was a name I could attach to the handsome man. My eyes left Evey's, once again drawn to Abraham. Upon closer inspection, I saw his thick, dark hair was wet, some strands sticking to the sides of his face. My gaze traveled lower, down his throat, and to his sculpted chest. As I watched, a single drop of water ran from between his pectoral muscles, following a trail down his torso, between his abs and disappeared at the waistband of the gray sweatpants he wore.

Abraham took a faltering step forward before he seemed to restrain himself. His hands tightened along with his jaw, and he swallowed, and closed his eyes. A second later, his denim blue eyes snapped open, and he stalked out the door to his right. It shut behind him and left the room in silence.

"Well, that was strange," Evey commented. "He's not very talkative, but he's usually much more polite than that."

I looked back and found her staring at the door Abraham had escaped through with a confused look. My eyes watched the door too, waiting (hoping) for Abraham to come back.

Get a grip, Montgomery.

"Abey said your name's Elizabeth?" Evey asked.

She looked remarkably like Abraham. Although there were many similarities, the main difference was all her softness compared to his hardness. Her features were small and delicate, but her hair and eyes were clearly a family trait.

"Yes. My name's Elizabeth." With another glance around the large room, I added, "How did I get here? Where *is* here anyway?"

Evey smiled. "Abraham brought you here. You're in our lodge near Asheville."

I let out a small sigh of relief. He hadn't taken me far at least.

"You and Abraham's lodge?"

A soft, tinkling laugh left her rosebud mouth. "Well, I guess technically it's Abraham's, but he shares it with all of us."

"*All* of you? How many are there?"

Evey's head tipped back as she tapped a dainty finger against her chin. "Let's see, there's us five, and then maybe another five or ten guards that live here full time? The rest of the pack live in their own houses on the property."

One word stuck out above the rest.

"Pack?" I asked incredulously.

Evey nodded her head slowly, her eyes serious and sad.

"Yes, pack."

I almost didn't want to ask, but knew I needed the answer.

"Pack of what, exactly?"

Evey's eyes searched my face, and she was silent for a minute.

With a sigh, she responded, "Pack of werewolves."

Chapter 4

Evey let out a wind-chime-laugh. "Catchin' flies?"

I picked my jaw up off my lap. "Beg pardon?"

She had to be joking.

Werewolves were *not* a thing.

Evey giggled again and rose gracefully to her feet. She couldn't have been more than 5'3".

"We're a pack of werewolves. Wanna see?"

Without warning, she reached for the hem of her shirt, and yanked it over her head. With her dark brown hair mussed, she stood there proud as a peacock in her lime green bra.

I shielded my eyes when she reached for the zipper of her jeans.

"Have you lost your mind?" I shrieked. "What are you doing? Keep your clothes on!"

Another giggle. "I gotta' take my clothes off before I shift if I don't wanna ruin 'em."

Dread churned in my stomach. Was this whole house insane? Who *were* these people?

"Shift?" I squeaked.

"Sure, silly. Into a werewolf."

My hand fell limp onto my lap.

This is insane.

There's no way this is real.

When Evey reached for her only remaining garment, her underwear, I turned my head the other way.

She giggled again. "You better get used to this."

"What does *that* mean?"

A loud *crack* filled the room, and I turned to Evey again. She'd crouched down on all fours, and I watched in equal parts horror and fascination as tufts of black-tipped gray fur sprouted from her smooth skin. She tipped her head back as her nose elongated and grew.

Bones shifted beneath her tan skin, and a few muffled snaps later, where

Evey once stood was now a very large wolf with dark blue eyes. I gasped, and scrambled backward on the bed, my heart racing.

For a moment I was back in the woods, broken and bleeding. I could almost feel the cold, wet leaves beneath me, feel the razor-sharp teeth tear into my skin.

I shook my head to clear those thoughts and centered myself in the here and now. This wolf has blue eyes-not black. This wolf hasn't tried to harm me. This wolf is apparently a werewolf. But if she's a werewolf, does that mean...

I lost that thought as the large carnivore came trotting over to the end of the bed. My back pressed against the headboard as I tried to get as far away from it, and its huge teeth, as possible. When it placed two big paws on the mattress, I finally got a good look.

The underside of the wolf was mostly white, with a similarly colored muzzle. Its back was covered in thick, coarse looking salt and pepper fur. As I watched, the animal cocked its head–big ears straight in the air, bright eyes focused on me.

Abraham came walking back in carrying a serving tray loaded with food and drinks, a small smile curving one corner of his lips. As soon as he saw the wolf standing there that smile vanished.

He set the tray down with a slam and turned to the beast with hands on his hips.

"Evelyn! What were you thinking?"

The wolf's ears flattened, and she let out a soft whine.

"Don't give me that. Look at her!" he demanded, thrusting an arm in my direction.

The wolf's big head swung my way, her eyes met mine as she let out a series of mournful yips.

Moments later, I watched incredulously as the fur receded into her skin. Her snout shrank, legs elongating, and stretching out. A minute or two later, there stood Evey, naked as the day she was born.

I averted my gaze again as Evey didn't seem to be in any hurry to cover up.

"What were you thinking?" Abraham repeated.

A soft sigh drifted through the room.

"I was just tryin' to show her I was tellin' the truth about werewolves." They were silent a moment.

"And what *truth* have you told her?" His voice was rougher than before.

"I just told her we're werewolves. Nothin' else," she answered quickly.

He responded with a long, masculine sigh. My skin tingled, and I *knew* he was looking at me. His gaze was like a physical caress. I fought off a shiver and kept my face resolutely turned away from the squabbling siblings.

"Can you at least put your clothes back on?" He tsked. "You're making Elizabeth uncomfortable."

My heart thumped an extra beat when he said my name.

Not the time, Montgomery.

"Sorry, Elizabeth," Evey said.

"It's okay," I replied automatically.

"No, really. That was stupid of me. You just found out werewolves were real and could probably have used some time to think that over before I shifted right in front of you."

Could I have used some time to process that information? Would it have mattered? Would *werewolves* have been an easier concept to swallow if I'd had time to think about it? Probably not. Truthfully, the idea is still pretty unbelievable.

But I *saw* it.

"You can turn around now."

Her soft voice broke through my endless questioning. I turned to see her clothed again, her face a picture of contrition.

"With all you've been through, I shouldn't have been so insensitive. Will you forgive me?"

I stared at her dumbfounded. I'm positive I'd never received such a sincere, and articulate apology. How could I not forgive her?

"Of course."

A brilliant smile lit up her face, and I mirrored her happiness. My eyes automatically sought Abraham's, and found him holding the tray again, his gaze fixed on me.

"Are you hungry? Thirsty?" He brought the tray over and slid it onto my lap. "I wasn't sure what you liked, so I brought a few different things."

A *few* was a gross understatement.

There were cups of water, juice, sweet tea, and soda next to dishes holding sandwiches, salads, pasta, and grilled chicken as well as three steaming bowls, each containing a different kind of soup.

"I wasn't sure what you liked," he repeated.

"Did *you* cook all that?" Evey asked incredulously.

Abraham narrowed his eyes at his sister. "Yes, I did."

"*All* by yourself?"

He let out a frustrated sigh. "Okay, I had help. But I *did* make most of it."

I tried to hide my smile behind the glass of sweet tea when Evey let out a satisfied guffaw.

"Thank you, Abraham."

His cerulean eyes found mine instantly. His lips tipped into a shy smile, and Evey gasped.

I looked back, but her laser gaze was not on me. She was looking at Abraham. Her eyes widened along with a megawatt grin, her face almost glowing with happiness.

"Oh, Abey!" She squealed.

"Evey! Can I see you in private for a moment?" Abraham didn't wait for an answer. He grabbed Evey's arm and dragged her out of the room.

The sudden silence was unnerving. But since when has being alone been weird for me? Maybe I had a head wound–

With a gasp, I slapped my hand over my forehead, harder than I'd meant to.

"Ow!" I yelped and rubbed my stinging skin.

Abraham abruptly opened the door and stuck his head in. "Everything all right?" His concern drew his dark brows together.

"How long have I been here?" I ignored his question.

He stepped through the doorway, and Evey peeked her head in after him.

"Since last night."

I'd been here a whole day?!

I pushed the tray away, and wrenched myself from the bed, gasping in pain when I put weight on my wounded leg. The room spun, and for a moment, I thought I might pass out again.

"Elizabeth?" Abraham's concerned voice rang out.

He took a step toward me, but I held up a hand in protest. I would get there under my own steam, or I wouldn't get there at all. I didn't need his help.

It took me a while, but I finally made it to the bathroom, and in front of the large vanity mirror. With shaking hands, I traced a butterfly bandage that partially covered an angry red line across my forehead. It didn't look as bad as I expected after smashing my face into the forest floor.

Upon further inspection, I realized I was also clean. My hair and skin held no reminders of my mad dash through the forest or my fight with the wolf/man duo.

A thought I should have had long before now popped into my head, and I met Abraham's eyes in the mirror. "Have you already called the police? We need to report my attack."

Abraham shook his head stiffly. "The police can't help."

I ran his words over and over through my mind until with sickening clarity, I finally understood. "It was a werewolf that attacked me, wasn't it?"

"We believe so," Abraham replied.

"But it wasn't you?"

He stiffened. "No. It was *not* me."

My mind was running at top speed as I rapidly made connections.

"You were the wolf with the blue eyes?"

Abraham relaxed slightly. "Yes."

"Then who attacked me?" I demanded.

He took a step forward but stopped dead in his tracks when I leveled him with a glare. His hands slowly rose in front of him.

"We don't know. We're working on it."

"How? How are you working on it? And who's 'we'? Are you working with the police?"

"No, I told you, the police can't help. My pack and I have been investigating this for a while now–"

"'A while'?" I interrupted. "As in, since a few hours ago when I was attacked?"

Abraham shook his head slowly, a lock of dark hair falling over one eye.

"No. 'A while' as in, since we found the first victim about a year ago."

First victim.

A year ago.

My heart stopped.

"How many?"

He knew exactly what I meant. "You were the fifth."

I staggered back, my behind hitting the granite countertop.

"He's attacked four other women? Where are they? Are they here too?"

Abraham's eyes turned hollow, and he shook his head again.

"No. They're all dead."

"And the police don't know about this?"

"The police know about the other murders, but they have even fewer leads than we do. We at least know it's a werewolf doing this."

My legs buckled, and only through sheer willpower did I remain standing. Four dead. I was supposed to be the fifth. I should be dead. Why wasn't I dead?

"How did I survive?"

"Calvin interrupted him."

"Who's Calvin? I only remember you," I admit.

"He's my cousin, and one of my pack enforcers. He took off after him, and I went to you."

I was quiet while processing all this. Someone had intervened when I thought I'd been all alone. Then Abraham showed up and brought me here. I looked in the mirror again and fingered my blonde hair.

"How did I get clean? Who dressed me? Whose nightgown is this?" I asked, pinching the white cotton material between two fingers.

His hands shot up again.

"It was Evey. I had her clean you up. You were filthy."

Heat rose in my cheeks, and I looked away. "Yeah, well, you try running for your life through the pitch-dark woods and see how you look at the end of it."

Abraham closed the distance between us and placed his large hands on my shoulders. I tensed at the contact, and he slowly released me. "It was more than that," he admitted. His electric blue eyes met mine in the mirror.

"What was?"

"You weren't just covered in dirt and leaves. You were also soaked in urine. We had to bathe you."

I whirled around to face him. "Covered in urine?!" I screeched.

His jaw ticked as he averted his angry gaze.

"It's how we knew it was the same guy. He marks all his victims."

I was shocked into silence. A rare occurrence for me.

"Come on. You're probably hungry and thirsty."

His supposition was correct, and as soon as he mentioned it, my stomach gurgled. A deep chuckle rumbled through his chest, and my breath caught in my throat. Damn that sound was appealing.

He followed me as I painfully made my way back to the bed, and once again placed the tray on my lap. I started out slow, but eventually ate everything on the tray.

I finally sat back, and rested against the headboard, my hand covering my full stomach. When I looked to the siblings, they were both staring at me.

"Still hungry?" Abraham asked, eliciting a bark of laughter from Evey.

My face heated, and I snatched my hand off my distended belly.

"Don't worry, we all eat like pigs around here," Evey reassured.

Or maybe she thought she was reassuring me. She wasn't.

"Thanks, Evey," I deadpanned.

Another laugh escaped her as she crawled onto the bed next to me. Personal space didn't seem to be something Evey was familiar with. "Anytime, babe."

I smiled begrudgingly. You couldn't stay mad at Evey.

"Really." I eyed both siblings seriously. "Thank you both for everything. You saved my life, patched me up, lent me your clothes, and even fed me. I'd be happy to pay for the clothes and accommodations if you'll let me."

Both of their mouths opened to respond, but they were interrupted with a soft knock at the door. Abraham groaned.

"Can we come in?" a female voice yelled.

"Would it matter if I said 'no'?" he muttered.

The door opened, and in walked two stunning women. One was tall and thin, with curly hair haphazardly thrown into a bun on the top of her head. The other was shorter, with wavy brown hair streaked with hot pink, and curves to spare.

"Nope. It wouldn't have mattered," the shorter one answered.

Had she heard him from out in the hall?

The two women's hopeful eyes bounced from Abraham to me and back again.

With a sigh, Abraham gestured to the tall woman, "Elizabeth, this is Callista," then the shorter one, "And Delilah."

I had that specimen-under-a-microscope feeling again.

"Hello."

"Hi," they replied in unison.

My eyes traveled from each new girl, to Evey, and back to Abraham.

"You're all related?"

Evey giggled next to me. "Yeah, those are our sisters."

"There's four of you?" As an only child, this concept was astonishing.

"Actually, we're quintuplets," Callista explained, her voice soft.

Quintuplets?!

I counted the people in the room.

"Where's the other one?"

Delilah cocked a hip, "Oh, Bea's around here somewhere. Don't worry, you'll get a chance to meet her too." It almost sounded like a threat.

I tried to stifle a yawn, but Abraham, always watching, saw right away.

"All right, ladies. Time to go. Elizabeth needs to rest."

Delila's mischievous eyes danced between me and Abraham. "Sure, Abey. We'll leave you two alone." She grabbed both Callista and Evey's arms and dragged them to the door.

Abraham let out a huge breath, and I couldn't help but laugh. His surprised eyes met mine, and he smiled a beautiful smile that made my heartbeat pound in my ears. Seconds passed as our eyes stayed locked, our smiles firmly in place, time standing still around us. Until another yawn escaped me. His brows dipped low, blue, blue eyes radiating concern.

"Get some sleep."

I nodded and scooted down until my head hit the pillow.

"Night, Abraham. Thank you," I muttered.

I was almost asleep when I heard his reply.

"Of course, Elizabeth. Anything."

Chapter 5

Bright sunlight gently roused me from my sleep. Unlike last time I woke up in this strange bed, this time I remembered exactly where I was.

In a house full of werewolves.

Only you, Elizabeth. Only you.

Because if there was trouble in a fifty-mile radius, it would inevitably find *me*. My sealed juvenile record could attest to that. I purposely led a boring, solitary lifestyle for that exact reason.

I'd been on vacation only a few *hours,* and already been attacked by a serial killer, and then rescued, and brought to a house full of werewolves.

Werewolves.

The rational part of me fought fiercely with what my eyes had *seen.* Evey, who'd seemed like an average woman, transformed into a wolf right in front of me. A lifetime of believing things like this only happened in books and movies was all wrong. Couldn't *be* more wrong.

I'd just met a whole family of them.

Elizabeth, Elizabeth. What have you gotten yourself into this time?

A soft snore came from across the room, and I jerked in surprise.

What is Abraham doing in here?

He was lying on a brown leather chaise against the far wall. One of his broad shoulders hung over the edge of the cushion, his bare feet jutting off the end. His normally expressive face was slack with sleep making him appear younger.

I had trouble forcing my eyes away from him. Every time I looked, I found something new to marvel at.

The dark hair covering his thick forearms.

A birthmark next to his right ear.

Tiny specks of stubble along his jaw and chin.

I could look at him all day, but I was feeling like a creep. What would he think if he woke up to find me sitting here drooling over him?

Not a good look, Montgomery.

Besides, he was a werewolf. Were we even the same species? When hazy images of his moonlit naked form crept into my head, I quickly shut down that train of thought. This was *not* the time to fantasize about a relationship with a mythical creature. And I wasn't looking for a relationship. Not now, and not any time soon.

I needed to get moving. Hopefully they won't mind if I took advantage of their hospitality a little further and had a quick shower before heading back to my cabin.

As quietly as possible, I swung my legs over the side of the bed and sat up. The room spun for a few seconds before I could see straight again. My temples throbbed with a slight headache, but I would manage.

With equal pressure on each leg, the wounded one hurt, but seemed a little better than last night. I took one half-shuffle forward and couldn't prevent the soft hiss that escaped my mouth when I put weight on my bad leg.

Abraham shot to his feet, and scanned the bedroom with quick, shrewd eyes. "What happened? What's the matter?"

Before I could answer, Abraham had assessed the room, and found the only threat to be my wounded leg. He frowned as he walked over.

"You look like you could use some help."

I straightened my spine and tipped my chin up.

"I don't need your help."

Abraham shook his head and grasped my arm.

"I didn't say you *needed* help, because I've already been informed that you don't." I met his cocky grin with a cool glare. He chuckled and continued. "I said 'you *could* use some help'. Which you definitely could. So just let it go and let me help you."

He didn't wait for an answer, just led me across the room.

With him helping to support my weight, I made it into the bathroom, and took a seat on the edge of the garden tub. I was out of breath, and desperate for him not to notice. His concerned frown told me I probably wasn't fooling him.

"Just wait a minute, I'll be right back," he tossed over his shoulder as he left the bathroom.

I turned on the faucets and propped my leg up on the edge of the tub so I could remove the bandage. When Abraham returned with a towel and a small pile of clothes, I was just peeling back the edge of the bandage. He emptied his hands and grabbed a washcloth from a cabinet on the wall.

"Wait a second," he said as he wet the cloth, and came to kneel in front of me.

I instinctively leaned back, my breath catching in my throat.

"I won't hurt you," he insisted.

He thought I was afraid of him.

I was.

Terrified.

But not in the way he thought.

I was terrified of how fascinating he was. Terrified of the way it felt like my life was spiraling out of control, and this man was the eye of the storm.

I wasn't afraid for my safety.

I was afraid for my peace of mind.

"I know you won't. You just startled me," I assured him. "What's the washcloth for?"

"It doesn't hurt as much if you wet the tape before you pull it off."

Abraham got to work pressing the damp terry cloth against my skin. When he was satisfied, he gently peeled the tape off, and removed the gauze.

The jagged puncture wounds dotted my skin like they'd been stamped there. They'd bled a little on the gauze but had scabbed over by now. It looked much better than the bloody pulp I'd been expecting.

"Did you do this?" I asked, gesturing to my leg. "The bandage," I amended. "You seem like you know what you're doing with this stuff."

He smiled and stood to wring the washcloth out in one of the sinks. "Most werewolves know basic first aid." A light blush tinged the apples of his cheeks. "Some of us can get pretty...rowdy." He chuckled softly. "Especially when we're younger. It's much worse then." His head tipped back as he squinted at the ceiling. "I can't think of a single wolf I know who's never broken anything."

I smiled. "I guess we're all guilty of doing dumb things when we were young. I haven't broken any bones, but I've had my fair share of trouble."

"I'd love to hear about it sometime," he said with a grin.

My smile slid off my face faster than butter off hot pancakes.

"Yeah, sure. Sometime," I lied.

I've never told anyone about my past.

Sure, my parents and gran, and even school officials were notified. But *I'd* never told anyone. And I wasn't about to start now. It was too shameful, and I didn't want to relive it. My past was locked up tight, and buried deep, and I intended to keep it that way.

If he noticed my lie, he didn't let on.

He jerked a thumb over his shoulder. "I brought you some clothes. They're way too big, but I thought you'd like something clean."

"Where are *my* clothes?"

He winced. "They were filthy and ripped. We threw them away. I can pay to replace them."

I shook my head quickly. "No, no. I don't need them replaced. Thank you though. I'll return these to you as soon as I get back to my cabin and get them washed."

And then run as far and fast away from you as I can.

I didn't need a distraction like Abraham in my life right now.

His blue eyes darkened. "We'll talk about that later."

"Talk about what?" I asked with a frown.

He ignored me and headed out the door. "There's some bath beads or bombs or salts or whatever under the sink if you'd like."

Once he was gone, I dug out some lavender bath beads, and liberally added them to the steaming water. Within moments, I was undressed, and submerged from the neck down. I let out a deep sigh and felt my sore muscles relax.

An hour later I emerged from the muggy bathroom to find Abraham with wet hair and clean clothes, sitting on the perfectly made bed. In his hands were rolls of gauze and tape. He rose and assisted me to the bed. His help was especially welcome since I needed to hold onto the shorts to keep them on my hips. I propped my leg up on the mattress, so he could have easier access.

"What did you use on it? It's working great. My leg is healing so fast."

Abraham froze for a moment and then shook his head. "I haven't put anything on

it. I just cleaned and wrapped it."

I frowned. "Then how is it healing so fast?"

He was quiet as he gently taped the gauze to my calf. When he didn't answer a

couple minutes later, I dipped my head to catch his eye. "Abraham?"

He sighed and met my gaze, his mouth open to speak, but only a sigh came out. "Elizabeth, I–"

"Knock, knock!"

Abraham leapt to his feet. "Come in, Evey," he hollered.

The woman came barreling in with a pile of light blue fabric in her hands. "Hey, Elizabeth. I thought you might like some clean clothes."

Abraham swiftly stepped in front of her. "She's already got clothes."

She looked incredulously from Abraham to me. Her critical gaze roved over the baggy clothes hanging off my frame. With a roll of her eyes, she gave him a shove, and to my surprise, he stumbled back a step.

"Don't be an idiot, Abey."

He gritted his teeth and watched me with serious eyes. A delicate snort from Evey had me look her way in time to catch another eye roll.

"Don't listen to him. You can't wear that, they're fallin' off you!" She tsked and shook out the dress she brought me. It was a pale blue, halter top sundress, with white daisies lining the hem. It was adorable. And *small*.

I eyed the dress critically. "Evey, I'm not going to fit in that."

"Nah, it'll look fine."

"Don't you have some pants I could borrow?" I was grasping.

She shook her head. "You're way taller, all of my pants would be too short. This dress is gonna look great on you, just wait."

I took the questionable garment in my hand, and suddenly Abraham was at my elbow, helping me into the bathroom.

"You don't have to wear that if you don't want to," he whispered.

Evey scoffed from across the room.

"It's all right. I can try it on at least."

Abraham guided me into the bathroom and left swiftly. I shed his too-big clothes, leaving only the borrowed underwear I'd woken up in, and slipped on Evey's dress. It was snug, making a bra unnecessary which was good since I didn't have one. I took a look in the mirror and frowned at my thighs. The dress was a little shorter than I was comfortable with, but it beat wearing clothes I had to hold up or risk losing.

"I guess I'll just return these to you now," I said to Abraham as I eased out of the bathroom. I was met with dead silence.

Both of them were looking at me though their reactions were much different. Evey had a smug smile on her lips, and Abraham's mouth was ajar. With a laugh, Evey gave him a tap under his chin, and it closed with a snap.

"Is it that bad?" I could feel the heat creeping across my cheeks.

The tiny brunette leapt to her feet. "Of course, it's not bad! Girl, are you crazy? You look amazin'!"

"It's too short," I complained.

She took a step back and eyed me up and down. "It's a little short, but not indecent. You're keepin' that dress by the way. There's no way I can wear it again after this. It'd look like a potato sack on me."

I shook my head in amazement. "Well, thank you for this. And thank you too, Abraham. For saving me and fixing me up."

He stood and took a step toward me. "You're welcome?" He replied, eyes confused.

"Nice meeting you two," I tripped over my words, and gave a halfhearted wave.

Not one for awkward goodbyes, I spun on my heel, and headed for the door I knew led to the hallway. As I reached for the handle, I realized I had no clue how to get out of this place. But how hard could it be?

"Elizabeth! You can't go!" Abraham called as he caught up to me.

My brows furrowed. "Why not?"

He swallowed harshly, his eyes darting around the room. "There's something I need to tell you."

I put a hand on my hip. "Okay, what is it?"

His frantic eyes met mine, and he opened his mouth, but no words came out.

"Maybe you should have a seat. You're still hurt, and this may take a while to explain," Evey said from behind me. She wrapped her arm around my shoulders and helped me back to the bed. I thought with the height difference she wouldn't be much help, but she surprised me. She was pretty strong for such a little thing.

"Okay guys, what's up?" I directed my question at Abraham who was still standing across the room, looking torn.

He took a deep breath, let it out slowly, and took a few slow steps toward me. "You asked me how your leg was healing so fast."

It wasn't a question, but I answered anyway.

"Right," I dragged the word out. "Are you trying to say you know why?"

He nodded his head but didn't speak. I looked from him to Evey, but neither of them continued. I sighed in frustration, and Abraham took another jerky step in my direction.

"Okay, how about this? I'm sure you've heard of werewolves before last night, right? Tell me what you've heard."

My forehead creased in confusion, but I thought back. "Um, okay. Well, uh, they turn into wolves during the full moon?"

Abraham nodded his head. "Yes, what else?"

"Uh... they're allergic to silver?"

His head shook side to side this time. "Not true, but good job. Keep going."

I wracked my brain but couldn't think of anything else.

"What about how werewolves are made? What do you know about that?"

"Oh! They're bitten right?"

Oh, no.

"Most werewolves are born, like me and my sisters, from werewolf parents."

An important skill I'd learned from being a lawyer is to hear what someone was saying, and also what they weren't. A lot of times, it was the unspoken words that told the real truth. So, I immediately picked up on the key word in his statement.

"Most?" I asked hesitantly.

He nodded and closed his eyes. "Almost all." With a deep breath, he opened them again, and speared me with his laser gaze. "But some are bitten."

And that storm I'd felt coming?

It had finally reached the shore.

Chapter 6

"Elizabeth!"

I heard my name being called but couldn't respond. Body frozen in shock, my world was spinning violently around me.

I'd been bitten by a werewolf.

How could I have not put the pieces together before now? *Everyone* knew if you're bitten by a werewolf, you turn into one. Then again, everyone also knew werewolves were make-believe. Boy, were we wrong.

"Why aren't I a…" I swallowed harshly, and spit out the next word like it tasted bad, "werewolf yet?"

The siblings looked at each other silently until Abraham approached me and took a seat on the bed. I immediately noticed the creases lining his handsome face, and the bags under his eyes.

"It won't happen until the next full moon," he explained.

The next full moon.

"And when is that?"

"Not for about another four weeks."

I nodded as my chest constricted.

I had a month until my life became drastically altered forever.

My impending change threatened to drown me in fear and anger, but I fought to keep my head above water. Besides, I'd never been one to sit and cry about a problem instead of trying to solve it, and I wasn't about to start now.

"Is there an antidote?" I asked.

This seemed to surprise them.

Another wordless conversation passed between the two before Evey speared me with remorseful blue eyes.

"Not that we've ever heard of," she breathed.

"Has anyone ever looked?" I asked, desperate for a way out of this nightmare.

She nodded her head slowly.

"No one's ever found anything. I'm sorry, Elizabeth."

Okay, so that option was a bust. What else? There had to be a solution. I wouldn't accept this fate without a fight. I wracked my brain in the quiet of the room, the only sound my harsh breathing as I hyperventilated.

"This is not okay," I whispered.

What an understatement that was.

Abraham reached out tentatively and wrapped his thick arm around my shoulders. I tensed a moment before I gave in to the comfort he was offering.

"It won't be that bad!" Evey insisted with a hopeful grin. "You'll like livin' here, we're like a big ol' family–"

"I'm sorry, *live* here?" I interrupted.

Her eyes flashed to Abraham. The man sighed next to me, and tightened his arm, as if he was worried I'd bolt.

"Yes, you'll have to live here now."

I jumped to my feet despite his hold. My leg screamed in protest, but I ignored it.

"The hell I will!"

"Elizabeth be reasonable," he pleaded.

I gave him my fiercest glare.

"*Reasonable?* What part of this is *reasonable,* Abraham? The part where I got attacked by a serial killer in the woods? Or the part where I woke up in a house full of storybook characters? Or maybe, it's the fact that I'm now apparently a part of this fucked up fairytale too? Which is it?!"

I never cursed. *Pretty girls don't say ugly words.* My mother had drilled that into my head from a young age. Well, this pretty girl was *pissed.* All bets were off.

Abraham remained seated, his face full of remorse. "I'm so sorry."

"You think *sorry* makes up for this? Sorry is for when you bump into someone on the sidewalk or forget a person's name. This is so far beyond a simple *sorry!*"

The anger and *unfairness* of the situation boiled inside of me. I was an active volcano, set to erupt at any moment. My stomach churned like molten lava undulating beneath the earth's crust.

With a very unladylike growl, I turned on my heel, and paced the length of the room despite my injured leg.

I felt trapped.

Like a caged animal.

"You can't keep me here," I told him. "I won't stay."

Abraham sighed, but remained silent. Smart man.

"I have a life back in Raleigh. A career." Another thought popped into my head, and I stopped dead in my tracks to level another glare at him. "I'm supposed to be getting a promotion on Tuesday!"

Abraham's eyes dimmed, but he stayed quiet.

With a snarl, I started pacing again. If I didn't get this pent-up anger out of my system, it would tear my body at the seams, and burst out of me. It was that intense.

What am I going to do?

I couldn't live here in this house full of werewolf strangers.

Was it even safe?

I wouldn't.

They couldn't make me.

A few more laps around the room, and I had enough control to speak again.

"I'm not staying here," I informed him.

Abraham took a deep breath and stood. With his hands raised in front of him, he cautiously approached me. "It's not safe for you to live off pack land."

"And why is that?" I asked through gritted teeth.

He ran a large hand down his face. "Your body will go through many changes. Things you won't be able to understand without our help. And when the full moon comes, you'll need to be somewhere you can safely shift. Away from any humans that might see you. I can't risk you getting hurt, or worse," he looked like the thought pained him.

The way he said "humans" was like a shock to my system.

He wasn't human, and now neither was I.

Oh my god, I'm a werewolf.

I paced again.

Think, Elizabeth!

My brain zipped at top speed searching for a solution. Anything that could make this situation bearable for me.

"What if I came back here on the full moon?" I stopped in front of Abraham.

He shook his head, but Evey piped up from behind me. "That could work."

He glared at her. "Not a good idea."

I cocked a hip and placed my hand on it. "Why not?"

He sighed in frustration. "I told you, your body will change in the time leading up to your first full moon. There will be things you won't know how to deal with. You need to stay here so we can help you through all that. This is what's best."

"I don't accept that," I informed him.

He let out a frustrated breath, and looked up at the ceiling, like it could give him the answers he sought.

"What if one of us went with her?" Evey suggested.

I spun to face her. That was a better option than staying here, but it still wasn't what I wanted. "That won't be necessary."

Evey shook her head slowly. "Abey's right. You'll be goin' through some changes you'll need our help with."

My hackles rose, and I spit out, "I don't need anyone's help!"

A heavy sigh from behind had me spinning to Abraham again.

"You seem like an independent woman who's used to only relying on herself, and I respect that. But just this once, Elizabeth, you really do need help."

I shook my head and looked away. "I disagree."

"Must you argue over everything?"

I scoffed and rolled my eyes. "I get along just fine with most other people. It must be something about *you* that brings this out of me."

A small chuckle sounded like it escaped him unwillingly. I turned to find his eyes light with humor. For some weird reason, it lessened the weight on my heart, and I sighed in resignation.

Sensing my defenses weakening, he went in for the kill.

"If you agree to take one of us with you, I'll let you stay at your place until the full moon."

And my fury was back.

"*Let me?!*" I shrieked.

Evey came rushing over, placing herself between us. She somehow made herself tall enough to interrupt my furious stare-down with her brother.

"He didn't mean it like that. He's concerned for you." She shot an annoyed look at the man in question. "He just needs to work on his delivery."

My chest heaved, fists clenched as I struggled to calm myself. I hadn't felt this out of control in a long time. Years and years of rigid self-discipline had flown right out the window. I needed to get myself together. If I wasn't calm, I couldn't think rationally, and I needed my brain firing on all cylinders right now.

With a few measured breaths, I brought myself back from the edge.

"Fine, but I'm staying in my cabin the rest of the weekend."

Abraham was shaking his head before I'd even finished my sentence.

"Why the hell not?!" I exploded, all my calming measures down the drain again.

He shot a disbelieving look at the leg I could barely stand on.

His eyes softened when they reached mine. "You're hurt. You shouldn't be alone while you're still healing. What if something happened to you, and there was no one there to help?"

I wasn't used to being cared for. Not since Gran. His attention was making my skin itch and my heart flutter.

"Why do you even care? You don't know me. You don't owe me anything. What's in it for you?"

Abraham's cerulean eyes scanned my face like he was searching for something. I kept my chin up, and my face open–I had nothing to hide.

His gaze dimmed, but a reassuring grin spread across his face. "You're pack. And we take care of our own."

A multitude of emotions clashed inside me.

Fear. Uncertainty. Trepidation.

What was I getting into being a part of this pack? What would it entail? How would I be able to keep living the life I'd work so hard to create for myself while also being a werewolf?

But beyond that, there was also a small glimmer of hope. And maybe a pinch of self-doubt. I hadn't been a part of something in so long. What if I screwed this up like I'd done before? What if they got to know me and stopped wanting me to be a part of their pack? But what if this was the family I'd always yearned for?

"Please stay?" Abraham asked, interrupting my thoughts.

I did *not* like losing arguments. In fact, I'd based my entire career on my ability to reason my way out of or into anything I wanted. The thought of conceding to his demands again had my stomach churning.

However, I prided myself on my logical reasoning above even my ability to win arguments. As much as it pained me, Abraham was right. Just the thought of climbing those stairs to the loft in the cabin made my leg ache. I wasn't sure how I'd make do on my own.

Would it be such a bad thing to accept help?

The defiant adolescent I never fully outgrew screamed: *YES, IT WOULD*. I didn't need help. I couldn't count on anyone but myself. If I let my guard down, I'd only end up being disappointed, or worse, hurt.

But the adult Elizabeth knew my adolescent self had gotten me into more trouble than I cared to remember. Maybe it was time to accept some assistance. And, what better time than now, when I really needed it?

And besides, he'd said *please*.

My shoulders sagged in defeat. "I need to get my things at least," I muttered.

Abraham spoke up immediately. "I can take you there now."

Evey frowned. "But Abey, don't you have that thing–"

"This is more important," he interrupted.

She shook her head with an indulgent smile.

I spun on my heel and stormed toward the hall door. Well, more like limped, but hopefully it looked like an angry limp at least. "Let's go," I grouched.

A small chuckle came from behind me, but I ignored it.

I whipped open the door to find another room, and not a hallway at all. The giant space looked like a private sitting room decorated in dark colors like the bedroom. There were overstuffed chairs, and a huge entertainment system alongside a pool table and a wall full of books. I took a quick look around and located a possible exit. By then, Abraham had caught up, and rushed ahead to open the door for me.

A wide hallway stretched out before us, the series of rooms we'd been in were at the far end. I struggled to hide my discomfort as I hobbled along the seemingly endless hallway.

"Can I help?"

I narrowed my eyes at him.

"Please?"

With an aggravated huff and my leg screaming in pain, I hooked an arm around his waist, and let him support most of my weight. We walked past door after door but didn't run into anyone else until we'd made it down the first set of stairs.

A pair of tall, light-haired men were coming up the staircase, so engrossed in their conversation they almost walked right past us. The taller of the two spoke up first.

"Alpha," he acknowledged with a reverent nod.

"Hey, Wyatt. How's your mom doing?"

The other man answered. "Better. Thank you for sending the pack doc to her."

Abraham waved a hand dismissively. "We take care of our own here, Wesley."

Both men nodded gratefully, their inquisitive eyes bouncing from me to Abraham and back again. It looked like they were waiting for an introduction or explanation, but Abraham offered neither.

"I'm off, men. Bea's around here somewhere, but if you need me, I have my cell," he told them, patting the front pocket of his dark jeans.

They nodded again and resumed their ascent. We walked quietly down another flight of stairs before he spoke up.

"Wes and Wyatt are new additions. They've only been with us a few months."

"Where did they come from?"

Abraham's shoulders tensed. "Another pack," he replied succinctly.

"How many *are* there?"

He chuckled. "In North Carolina? Or in the world?"

My brain short-circuited for a minute. I'd been so immersed in this house, and my own pending transformation, that I hadn't even stopped to consider how many more werewolves there might be. How had they gone undetected for so long?

"Um, both?"

"There's about ten different packs in the state. Maybe a few hundred in the country? And who knows about the rest of the world? I *can* tell you, we're on six out of the seven continents and every country in them."

I blinked slowly, trying to process what I'd just heard.

He laughed, but said nothing else, and I appreciated that. It was like he knew I needed time to digest that thought before I learned more.

"Where did you all come from?"

I caught his brows furrowing out of the corner of my eye. "All over I guess." He scratched the back of his head. "My siblings and I were born and raised just a few hours from here."

I shook my head. "No. Werewolves. Where did they come from? Are you an evolutionary anomaly? An unidentified species? Aliens?"

Abraham's laugh echoed off the walls and high ceilings.

"Aliens? Really, Elizabeth?"

Indignation heated my blood for a moment, but I couldn't help the smile that spread across my face. Okay, maybe that was a silly question.

"Never heard that one before," he mused.

I rolled my eyes. "Okay, I get it. But really, what are you?"

"We're human," he insisted. I arched a brow. "With a twist," he added.

"Yeah, some twist," I mumbled.

He laughed again. "No, really. We are. It's a long story–one I'll absolutely tell you sometime. The short answer is: we're descended from a man who'd been spelled by a witch to turn into a wolf. Over the centuries, the magic mutated and evolved into what we are today."

My jaw fell open, and a small gasp escaped my lips. When would I stop getting pitched curve balls?

"Witch?" I croaked.

He nodded affirmatively. "Witch."

"Are they still around too?"

"Oh sure, they're all over. You've heard of psychic hotlines, right? Most of 'em are witches. Not all witches are strong enough to be very accurate though, and that's why they have a bad reputation. If you want a real divination, you need to find a powerful witch, and they definitely won't be working for a 1-800 company," he chortled.

My mind went blank.

What do you say to that?

I finally went with the first thought I could fully form. It was an old saying of my Gran's that had never seemed more appropriate than right now.

"Well butter my ass and call me a biscuit."

Chapter 7

"Don't you have a car or something?" I asked, eyeing the 4-wheeler he'd led me to.

Abraham scoffed. "First of all, I don't have a *car*. I have a truck. A big one," he winked, and my face heated. "But this will be much faster." He pulled a black helmet off the seat and handed it to me.

I took it and shot him an irritated look. "Where's yours?"

He shook his head. "I'm a werewolf." He rapped his fingers against his skull. "And I've got a hard head. You're still human, and fragile so you need to wear it. I'm not risking your safety."

I frowned but slid the helmet on. He was right. I was beat up enough as it was and didn't need another head injury this weekend.

I eyed the vehicle warily. The seat we were sharing looked *awfully* small. With a glance at my bare legs, I remembered my dress was pretty tiny too. Warmth spread further across my face.

"Do you need help?"

I frowned at him.

Shouldn't he know better by now?

As if he'd read my mind, he grinned, and shook his head. "I know, I know. You don't *need* help." He came to stand right in front of me. "But I'm going to help you anyway, so get over it."

A startled squeak escaped my lips when he wrapped his hands around my hips and lifted me more than a foot off the ground. "What are you *doing*?"

He turned to the ATV with me still suspended in midair.

Since I was at eye level, I could see the twinkling of mirth in his gaze. "I told you. I'm helping."

I growled deep in my chest. He ignored me, and lifted my body higher, so I was hovering over the seat. He paused for a loaded moment before lowering me with sure arms until my backside rested on the black leather.

He glanced down, and I followed his gaze. With a startled squeal, I slapped my hands over the juncture of my thighs. The already short dress had ridden up and was dangerously close to exposing my bits and pieces.

Abraham laughed quietly as he took his seat in front of me. The good news was, he helped protect my modesty. The bad news was, I found myself pressed tightly against the man that could tempt me from across the room. How was I going to control myself with my legs straddling him, and my chest mashed against his broad back?

Please, god, let this be a short ride.

"You don't need to worry about that stuff anymore. It doesn't matter to anyone around here."

I repeated his words over and over again, but I had absolutely no idea what he was referring to.

When I was silent for too long, he added, "Nudity. None of us pay any mind to it. We've all seen each other naked many, many times."

My jaw hit my chest as my skin warmed painfully with a fierce blush. A blurry image of Abraham naked in the woods flashed through my head. I sputtered a few times before I could spit out a reply. "That will *not* be happening. Ever."

Abraham chuckled. "We'll see."

"No, Mr...?"

"McCoy," he supplied.

"Mr. McCoy, I am certain it will be *you* who will 'see'," I informed him, crossing my arms over my chest.

He let out a loud, mocking sigh. "Always arguing."

"You've been getting your way far too much recently. I can't have that."

He let out a deep-belly laugh that I felt all the way to my bones. I searched for the indignation I should have been feeling with him laughing at me, but it was nowhere to be found. Instead, I ducked my head to hide a smile.

The ATV roared to life.

"Better hold on," Abraham called over the engine.

I wrapped my arms around him, keeping my hands fisted so they wouldn't be tempted to search out each individual muscle on his toned stomach. My leg throbbed slightly with the vibrations, but I ignored it.

He started out slow as he drove down his long, steep gravel driveway. It twisted and turned through the trees until the massive lodge disappeared from view.

"Hey, how do you know where you're going?"

"There's only one rental cabin within hiking range of where I found you," he explained loudly.

"You must know this area well."

"I've lived here for over fifteen years. I know these woods, and those mountains," he nodded his head toward where I knew the Blue Ridge Mountains stood, "Like the back of my hand."

I digested that information while Abraham turned off his driveway, and onto a smaller path that led through the forest. We relaxed into a comfortable silence as he expertly navigated the woods for the next few minutes.

When he slowed to a stop in the middle of what looked like nowhere, and turned to face me, he instantly had my attention.

"I need you to do something for me," he said seriously.

This was the first opportunity I'd had to return the innumerable favors I owed him.

"Of course."

He searched my face. "I want to take you back to where we found you. I was hoping you could walk me through your attack. Anything you remember could help us find out who this guy is."

My stomach dropped as the sunlit trees faded, and in its place, only a dark and sinister forest remained. I shook my head to rid myself of the false image. If I was going to help, I'd need to toughen up.

I straightened my spine. "Sure. Do you know where it happened? Because I don't think I could find it again on my own."

He nodded. "I had some of my men scout the area." His denim eyes searched my face for another moment before he turned back around.

Thin pine trees flew past in a blur as we made good time on the 4-wheeler. Before long, Abraham stopped the vehicle again, and helped me off. As soon as my feet were on the ground, I took a quick step away from him. The ride here had been torture. My body felt like it was boiling from the heat that spread from every place it touched his. I desperately needed some space from this man.

I took a look around, hoping to see something I recognized.

"This is the first place we picked up his trail intersecting with yours. Before now, he'd kept his distance from you." His voice was hard as steel.

"He was stalking me." My voice didn't sound like my own. Instead it was a pale, lifeless monotone I didn't recognize.

I walked around the space, trying to get my bearings. A few feet away I spotted a patch of the leafy carpet that had been disturbed.

"This is right where they meet," he breathed from close behind.

Focusing on the displaced leaves, I tried to remember the order of events from the night before.

"I found a small meadow near here. I think that's when he started following me." The story played out before my eyes like a movie. "That's the first time I heard anything unusual. It was quiet for about ten minutes before I heard something else in the woods. I started running down the trail when I heard a growl."

The sounds from that night played over and over in my head, drowning me in the fear I'd felt. My chest was hollow. Like all the blood in my body had finally abandoned my poor heart, leaving that organ empty of any kind of hope.

The sudden warmth of two hands wrapping around my upper arms broke through the fear those memories had elicited.

"Hey. Stay with me. You're safe now. Nothing's ever going to happen to you with me around. Got it?"

Against my wishes, my traitorous body relaxed, leaning into Abraham's chest. I could feel his heart beating against my back, and I concentrated on the steady rhythm until mine matched it.

His hands rubbed my arms from bicep to elbow, the sensation soothing me even further.

"You're okay now." That sentence wasn't a question coming from Abraham, it was a statement. He knew the moment I'd calmed down. I'd been able to feel him relax with me.

How was he so in tune with my body already? He didn't even know my last name but knew exactly how to calm my fears and comfort me. I couldn't tell if I was terrified or thrilled by that. Those emotions felt so similar.

"Yes. Thank you," I said, and stepped away. As appealing as Abraham's arms were, I still wasn't comfortable with affection like that.

"Okay, so, he growled at me a few times, and I ran again. A few minutes later, I tripped and fell, smashing my head on a rock or something. That's how I got this," I pointed to my forehead. "The wolf caught up to me. I tried to scare it off, but obviously that didn't work."

"How did you try to scare him?"

My chin tipped up. "I waved my arms and yelled." He didn't look convinced. "I've read if you appear bigger than the animal, it'll get scared and run off. If he'd been a real wolf, it would have worked," I informed him defiantly.

"I'm sure it would have," he placated. "What was it you did?"

I hesitated, not sure if he was mocking me or not.

His eyes were wide, and earnest when he asked, "Can you show me? This might be important."

I stared at him incredulously. He really needed a reenactment?

"Please," he added. "Anything could be useful."

I huffed out a breath. Well, if it might help, I guess it couldn't hurt.

"Okay, so I stood on my tip toes, flapped my arms in the air like this," I waved them like I was making a snow angel. "And I yelled something like: HEY WOLF! GET LOST!"

Abraham nodded solemnly, his head down. "Was that exactly what you yelled?"

I thought back. "I'm not sure. It could have been more like: HEY YOU," I waved my arms again for effect. "GET OUT OF HERE!"

"Mmm hmm. Okay, I think I'm getting it. Could you show me that one more time?"

When I didn't answer right away, he finally slipped up, and met my eyes.

"Damn you, Abraham McCoy!" I stomped my good foot while he howled with laughter.

"Oh my god, that was too funny," he panted out between chuckles.

"This is serious!"

Ugh! This man was going to drive me to drink! I stomped off toward the

ATV.

"Hey! Where you going?" He jogged after me.

"*I'm* trying to go look for clues. Where are *you* going?" I snarked.

He flashed an irresistible grin. "Anywhere you go, babe." With a wink, he settled me back on the seat before we took off again.

"I'm not your 'babe'," I muttered behind him. His shoulders shook with silent laughter.

What had gotten into him?

This sudden playfulness was making my insides churn. Trying to categorize that emotion was absolutely not an option. We only needed to spend the weekend together while I healed. After Monday, I wouldn't have to see him again for another four weeks. Surely, I'd be able to get myself under control, and my priorities back in order by then.

Abraham slowed the vehicle again. "This is where you fell," he said roughly.

"And also, where I tried to scare the wolf," I reminded him, sacrificing my dignity to lighten the mood. I was rewarded with a low chuckle.

"How *did* you get away from him here?"

I furrowed my brow as I traced through the events. "Oh yeah! I used the flash on my camera to stun him and then took off running. I wonder if I got a picture..."

He turned around, his big blue eyes incredulous. "That's really smart." He sounded impressed, and oddly, proud as well.

"Yeah well. *Some* of my ideas are good ones," I groused.

"I was just messin' with you. That actually might have worked if it'd been a real wolf. But do me a favor? In these woods, always assume it's a werewolf. At least until you're able to tell the difference."

"How can I tell the difference?"

"Werewolves are bigger than regular wolves, and when your heightened senses manifest, you'll be able to smell the difference between the two."

This news stunned me. What other changes did I have to look forward to? Before I could voice my questions, Abraham spoke again. "By the way, we found your camera and phone out here. I have them in my office. They're both in pretty bad shape, but maybe there's something on the camera's memory card."

When we stopped a third time, Abraham helped me off the quad. Right away I found the dark spot where I'd lain, thinking I was going to die. A shiver ran through me, and I wrapped my arms around my torso. Predictably, Abraham's solid arm enveloped my shoulders, infusing me with his strength when my own felt depleted.

With a deep breath, I closed my eyes, and recounted the rest of the story. "I ran for as long as I could, but he still caught up. He attacked me from behind, tearing into the back of my leg." The aforementioned limb seemed to flare with pain, like my body was reliving the memories with me.

"I tried to fight him off, but he was too strong. Nothing I did made any difference," I sniffed. "Then suddenly, he stopped, and just walked away. I didn't know why, but I took that opportunity to crawl forward on my stomach. My only thought was to get as much distance between us as possible. If I'd known he was coming back, I'd have stayed face up, so I could have gotten a look at him. I'm a criminal lawyer, I know how important victim I.D.'s are. That was so dumb," I chastised myself. My head was starting to ache.

"You were being attacked," he insisted. "You did what you could to survive. If you'd seen his face, maybe he would have snapped your neck instead of running off." He paused for a moment, like he was collecting his thoughts. "'What if's are like cancer. They eat at you from the inside, turning everything good black with death. Take my word for it, let 'em go."

My eyes roved over his face, watching the story being told by his mouth also play out in his eyes. In that instant, I recognized something that echoed inside my own heart: regret. But watching him, I knew one thing for certain. Abraham was much closer to acceptance, and forgiveness than I was.

Chapter 8

"So, what happened after the wolf left?" Abraham prodded.

My body tensed painfully at the memories. "I'd only crawled a few feet maybe, when he grabbed me by the hips, and pulled me backward. I screamed, and fought, but he was even stronger than the wolf…" My voice trailed off as the sound of my pounding heart filled my ears and drowned out my words.

A warm hand on my shoulder pushed through the noise. "What happened next?"

I shook my head, and closed my eyes, taking deep breaths until my heart rate slowed. "He said something." I bit my lip anxiously as I tried to recall his exact words.

A violent shiver wracked my body as his cold voice played in my head. I wrapped my arms around myself again. "He said 'there's no use fighting, princess'," I whispered.

My eyes were still closed, but it felt like I could almost feel the anger radiating off Abraham, like a low-wave frequency. I opened my eyes to see his tense face staring over my shoulder, jaw clenched, and eyes dangerous.

"We need to find this guy," he growled.

I shivered again at his tone. Although I wasn't at all afraid of him, I was certainly happy I wasn't on the other end of his rage.

"Is there anything else you remember?" he asked, his tone only slightly softer. Like it went from diamond to granite.

"I kept fighting and yelling until he wrapped his arm around my neck," I gulped harshly, the action hurting my still-raw throat. "Everything went black after that. The next thing I knew was a wolf–you, I guess–nudging me awake." The idea that he was the second wolf in the forest was still so hard to grasp. When had I fallen down this rabbit hole, and how was I going to get myself out of it?

You're one of them now, Elizabeth. There's no getting out.

So much had happened in forty-eight hours, I was having trouble getting my head around it all. His warm arm wrapped around my shoulders and pulled me to his side. Abraham's touch was becoming familiar, and that was a problem.

"Come on, let's go get your things, and get back to the lodge. You're still healing and could probably use more rest."

We got back on the ATV, and a few minutes later, pulled up to the cabin I'd rented. Abraham helped me up the walkway, and that's when I remembered I'd left the back door unlocked when I went for my hike.

What if my attacker was in there waiting for me?

I dug deep for that steely resolve I'd relied on all my life, but found it riddled with holes, and warped from fear. Real, bone-deep fear. I'd never felt anything like it before in my life, and it left me feeling adrift.

A quiet shuffling noise from behind had me jumping in alarm before I realized it was only Abraham. That's when I remembered I wasn't alone, and I didn't have to do this on my own. I had backup. I had *help*.

"Everything okay?" His voice was quiet and concerned. Whether it was over my skittishness, or because of how long I'd been standing here, looking at the door, I didn't know.

I took a deep breath, exhaling slowly. This wasn't easy for me.

"Yeah, I'm fine," I said, my back still to him, "I'm just a little worried, because I left the door unlocked. Maybe you should go in first?"

The words hadn't finished leaving my lips before he sprang into action. He stepped in front of me, his body tight with tension, and knees bent as if waiting for an attack.

"I'm glad you told me. Wait out here."

With that, he stalked over to the door, and yanked it open. Once inside, he stopped, and cocked his head to the side, like he was listening intently to something. He glanced between me, and the rest of the house before walking back over and leading me inside.

"I don't want you out there by yourself. This immediate area is clear, so I want you to wait here for me, okay?" He positioned me inside next to the locked door and eyed me seriously.

"Okay."

Abraham nodded once, and took off for the bathroom, the only walled-off room on the first floor. When satisfied, he took the stairs two at a time, and was in the loft in record time. Seconds later, he appeared over the half wall overlooking the downstairs.

"Is this all you brought?"

"Yeah, I didn't even have a chance to unpack."

"Can I just bring it down to you?"

I pressed my lips together. "I know you're in a rush, but I really wanted to change into something a little more... modest. Do you mind if I do that real quick, and then we can get going?" He was the alpha, I'm sure he had better things to do than cart me around.

He descended the stairs even faster than he'd ascended them and stopped a few feet away from me.

"I wasn't trying to rush you. There's nothing more important to me right now than... this," he finished awkwardly, and ran a hand through his dark hair. After a big sigh, a grin broke out across his perfect face. "I was just trying to help."

I rolled my eyes. "Don't *need* help, remember?" With a wary glance at the narrow stairs, I straightened up, and grit my teeth. This would suck.

I had only taken one painful step, before I was lifted off the ground, and into his arms. My free hand slapped against my backside, stretching the short dress down as much as possible. I silently thanked that angel, Evey, for the underwear again.

"Abraham McCoy put me down right this instant!"

He only shook his head. "I'm a quick study, and what I'm learning about you, is to never *ask* if you need help, because you're stubborn as hell, and would deny it to your last breath." I huffed, and glared at the side of his face, noticing he needed a shave. "So, from now on, if I see you need my help, I'm going to give it to you." He smiled down at me, and it took all my willpower to not return it. That smile of his would be my downfall, I just knew it.

"Whatever," I muttered mulishly. He carried me up the stairs as if I weighed next to nothing. Wasn't even out of breath by the time we reached the loft.

He placed me on the bed and backed up a few steps.

"I'll wait for you downstairs. Holler when you're ready." He said before making himself scarce.

I glanced morosely around the beautiful rustic room. I'd been really looking forward to a quiet weekend in the mountains. How had things gone so far off course? If I'd never gone for that hike, I could have been reading peacefully on the front porch with a cup of coffee right this minute.

But then I never would have met Abraham. I couldn't decide if that was a good thing, or not. Or maybe, I just didn't want to admit the answer.

Struggling to my feet, I limped over to my bag, and rummaged around for something to wear. I pulled out a pair of khaki shorts, a white long sleeve t-shirt, and a fresh bra, and panties.

When I bent to pull up the shorts, a wave of dizziness hit me at the same time the rough material scraped against the bite wounds. I dropped the bottoms, and straightened to alleviate the vertigo, but that made it worse. Stumbling backward, I caught myself on a nearby dresser, but not before one of the knobs dug painfully into my injured calf. I let out an involuntary yelp of pain, and staggered forward, my leg throbbing bursts of flames that took my breath away.

"Elizabeth?" He sounded close, maybe at the bottom of the stairs.

"I'm fine! Don't come up!" I wheezed.

Thankfully, he listened, and I waddle-limped over to sit on the bed with the shorts still around my ankles. Once seated, I bent to pull the bottoms up when another sharp wave of dizziness hit me, threatening to eject the contents of my stomach. I yanked the shorts over my hips and fastened them before flopping backward onto the bed. That sent a stabbing pain through my head, causing an instant headache. I squeezed my eyes closed and slowly counted to ten waiting for the worst of it to pass.

I must have overexerted myself because *everything* hurt. My eyes teared, and I sniffed softly. The attack, the revelation that I would become a werewolf, the pain that was almost incapacitating me, all bubbled to the surface, and leaked out my eyes.

It was too much for one person to handle in such a short period. My brain had almost been on autopilot, only allowing me to worry about one thing at a time. But the controls had been reset to manual, and everything was bombarding me at once.

What would happen to me? How would I change when I became a

werewolf? Would it alter my personality too? What kind of life could I expect now? Could I continue to be a lawyer after the next full moon? Would it be safe for me, and everyone else? Am I safe from any more attacks by this serial killer? Or was he looking for me even now?

My thoughts swirled like a tornado through my mind as the tears fell steadily, rolling down my face, and into my hair.

A creak on the stairs interrupted my pity party. Abraham stood there, large, and imposing, but with soft, gentle eyes. I sat up, and wiped my face, but the tears continued to fall.

"Elizabeth?"

I waved him away. "I'm fine," I choked out.

He hesitated only a moment before he was across the room. This big, strong man knelt on the hardwood floor at my feet, and wrapped his arms around my body, pulling me into his warm chest.

With that, the damn broke, and I sobbed into his shirt.

Abraham's large hand stroked over my hair, and down my back, over and over while I cried out my frustration and sorrow.

"What happened? What's the matter?" He pressed his face against the top of my head.

"I hurt myself getting dressed," I confessed, my voice cracked, thick with phlegm. "I think it's just all catching up to me."

He sighed into my hair. "I'm so sorry."

I leaned back so I could see his eyes. "For what?"

He looked away and ran a hand down his face. "This guy's been killing humans near my territory for months, and we haven't been able to do anything to stop it." He stood to pace the old wooden floor. "I should have already caught him. A long time ago. You, and all those other women had to pay the consequences for my failure. He hurt you," his somber eyes met mine, "and almost killed you." His throat bobbed up and down, fists clenched tight.

I climbed to my feet. "You can't take the blame for this. The authorities haven't found him either–"

"The police don't have the knowledge of werewolves that we do," he interrupted. "Or the heightened senses to track him." He started pacing again.

"We need to up surveillance and security. Maybe call in a favor from another pack," he mused.

"It's not your fault," I insisted.

He stopped, and turned, soft eyes tracing the tracks my tears had left across my face. Approaching slowly, he swiped his rough thumb across my cheek, gathering my sorrow, and easing some of the pain. A sigh of contentment escaped my lips before I could stop it, and he smiled, leaving his hand cupping my face.

"Better?"

I gave him the fake smile I'd perfected at the office. "Better," I lied.

His eyes scanned my face, and he shook his head, lowering his arm. "What else is bothering you?"

Guess I needed to work on making that smile more believable. Did everyone see through it like Abraham did?

I let out a big sigh and dropped my head. "I'm scared," I confessed.

Those words tasted awful in my mouth, but they were the truth.

"I told you, I'm not gonna let anyone hurt you."

I shook my head. "It's not just the threat of the killer werewolf returning. I'm also scared about what's going to happen to me. What my future holds. I've had my life planned out perfectly for the past ten years and suddenly, I don't even know what's going to happen a month from now. Or in the weeks leading up to the full moon. My entire future is a giant question mark, and that's terrifying for me."

His fingers slid under my chin and lifted my face to meet his. Blue, blue eyes stared back at me, knotting my stomach with their intensity.

"I know how hard this must be for you, and you've been so strong this whole time. If you can just keep your chin up, I promise, I'll handle everything else." He pulled me into his arms and held me for a long time.

I stepped out of his embrace as soon as I felt strong enough. I couldn't afford to get comfortable in his arms. I was leaving, and he was staying, and then I'd get to work on straightening myself out where this man was concerned. I just needed to keep a clear head until tomorrow when I went back to Raleigh.

He took a look around the loft and clapped his hands together. "You got everything?"

I nodded, and Abraham stooped to grab my bag before I could. He gathered the rest of my things and then picked me up once more. Even carrying me and my stuff, the man didn't break a sweat. I wonder if I'd be this strong when I became a werewolf.

He set me on my feet in the middle of the living room, and stood in the entryway, sharp eyes following every move I made. With a last look around the cozy cabin, we stepped onto the front porch, and I locked the door, tucking the key back into the lockbox.

"What are we going to do with my car?"

"We'll drive it back to my place now, and I'll have one of my men come pick up the ATV later."

I nodded and made my way to the driver's side door.

"What do you think you're doing?" Abraham asked suspiciously.

"Getting in my car?"

Next thing I knew, his large, warm body was pressed against mine, my breath catching in my throat. With his lips millimeters from my ear, he whispered, "I don't think so, Ms…?"

I gulped and closed my eyes. "Montgomery," I whispered.

"Ms. Montgomery," his breath tickled the shell of my ear, and I fought off a shiver of pleasure, "I did not save your life to let you run us into a ditch because you're trying to drive with a head wound."

The spell broken, I spun around as fast as my injured leg would let me and put my hands on my hips. I had to tip my head all the way back to meet his eyes. "I'm perfectly capable of driving," I informed him obstinately.

He took a step closer, his chest brushing against mine, but I held my ground. "That may be. But I'm not willing to risk your safety. Now, get your cute butt over to the passenger side, or I'll take you there myself."

Abraham's eyes were serious, although a taunting grin played across his face.

I growled, but he was right. After that dizzy spell I had in the loft, I had no business driving a car. That didn't mean I appreciated his high-handed attitude, or that "cute butt" comment. I turned and stomped around to the other side of the car. My leg screamed in pain, but I ignored it.

"Knew you'd see it my way," he called gleefully.

I met his eyes with a glare and flipped him the bird.

"Ms. Montgomery! I'm appalled at your manners. Is that any way for a lady to act?"

I intensified my glare before climbing into the car. "I'll show you how a lady acts," I grumbled.

His loud laugh echoed around the clearing until it sounded like even the trees were mocking me. When he climbed in the car, I was staring straight out the window with my arms crossed.

"All teasing aside," he began, his serious tone making me turn my head to look at him, "Thank you for letting me drive. I wouldn't let you get hurt again, but I'm sure you'd be pretty upset if you wrecked this little car of yours."

"Don't be condescending toward my car. Not all of us like driving *big* gas guzzling redneck mobiles like you."

His laugh filling the small space between us was like a balm on my heart. Soothing, comforting, and somehow healing.

And I knew.

Just *knew* this man would be trouble for me.

I just didn't know how much yet.

Chapter 9

"So, tell me about your life back in Raleigh," Abraham requested as he pulled onto the gravel road leading away from the cabin.

"Okay, well, I'm a junior associate at Hildebrandt & Moore in Raleigh. Hopefully, the meeting on Tuesday is for my promotion to senior level."

"And what comes with this promotion?"

"Well, more pay for one. I'd also get a bigger office, more say in which cases I take, things like that." I thought hard for a moment before continuing. "When I make senior associate, there'll be no question about whether I can pull my weight. Everyone knows you only make senior if you work your butt off and have a great win rate. A boob job, and a bottle of bleach might be enough to land a job as a junior associate, but that's about it."

He shot me a sidelong glance. "You don't seem like the type to get a boob job, and I can see from your roots you don't need bleach."

I laughed. "No, I am not the type to get a boob job. Besides, you think I'd spend twenty grand for a B cup? Not likely."

His knuckles turned white as they gripped the steering wheel.

"And how do you know anything about roots?"

The corner of his lip twitched. "I have four sisters."

"Ha. That's right."

"So, you're obviously intelligent, and it sounds like you've worked hard enough to earn this promotion. Who's doubting that?"

I rolled my eyes. "Just about everyone there. That's what I get for taking a job at a firm with only four other women associates. Don't get me wrong, there's a few genuinely good guys there, but most are chauvinistic, narrow-minded Neanderthals that are about as useful as a trapdoor on a canoe."

Abraham's deep laugh reverberated through the confines of the sedan. The sound satisfied me in a way I couldn't explain. Like crawling into your bed after a long day. Peace, security, and familiarity swirled around me, and I relaxed muscles I didn't know I'd been tensing.

"What else is in Raleigh?"

"Well, there's Charlie."

The car swerved violently to the right for a split second before regaining its place between the lines.

"What the hell is wrong with you?!" I screeched.

"Who the hell is Charlie?!" He yelled at the same time.

I stared at him in shock. His jaw clenched so tight, I swore I could hear his teeth grinding from where I sat. His knuckles were ghostly white, and I feared he'd break the wheel in two.

"I'm sorry. I thought I saw something on the road," he answered through gritted teeth. "Who's Charlie?" He repeated only slightly calmer than before.

"Charlie's my cat, Abraham. What's wrong with you?" I repeated.

He released a huge sigh, and his entire body relaxed. "Nothing's wrong with me. I'm sorry, I didn't mean to scare you. You just surprised me. I thought Charlie might be a boyfriend of yours." His words were phrased as a statement, but I knew they were meant as a question.

I scoffed. "No. Charlie is not my boyfriend. I don't have a boyfriend." *And I don't* want *one, either.* "What about you? What do you do?"

Abraham's demeanor had completely changed from just a few minutes ago. His smile was wide when he responded.

"I own a construction company. We mostly flip houses, but we also do reno's whenever they come along. We have enough men now that we can work on multiple projects at once."

"You seem too young to own a big construction company."

He shrugged modestly. "Well, we started out pretty small, just me and my cousins taking on projects in the surrounding counties. But we've expanded to South Carolina, and plan to move into Tennessee and Virginia in the next three years."

Strangely, I felt proud of him. "That's pretty impressive, Mr. McCoy. You must be really good at what you do."

He shrugged again, but his pink cheeks told a different story. "You tell me."

My brows furrowed. "What do you mean?"

Abraham jerked his chin forward, and I turned to peer out the front windshield. Up ahead loomed his massive lodge. When we left earlier, it had been from the side entrance and I hadn't been able to see much. Now, however, I could see the house in its entirety, and it was magnificent.

A large wrap-around porch jutted off the main floor, with intermittent wall sconces between the various doors. Those walls were covered in river rocks while the rest of the house was red cedar with a gray shingled roof. The large home looked like it might have had more windows than walls, and they all reflected the afternoon sun brilliantly. Beyond the house sat a serene-looking lake, and a long dock leading out into its depths. A warm breeze blew through the open windows, bringing with it the smell of lake and pine.

"You built this?" I asked in awe.

He nodded. "It's the first home I built."

When we pulled around back, there was a tall woman with short, straight, brown hair pacing in front of the garage doors. Her beautiful features were pinched in disapproval, and I shrank in my seat.

Abraham unfolded his large frame from the car, and strode around to the other side, calling to her over his shoulder, "Hey, Bea."

The woman stopped in her tracks, and I felt like I could feel the flames from her icy blue eyes.

"Hey, Bea? You bail on an important meeting, and are gone all afternoon gallivanting around with…" her harsh gaze raked me up and down, "*her,* leaving *me* to clean up after you and all I get is a friggen' 'Hey, Bea'?"

Abraham ignored her, helped me stand from my seat, and lead me toward the house. We were about halfway there when Bea stepped in our path.

With a sigh, Abraham introduced us. "Beatrice, this is Elizabeth. Elizabeth, this is my sister, Bea." I nodded my head, and tried for a tentative smile, but felt like my effort probably fell flat judging by the look on her face.

She glanced at me before turning to Abraham. "This her?"

He nodded.

Her eyebrows rose until they disappeared beneath her bangs. "And how do you suppose this will end?" Her tone was biting and sarcastic.

Abraham took a menacing step forward, a low growl rumbling through his chest. "It'll be fine. There's no other option."

Bea's eyes widened, her eyebrows still hidden from view. With her jaw slack, her gaze darted from me to Abraham, and back again a few times before she closed her mouth and shook her head. "Oh, Abey. What did you do?" she asked sadly.

"It's none of your business, Bea, so stay out of it. Just do your job, and I'll take care of everything else. I assume the meeting went well, and there were no disasters while I was gone?"

She huffed and rolled her eyes. "Yes, the meeting went well, and no, there were no disasters. I just like being kept in the loop."

Abraham nodded. "I can do that. If that's all, I'll see you later, and you can brief me. I'll call you when I'm ready."

Bea jerked her head once in agreement and left without sparing me another glance.

With a sigh, Abraham placed a hand on the small of my back and led me toward the door. "Don't worry about Hurricane Bea. Her bark is worse than her bite. Most of the time."

That was not reassuring at all.

It took us a while to get to the third floor because I refused to be hauled around like a sack of potatoes any longer. When we finally made it, Abraham stopped a few doors down from the one we'd left earlier and led me inside.

The room was smaller than the other, but still large with soft looking tan colored sheets, and light blue walls except for the one made of glass. From vaulted ceiling to thick carpeted floor, the giant windows stretched, and above me, skylights were carved into the sturdy wood.

"Is this room all right?" Abraham asked.

I turned incredulous eyes toward him. "All right? It's gorgeous! But why aren't I sleeping in the room I was in yesterday?"

His cheeks darkened, and he averted his gaze. "That wasn't a guest room."

My mind raced to figure out what I was missing.

"Whose room was it?" I prodded.

He met my eyes. "Mine."

I gulped, my breath catching in my throat, and threatening to choke me.

I'd slept in Abraham's room. *I'd slept in Abraham's bed.* Is it wrong that it was making me hot just thinking about it?

Bad, Elizabeth.

I saw the heat in my blood reflected in his sky-blue eyes, and my legs shook beneath me. He smirked and took a slow step forward. "I didn't mind letting you have the bed the past two nights, but I have to admit, I didn't sleep so well with half of me hanging off the sides of that little couch."

Another step.

"If you're willing to share, you could stay in my room again tonight," he offered, his voice deep, and rough.

I inhaled a shaky breath and shook my head. "No, thanks," I squeaked before clearing my throat, and trying again. "This room is just fine," I assured him.

One last step, and he was inches from me, his warm breath rustling hairs on the top of my head, tickling my skin, and making my pulse pound in my ears.

He has to hear it.

"Are you sure?" he whispered, voice husky.

With jerky movements, I nodded my head, and squeezed my eyes closed. If I saw that heated look in his eyes one more time, I'd lose all control.

A feather light touch caressed my cheek for a second before disappearing. When I finally opened my eyes, Abraham was across the room, opening the door to leave.

"And," he said with a mischievous grin, "in case you're as curious about me as I am about you, you might like to know I'm not seeing anyone either." He walked through the door, and called back, "I'll be across the hall if you need me."

With a soft click, I was alone, my heart beating painfully, and my legs just strong enough to get me to the bed before they gave out.

I eased back on the pillow-soft mattress and scrubbed my face with both hands. This is out of control. *I'm* out of control. A couple hours with the man, and I can hardly string two words together.

But if I'm being honest, I'd had similar feelings as early as last night. The second he walked out of that steamy bathroom, my eyes had been drawn to him, and they'd barely moved an inch since. And if I thought back hard enough, I could remember feeling a kinship with him even in the woods. As I lay broken, bleeding, and dying, this man had moved me.

I was in so much trouble.

I needed to stop thinking with my hormones and start using the brain I'd grown and nurtured for years. Lusting after this man would get me nowhere.

And besides, he was my...*alpha* now. It still felt weird thinking about it, and to be honest, I didn't even have a clear definition of what an alpha *was*.

Was he similar to a father figure? *Gross.*

A boss? *Weird.*

Was he like, the mayor of Wolf Town?

I needed questions answered, and I think I knew the right person to ask.

A knock interrupted my thoughts.

"It's Evey!" The vivacious woman called.

I smiled. Evey was *just* the woman I'd planned on hunting down.

"Come in!"

When the petite brunette walked through the door carrying all my heavy bags in one of her tiny hands, I almost laughed out loud. "Those bags are about as big as you are! Why did you lug them all the way up here? I could have helped." Which was a lie since I could barely walk across a room without assistance.

Evey didn't seem fooled and arched a dark brow. "This?" She lifted my luggage. "Is nothin'. In fact, I coulda' taken you *and* these bags from the car to here faster than you made it on your own."

My cheeks heated. "I'm injured."

"You're stubborn," she countered.

I could have argued–hell, I'd done nothing *but* bicker with Abraham most of the day, and it was just past noon–but shrugged my shoulders instead. She was right. I was stubborn.

Her eyes widened in disbelief at my concession and I couldn't help but giggle. "Oh, shut up," I said.

Evey grinned and walked closer to sling an arm around my waist. "How you feelin' today?" She asked, concern clouding her pretty eyes.

"Better, for sure."

Evey's rubbed my side before giving me a squeeze. I found it odd how comfortable these people were with me, a perfect stranger. Did she go around hugging everyone she meets? Does Abraham hold and console every new member of this pack? These people were so far from my norm, I was having trouble keeping up.

That reminded me. "Evey, I was hoping you could help me."

The bubbly woman nodded vigorously. "Of course. What's up?"

"I feel like I'm completely in the dark here. I'm confused about what I am now, how things will change for me, where I fit in here…" I trailed off. *Fitting in* was not something I usually worried about. But it was becoming clearer every minute, that I was connected to these people, whether we liked it, or not. And, I could tell some were more accepting than others.

I needed all the information I could get if I had any hope of keeping my head above water. And I desperately needed to do that. I couldn't afford to go under again. Last time, I almost hadn't found the shore while the crushing riptide threatened to drag me into its watery depths. I'd crawled onto land with barely any life or sanity left. I feared next time, I'd sink instead of swim.

Chapter 10

Evey climbed onto the large bed and patted the spot in front of her. "Hop on up and let's chat."

Hopping was out of the question, so I carefully climbed up, and took a seat in front of her. She reached out and laid a comforting hand on my exposed knee. I wasn't used to being touched by strangers, but Evey's made it comforting instead of awkward.

"Now, what's goin' on?"

I sighed and rubbed two hands through my windblown hair. With a cringe, I lowered them, and vowed to find a hairbrush ASAP. "I have about a million questions," I confessed.

Evey chuckled, "Well that's no surprise. What's botherin' you most?"

Your brother.

I cleared my throat. I'm not opening with that. "Let's start with these 'changes' you guys keep talking about. What exactly is going to happen to me?"

"Oh, sure! Well, let's see...your senses will be enhanced–"

"Enhanced how?"

"Your vision will be clearer and stronger, your sense of smell will be more advanced, and you'll be able to hear much better, and from longer distances than ever before."

"That doesn't sound so bad," I admitted.

"No, it's not bad at all! I can't remember everything from when I first shifted because it's been so long–and don't you dare ask how long it's been!–but I know it was exhilaratin' bein' able to see, and hear, and smell so much more than I could before."

"Wait, I thought you were born a wolf…"

"Of course, I was! But we don't come out of the womb with fur and fangs," she giggled. "A natural wolf doesn't make their first shift until around the time they reach puberty. As if all those hormones weren't bad enough, we have to deal with the changes that come with shiftin' into a wolf too." She shook her head in exasperation.

"Was it really bad?" I asked in a small voice.

Evey looked at me seriously before continuing. "No, it wasn't that bad. It wasn't *fun,* but it really wasn't that bad." I sighed in relief. "*But.*"

Uh-oh.

"*You're* not a natural wolf."

I raised my eyebrows. "What does that mean?"

"You're a bitten wolf. So, things will be a little different for you." She bit her lip and studied me.

"How different?" I asked warily.

"For starters, natural wolves usually go through the physical changes over the course of a few months. You'll be doin' it in just one."

I gulped. "Okay, what else?"

Evey averted her eyes. "Uh, well, it's also a bit more difficult for your body since you weren't born to shift into a wolf. It'll be a bigger shock to your system." She paused to study me. "But hey! You also get super-fast, and strong so that's pretty cool!" Evey added.

"Will I be as strong as you?"

Evey scoffed and pulled up her short sleeve to expose a thin bicep. She flexed her small muscles and gave me a cocky look. "You'll be strong, but I don't know if you'll be able to compete with *this.*"

I looked at her incredulously until she broke out in peals of laughter I couldn't help but mimic.

"Girl, *yes* you'll be as strong as me! Probably stronger since I'm a runt."

"Don't talk about yourself like that," I admonished.

She waved me away. "No, it's true. I'm the runt of our family. It's okay, though, cause' I'm the prettiest." She grinned widely, and I laughed again.

"All right, all right, I get it," she grumped.

I shook my head at the lovely woman in front of me. "Don't be silly. You're gorgeous, Evey."

She perked up and flashed me a brilliant smile.

"What about Abraham?" I asked tentatively.

"What about him?"

"Will I be as strong as him?"

Evey chuckled. "No. No one's as strong as the alpha."

"Why's that?"

"To keep order. If anyone else could be as strong as the alpha, they'd constantly be challengin' him for his position. The pack would destabilize, puttin' the weaker wolves in danger, and causin' chaos."

"How does he make sure he's the strongest then? What if you accept a new member, and they're stronger than him?"

"Good question. First of all, Abey's always been the strongest out of all of us. It was clear, even when we were young, he was meant to be an alpha. Secondly, the larger our pack grows, the stronger he becomes. Our fealty to him strengthens his wolf and makes him a better leader. And as for new members, Abey's very careful to not allow another alpha into the pack."

"So, he would just turn them away? That doesn't seem fair."

Evey shook her head. "You don't understand how packs work. If Abey let another alpha in, it would only be a matter of time before they challenged him for his position. That other wolf wouldn't have a choice. It's in an alpha's nature to dominate and lead the wolves around him. This would cause fightin' and threaten the stability of the pack. He doesn't deny those wolves for himself, he does it for the rest of us."

Their way of life was so foreign to anything I'd ever experienced. I knew I still had a lot to learn. Dozens of more questions bubbled to the surface, and I struggled not to blurt them out all at once.

"What is an alpha exactly? It seems like he's in charge around here, but what does that entail?"

Evey leaned back onto her hands and blew out a big breath. "He's a lot of things. He sets the rules we abide by, settles any disputes that arise within the pack, and makes sure everyone is taken care of. It's his job to make sure we're fed, clothed, housed, and healthy. He also protects us by makin' alliances with other friendly packs or protectin' us from malicious ones."

"That's a lot of responsibility," I mused.

Evey nodded. "It is. Especially for such a young wolf with such a large pack."

"How large *is* it?"

"Currently, we've got thirty-three wolves in our pack. And we're growin' all the time."

"Where do they all come from?"

She looked away. "Some move here for whatever reason, and are so far away from their old pack, that it doesn't make sense to stick with them. Others leave their packs for whatever reason and come this one because of our reputation."

"What kind of reputation?"

"We're a young, up and comin' pack which is appealing to wolves lookin' for a new place to be a part of. And, our alpha is well known for bein' capable and fair. Unfortunately, that's not so common."

"Not all alphas are like Abraham?"

Evey's blue eyes turned grave. "Not at all."

A knock on the door interrupted us.

"Come on in, Del!" Evey called.

The petite woman entered the room, arms laden with a giant tray full of food and drink.

"What's all that?" I asked warily.

She set it on the nightstand next to me and placed a hand on her cocked hip. "*That* is your brunch. Abey said since you stalked off in such a huff earlier, he didn't get a chance to feed you."

Evey looked at her incredulously. "Don't tell me he cooked *again*!"

"Abey cooked?!" Delilah screeched.

Evey nodded with a laugh. "He did. I was just as surprised as you."

Delilah eyed me. "Seems a lot of things are changin' 'round here."

"I was just tellin' Elizabeth about becomin' a wolf."

The other woman's eyes lit up. "Are you so excited?"

"Um. I'm not sure if 'excited' is the word I'd use."

She waved my words away. "It'll be so much fun! You'll see."

I nodded but wasn't entirely sure I believed her. When my stomach rumbled, Evey scooted off the bed, and retrieved the tray full of food.

"You need to eat," she admonished, sliding the feast onto the mattress in front of me.

My first instinct was to argue, but I found I didn't have it in me. She was right. I needed to eat. I just wasn't used to other people telling me what I needed to do or not do. For some reason, Evey's concern didn't ruffle my stubborn feathers. In fact, I found I liked that she cared enough to worry about my wellbeing.

Without another word, I dug into the food while the sisters chatted to themselves, and at me. I occasionally gave them a nod or shake of my head, but my mouth was too full to give them any proper answers. They seemed to understand, and I was thankful because once I started eating, I couldn't stop. Before I knew it, all that was left on the tray were empty dishes and cups.

"You sure got that wolf appetite down, don't ya?" Evey asked with a little giggle.

My cheeks warmed at her words. "I was really hungry," I admitted.

"Elizabeth," she admonished. My eyes met hers involuntarily. "You're in a house full of werewolves, and we know how to *eat*. Don't be upset that your appetite's increased. You'll see you're in good company tonight."

"What's tonight?"

"Weekly pack barbecue," Delilah answered. "It's not mandatory or anything, but Abey has a cookout open to all the wolves at least once a week. We usually only get about half of 'em to come, but I have a feeling we'll be seein' just about every wolf tonight," she laughed.

"What's different about tonight?"

Evey scoffed. "*You* silly. Everyone's comin' to see you."

I gulped. "Why?"

The sisters rolled their eyes in unison. "You're the girl who lived," Evey said, eyes wide.

Delilah snorted. "Nerd."

"Illiterate," Evey shot back. Del just shook her head. "We've all known about the wolf that's attackin' women in our woods," Evey continued. "The fact you survived is a small miracle. Besides, you're the first bitten wolf most of us have ever met. You're like a celebrity!" Evey laughed, but my stomach dropped.

I didn't want to be a celebrity. I didn't want to attract any extra attention. In fact, I didn't even want to be here. This should have been a quiet, solitary weekend in the mountains. And now, I felt like a sideshow at a circus, and soon I'd be on display for everyone to gawk at.

Another knock on the door interrupted my thoughts.

"Come in, Abey," Evey called.

She loved inviting people into my room.

The man in question opened the door and stuck his head in. When he saw his two sisters on my bed, his brows furrowed, and he stepped inside.

"What are you two doing in here?"

"I brought her bags up," Evey answered.

"And I brought her food like you asked me to," Delilah added.

He shook his head good-naturedly at the women. "I didn't tell you to stay and bother her."

Both women gasped in indignation. "We are not botherin' her," they yelled in unison.

"We're gettin' to know our new sister," Delilah added.

Sister? Was that how they referred to their fellow pack members?

Abraham's eyes jerked to my face and frowned. He dragged his gaze away from mine for a quick moment while he inspected the empty tray. "Did you have enough to eat?"

I couldn't help the incredulous laugh that escaped me. "That was enough food to feed me for a week."

He smiled and walked closer. The less space there was between us, the harder my heart pounded. My eyes were riveted on his as he came to a stop at the side of the bed. "Your body is changing." He paused and raked his heated gaze down the length of me. "You'll need more food as a werewolf. This is all perfectly normal."

"Well, my werewolf body better burn calories faster than my human one did, because I can't afford for these hips to get any wider than they already are."

His denim blue eyes heated, and he shook his head. "Don't worry about that. You're perfect."

My cheeks heated painfully, but the spell between us broke when one of the women on my bed cleared their throats. I severed my stare with Abraham to turn to the sisters, both of which had smug grins spread across their faces.

"Did you say something?" I asked, embarrassed I'd been caught staring.

"Oh no, we didn't say anything. I was just wonderin' if we should excuse ourselves," Delilah said with a smirk.

I didn't think it was possible, but my cheeks burned hotter. "Um, no. No, that's not necessary," I stammered.

"I can't stay," Abraham spoke up. "I have a lot more work to get through before the cookout tonight." His eyes raked me again, seeming to see right through me. "You should take a nap before then. You're probably tired. Your body's still healing." He gave me a knowing smile and turned to his sisters. "Will one of you take the tray back down to the kitchen?"

The sisters smiled and nodded. Evey grabbed the tray, and they made a hasty retreat. I watched them go with trepidation. Alone with Abraham in a bedroom was a very dangerous place to be.

"How are you feeling?" His deep voice broke through my thoughts.

I turned to him, marveling once again at how incredibly handsome he was. At least I knew my attraction to him wasn't some weird Stockholm Syndrome. This man would have tempted me in any situation.

"Elizabeth?" His voice sounded concerned. It was then I realized I'd just been staring and hadn't answered his question.

"Yes. Sorry. I'm feeling fine. My leg's still sore, and my throat's a little raw, but I'm feeling much better than I expected to."

He nodded. "Fast healing is another werewolf perk."

"Really?" Evey hadn't mentioned that.

"Really. In fact, right now you're healing pretty slow for a werewolf. After you've shifted, a wound like this will be gone in a few hours."

"So, I'll be fast, strong, have better vision, hearing, and sense of smell, and I'll also heal super-fast? Is that everything I need to know?"

Abraham's eyes left mine, and I knew, without a doubt, he was keeping something from me. "Pretty much."

Another yawn escaped, and I didn't bother to stifle it.

"I'll let you get some rest." He turned for the door, but hesitated. It seemed like he didn't want to leave, or he had more to say. Something was stopping him from walking out the door.

I sat quietly and waited for him to do, or say, whatever was holding him up. After a few moments, I was disappointed when he said only, "Sleep well," before retreating through the door and closing it quietly behind him.

Chapter 11

I was running.

My feet pounded against the soft forest floor as I raced between trees, and over fallen logs. Heart thumping, and lungs screaming, I pushed myself faster, and faster.

Something was after me.

I could feel it. Just out of reach, but always keeping pace. And I knew, if I were to slow down for even a second, it would be on me. I couldn't let that happen. Couldn't let it catch up.

With a quick look over my shoulder, I finally identified my pursuer. It was a large, light gray wolf with brown eyes. This wasn't the one that attacked me in the woods last time. I knew with every fiber of my being I'd never seen this wolf before.

Then who was it?

That split second, I'd turned my head was enough for me to lose my balance and catch my foot on something. My ankle twisted, and I hit the leafy floor with a thud, knocking the breath from my lungs.

"Not again, not again," I chanted the words over and over, desperately wishing they were true.

I couldn't be here again. Couldn't be in the woods, at the mercy of an unknown wolf again. My heart couldn't handle it. My mind couldn't absorb it.

I lay on the forest floor, my face pressed against prickly pine needles, and dirt. Although I wasn't running any longer, my heart raced faster, breaths becoming more shallow. I knew I needed to roll over, and face this new threat, but couldn't bring myself to do it. Because I knew, when I saw the unknown wolf, it would all be over. My luck would finally run out.

For a moment, I was five years old again, hiding under the blankets because I thought if I couldn't see the monster, the monster couldn't see me.

Over the sound of my harsh breathing, I tried to pick up any other noises, but the woods were quiet. Too quiet, in fact. Where were all the little forest creatures? The cicadas, and owls, and bats? Was it just me, and this wolf, all alone out here?

That thought scared me worse than anything else.

I lay there for what seemed like hours, listening, and waiting for the attack I knew was coming. My leg throbbed where I'd received my last wolf bite, as if the brutalized flesh was preparing for another onslaught.

When I couldn't take the silence any longer, I rolled over, and sat up. The brown-eyed wolf was sitting a few feet away, staring. Dark eyes raked me up, and down as if taking my measure. Its unimpressed expression made it clear it found me lacking in some way.

"What do you want?" I yelled.

The gray wolf sat there and continued to stare.

"Are you going to attack me?"

Still no answer. Not that I was really expecting a wolf to talk, but still. Some reaction to my words would be nice.

"Who are you?" I demanded.

The wolf let out an odd barking cough and stood up. With slow, precise movements, the animal stalked forward. One paw after another, closer and closer.

I scrambled away until I hit something solid. With a quick glance, I saw I'd backed myself up against a large boulder. I looked back at the wolf to see it still approaching. My stomach dropped with the realization I'd trapped myself.

"Please don't do this."

The wolf didn't listen. Or didn't care. It didn't matter either way because the beast was still moving closer.

"Please, just let me go."

My poor heart raced out of control, and I thought I might pass out from fear. "Please, please, please," I begged, over and over. I pushed back as far as I could and tucked my limbs close to my body. While keeping the wolf in sight, I searched frantically for any sort of weapon, but came up empty-handed.

I was trapped, hurt, defenseless, and alone. The first wolf in the woods hadn't finished the job, but here and now, this wolf would.

When it was only a foot away from me, it suddenly stopped. I stared at it, taking in its thick coat, and intelligent eyes.

"Please," I whispered one last time.

My plea seemed to enrage the wolf, and it snarled viciously before leaping toward me.

In my fear and hysteria, I screamed out the first thing that came to mind. The only thing I thought could save me. "Abraham!"

I opened my mouth to scream his name again when the wolf's paws landed on my shoulders and tackled me to the ground. The wolf shook me violently, rattling my teeth, and blurring my vision.

"Elizabeth!"

My name being said in that deep, gruff voice was like a sweet symphony. He'd come for me.

"Abraham?"

I searched frantically but couldn't find him anywhere; the forest was too dark, and the wolf's body was completely covering me now.

"Please, please! Abraham!"

"Elizabeth, wake up!"

The forest dissolved, and in its place, was the guest bedroom in Abraham's lodge. I gasped for air as my mind raced to understand the change of scenery.

"Elizabeth? You with me?"

The room was lit with morning light, illuminating Abraham's concerned eyes.

"Abraham?" My voice trembled.

His large, rough hand smoothed the hair off my sticky face. "Shh, I'm here. You're okay."

I let out a tired breath, and without thinking, wrapped my arms around his neck pulling him close. My body trembled beneath his large frame, and I squeezed tighter. He was still for only a moment before sliding one hand into the hair on the back of my head, and the other around my waist. Abraham lay there, holding and shushing me until the tremors subsided, and my exhausted body finally went limp.

He pulled back and propped his weight up on his elbows. His eyes traced the lines of my face, searching for something. I lay there completely open, too tired to hide behind the wall I'd built to keep myself safe.

"What happened?" His voice was quiet, warm breath caressing my face.

"It was a wolf." I gulped and closed my eyes. "I was being chased by a wolf."

"Was it the same wolf from the other night?"

I shook my head. "No, this one was smaller."

"Did you recognize it?"

I shook my head again. "What do you think it means?"

He cupped my face, using his thumb to trace small circles on my cheek. "Probably nothing. It was just a dream."

Just a dream.

Of course, it was just a dream. What was I thinking? I exhaled and sank further into the mattress. "You're right. It was just a dream. I don't know why I reacted like that. It's kind of embarrassing." I tried to turn away from his all-seeing gaze, but he held me in place.

"There's no reason to be embarrassed. You had a nightmare. After the past couple of days you've had, I think you're entitled to a bad dream or two."

I shook my head. "I never dream. Or at least I never remember them once I wake up. And this felt so *real*. I could smell the pine trees. I tasted the dirt when I tripped and fell. The wolf was so realistic, I swear I could draw it for you right now."

He pulled back another couple of inches. "Do you think that would help?"

I sighed and covered my eyes with my hand. "I don't know. I'm probably just making a big deal out of nothing."

Abraham gently pried my hand off my face. "You aren't. I was here, I saw how frightened you were. It took me a few minutes to even wake you up."

"Really?"

He nodded slowly.

Realization dawned on me then.

Holy hell, I'd yelled his name.

And just like that, flames erupted under the skin on my face, and I gulped. "You've been in here a while?"

"Yeah, I heard you screaming from across the hall, and rushed over to see if you were all right."

I nodded and squeezed my eyes closed. "Did I–um." Deep breath. "Did I say anything?" I asked.

When Abraham didn't respond, I took a peek in his direction. A huge smile had spread across his handsome face, and I groaned in mortification. "I did, didn't I? Aw, crap."

His chuckles vibrated through his chest, and into mine. I felt his heat come closer as he leaned his head toward mine. "As a matter of fact, you did."

"Oh, my god."

"That's not what you were screaming a minute ago."

"Abraham!"

"That's it! Only it was a little louder."

I slapped his rock-hard chest, hurting my hand in the process, but I was too irritated to care. "You're the worst. Couldn't you have just pretended to not have heard that?"

"Elizabeth," he admonished. "Where's the fun in that?"

"I'm glad *you're* having fun."

He laughed again, pulling me into his arms, and rolling over so we were on our sides facing each other. "Oh, it's not that big a deal."

"That's easy for you to say," I grumbled.

He chuckled again, eliciting an unladylike growl from me which made him laugh harder. I moved to get up, but he wrapped an arm around my waist, and pulled me closer to him.

Our intimate position suddenly registered in my brain, and my body froze. I couldn't believe I was lying in bed with a strange man's arms wrapped around me. Where the hell had my decorum gone? My morals? My standards?

"Why were you yelling my name anyway?" Abraham interrupted my inner dialogue.

I tipped my face up to meet his and regretted it. His soft-looking lips were only inches from mine, and suddenly the most fascinating thing I'd ever seen. The stubble that dotted his jaw earlier was now a full-blown five o'clock shadow, making him even sexier in a rugged way. His strong jaw, and prominent chin begged to be kissed, and nibbled, and I was having trouble denying the impulse.

"Elizabeth?"

I snapped my eyes up to his. "Huh?"

He smiled knowingly. "Why did you yell my name in your dream? Was I in it?"

I shook my head. "No, you weren't in it. I yelled your name when the wolf lunged at me."

His brows furrowed. "Why's that?"

I studied his eyes, first the right, then the left, back and forth, over and over. I didn't want to tell him the truth. I didn't want him to know what I knew. That I'd come to see this man as a protector. *My* protector.

"I... um..." I stalled, hoping for a distraction that would get me out of answering this question.

He inched closer until his warm breath blew against my cheek. One of his thick fingers traced the edge of my jaw from ear to chin and back again. "Will you please tell me?"

"I..."

His cheek met mine, the rough hair scratching my skin deliciously, and sending a shiver down my spine. "Please?" he asked again.

I sighed in irritation. He wasn't going to let it go, and I needed to gain some distance from this man before I lost all my sensibility. I leaned back, breaking the contact with his face. "Fine. I'll tell you." Deep breath. "The answer is: I don't know."

"That's not an answer–"

"I'm not done." He shut his mouth with a snap, and I continued with my confession. "I was alone, and scared in the woods again, and your name was the first thing that popped into my head."

His smile almost split his face in two.

"It's probably because you found me last time, and my frightened, adrenaline-filled brain was hoping you'd save me again," I rushed to explain.

He kept smiling.

"I don't even know why I did it. It was just a fluke. I don't need or expect you to save me again. That was a one-time deal."

He shook his head, his smile just as bright. "You're wrong." His face lowered to mine until his lips were against my ear. "I'll always be there to save you," he whispered.

"I don't need saving." My voice was breathy, and almost unrecognizable.

He shook his head again, his nose brushing against the shell of my ear. "Everyone needs saving sometimes."

I opened my mouth to object again but was interrupted by a knock at the door.

"It's Evey!"

"Come in," Abraham yelled before I could respond.

I squeaked in horror and scrambled to get out of the compromising position I was in. Unfortunately, Abraham was not as concerned, and I had to remove his hand from my hip before I could sit up.

The overhead lights blazed to life, blinding me as I struggled to crawl off the bed.

"Well, well. What do we have here?" Evey's smug voice came from somewhere near the door.

"Nothing!"
"Elizabeth had a nightmare."

We answered in unison.

My vision cleared enough to see the pint-sized woman, standing in the doorway with arms folded across her chest, and lips spread into a huge smile. "Uh-huh," she drawled.

"He's right. I had a nightmare. He woke me up from it. That's all."

"He needed to get in the bed with you to wake you up?" she asked with an arched brow.

"No. Yes. No. He–"

"She was upset. I was comforting her," Abraham piped up.

"Oh, *comforting* her, were you? Is that what the kids are callin' it these days?"

Abraham's deep laugh echoed around the room while my cheeks burned painfully. I covered my face with both hands, praying for invisibility. Or maybe a sinkhole. A tornado? Anything to get me out of this.

"I was just comin' to see what Elizabeth wanted for breakfast, but I see you got things handled here, Abey."

I heard the bed sheets rustling, and moments later, his warm hand was resting between my shoulder blades.

"Are you feeling better now?" he asked.

"Define *better*." I grumbled.

He chuckled. "There's the Elizabeth I've come to know and love!"

Love?!

He gently mussed my hair before walking away.

"I'll see you later at the cookout," he called over his shoulder.

"Abraham McCoy! Have you lost your damn mind?!" I hollered after him, but he only chuckled, and shut the door behind him. "Ooh that man! He drives me crazy," I grumbled while trying to put my long hair back into some sort of order.

"Mmm hmm. I'm sure that's not all he drives you."

I leveled her with a glare. "What's that supposed to mean?"

Her hands raised in surrender. "Nothin', nothin'. Jeez. Did you wake up on the wrong side of the bed or somethin'?"

"No."

"Oh, that's right! You woke up underneath Abey!"

With a growl of frustration, I picked up one of the many pillows on the bed and hurled it at her head.

Evey laughed and deflected the projectile with ease. "Girl, that temper's gonna get you in trouble come the full moon."

"I don't have a temper," I spat.

She raised both brows and looked from me to the pillow laying on the floor, and back again. "Right," she said slowly.

I rolled my eyes, but couldn't help the way my lips twitched, begging to turn up in a smile. "You had it comin'," I insisted.

Evey shrugged her shoulders. "You're probably right. I'll have to watch it once you shift, and your aim gets better."

I couldn't help but laugh at that. You really couldn't stay mad at Evey for long. "Moving on! What does one wear to a werewolf barbecue, anyway?"

Chapter 12

Although my leg was feeling much better, it still took me a long time to make it down the two flights of stairs on my own. Evey's moaning and groaning did little to help the situation.

"I don't understand why you won't just let me carry you."

"Evey, you're half my size, that's ridiculous."

"I'm a *werewolf!* My size has nothin' to do with my strength. We could already be outside eatin' deviled eggs and fried pickles. I swear, if they're all gone by the time we get there, you'll have me to answer to. And trust me, you don't want to deal with a hungry werewolf."

"Deviled eggs?" My mouth watered.

"Yup. Miss Elsie makes the best I've ever tasted. And at this rate, we'll be eatin' next week's deviled eggs instead."

I rolled my eyes. "Stop being so dramatic, we're almost there."

A minute or two later, we finally made it to the ground floor. Evey led me behind the grand staircase, and down a long hall to sliding glass doors. Out past the back deck were a bunch of wooden picnic tables with at least two dozen people sitting, standing, and loitering amongst them.

"I knew we'd have a big turnout today," Evey muttered beside me.

We stepped onto the back deck to find a long stretch of tablecloth-covered tables, holding what looked like enough food to feed half of North Carolina.

One table held plates piled high with hamburgers, hotdogs, ribs, brisket, fried chicken, and pulled pork. Next to that sat potato salad, coleslaw, hush puppies, cornbread, corn on the cob, fried pickles, mac and cheese, and the most delectable looking deviled eggs. Last was the dessert table. A half dozen pecan pies joined about as many apple, and sweet potato pies. Beside that was a large bowl of fruit salad, a couple tiered cakes, and a large plate full of a variety of cookies.

To my astonishment, most of the dishes were already half gone.

"You are *so* lucky there's eggs left!" Evey huffed before sprinting away from my side, and over to the food laden tables. She popped a deviled egg into her mouth before grabbing a paper plate and piling food onto it.

I limped over to join her when Abraham appeared next to me. "I got you a plate already." Without waiting for a response, he grasped my elbow, and led me down the deck stairs, and onto the lush grass.

He directed me toward a mostly full table up front and motioned for me to take one of the remaining spots. When I sat down, he slid a mountainous plate of food in front of me.

My eyes widened. "I can't eat all that!"

"You don't have to," he assured me, "I didn't know what you liked, so I got you some of everything."

"We clearly need to have a talk about my food preferences," I mumbled.

He chuckled and leaned closer to my ear. His warm breath tickled the sensitive skin there. "I look forward to learning anything I can about you."

I fought off a shiver and kept my gaze fixed on my monstrous plate. When I spotted a paprika-speckled stuffed egg, I scooped it up, and stuffed it in my mouth. Evey was right, they were delicious.

As soon as my mouth was full, Abraham took that opportunity to introduce me to the rest of the table. "Elizabeth, I want you to meet some of the pack." I turned to a thin, strawberry-blond man with a smattering of freckles spread across his face. "This is our healer, Dr. Monroe, and his mate Doreen." The olive-skinned woman next to him gave me a warm smile which I returned.

"Please call me Kyle. It's a pleasure to meet you, Elizabeth, although I'm sorry for the circumstances."

I couldn't help but like the exceedingly polite man. "Thank you, Kyle. It's nice to meet you too."

"If you wouldn't mind, I'd like to take a quick look at your wounds after dinner. I know Abraham treated them, and he's perfectly capable, but you *are* still human, and I want to make sure there's no infection we need to worry about."

"Thank you, Kyle, that's very kind of you to offer."

He waved my gratitude off, and his wife shook her head indulgently. "He can't help it, he's been beside himself since you got here, and Abraham wouldn't let anyone see you."

"You're the only survivor we've come across. And although you'll be a werewolf soon enough, you're still human, and very susceptible to infection," the doctor added.

I turned a questioning eye to Abraham, but he was ignoring me. Instead he turned to the other two men at the table. Their features were similar, but their expressions were vastly different. The one with long, shaggy brown hair just grazing his shirt collar had an open expression, and friendly hazel eyes. Next to him sat a larger man with a buzz cut, and a severe look on his face.

"These are my cousins, Calvin and Clyde," Abraham gestured to the men. "Calvin's the one who found you in the woods."

I smiled gratefully at the friendly looking man. "Thank you, Calvin. I would have died out there if you hadn't found me."

"You should have," Clyde interjected.

I felt Abraham tense beside me, and a low, menacing growl come from deep in his chest.

Calvin turned angry eyes toward his brother before giving me an apologetic smile. "You'll have to forgive Clyde, he's got a way with words. Unfortunately, it's a bad way."

Clyde slammed his palms against the table and stalked off. Calvin sent a worried glance in Abraham's direction before excusing himself and following his brother.

"Don't worry about him," Abraham said between gritted teeth. "He's just upset we haven't found this wolf yet and doesn't understand why he left you alive. It's nothing personal."

I nodded mechanically, but underneath, Clyde's words had shaken me. Was he unhappy to have me as an addition to his pack? Was he mad that I survived when so many others hadn't? But that doesn't make sense, he should be happy there was one less body left in this killer's wake.

Loud chatter interrupted my musings and Evey, Delilah, and Callista squished into the seats left unoccupied by Calvin and Clyde. I smiled weakly at the women and returned my attention to my plate. I'd hardly eaten anything, but found my appetite was missing.

"Do you want something else to eat?" Abraham asked softly.

I couldn't help the small smile that lifted my lips. Nothing got past him. "No, this is all delicious. I'm just not that hungry anymore." I met his gaze and saw the concern in his blue eyes.

"Did you like the deviled eggs, Elizabeth?" Evey piped up from the other end of the table.

I turned to her with a forced smile and nodded. "You were right, they were amazing."

Evey smiled knowingly and opened her mouth to speak but was interrupted by shouts coming from the other end of the yard. We all swiveled to see Calvin and Clyde arguing. Clyde's fists were clenched as he towered over his brother whose hands were up like he was trying to placate the angry man.

"Looks like Jekyll and Clyde is at it again," Delilah muttered.

"Del," Abraham snapped.

The spunky woman raised her hands. "I'm sorry, but that man is unhinged."

"He's your cousin."

Del scoffed. "Right and bein' a part of our bloodline makes you a paragon of sanity?"

Abraham didn't reply, but his thinned lips spoke of his displeasure.

"How are you feeling today, Elizabeth?" Callista's soft voice broke the silent tension.

I turned gratefully to her. "Much better, thanks."

She smiled sweetly and turned to talk to Doreen.

Abraham's calloused hand wrapped around my arm. "Would you like to meet some more of the pack?"

I gulped. I hated being the new girl. Making a good first impression in a social setting was difficult for me. Put me in front of a judge and a twelve-person jury of strangers, and I excelled. Ask me to make small talk, and I had a bad habit of sinking. But these people were a part of my future, and it would be a good idea to make friends.

I nodded. "Sure." My smile was brittle, but it was there all the same. If Abraham noticed, he didn't comment on it.

He led me to the next table over. "You've already met, Bea," he motioned toward his sour-faced sister. I gave her a smile despite her obvious aversion to me. What I'd done to the woman, I wasn't sure, but although she intimidated me something fierce, I'd never let it show.

"Hi, Bea. Nice to see you again."

"It's Beatrice," she snapped.

"Bea!" Abraham growled.

The woman just rolled her eyes and turned to the black-haired woman next to her.

"That's Bea's best friend, Peyton," he motioned toward the woman Bea was speaking to. Peyton gave me a brief inspection from head to toe before returning her attention to Abraham's irritable sister. She seemed to like me as much as Beatrice did.

Making friends already, Montgomery.

Abraham then gestured to a short, black-haired man next. "That's Peyton's brother, Paul and next to him is his mate Annalise."

I smiled, and greeted both of them, and was given only slightly warmer welcomes. The next few tables Abraham dragged me to were very different. It seemed like the majority of the pack were both happy to meet me, and curious about my encounter with the elusive serial killer. Abraham squashed any questions that arose, telling them it was too soon for me to talk about any of it.

I was torn. Letting a man make decisions for me about what I did or didn't want to talk about was against my nature. I didn't let others speak or decide for me. *Especially* not a man. But I really *didn't* want to talk about the attack yet. It was still so fresh in my mind, and after the nightmare I'd just had, I was feeling even more raw. Besides that, I was at a party full of people that I'd never met before, and I felt very much out of my element.

With my feelings in turmoil, I decided to just stay quiet instead of kicking up a fuss about it. Besides, I was learning that Abraham didn't have any ill intentions. He was trying to protect me, and it wouldn't hurt to let him, would it?

Once I'd been introduced to dozens of pack members, Abraham led me to the dessert table, and insisted I try a piece of Miss Elsie's famous pecan pie. I'd had a chance to meet the older woman herself and could confirm her personality was as sweet as her pie.

"Oh my god, this is good," I groaned around a mouthful of pie.

Abraham chuckled. "I know right? Elsie joining this pack was a godsend."

I swallowed a large bite before speaking again. "How long has she been with you?"

He squinted up at the darkening sky. "Hmm must be about five years now. After her husband passed away, she left her old pack and came to ours."

"How come?"

Abraham frowned. "She didn't agree with that alpha, and once her sick husband was gone, she had nothing keeping her there."

"How did she find you?" I asked, eyes still on my dessert.

"I knew her from our old pack."

I met his gaze, my brows furrowed. "And she didn't leave with you at first because her husband was sick?"

Abraham nodded.

"Why *did* you leave your old pack?"

He opened his mouth to speak but was interrupted by a joyous declaration from someone on the lawn. "Bonfire!"

Abraham smiled and shook his head. "That's a long story for another time." He grasped my arm, and led me back down the stairs, and over to a series of rocks and logs encircling a large fire pit. The orange and red flames were growing, licking, and snapping toward the twilit night.

He led me to a large petrified log, and I took a seat, grateful to be off my injured leg. I closed my eyes and luxuriated in the warmth emanating from the fire. Abraham's large hand rubbed small circles across my shoulder blades, and I had to stop myself from moaning in pleasure.

That realization snapped me out of my stupor, and I sat up straighter. Abraham's hand fell away from my back, and I stared straight ahead, unwilling to see if my actions had upset or disappointed him.

Since when did I start caring about his feelings?

"How's your leg?" he asked quietly.

I turned to him, but another face caught my attention. Across the circle from us sat Beatrice and Peyton. The latter's face was pinched in fury, her glare even hotter than the fire. My eyes widened in shock. What could I have done to make her so upset?

"Elizabeth?"

Abraham's deep voice broke through the staring contest I was having with the irate werewolf. "Huh? Oh. Right. I'm fine, thanks. A little sore, but much better."

He nodded thoughtfully. "Kyle's right, I should have had him take a look at your leg a long time ago. If you have an infection, we could have caught it days ago." His worried voice rumbled in the space between us.

"I'm pretty sure it's not infected. Stop worrying so much."

He shook his head and leaned in closer. "It's my job to worry about you."

"Because you're the alpha?"

When he didn't answer right away, I turned to meet his eyes. They were dark blue in the early evening light and so deep, I swear they were bottomless. We stayed locked like that for an immeasurable amount of time. I felt my body sway toward his, as if he were a magnet and I was a pile of iron filings, helpless to deny the attraction I felt. Gravitating toward him as if that's where I belonged.

"Who wants to hear some music?" A voice yelled nearby, breaking the spell. I leaned back and took a deep breath to steady my nerves. My eyes sought Peyton without my permission and found both her and Beatrice still glaring at me, their eyes brimming with hatred.

I looked away, remembering you weren't supposed to stare down an angry animal. The comparison elicited a dark chuckle from me that had Abraham shooting a questioning look in my direction.

Del was sitting nearby fiddling with the tuning pegs on a tan acoustic guitar.

"Del's really good," Abraham whispered near my ear.

I ignored the chill his proximity sent down my spine. "Oh yeah?"

"Yeah. She has gigs around Asheville all the time."

"Anyone have any requests?" Del called over the chatter.

Abraham cleared his throat and stood. "Do you mind if I join you?"

My wide eyes traveled from him to his equally surprised sister and back. "You wanna play with me?" she asked incredulously.

He laughed. "Let me go get my guitar," he called as he hurried toward the house.

Evey slid into his empty seat and leaned toward me. "Abey hasn't played in years. Him and Del used to write music together all the time. It's been years though. I can't believe he's decided to play tonight. I wonder what's changed," she mused. I could feel her eyes on me, but I ignored her, refusing to entertain her insinuations. There was no way I was responsible for his sudden change of heart. He'd just met me. How could I have had such a big impact in such a short time?

As I tried to believe my own words, a little voice in my heart whispered: *look how much he's changed you already.* I ignored it too.

Chapter 13

Abraham returned and took a seat near Del. He fiddled with the strings on his black acoustic guitar while his sister plucked a few chords.

"You have a song in mind?" she asked.

He shot me a quick glance and turned back to his guitar. "Let me back you up first, and then I'll play after you."

Del nodded and adjusted her fingers on the strings. She took a deep breath and strummed a steady beat. After a few moments of Abraham watching her movements, he joined in with perfect synchronicity.

Delilah's voice was high and clear, with beautiful pitch, and perfect control. The first few lines of the song sounded familiar, but it wasn't until the chorus that I recognized Sheryl Crow's "If It Makes You Happy". A small rasp deep in her throat gave the song some dimension and grit. She was amazing.

Soon, my foot was tapping in time to the beat, and I was mouthing the words along with her. When she got to the second chorus, Abraham lent his voice, and I was astonished at the clarity and tone. Both siblings were incredibly talented.

I watched Del lose herself in the song. She sang as if she'd lived the words and composed it herself. In the dim light, this spunky woman's passion shone brightly, and I could see how much music meant to her.

By the third chorus, most of the pack had joined in to sing with them, myself included. I'd never sang in public before, and if there weren't dozens of other voices to drown mine out, I wouldn't be. I felt strangely at ease with these people. Besides Clyde, Beatrice and Peyton, everyone had welcomed me with a warmth I hadn't expected.

The song came to an end, and we all broke out in cheers and applause for the duo. Del's eyes glittered, and when she looked over at her brother, the happiness on her face doubled. "Your turn?"

He nodded and rearranged his fingers on the strings. With eyes closed, the first words of the next song confidently slipped from his lips. Before when he'd sang with Del, I wasn't able to hear the full depth and timber of his singing voice, but now with him center stage, I was transfixed.

The words he sang sounded familiar, but I couldn't place the melody. After a few lines, I realized he was singing a slow and stripped-down version of the classic Beatles song "I Want To Hold Your Hand". After a while Del began to sing backup, but her voice barely registered with me.

When he reached the second verse, his eyes found mine with pinpoint precision. His laser focused eyes gleamed in the moonlight, drilling straight into my soul. I was lost as his deep voice hollowed out my center, refilling it with a yearning I didn't understand. I wasn't sure what was happening, or what I was feeling, but I couldn't deny the delicious warmth that spread from my chest to every corner of my body. I was slowly being filled up by this man, and in very real danger of overflowing.

With the third verse came the climax of the song, and Abraham sang it flawlessly. I felt like a passenger he'd taken along on this ride. He'd driven me up this incredibly high mountain, and coaxed me back to the ground, ending the song on a prolonged note that swirled around me, and dissipated into the warm evening air.

The pack erupted in cheers and chants, but all I could see was Abraham, his eyes locked on mine. The breath in my lungs froze as my heart galloped ahead. My brain was past all functionality. If it hadn't been, I know it would have told me to run as fast as I could away from this man. Because the look in his eyes was unraveling my well-constructed world, and if I didn't watch my step, I'd entangle myself in the loose strands.

My staring match was interrupted when a thin, dark-haired woman stepped in front of Abraham, cutting off our connection. I took my first real breath since he'd started singing, and felt my tightly wound insides recoil, and reconfigure themselves into the order I'd learned to master.

"Oh my god, Abey, that was amazing!" A high-pitched voice rang out above the cacophony. It was Beatrice's friend, Peyton. My stomach pinched sharply for just a moment before I shook it off. Peyton was none of my business. *Abraham* was none of my business.

I turned to Evey who was surprisingly quiet beside me. Her eyes narrowed in the direction I'd been looking, and in that instant, I liked her even more.

"Do you sing too?" I asked her, desperate for a distraction from the annoyingly flirtatious voice I couldn't seem to drown out.

Evey scoffed. "Girl, I couldn't carry a tune if I had a bucket with a lid on it. I'm afraid our parents' gift for music didn't make it down to me."

"Your parents were musicians too?"

"Not professional or anything, but they played a lot of music when we were younger. That's how Del and Abey learned. They tried to teach all of us, but only those two were ever any good. Bea wasn't too bad on the drums and Callie played violin throughout school. I was always put on the triangle," she sulked, and I couldn't help but laugh.

"Don't worry, I'm with you. I'm not very musically inclined either though not for lack of trying. The day I had to finally admit to myself I wasn't the next Christina Aguilera was a dark one."

Evey erupted in peals of infectious laughter. We were still giggling when Kyle found me.

"Elizabeth is this a good time for me to take a look at your leg?"

"That'd be great, thanks."

"Let's move into the lodge so we have better lighting."

"I'll catch up with you later," Evey said before disappearing into the crowd.

I began limping toward the house when Kyle tsked. and wrapped a thin arm around my shoulders.

"I'm fine," I assured him.

He shook his head, a lock of strawberry-blond hair falling across his forehead. "You are not fine. You were bitten by a werewolf. One that has killed numerous other women. You're lucky to be alive, and frankly, lucky I'm not making you use crutches until you're all healed up. Now, cooperate with me."

Feeling chastised, I grumbled, "Some bedside manner."

The middle-aged doctor laughed heartily. "Werewolves are notoriously stubborn. I've had to learn to be stern, or I'd get nowhere with them. And although you aren't a full-fledged werewolf yet, your stubbornness could rival even the prickliest of our kind."

I wasn't sure if I should take that as an insult or not, so I kept quiet.

Minutes later, we were in a large, well-lit living room in the lodge. Kyle eased me onto a brown leather sofa and had me set my injured leg on a nearby ottoman.

"May I?" he asked, gesturing toward the gauze around my calf.

I nodded, and he gently peeled the bandage off. He studied the wounds, turning my leg this way and that to hit the light at different angles.

"Everything looks good. Thankfully the werewolf venom in your system is already helping to speed up the healing process."

His words struck me. Although I'd been told my body would change, and that I'd eventually shift into a werewolf, the idea that there was already a physical difference drove that point home. I was no longer an average human. I would really turn into a werewolf someday soon.

"Now, what about that head injury?"

"Uh, it's been fine, actually. I had a headache earlier, but it's gone now."

He nodded, and reached out to touch my face, as he examined the cut.

"What's going on here?" a deep, menacing voice interrupted.

I looked up to find Abraham in the doorway, shoulders tensed, fists clenched, and eyes bright with anger. His gaze raked my body, halting on where the doctor still held my face. The next minute he was standing beside Kyle with his hand gripping the older man's shoulder. He yanked him backward, and Kyle almost lost his footing, catching himself just in time.

I struggled to my feet. "Abraham, what the hell is wrong with you?"

He ignored me. Instead, he placed his large frame between me and Kyle, and I watched his shoulders rise and fall with his rapid breaths. I peeked around him to see Kyle with his eyes on the ground, and his hands held up in surrender.

"I was just checking her wounds, Abraham. You heard me offer that earlier."

"Why didn't you come get me?" His voice was still deep, and deadly.

"You were busy, and I didn't want to interrupt. I meant no harm. I was only trying to make sure she was healing properly." He chanced a quick look at Abraham's face. "You wouldn't want her to have an infection that went untreated, would you?"

Abraham remained quiet for a few endless minutes while I watched the muscles in his back slowly uncoil, his arms falling limp to his sides. He ran a rough hand over his face and reached out to pat the doctor on the back.

"You're right, friend. I apologize. When I couldn't find her, I panicked. Forgive me."

Kyle smiled genuinely. "There's nothing to apologize for. After all, she is your m–"

"Newest pack member!" Abraham interrupted. "She's my newest pack member, and you know how protective I am of them."

The doctor looked confused for a moment before clarity washed over his features. He opened his mouth to respond, but I interrupted this time.

"Could you two stop talking about me like I'm not here?"

Abraham tensed, but Kyle only chuckled. "Good luck with your...newest pack member. I have a feeling you'll need it." With that cryptic remark, he took his leave.

Abraham released a big breath and turned to me.

"What was that all about? You could have hurt him."

He shook his head slowly. "I know. I'm sorry. Like I said, when I couldn't find you, I panicked. Then when I found you alone in here with him…" His voice trailed off, Adam's apple bobbing up and down.

"I don't understand you," I confessed.

He chuckled darkly. "That makes two of us."

He smiled and held out an arm. "Come on, let's get back to the bonfire. I think someone brought out marshmallows, and I'm craving a s'more."

Remembering the doctor's threat, I latched onto Abraham's arm, and let him lead me out of the room.

"I can't remember the last time I had a s'more," I told him.

We stepped out onto the back deck, and the sound of singing, and laughter filled the cool night air.

Abraham ducked his head and spoke softly in my ear. "Then it's a good thing you're here."

I fought off a shiver, and nodded, not trusting myself to speak. Del was just finishing another song when we arrived back at the bonfire. Abraham found us two seats and tracked down the necessary s'more supplies.

While he speared a couple marshmallows onto the end of a long stick, I scanned the faces in the surrounding crowd. Some I could identify from the introductions Abraham had made earlier, but most I couldn't. As I looked around, one thing struck me as odd.

"Do you not allow children into your pack?"

Abraham did a double take. "Why would you think that?"

"It seems like you have people of all ages here except kids."

He stared into the flames that licked at the soft white puffs he held above the fire. "A pack is only as secure as their alpha."

I waited a beat, hoping he'd continue. When it was clear he wasn't, I spoke up. "And you aren't secure?"

He met my eyes briefly and sighed. "There are tons of couples in the pack in their childbearing years, but they won't feel comfortable having children until I do."

I frowned. "Why do they have to wait for you? Is that some kind of weird wolfy rule?"

A reluctant chuckle fell from his lips. "No. It's nothing like that." He paused for a moment. "Werewolves are very protective of their young, and they'll only bring a child into a pack if they're sure it'll be a safe place to raise them. The ultimate sign of safety is when an alpha has children of his own. If the alpha is unwilling to have children that signals to the pack that things aren't stable enough for him. And if the alpha isn't strong enough to protect his own young, the rest of the pack knows he couldn't protect theirs either."

I digested his words for a few minutes before responding. "So, you're not willing to have children?" I wasn't sure why that thought saddened me but couldn't deny that it did.

He shook his head. "No, I'd love to have children."

"Then what's stopping you?"

His gaze met mine, the yearning clear even in the dim light. Without my permission, my heart beat faster. Deep inside, I had this undeniable craving to be or find or do whatever he was looking for.

"Just waitin' on the right lady to come along." The carefree words were at odds with his serious eyes. I cleared my throat nervously, and the browning marshmallows drew his attention again. "I've had my fair share of... options. Some folks think I should have settled for one of them."

A sudden heat swelled in the pit of my stomach, and I clenched my fists in my lap. "Options?" I asked slowly.

"A few." He shrugged.

I nodded and looked away. My chest felt tight as my insides churned. The idea of him with another woman filled me with an emotion I was having trouble identifying. I quickly reasoned that it was just the thought of him being pushed into a relationship against his will that bothered me.

Keep telling yourself that, Montgomery.

Abraham's voice broke through the turmoil swirling inside me. "I'm glad I held out."

I looked away, desperate to cling to anything that could keep my feet on level ground. But the dirt beneath me was slowly crumbling, and I knew it was becoming more and more unlikely I would escape this man unscathed.

"You are?" I asked against my better judgement.

He busied himself assembling the gooey confections and handed me one before finally answering. "I really am."

Chapter 14

"We!" the crowd chanted back at Del, the sound of our combined voices echoing in the clearing.

We were in the midst of a lively rendition of Taylor Swift's classic "We Are Never Ever Getting Back Together". As I sang along, I looked around the group of people, and saw every one of them knew all the words. When Del's sweet voice rang out with the last note, they all erupted in cheers.

I turned to Abraham. "Taylor Swift? Really?"

He shot me a comically offended look. "Don't tell me you're not a Swiftie." A loud laugh shot out of me, and I slapped a hand over my mouth. His answering smile was brilliant. "Are you having a good time?"

"I really am. Thank you for inviting me."

He shook his head. "You're pack now. That means you're family."

Family.

That word was still so foreign. It'd been so long since I could say I was a part of one. The encroaching sadness was cut short when a small group of people approached us.

"We're heading home, Abraham. Thanks for the cookout."

He reached out to pull the man into a brief hug. "Anytime, you know that. Elliot, this is our newest pack member, Elizabeth."

I held out a hand, but he knocked it aside in favor of pulling me into a brief, but fierce embrace. "Welcome to the pack, little lady. I look forward to gettin' to know ya'."

With heated cheeks, I stuttered out my thanks. The rest of his group also enveloped me in big hugs before taking their leave. Feeling self-conscious, I tried to step behind Abraham, but he wrapped an arm around my waist, and stood me next to him. His touch was becoming familiar and almost expected at this point.

It felt like there was more to his touch than simple friendship. But I had *zero* time for a relationship, so that thought got folded up, and stuffed in a closet somewhere in the back of my mind.

Person after person streamed by us, offering thanks to Abraham, and welcomes to me. I hugged more people in that fifteen-minute span than I had in the last fifteen years of my life. To my surprise, it got easier as time went by. I went from feeling awkward, and out of place, to holding out my arms without being prompted.

When most of the pack had gone home, the only ones left were the McCoy siblings, and unfortunately, Peyton.

The latter slithered over to us and wrapped a thin arm around Abraham's bicep. "Abey," she cooed, "Some of us are gonna have some moonshine down by the lake. You're comin' right?" Her fake eyelashes were fluttering so fast, they looked like they were in danger of flying off.

Abraham extricated himself from her grip and took a small step back. "Thanks, Peyton, but I'm good tonight."

Her angry eyes flashed in my direction before she stuck out a lip. "C'mon Abey. It'll be fun."

He shook his head resolutely. "No, thanks."

She pouted harder and actually stomped her foot. "Fine. We'll have fun without you then." Spinning on her heel, she stomped over to Beatrice who shot a scathing look my way before wrapping an arm around Peyton and leading her away.

Evey, Delilah, and Callista wandered over next.

"You two aren't comin'?" Evey asked.

"Elizabeth can't drink moonshine."

I turned angry eyes in his direction. "Says who?"

"Says me," he retorted.

I spun on my heel and poked him in the chest. "Who do you think you are tellin' me what to do?"

Callista stepped forward. "He's right, Elizabeth, you can't drink this moonshine."

I redirected my ire her way.

"Hear me out," she entreated.

I sighed, but kept my mouth shut.

"The moonshine we have here is a lot stronger than anything you've ever had. It has to be to affect us in any way. If you drank it, there's the possibility you'd get really sick. We don't know for sure what effect werewolf moonshine would have on a human, but none of us are willing to take that risk with you."

The other two women nodded seriously, and the anger left my system all at once, deflating me like an old birthday balloon.

"Okay, that makes sense." I turned to Abraham. "Why didn't you just say that in the first place?"

He laughed humorlessly and shook his head. "I would have if you'd let me get a word in."

I opened my mouth to argue, but thought better of it, and snapped it shut.

"No sarcastic retort?" he asked.

With narrowed eyes, I warned him, "Don't try me."

He laughed again and turned to say goodnight to his sisters. They each hugged me tightly before melting into the dark night.

And suddenly, I was alone with Abraham.

My heart was the first one to react, thumping wildly in my chest, almost drowning out the noisy crickets and cicadas around us.

Abraham either didn't hear my wild heartbeat or was choosing to ignore it. Either was fine with me. He held out his strong, tan arm, and I wrapped my hand around it.

While we made our way back to the house, Abraham tried to help me identify the members of the pack I wasn't familiar with. He had a different funny or interesting story for each one, and it was obvious how much he cared for his pack. They really were like a big family.

When we made it to the staircase, I looked up the steep steps with trepidation. My leg was feeling better, but walking up these steps to the back door, and then another two flights to my room would be tough. Abraham sighed from behind me before my feet left the ground, and I found myself cradled in his strong arms. We were up the first flight, and in the house before I had a chance to protest.

"Abraham, put me down!"

He shook his head. "I spoke with the doc, and he told me to keep you off that leg as much as possible."

"It's feeling better. I don't need to be babied like this."

He shook his head again. "He said you'd try to argue your way out of it."

I crossed my arms over my chest and huffed in defeat. They were all conspiring against me.

Or they're just concerned.

I pushed that thought away and locked it up in the back of my mind. I didn't need anyone's concern. Or help.

Or worse, their pity.

I expected him to set me down once we made it to my room, but he swung open the door, and walked over to my bed before I could protest. He gently sat me on the edge of the bed and took a big step back.

His breaths were even and measured as if he hadn't just lugged my butt up three flights of stairs. But as he stood there, his chest began to rise and fall more rapidly. How was it that he was out of breath *now*?

"Do you need anything?" His voice was full of grit.

I shook my head, unable to form words at the moment. I watched him brace himself before closing the distance between us.

"Abraham," I breathed. With my eyes squeezed closed, I took a big breath. "Whatever this is," I wagged a finger between the two of us, "cannot happen."

There. I'd said it.

He reached out a hand to tuck a lock of thick blonde hair behind my ear. When he leaned his face down toward mine, my breath caught in my chest, and I swear, my heart stopped all together. His clean scent enveloped me, and I felt the heat radiating off his body. His warm lips pressed gently against my temple for a moment that felt both brief and infinite.

The room spun, and I wasn't sure if it was from his proximity, or the lack of oxygen. He took his time walking toward the door as if reluctant to leave. When he turned to face me again, I saw my conflicted emotions mirrored on his handsome face. He gave me a small smile. "Sweet dreams, Elizabeth."

Just before he closed the door behind him, I squeaked, "Night."

The door closing echoed throughout the dark, empty room like the heartbeat in my hollow chest. It begged me to call him back, but I resolutely ignored it. I hadn't let my heart make decisions for me in over a decade, and I wouldn't start now. My sanity depended on it.

I woke the next morning feeling much better than the day before. My head was clear, and my leg almost completely healed. I was already showered and dressed when there was a knock on the door.

I called for them to come in, expecting Evey carrying an overly large tray of food. Instead, Abraham's massive frame entered the room, somehow tentative and confident at the same time. I took a minute to admire his casual clothing that seemed tailormade for him. His thick, dark hair was wet as if he'd just showered. He jerked his head to the side flinging an errant lock back into place.

I stood there like an idiot for so long, he had to clear his throat to get my attention.

"Ah. Um. Sorry. Did you say something?" I stuttered. Embarrassed that I'd been caught practically drooling over him. I turned around and continued to towel-dry my hair in the large mirror hanging on the wall.

He chuckled softly. "No, I didn't yet. I was just coming to invite you down to breakfast."

"That sounds great." When Abraham remained quiet, I turned to find him still standing in the doorway, looking like he needed to say something.

"Is there anything I can say to get you to stay here?" he asked quiet, but firm.

Yes.

No.

Probably.

"I have an important meeting I can't miss Tuesday morning," I insisted instead of answering his question.

His eyes dimmed. "What time do you have to leave?"

I couldn't stand to see the look of disappointment on his face, so I turned back to the mirror, and ran a mascara wand over my light lashes. "Probably around noon."

"So soon."

It wasn't a question, but I answered him anyway. "Yeah, I don't want to hit holiday traffic getting back into Raleigh, and I want to get caught up on some paperwork."

"I see." He was silent for a moment while I quickly wove my hair into a thick plait. "Oh! I almost forgot. I still have your camera and phone in my office. We'll get them on the way back up from breakfast, that way you don't have to carry them around all morning."

I gave myself one final look in the mirror. "Sounds great, let's go."

To Abraham's dismay, I insisted on getting down the stairs on my own. He only let it go when he saw how well I was walking on my injured leg today. As we neared the ground floor, the sounds of many people talking, and the clanking of dishes could be heard several rooms away.

He led me down a new hallway to a massive kitchen that overlooked the back of the house. There had to be at least twenty people, mostly men, in various stages of their morning meal.

A large, granite-topped island held large platters of breakfast foods. There were several styles of cooked eggs, a variety of meats, toast, muffins, and breakfast pastries alongside large pots of oatmeal, grits, and cream of wheat. Clear glass pitchers held a few different fruit juices and milk which sat next to a couple carafes of coffee.

"I'm seeing a mealtime pattern," I commented dryly.

Abraham chortled next to me. "We like to eat."

Even though I scoffed at the understatement, I wasted no time locating a clean plate, and loading it up with the delicious smelling food. Abraham was never far away, and once we had full plates, he led me over to the massive wooden table. We found a couple seats near the end, and he held out my chair for me.

Once seated, Abraham made a few introductions to the men sitting closest to us. They all greeted me with friendly smiles, and words of welcome. It wasn't long before I caught the eye of one of the few people who'd been less than hospitable toward me.

Clyde sat on the other side of the table, a few chairs down. He sat hunched over a large plate of food, eating like he hadn't in days. As if he felt my prying eyes, Clyde's gaze snapped up to mine. I quickly looked away but knew the damage had already been done.

Embarrassed, I focused all my attention on the cooling food on my plate. A few moments later, a masculine throat-clearing from behind made me jump in my seat. I spun around to find Clyde just a few feet away, hazel eyes significantly warmer than I'd ever seen them.

"Elizabeth?" His rough voice was like sandpaper against my skin.

I nodded tentatively.

"I want to apologize for my behavior yesterday. I was rude, and I'm sorry."

He stood there waiting for my reply, but I found my tongue absolutely useless. Instead of an actual response, I nodded again.

His jaw clenched almost imperceptibly before continuing. "I was hoping you had a minute to go through the details of your attack with me. Anything you can remember will be useful for me."

I finally managed to unstick my tongue from the roof of my mouth. "Sure."

He smiled widely, and I swear, I could see all thirty-two of his teeth. "If you have time after breakfast, you could come to my room, and we can talk there."

My stomach tightened at the suggestion, but before I could respond, Abraham piped up. "We'll be in my office after breakfast having a look at her phone and camera we recovered from the scene. The camera's damaged, but we're hoping to retrieve something from the memory card. You're welcome to join us."

Clyde nodded his head a few times, his eyes focused on something in the distance. "Sure, sounds good. I'll meet you up there in thirty?"

Abraham took a quick look at my plate. "That should be good."

Clyde nodded once more before making a hasty exit. I watched the doorway he'd disappeared through, trying to understand the unease I felt.

"Sometimes I worry about him." Abraham's voice pulled me out of my thoughts, and I turned to face him.

"Really?"

He nodded seriously. "He had a rough childhood, and it kind of messed him up. Made him real angry all the time. I put him on this case because I thought it would keep him out of trouble. Give him a purpose. Something to be proud of. Instead, it seems like he's become almost obsessed with finding the killer. He spends night after night, combing the woods for any sign of him. It's made me wonder if I made the right decision assigning him to this."

The concern for his cousin was clear in his deep blue eyes. I'd bet just about anything that while Clyde had been out searching for the killer, Abraham had been here worrying about him.

"I think you made the right choice at the time. Keeping his mind off his personal life was probably helpful for him." I was quiet for a moment while images of my own experiences with tough investigations floated through my mind. "It's real easy to let the senseless death and violence get to you. It can change who you are if you're not careful to compartmentalize your work, and your personal life. Maybe Clyde just needs a little break. Some time to step back and clear his head for a while." I laughed humorlessly to myself.

"What's funny?"

"That's what this weekend was supposed to be for me. A time to just relax and let all the stress of my work take a backseat for a few days."

Abraham was quiet for a long time before he asked another simple question. "Do you regret it?"

His words struck me. If he'd asked me this two days ago, my answer would have been an easy *YES*. But now, that answer didn't have the ring of truth it once did.

Did I regret it?

My life had changed irrevocably. Taken a direction I'd never planned for–never even imagined possible. I'd be a werewolf for the rest of my life. A slave to the full moon until the day I died. I'd change in incomprehensible ways.

I took a look around the beautiful kitchen, and out to the backyard. The large ring of seats around the charred logs from last night's fire reminded me of all the wonderful people I'd met. People who'd welcomed a stranger into their fold with no questions asked. I thought about Callista and Delilah. About Evey. And lastly, I met Abraham's true-blue eyes, lit with the tiniest spark of hope.

The answer wasn't *yes* anymore. But I wasn't entirely sure it was *no* either. So, I gave him the only response I could give with absolute certainty.

"I'm not sure."

Chapter 15

When we finished eating, we passed our dirty plates to a surly looking Peyton. She took our dishes, and dropped them into the sudsy water, making dishwater splash her shirt. Her hands curled into fists, and she growled.

"Everything all right, Peyton?" Abraham asked.

"I'm great, Abey." Her tone was honeyed, but her knuckles were turning white with how tightly she had them clenched.

When I thought we were out of earshot, I asked, "Why is Peyton doing the dishes?"

"As of a couple weeks ago, she works here." Abraham's lips pinched. "I employ as many pack members as I can to look after the house and grounds."

My stomach clenched. I didn't like the idea of Peyton working here, but what could I say? It was none of my business who he hired, and I really didn't have a reason to not want her here. It just didn't sit right with me.

We made our way up the stairs in a comfortable silence. Thankfully, my injured leg didn't hinder our progress too much. Once upstairs, we found Clyde leaning against the wall next to Abraham's office door. Abraham unlocked it, and we all took seats around his large mahogany desk.

"So, Elizabeth," Clyde turned to me, "tell me what you can remember from the other night. And keep in mind, any detail might be important, so try not to leave anything out."

With hands folded in my lap to keep them from fidgeting, I reluctantly dug up the painful memories, and laid them out for Clyde. I relayed the story in monotone, afraid that my voice would shake if I gave it any kind of inflection.

Clyde seemed entranced by my story, practically hanging onto every word. Several times, he asked me to repeat, or to go into deeper detail about something I said. I had to admit, after having worked with so many law officials, I'd been expecting Clyde to do a poor job of interviewing. But to my surprise, he was thorough, and exact, asking great follow up questions, and even helping me remember things I hadn't when I'd told the story to Abraham.

Clyde insisted we exchange contact information in the event I remembered anything else. I recited my number, and both Clyde, and Abraham typed it into their phones.

I would have thought spending a weekend without my phone would be torture, but I didn't miss it. There was no one who'd be calling or texting for anything besides work, and I'd promised myself a weekend off. I was almost reluctant to get it back.

After Abraham finished saving my number, he opened his top desk drawer, and retrieved my phone and camera. I took them from him to inspect the damage they'd sustained.

My phone looked intact but was powered off. I didn't know if that was because the battery had died, or the phone had. Abraham offered to plug it into his charger, so I handed it back to him.

Unfortunately, my camera hadn't fared as well. The display on the back was shattered, and as I inspected it, a few drops of water slipped from the seams. I sighed in frustration and slid open the slot where the memory card went. It was empty.

"Huh."

"What's wrong? Is the memory card damaged?" Abraham asked.

I shook my head as I examined the empty slot. "No. It's not in here."

"Do you think it fell out?"

I shook my head again. "No, the latch was still closed, and it doesn't pop open easily. You have to use your nail to slide this tiny piece aside to get the door open." I held the camera up for his inspection and mimed the process for him.

"You must have forgotten to put it in last time you used it?" Abraham's words were half statement, half question.

I shrugged and frowned as I tried to think back. "I guess so."

"Can you turn it on and see if there are any pictures on the camera's internal memory?" Abraham asked.

I shot him a doubtful look, but obliged. Pressing my finger on the power button, I held it for about twenty seconds before releasing it. When nothing happened, I tried it again. And again, this time for longer. With dismay, I had to admit, it looked like the camera was broken.

"It won't turn on?" Clyde asked from beside me.

I shook my head. "Nope. Looks like it's dead."

Abraham sighed in frustration. "That would have been a great lead if we got a shot of the wolf."

I nodded in agreement. "I suppose I can let it dry out, and try plugging it into my computer at home," I offered uncertainly. "It probably won't work, but I guess it's worth a try?"

Clyde clapped his hands together and sprung from his seat. "Well, it looks like we're all done here. If you need me, I'll be on patrol," he said to Abraham, and left.

I kept my eyes trained on the broken camera in my lap, shoulders hunched. "I'm sorry."

"For what?"

I peeked up at him. "I should have kept a better hold of this," I held up the useless contraption. "That picture could have been the big break in this case."

Abraham's large frame rose from his burgundy leather office chair and came around to sit on the desk in front of me. His rough fingers slid underneath my chin, lifting my face to meet his. "You have nothing to be sorry for."

"But–"

"No," he insisted firmly, and my mouth closed with a snap. "You survived. That was all you were responsible for that night."

I sighed. "It doesn't seem like enough," I admitted.

He slid off the desk and crouched in front of me. His eyes were an intense, brilliant blue that tore into my chest, ripping me apart from the inside out. The pain was a delicious agony.

"It's everything," he assured me.

Unfortunately–or maybe fortunately–a knock on the door broke the spell between us. He stood and called, "Come in."

Evey came bursting through the door, mouth first. "Abey, have you seen Elizabeth? I've been lookin' all over and can't find her. She can't have left already cause' her things, and her car are still here. I need to ask her–"

She stopped short when her eyes reached mine. Her gaze traveled from me to Abraham and back again. A sly smile spread across her face. "Am I interuptin' somethin'?"

I sprang to my feet. "Not at all. What was it you wanted to ask me?"

Her mischievous eyes gleamed. "Oh, nothin'. I can come back later."

She turned to leave, and I cleared the distance to the door in record time. "No really. We're done here. I need to finish packing, anyway."

Evey turned questioning eyes toward Abraham who nodded. "All right then. I was just comin' to ask if I needed to pack toiletries like shampoo, and toothpaste or if I could just use yours."

"You're coming home with me?"

She rolled her eyes. "Duh. You think I'd let anyone else get to go first?" She scoffed, and wrapped an arm around my waist, leading me into the hall. "It's gonna be so fun. Like a weeklong sleepover!"

A sleepover? I hadn't had one of those in *decades*. With a look at the bubbly brunette next to me, I knew this week was going to be an interesting one.

About an hour later, the car was packed with mine, and Evey's belongings. Abraham snapped the trunk shut, and walked over to where me, and his siblings stood. Well, all but Beatrice of course. I hadn't seen her since the night before and was extremely grateful for that.

Abraham reached into the front pocket of his jeans and withdrew my cell phone. "Almost forgot this."

I took the device from his hand, threw up a silent prayer to the cellphone gods, and pressed the little power button. A few seconds later, the screen came to life. "Finally! Something that went right this weekend!"

As my phone loaded, I saw Evey shake her head out of the corner of my eye. When I turned, her expression was neutral. I took a peek at Abraham, and found him staring into the woods, a pensive expression on his face.

Missed messages, and calls flooded my notifications as I caught sight of the time. "It's getting late. We should really hit the road," I said to Evey. She nodded and walked off to hug her sisters goodbye.

"May I?" Abraham's deep voice asked from close by. I looked up to find him only a foot away from me, with his hand outstretched. I handed over my cell and watched his thick fingers fly across the screen. "I'm putting my number in your phone. It's saved under 'Sexiest Man Alive' so you'll know where to look for it."

A loud bark of laughter flew out before I could stop it. I used one hand to cover my still-grinning mouth, and the other to slap his muscled shoulder. He shot me a lopsided grin that made my heart do a quick backflip in my chest.

Delilah and Callista approached us, and each took a turn enveloping me in long, warm embraces. After this weekend, you'd think I'd be a hugging master, but I still felt a little awkward. Physical affection wasn't something I'd had a lot of in my life.

When the last woman released me, they both retreated to the house. Evey had taken her spot in my passenger seat, and that left just me and Abraham.

I peered up into his deep blue eyes, and watched as they swirled, and undulated with a mixture of emotions. They were impossible to untangle, and identify, but strangely, it felt like if I had a mirror, I'd see a similar expression staring back at me. This man dug up feelings, and emotions I didn't know what to do with. And frankly, had no place in my life for.

With the weekend coming to a close, I felt the pull of my life in Raleigh tugging me back. The normalcy begging for me to return. But I wasn't normal, anymore was I?

"Please drive safe," Abraham's pleading voice cut through my inner monologue. "And you or Evey text me when you get there. You're sure you're all right to drive, right? Cause' Evey can drive you guys back if you're not feeling up to it. In fact, let me talk to her–"

He made a move to walk around me, but I stopped him with a hand to his chest. Well, I probably couldn't have stopped him if he hadn't wanted to, but he paused all the same. "Abraham. Stop worrying, I feel fine. Haven't had a headache or any dizziness since yesterday afternoon. And the doc said I was clear to drive."

He sighed heavily; the motion pushing my hand, reminding me it still rested on his chiseled chest. I snatched it back and tucked it behind me.

"I wish I were going with you," he admitted softly. "If I didn't have so much work piled up, I would." He closed his eyes and took a deep breath. "Just call me when you get there."

I rolled my eyes. "I promise. We'll let you know when we get to my place."

He nodded, but his eyes were still full of concern. I placed a hand on my hip and poked him once in the chest. "You know, I got out here just fine without you. I'm sure I can make it back just as well."

His eyes traveled from my irritated expression down to my cocked hip, and he smiled. "You know, I think I'm even going to miss that attitude of yours."

"*Attitude?*" My voice was incredulous, eliciting a loud guffaw from him.

"Come here," he beckoned. Without waiting for a response, he wrapped one arm around the back my neck, and the other around my waist, pulling me into his large, warm body. His face tucked in next to mine, and his chest expanded with a large inhale. When he exhaled, his breath blew the hair around my ear, tickling the sensitive skin.

After a few moments, my traitorous body relaxed into his embrace. I raised my arms to wrap around his broad shoulders and felt them tense for the briefest of seconds before he tightened his hold around me. It was almost too tight, but not quite.

For one long minute, I let myself drown in this man. In his scent, and his presence. In his affection, and warmth. Everything that made him Abraham swirled around me, tucking itself into the deepest darkest corners of my soul. Branding me in a way I'd never experienced before.

When I couldn't stand the tornado of emotions inside me any longer, I reluctantly pulled out of his arms. His lingering touch said he was as averse to the separation as I was. But it had to be done. My world had no place for sweet hugs from a man like Abraham.

Because it would never just be a hug with him, would it?

Abraham McCoy was the kind of man who swallowed you up whole. There would be no part of my heart that could be kept safe from him. He'd completely eclipse my life, and I'd be left in the blinding darkness.

No. Abraham needed to stay on this side of the state while I scurried back to mine. There was just no other way.

Chapter 16

We made great time and slipped past Raleigh city limits before the holiday traffic kicked in. I pulled into a parking spot near my building with a confusing swirl of emotions. It felt like I'd been gone for months rather than a long weekend. I looked around the complex and felt as if I was seeing things through different eyes.

"This it?" Evey asked from beside me, interrupting my introspection.

She'd been a great road trip companion. Turns out we like a lot of the same music, and had a great time splitting our favorite songs into duets that we sang loudly, and off-key. In between performances, we found endless topics to chat about, and I felt the friendship between us swell, and solidify.

It was strange, I'm not sure if I consciously avoided it, but I hadn't gotten close to anyone in a long time. In just a few days, Evey had broken down that boundary. If I was being honest, she wasn't the only one. But I was keeping that locked up tight.

"Yep. Home sweet home."

We grabbed as much as we could for this first trip, and I led her up the stairs to my second-floor apartment.

"Where's my handsome man?" I called.

"Whoa," Evey muttered behind me.

Charlie came streaking through the living room, misjudging the distance, and slamming into my shins as usual. His little body vibrated with a purr as he rubbed his soft fur against my legs.

"You have a cat," Evey deadpanned.

"This is my main man," I confirmed. He reared back, and placed his little white paws on my knee, signaling he wanted up. I pulled him into my arms and turned to my new house guest.

Evey's eyes were wide as she surveyed my living room from the doorway. I turned to look at what she was seeing. Multiple tapestries hung from the walls surrounding the ornate hot pink velvet couch in the center of the room. Fairy lights lined the ceiling that when turned on, gave the room a soft glow.

"You have a very... colorful home."

I laughed. "Is it really that bad?"

Evey's eyes were still darting around the space. "I wouldn't call it *bad*. Just suprisin' is all. I didn't figure you for the type."

"Well I guess that just goes to show you can't judge a book by its cover, huh?"

Evey giggled. "I guess you could say that."

I walked over to introduce her to Charlie, but both had very adverse reactions to the meeting. My cat's spine stiffened as his hackles rose, and a warning sound rumbled in his chest. Evey backed up a step, eyes widening in what looked like fear.

I looked between the two trying to figure out the problem. "Charlie isn't the most welcoming to guests, but he's never acted like this before," I mused aloud.

"Werewolves and cats don't mix. I don't even think I've ever been this close to one before." Her delicate shoulders shook with a shudder, and I couldn't help but laugh.

"Oh please. This is about the most gentle cat you could ever meet. Don't tell me you're scared of him."

Evey shook her head adamantly, eyes wide with trepidation. I sighed and set Charlie on the ground. The feline immediately took off for his favorite hiding spot, the fuzzy purple flower cat house. He slipped inside, only his lime green eyes visible.

"Well, you don't need to worry about him. He's not good with strangers, so I imagine he'll spend the week avoiding you too."

Evey didn't look convinced, but she relaxed once the cat had run off. I shook my head in exasperation. "Really, a big, bad werewolf afraid of a little kitty. I've never heard of something so ridiculous." She shot me a glare but ignored my ribbing.

On the second trip, we had the car emptied of our things, and I showed Evey to the guest room/office.

"I'm sorry, I have some work to do in here tonight, but for the rest of the week, I'll try to make sure I finish up before coming home so I don't bug you."

She snorted. "Girl, I shared a room with three sisters until I was sixteen. You comin' in and doin' some paperwork ain't gonna bother me. Do what you need to do. I'm not here to get in your way." I nodded, but silently vowed to do just what I said.

After Evey placed her things in the spare room, I gave her a tour of the rest of the apartment. It wasn't very big, so it didn't take long.

"It's not much, but I don't need much. I didn't see the sense in paying for a big old house when there's only me."

Evey waved me away as she searched through the kitchen cabinets. "Don't worry about it. You've got a nice place here. And you're right, if it's just you, you don't need much." She eyed me critically. "But how come it's just you?"

I averted my gaze. "What do you mean?"

"No boyfriend?"

I shook my head. "No time for boyfriends."

"Hmm. What about girlfriends?" I shot her an incredulous look that made her laugh. "Not like that! I just meant friends who are girls."

"Don't have much time for any of those either."

"Family?"

I shook my head. "No family."

Her eyes widened. "You don't have *any* family?"

My shoulders rose with a half-hearted shrug. "I have a mom and dad, but we're not close. I got along great with my gran, but she passed away years ago."

"You're an only child?"

I nodded.

"Wow. What that must be like."

Lonely.

She cocked a hip and rested a hand on it. "So, I get you don't entertain much, but where's all your food? You gotta' eat right?"

I shrugged again. "I don't eat at home much. Maybe a quick yogurt, or protein bar before work, and then I'll pick up takeout, or get delivery at night. I'm usually too tired to cook."

"Delivery?" Her eyes lit up. "I've never gotten delivery before."

"I'd pretty much starve if it wasn't for Postmates."

"What's Postmates?"

My jaw dropped, and I slung an arm around her shoulders. "My dear Evelyn, I have so much to teach you."

An hour later, there was a knock on the door, and Evey jumped from the couch to answer it. With childish glee, she thanked the driver profusely, and even invited him to stay for dinner. He declined, but her enthusiasm couldn't be dampened.

"We've always lived so far outside of town that no place would deliver to us," she explained as she gathered up plates and utensils for our Chinese food. "Besides, it wasn't safe for random humans to show up on pack lands. Never know who'll be out runnin' around as a wolf."

Her excited chatter kept up throughout our meal, and I found it was nice to have something besides the television to keep me company. We finished, and I reluctantly retreated to the office to tackle some paperwork. It was strange, I couldn't remember the last time I *didn't* want to work. I was always the first one in the office, and the last one out, only to come home, and do more.

I finally settled down to read through some case files when my phone chimed with an incoming message. I'd been purposely avoiding all the missed calls and emails I had piled up, but when another new message came through, I bit the bullet, and checked.

Sexiest Man Alive: Hey

Sexiest Man Alive: How was your drive?

A bark of laughter shot out unexpectedly, and I shook my head.

Me: It was fine, sorry I forgot to text you.

Me: Btw I can't believe you actually saved your number in my phone as "Sexiest Man Alive". You're ridiculous.

Sexiest Man Alive: It's all right. Evey texted me.

Sexiest Man Alive: And I told you I did that. Now you know I mean what I say.

I shook my head again, a stupid smile still pulling at my lips.

Me: I suppose there's no denying that now.

I set my phone aside and focused on my work again. It was only a minute or two before another text came through.

Sexiest Man Alive: What are you doing?
Me: Getting some work done.
Sexiest Man Alive: Do you work from home a lot?
Me: Unfortunately, yes.
Sexiest Man Alive: Why?

I had to think about that for a minute. Why *did* I always bring my work home? Sure, there were the times when I needed to make a call after business hours or had a court date in the morning I needed to prep for. But I brought home work even when it wasn't that important. Grudgingly, I answered as honestly as I could.

Me: Working the extra hours at home gave me the edge I needed to get ahead. Now it's just habit.
Sexiest Man Alive: I think you work too hard.
Me: I think you're right.

I watched the phone's screen for a few minutes before I locked it and turned back to my computer. The blinking cursor was like the second hand of the clock, ticking away the time. Before, I'd had nothing better to do than to work. But here I was, with someone in the other room who was shaping up to be a good friend, and I'd sequestered myself in my office, doing work that could wait. I straightened my spine and snapped my laptop closed.

When I got out to the living room, Evey was spread across the bright velvet couch, idly clicking through channels.

"Wanna watch a movie?" I asked.

Her blue eyes lit with tentative excitement. "Thought you had work to do."

I shook my head and walked over to the couch. With a swipe, I shoved her legs off the end, so I could have a seat. "It's not important. Let's watch a movie on demand instead."

Evey sprang up and clapped her hands. "Yay! What kind of movie do you want to watch?" She asked as she flipped to the on-demand screen and scrolled through our options.

My usual go to movie genre was crime drama, but I was in the mood to branch out. "How about a RomCom? I think there's a new Matthew McConaughey movie out."

"All right, all right, all right." Her impression of the actor was awful, but it still made me laugh.

For the first night in a while, I just relaxed, and enjoyed myself. Even more rare was that I was spending it with a friend. Someone besides my cat.

That night turned out to be one full of firsts. The first time I'd had someone sleep over my apartment, the first time I'd laughed so hard I cried, and the first time I'd received a goodnight text from a man.

Sexiest Man Alive: Sweet dreams, Elizabeth.

The next morning, I emerged from my bedroom, pressed, dressed, and ready for that promotion. A stomach-rumbling smell had me wandering into the kitchen. To my surprise, Evey was already awake, and at the stove cooking something.

"Mornin'," she called over her shoulder.

"Morning. What are you up to so early?"

She waved a hand in my direction. "I'm used to wakin' up early. I thought I could cook you some breakfast before you left."

My heart warmed, swelling in my chest.

"You didn't have to do that," I told her meekly.

She waved another hand and turned the stove off with a click. "I'm takin' up space in your home, the least I can do is cook you a hot breakfast." She whirled around my kitchen like it was her own, fetching bowls and utensils, and scooping up steaming hot oatmeal with a ladle.

I didn't even know I owned a ladle.

She sprinkled brown sugar on top and passed me the bowl. I thanked her, but she'd already turned to prepare her own. I stood there awkwardly, not knowing what to do with myself.

Do I help her?

Do I wait for her?

Do I go sit down?

Evey helped me decide. "Go sit. I'll be over in just a sec."

When we were both seated, I once again thanked Evey for her

thoughtfulness, and dug into my breakfast. We spent a few minutes in companionable silence, the only sounds our spoons clanking against the ceramic bowls.

"I didn't even know I had oatmeal in the house," I mused aloud.

Evey snorted. "Girl, I almost had to call in a backhoe to dig up this food. Your cabinets are *bare*!"

I laughed. "Shut up!"

She shook her head and tucked back into her breakfast. A few minutes later, we were both done, and I stood to bring the dishes to the kitchen. Evey jumped from her seat and snatched the bowls before I could.

"You gotta' get to work. Don't worry about the cleanin', I'll take care of it."

I shook my head. "But you cooked. You shouldn't have to clean too."

She scoffed. "Like I strained myself boilin' oatmeal. Go on and get that promotion girl. I wanna hear all about it when you get home."

My chest tightened again, and I couldn't help the smile that broke across my face. When was the last time I had someone to come home to and share my day with?

I scooped some food into Charlie's bowl before gathering my things and leaving the apartment. It felt so strange to be leaving my place with someone else still inside it. So weird knowing I wouldn't be coming home to an empty apartment.

Last night I'd finally cleared out the missed calls and texts from my forgotten cell phone, so when a chime signaled an incoming message, I didn't hesitate to check.

Sexiest Man Alive: Good morning, Elizabeth. I hope you slept well. Good luck at work today.

With a grin, I typed out a quick message, and sent it off to him. I couldn't remember the last time I'd smiled so much before eight in the morning.

The firsts just kept on coming.

Chapter 17

"Congratulations, Ms. Montgomery. We know you'll be a fantastic addition to our senior associates."

I smiled wide and gave my boss a firm handshake. "Thank you, Mr. Hildebrandt. I won't let you down."

"We know you won't. You just keep doing what you've been doing, and there's no telling where you'll go in this company. We've got an open office for you on the senior's floor, so why don't you go pack up your things, and take the morning to get yourself settled?"

I nodded. "That sounds great. Thank you again.".

When I'd escaped to my cubicle, I finally let my rigid posture slip, and closed my eyes, letting my head rest against the flimsy wall. There were two thoughts that were most prevalent in my head, and both concerned me equally.

First, I had people to share this news with, and I couldn't wait to do so. I had to restrain myself from texting Abraham right away, and knew when I got home, Evey's excitement would be almost uncontainable. The last time I had someone rooting for me like this was my gran. The swelling of emotion that came with thoughts of her took me by surprise.

The second concerning thought was, I wasn't as excited as I thought I would be. This is what I'd worked toward for years, and if I was being honest with myself, it didn't feel like I thought it would. Maybe I'd built this up too much? Maybe since I'd known since Friday that I'd be getting this promotion, the actual news wasn't as exciting?

I wasn't sure what it was, but I suspected that my weekend away had something to do with my change of heart. Was this a side effect of becoming a werewolf? Would I be unable to feel strongly about anything anymore?

I shook my head. That can't be the case. Evey spent half her life excited over something, or other. So, if that wasn't the culprit, what was?

A knock on the wall rattled my head still resting against it. I jumped a few feet away, and turned to find Ben in the hallway, slimy, fake smile pulling at his thin lips. Wire rimmed glasses magnified his dark brown, almost black eyes in a bug-like fashion. His sandy-blond hair was slicked back with far too much gel. I had a feeling he was covering a bald spot but had yet to prove it.

"Hi Ben."

His smile grew as he waltzed into my cubicle uninvited. I gritted my teeth but kept quiet. Soon I'd be a floor away from him and wouldn't have to put up with his intrusions all the time.

"Heard they made you senior associate," he remarked as his shrewd eyes assessed my space.

"That's right."

He laughed humorlessly and picked up a glass paperweight from my desk. "Wonder what you had to do for *that*."

I narrowed my eyes and crossed my arms over my chest. "I had to have a stellar win ratio, Ben. How has yours been lately?" I didn't need him to answer because I knew he'd been doing terribly. It was rumored he was one bad loss away from losing his job.

He turned, rage barely concealed in his dark eyes. "I've been doing just fine. Although I'd probably be doing better if I looked like *that* in a skirt." He jerked his chin in my direction, eyeing me from head to toe. It was almost like I could feel his red-hot gaze on my skin. Goosebumps broke out across my body in revulsion, but I stood firm.

"I don't believe a jury cares *what* I'm wearing, Ben. My win ratio is based on how well I do my job, and nothing more. But if you have doubts, I'm sure you could take them up with Mr. Hildebrandt."

Ben shook his head. "Of course not. I'm sure you've gotten just what you deserve." His words were benign, but his eyes belied the sentiment. "I wanted to come congratulate you and see if I could interest you in a little celebratory dinner tonight, my treat." He stalked closer until I could smell the overpowering smell of his cheap cologne.

"I have plans tonight, Ben."

He shook his head. "You always have plans, Montgomery. Why don't you blow them off and spend some time with me? I promise I'll make it worth it."

I fought off a shiver of disgust and shook my head. "I'm sorry, I can't. And I need to get packed up and moved into my new office. So, if you don't mind…" I jerked my head toward the hall, hoping he'd get the hint. I was a well-mannered Southern woman, but he was working my last nerve.

"Where are you going?" he asked belligerently

"The senior associate floor." I was about fed up with his questioning and my words were becoming terser by the second.

"Of course." He shook his head and sauntered toward the hall. "If you change your mind about dinner, you know where to find me."

"Thanks, Ben." I waited until he was out of sight to turn back toward my desk.

I really should report that arrogant asshole.

I wasn't sure what made me keep putting up with his crap.

That's not true–I did know.

It has always been more important for me to get along and not make waves in the office. No one will to promote the person who can't play nice with her colleagues. And, for whatever reason, women were expected to be even more mild-mannered, and acquiescent than men were.

But lately, my patience was running thin with him. Maybe it was because I'd already gotten the promotion I'd been working toward. Or, maybe I was just plain old sick of his bullshit.

About a half hour later I was in my spacious new office. It didn't take long at all to unpack as I didn't have a ton of personal items at work. I preferred to keep my office professional and allow my home to be a more accurate expression of my tastes.

My phone chimed, and I reached for it, unwilling to admit that I'd been hoping for a text from a certain werewolf.

Sexiest Man Alive: How's your day?

I tried to wipe the stupid smile off my face but was unsuccessful.

Me: So far so good. I just got settled in my new office.

Sexiest Man Alive: New office?

Me: Came with the promotion!

When it'd been a couple minutes with no new messages, I reluctantly set my phone down, and got back to work. I was having trouble concentrating on the documents in front of me and was thankful when my phone rang. When I saw the caller was "Sexiest Man Alive", my stomach did a back handspring, and I had to pull myself together before answering.

"Hello?"

"Elizabeth." His deep voice rumbled through the speaker, and straight to my core. "Congratulations on your promotion. I'm so proud of you."

His words stopped me short, conflicting emotions warring inside of me. My brain questioned why a practical stranger would bother being proud of someone he barely knew while my heart soared at his praise. I didn't know which one was thinking straight at this point.

"Elizabeth?"

I shook my head. "Sorry, I'm here. Thank you, I appreciate it."

"I wish I could be there to celebrate with you."

My heartbeat stuttered a few times as what felt like a whole flock of butterflies took flight. "You do?" I asked quietly. As soon as the words were out of my mouth, I winced. I sounded like a lovesick teenager.

"Absolutely." His voice was deep, and serious.

My heart raced, but doubt crept in. "Why though? Why would my promotion be so important to you?"

Abraham paused for a moment before answering, his voice ringing with sincerity. "Because *you're* important to me. You mentioned how much you were looking forward to this promotion, and I'm proud you got it." He paused again, this time his almost hesitant. "I actually did some research on your law firm. It's supposed to be one of the most competitive offices in North Carolina. The fact that you've gotten so far already is really amazing."

I took a deep breath in the hopes it would steady my racing heart. How could this man affect me like this from so far away?

"I have to run, but I'll see you soon."

"What?" I asked, but he'd already ended the call.

How would he be seeing me soon? We had no plans to see each other. I suppose he'd have to come get Evey, or I'd have to take her back home at some point. But we hadn't discussed that far in advance yet. Maybe it was just a vague send off, a phrase that people say, and don't necessarily mean?

I shook thoughts of Abraham McCoy out of my head. If I was going to get anything done today, I couldn't have him taking up prime real estate in my brain. I had a big case I was working on that needed all my concentration if I was going to earn my keep on the senior associate's floor.

The rest of the afternoon sped by, and before I knew it, it was five. I immediately packed up and headed out of the office. I couldn't remember the last time I'd left work on time. Maybe it had something to do with the house guest I had waiting at home for me. For once, I had something to look forward to after work besides more work.

I made it home in record time, and when I walked in my apartment, a delicious mixture of spices greeted me, instantly making my mouth water. Following the smells into the kitchen, I found Evey hard at work stirring a variety of pots on the stove. Did I even own that many pots?

"Hey Elizabeth! How was work?" Evey greeted with a big smile, and bright blue eyes.

I returned her grin. "Great. I got the promotion and a new office."

She squealed in glee and rushed over to wrap her arms around me. "That's amazing! I'm so proud of you!" There was that word again. And like before, it warmed me in a way that was unfamiliar. "I got us a bottle of wine. I figured we'd be celebratin' or commiseratin', and either way, it'd be better with wine."

I laughed at her exuberance. "Good thinking." I looked around the kitchen at the food lining the counters and frowned. "Where'd all this food come from?"

"Well, obviously not your cabinets," she mumbled. Then louder, "Did you know Postmates delivers groceries too? And even alcohol?"

I shook my head with an indulgent smile. "I think I've created a monster," I deadpanned. Evey broke out in peals of laughter I couldn't help but echo.

"I only got a few things delivered, so tomorrow I'll have to go shoppin' myself."

"Oh, if you want, you can drop me off at work, and use my car for the day."

"I was plannin' on takin' an Uber."

My eyes widened in shock. "You know what Uber is?"

She rolled her eyes and turned back to the stove. "I'm a werewolf, not a hermit. Of course, I know what Uber is."

I laughed and shook my head. "Is there anything I can help with?"

She waved me away. "Nah, I got this all covered. Go change into somethin' more comfortable than that monkey suit, and I'll have dinner on the table in a few."

I frowned and looked down at my pinstriped pantsuit. "This is not a monkey suit."

Evey scoffed. "Whatever you say."

I grumbled good-naturedly but did as she requested. Once I was in a comfy pair of sweats, and an old t-shirt, I went looking for Charlie. To my surprise, I found him sitting in the dining room just off the kitchen. He was keeping his distance, but a lot closer to Evey than I'd expected to find him.

I walked over to pick him up and scratch his head. "Were you a good boy today?" I asked him.

"He finally got curious, or maybe hungry, and came out of his little hidey-hole. I've been tossin' him scraps, and he keeps creepin' closer, and closer. I think we'll be best friends by the end of the week," she declared with a satisfied smile.

I widened my eyes in shock. "You, a big, bad werewolf, friends with my little bitty kitty?"

Evey rolled her eyes. "Yeah well, if we're gonna be roommates this week, we might as well learn to get along." She turned the burners off and opened the oven. "Now get out of my kitchen and go have a seat."

Technically it was *my* kitchen, but since she'd done more cooking in it in the past twelve hours than I'd done in the four years I'd lived here, I figured it was probably more hers than mine at this point.

Minutes later, she had several platters of food, and two chilled glasses of white wine laid out for us. My eyes widened as she set plate after plate of food on the table. "Evey, how many people are you expecting for dinner?"

She laughed. "I'm used to cookin' for a lot of people at a time. I guess my calculations were off," she frowned. Her shoulders rose with a shrug. "No worries, I can make you lunch with the leftovers."

I opened my mouth to protest, but her glare had me snapping my mouth closed. "Okay, thanks, Evey."

We indulged in her tender pot roast and chatted easily throughout dinner. When I'd finally stuffed myself, I leaned back in my chair, thankful I'd changed into less restricting clothes. "Evey, this was all *so* good. Thank you so much. I can't remember the last time I had a home-cooked meal after work."

She shook her head. "That's a damn shame, Elizabeth. I plan to make sure you get a lot more of 'em while I'm here."

That warmth was back, heating me from the inside, starting in my chest, and spreading outward. Or was that the wine? Either way, I couldn't remember being this happy, and satisfied in a long time.

I searched for a name for these feelings, and when I came up empty handed, I settled on a concept instead. This must have been what it was like to have a family.

Chapter 18

The next morning, the smell of bacon roused me from my sleep. Although the delicious scent was a welcome one, if it'd just come a few minutes later, I could have finished the amazing dream I'd been having.

My cheeks heated, and I was glad I was alone in my bedroom.

Or, was I glad to be alone?

The steamy scenes from my dream slid through my sleepy brain, and I relished them. Abraham had starred, and I'd played a supporting, but extremely essential role. A small chill sped down my spine as I remembered the way he'd touched me in the dream, how his lips skated across my skin, the taste of his mouth on mine–

"Elizabeth, you up?" Evey called through the door.

I sprang out of bed like it'd shocked me and covered my face with shaking hands.

Calm down, Elizabeth. She doesn't know what you were just thinking about. The girl just has crap timing.

"Elizabeth?" she called again.

"Yea–," I cleared my throat, "Yes. I'm up. I'll be out in a few."

"Okay good. Eggs are gettin' cold!"

"Okay thanks!" I called before making a hasty retreat to my en suite bathroom. I could definitely use a cold shower after that dream and the consequent embarrassment of almost getting caught swooning by his sister.

Without permission, my thoughts turned back to the racy scenes from the dream. It'd felt so real. Like he'd been there with me. When I'd awoken, I'd almost expected him to be lying there next to me.

As the cold water cooled both my insides and outsides, I finally started to get a grip on my raging hormones.

Sure, I was attracted to Abraham, who wouldn't be? The man was a rugged Adonis complete with the perfect physique, and that strong, alpha personality that both annoyed and excited me. Even more troubling was that I was getting to know him and discovering he was just as beautiful inside as he was outside.

We'd stayed up texting well into the night, and I blamed that for the crazy dream I'd had. Why else would I be thinking of him in that way? He had a pack to run, and I had a corporate ladder to climb. Neither one of us had time for a relationship. And besides, all of our conversations had been more friendly than anything else. Sure, there was the occasional light flirting, but I assumed that was his personality. Some people couldn't help themselves.

Keep telling yourself that, Montgomery.

I ignored my catty inner voice and rinsed off beneath the cold stream of water. With a towel, I did my best to dry my long, blonde locks before twisting them into a single French braid. Choosing what to wear wasn't hard. My closet looked like that of a cartoon character's–the same top and bottoms lined the racks from end to end.

I grabbed a skirt suit and slipped it on along with a pair of sensible pumps. With a glance at the clock, I saw my dream sexcapades left little time for makeup, so I swiped on some black mascara, and a little bronzer before I followed my nose to the kitchen.

Evey was where I found her yesterday morning, but this time, instead of her furry pajamas, and house slippers, she was in jeans and a t-shirt. It was then I remembered I offered her my car for the day.

"Mornin'," she called over her shoulder.

"Hey Evey. Breakfast smells delicious." Guilt ate away at me until I added, "You know you don't have to cook for me, right?"

Her light blue eyes met mine, and the glare she pinned me with had me swallowing any further protests.

"I already told you. If I'm stayin' in your house, the least I can do is cook you a few meals. Besides, do you think I'm gonna starve myself?" She raised a brow at me before turning back to the stove. "If you hadn't noticed already, werewolves can *eat*. I can't survive on the bird food you had hidin' in those cupboards of yours." She waved a dismissive hand at my cabinets. "So, if I'm cookin' for myself, that means I'm cookin' for you too. You're my sister now, and we always take care of family."

Her words formed a lump in my throat. I'd never had a sister.

She pulled a plate full of food from the oven. "Now, have I heard the last about this nonsense, or what?" She held the plate like she'd take it back if I disagreed.

Fried tomatoes, fluffy scrambled eggs, and bacon were squished alongside a pile of grapes, and a large scoop of cheesy grits. My mouth watered, and I nodded my head. "Sure, Evey. I won't mention it again." I held my hands out for the plate, and she eyed me seriously before finally relenting, and handing the food over.

I popped a piece of bacon in my mouth and groaned at the salty taste. "Anything I can do?" I asked around a mouthful of food.

She laughed. "No, I'm good. Now go eat at the table. What, were you raised by wolves?" She winked and laughed again before pulling out a second plate for herself.

I chuckled around another mouthful of bacon and took my seat at the now well-used dining table. She'd already set it and had steaming mugs of coffee and glasses of orange juice for us.

In between bites, I commented, "I could get used to this."

Evey had already taken care of at least half her plate. "And you should. You're a growin' wolf, you need to eat." She smiled widely at her little joke.

"It seems the only growing I'll be doing is in width."

She laughed. "Don't worry, our metabolisms are super active. You won't gain a thing except for muscle."

I lowered the hunk of tomato from my mouth. "You mean to tell me, I'll be able to eat like this, and not gain any weight?"

She nodded, her smile wide.

"This werewolf thing keeps getting better and better."

Evey shook her head with an indulgent smile, and we finished the rest of our breakfast in silence. When we were done, I helped her load the dishwasher, but she had me leave the pots and pans in the sink to soak.

"I'll get to those when I get back from shoppin'. You ready to leave?" she asked.

"I just need to feed Charlie and we can go."

"Already did it."

I stopped in my tracks. "For real?"

She giggled. "For real. I'm not gonna feed us, and not him. Cats and wolves might not get along, but I'm not lettin' anyone go hungry on my watch."

My affection for the small woman swelled in my chest. She was such a genuinely caring person. I don't know how this werewolf thing would turn out, but either way, I was lucky to have her in my life now.

When we made it to my office building, she walked around to the driver's side, and handed me a brown paper bag.

"Your lunch," she explained.

My chest warmed again, and I gave her a grateful smile. "Thanks so much, Evey. I rarely have time to even stop for lunch."

Her outraged face had me laughing out loud. Without thinking, I wrapped my arms around her narrow shoulders, and gave her a big squeeze. She only hesitated a moment before returning my embrace.

"Have a good day at work, honey. I'll be here at five to pick you up." She blew me a kiss and batted her eyelashes.

I laughed again and shook my head before stepping through the revolving front door. The smile instantly died on my face when I was met with a sour looking Ben. I tried to walk past him, but he grabbed my wrist.

"Is that why you won't ever go out with me? Playing for the other team?" His voice was barely held contempt.

I broke out of his grasp. "That's none of your business, Ben," I replied through gritted teeth.

It wasn't the insinuation about my sexuality that was raising my blood pressure. No, that I couldn't care less about. Gay, straight, bisexual, transsexual, none of it mattered to me. His snide attitude, and assumption that a relationship with a woman was what kept me from dating him was my problem.

"So, if you're not a lesbo, why won't you go out with me? Think you're too good or something?"

I swear I saw red.

"You listen to me, I don't want to date you, because *I don't want to date you*. It has nothing to do with anyone else, and everything to do with you." I took a step closer and jabbed a finger in his chest. "And, if you ever grab me like that again, I promise to make you regret it. Are we clear?"

Instead of the fear and resignation I should have seen, I only saw more anger. "Sure thing, Montgomery." With that he spun on his heel, and stalked through the revolving door, into the warm Carolina morning.

I pulled on the cuffs of my blouse and patted my hair. My patience was about used up with that man. He seemed to be getting more and more insistent with his advances. If things continued like this, I might have to report him to human resources, something I really didn't want to do. No one wanted to work with the woman who made waves, no matter how well deserved they were.

The rest of my morning went smoothly, and around noon, I was immensely happy to have that packed lunch from Evey. I'd exchanged a few texts with Abraham but was disappointed they weren't as frequent as yesterday. The afternoon was busy with meeting after meeting, and when I finally caught sight of the clock, it was a quarter after five.

"Shoot!"

Like a twister, I spun around my office, clearing the desk, and collecting documents I wanted to bring home with me. A couple minutes later, I was down in the lobby, rushing through the doors only to come to an abrupt stop on the sidewalk outside.

My ride for this evening wasn't Evey with my car, but Abraham, with his giant black pickup. I was struck dumb, my brain disconnected from my mouth, and I stood there like a fish gasping for breath on land.

"Hey, Elizabeth," he greeted, his deep voice sending delicious chills down my spine.

"Hi," I squeaked.

He covered the distance between us in a few long strides, and before I knew it, I was wrapped in his strong arms. His scent overwhelmed me as he lifted me a few inches off the ground.

"I missed you," his voice rumbled in my ear.

I missed you too.

"It's only been a couple days since you saw me," I breathed instead.

His chuckle reverberated through my chest, and he set me down, but didn't remove his arms from around me. There was less than an inch between us, and it still felt like too much.

"Is that all it's been?" he asked with a smile.

I nodded stupidly, and his eyes twinkled with mirth. He spun around and led me to his monstrous truck.

"You weren't kidding about that big truck, huh?" I commented.

He leaned down to whisper in my ear. "There's two things I never kid about, and one of em's my truck." His warm breath made the loose hairs around my ear flutter and tickle my skin.

"What's the other thing?" I asked barely above a whisper.

"My women."

I turned around and leveled him with a glare. "*Women?*"

Where the hell had that spark of jealousy come from?

He laughed and spun me back around toward the truck before opening the door. "Well, in this case, it's just one woman."

I glanced over my shoulder. "Is that so?"

His eyes were dead serious. "It is indeed."

I didn't want to assume he was talking about me or let on that I'd be insanely jealous if he wasn't, so I did the smart thing, and shut up.

With a dubious look at the height of the truck, and another at my tight skirt, I tried to figure out how I was getting onto the seat when I heard a chuckle from behind me.

"That skirt's a little tight, huh?"

"It's not that tight," I responded indignantly. "It's not my fault you've got a massive monster truck. If I'd known you'd be picking me up today in *this*, I'd have worn pants instead."

His hands gripped my waist, lifting me with ease, and settling me on the tan leather seat. "I like the skirt," he admitted gruffly, before shutting the door, and giving me a much-needed reprieve from him.

Damn. I'd only been in his presence for a few minutes, and I was already a mess. Maybe it was because of that dream I'd had.

Oh, no.

My dream.

Instantly the sexy images of the two of us raced through my mind, heating my blood and face. My pulse pounded, and my breaths came in short gasps.

I needed to get a hold of myself. Quickly.

Baseball.

Corn dogs.

Butterflies.

Grandmas.

Donkeys.

I desperately tried to think of un-sexy things in an attempt to dampen my hormones before it was too late.

Abraham climbed in the cab and turned to me with worried eyes. "You all right?"

"Daffodils."

He raised a dark brow. "Beg pardon?"

Oh my god, I said that out loud.

"Uh. Um. Have you seen the daffodils blooming yet?"

He looked at me suspiciously, tilting his head to the side, and taking a deep breath. His nostrils flared, wide eyes pinning me to the seat.

"Uh, can't say I've noticed," he responded, reaching up a hand to scratch the back of his head. "You got a thing for daffodils?"

I shook my head. "Not particularly. I prefer peony's."

He looked even more confused. "Then what were you talking about daffodils for?"

I shrugged my shoulders in what I hoped was nonchalance. "Just making conversation." With a glance out the window, I took a deep breath, and faced him again. "So, what brings you out here, anyway?"

Less than five minutes. That's how long it took you to lose your cool, Montgomery.

I needed to get myself together ASAP.

Chapter 19

Abraham's face solidified into a mask, shutting me out as if he'd closed a door between us. "Something's come up, and I needed to speak with you, and Evey about it."

"It's something bad."

He nodded and continued to drive through the rush hour traffic.

"Hey, how do you know where you're going?" I'd just realized I hadn't given him directions. Without waiting for an answer, I posed another question. "And, how did you know where I worked?"

His posture relaxed slightly. "Evey gave me your address, and when I got there, she was on her way to get you. I offered instead, and she gave me directions. It's a good thing you're a lawyer, and not a detective." His teasing tone belied his less than stellar assertion of my wits.

"Lawyers don't make assumptions, Mr. Smartypants," I grumbled.

His deep laughter rolled through the space between us, and I couldn't help the smile that spread across my face.

Minutes later, he pulled into my complex, and parked in front of my building. I tried to slip out of the giant truck without his assistance, but he was there in a flash, catching me, and slowly lowering my feet to the ground.

"Thank you." I stepped away from him as fast as I could without seeming rude and walked up the path to my building. When I realized he wasn't following, I spun around to find him staring at me. I was too far away to tell what he'd been looking at, but I had a hunch. "Abraham McCoy were you just checking me out?"

I placed a hand on my hip, and enjoyed the way his face reddened, and he floundered for a response.

"N-n-no! I wasn't! Well, I was, but it's not what you think." I raised a brow but remained silent. Another trick I'd learned as a lawyer was to let people talk without interruption. Usually, they didn't need prodding to tell me what I wanted to know.

Abraham blew out a big breath and ran a hand through his dark hair. "I was watching you walk, but not in the way you think. I was checking to see if you were still limping since I haven't seen you in a few days, and you haven't mentioned any pain."

Now I was struck dumb, searching for an appropriate response. To tell the truth, I'd all but forgotten about my injuries. I suppose if I thought back, the last time I'd had any pain had been Monday night. Then with the promotion, and excitement of having a roommate, I hadn't given it much thought.

"I've felt fine honestly," I told him.

His full lips turned up into a smirk. "You look fine."

I rolled my eyes, and continued up the stairs, his heavy steps thumping behind me. Once again, I opened my apartment door to mouthwatering smells that had my stomach rumbling.

"Hi Evey! Where's my handsome man?"

"I'm right here," Abraham answered from behind me.

I chuckled and shook my head. The man was incorrigible. Charlie came running full speed out of the kitchen, and like always, didn't have enough time to stop before he collided with my stockinged legs. I picked up the black and brown tabby and gave him a good head scratch. "There's my handsome guy. Did you have a good day today? Hmm? Were you behavin' for Miss Evey?"

"So, this is Charlie."

"Yep. This is my main man."

Abraham's eyes held barely concealed disgust, but he reached out a tentative hand, and gave him a pat on the head. "Never thought I'd be jealous of a feline," he muttered.

Abraham's eyes widened as he took in my colorful apartment. Like I'd done with Evey, I turned to scan the tapestry-covered walls, and colorful mandala carpet designs with him.

"Colorful place you got here."

"So, I've heard," I deadpanned.

I wandered into the kitchen to find out what Evey was cooking today. The petite woman peered over her shoulder at me while she basted the massive chicken she'd roasted.

"How was your day?" she asked.

"Busy," I responded as I snuck a potato out of the pan and popped it in my mouth. It was piping hot, but that didn't detract from the flavorful taste. I moaned out loud, and Evey chuckled while Abraham cleared his throat behind me.

"Do you need any help, Evey?" he asked, his voice sounding strangled.

She waved him off like she'd done me so many times. "Nah, I'm good in here. If you want to set the table while Elizabeth gets changed, dinner will be ready in just a few."

When I returned from changing, the siblings were already seated, and I took the chair across from Abraham. They'd both piled their plates high with the feast Evey had made, and I followed suit. "Evey, this all looks amazing."

Her smile beamed across the table. "Hope it tastes as good as it looks."

"You're being modest, Evey," Abraham lightly reprimanded. He turned to me. "Evelyn was always in the kitchen cooking with our mom when we were younger. That's where she learned all her tricks. Our mom was an amazing cook."

Evey nodded, her mouth already full of food.

"Well, that explains why I'm so hopeless in the kitchen. My mother never cooked."

Both sibling's mouths fell open. Thankfully, they'd swallowed their food beforehand. "Never?" Evey clarified incredulously.

I shook my head as I cut up my chicken. "Nope. We had a cook. She wouldn't be caught dead in the kitchen except to give out orders."

When I looked back at the pair, Evey's eyes were still incredulous, but Abraham's looked a little sad. "That's certainly a different upbringing from what we had," he commented.

I shrugged. "I'm learning that a lot about my childhood was different." On that solemn note, we all dug into our food, and were silent except for the scrape of forks and knives on our plates.

Not much later, I finally set my utensils down, and waved the proverbial white flag. I couldn't possibly fit another bite in my mouth. "That was *so* good."

Evey smiled wide as she took a sip of white wine. "Glad you liked it. I got a sweet potata' pie coolin' for later."

I groaned but couldn't wait until I'd digested enough to fit a piece of pie in too.

"So, Abey," she turned toward her brother, "I know why you're out here." Her eyes cut to me and back so quickly I might have imagined it. "But what is it you had to talk to us about?"

Abraham set his fork down and took a long sip of water. I watched in fascination as his prominent Adam's apple bobbed up and down with his swallows. I was so entranced, when he finally spoke, his voice almost startled me.

"There was another attack."

Evey gasped. "Wait, what?"

Abraham nodded solemnly. "We found her this morning. It was just like all the others." He glanced at me. "She was found strangled and covered in wolf urine. Must have only been there a day or so before we found her."

"Isn't that a little soon to fit the profile?" Evey asked.

He nodded again. "He's accelerating."

"Why do you think that is?" she asked.

Abraham ran a rough hand through his hair and leaned back. "My best guess is he was frustrated he was interrupted with Elizabeth, and to make up for that, he attacked again."

My heart dropped, and my mouth went dry. "Another woman's dead because of me?" I asked quietly.

Both siblings instantly denied it, but Abraham's voice rose above the white noise in my head. He placed a hand over mine, and my eyes met his. "No. That's not true. You did nothing wrong by surviving. Never be sorry for that. Nothing this guy does is anyone's fault, but his."

I heard his words, and they made sense, but deep down, I knew this woman wouldn't be dead if he'd been able to kill me. I couldn't wish I'd died, but was my life worth more than hers? Should I have lived while she died? Those questions and a hundred more whirled through my brain like a tornado, tearing apart anything in its path.

Abraham's warm hand was still on top of mine, and he squeezed gently. "Elizabeth, listen to me. Do not blame yourself."

I pulled my hand away and sat back. "I hear what you're saying,

Abraham, and I know you're right. But you can't deny this woman would still be alive if I'd died. Sure, he would have killed again, but not this soon after. Who was this woman? Are her parents looking for her? Does she have a husband she'll never come home to? Kids that will have to grow up without her? I have none of that. Why should I have lived while she died? It doesn't make any sense."

Abraham shook his head, but it was Evey who spoke up first. "His pattern has been escalatin' all this time. Sure, he's never attacked two women in one week, but who knows? He might have done that, anyway. He's a serial killer, Elizabeth. You work with criminals and know how they are. His motives are his own, and you can't take any blame or responsibility for them, you hear me?"

I nodded but didn't comment. She was right. They both were. But I couldn't help the way I felt. Couldn't help knowing I shouldn't be alive, and that someone else was dead because of it.

All I could do was live my life in part for that woman who lost hers. I'd make sure I took nothing for granted anymore and pull myself out of this self-imposed isolation I'd been living in for years. With a quick glance at the only two visitors I'd had in this apartment in the four years I'd lived in it, I knew I was on my way.

"There's more." Abraham's voice rang out in the silent room, and my stomach fell. He stared at the wall, not meeting any of our gazes when he dropped his next bomb. "We found a new piece of evidence at this last crime scene."

Evey's eyes met mine before turning back to Abraham. "What was it?" she asked.

He shook his head and lowered his gaze to his hands clenched on the tabletop. "An empty jar, with a rope tied around the top. Almost like a necklace. It was empty, but it was clear it used to hold wolf urine." He took a deep breath and looked up at Evey. "It was the same scent that's been on all the women."

I furrowed my brow in confusion. "So, he pees in a jar, and then dumps it on his victims? That doesn't make any sense."

Abraham shook his head slowly. "No. It's not his urine in the jar."

Now I was even more confused. "Why would he pour someone else's urine on his victims?"

Evey gasped, blue eyes wide. "To mask his scent," she whispered.

Abraham nodded solemnly. "Which means, one, or maybe all of us, would have recognized his scent had it not been covered by this other wolf's urine."

I struggled to connect the dots. "So, this is someone you all know?" He nodded. With a stroke of insight, I finally understood. "He's probably a member of your pack." I didn't need to ask, it was clear in the distraught faces of the two siblings.

Abraham sighed and met my eyes. "That's what we're thinking. Of course, it could be someone from a neighboring pack, too. Someone we've had dealings with before"

We sat silently for a long while, before Evey finally stood from the table, and began slowly clearing it. Abraham and I followed suit, and the three of us worked to clean the kitchen, all while lost in our own thoughts.

I was having trouble getting around the fact that my attacker might have been close this whole time. Have I met him? Had he been at the cookout? Does he live in the lodge with Abraham?

Evey's sweet potato pie did little to lighten the mood, even though it was just as delicious as I thought it would be. The petite woman did her best to keep our minds off the recent discovery, but the black cloud over our heads persisted.

"So Abey, you're going home, and then coming back to pick me up tomorrow?" Evey asked.

We'd settled on the bright pink couch in my living room with warm mugs of coffee in hand.

"That's the plan," he confirmed.

"Who's coming to stay next?" I inquired over the rim of my cup.

Abraham blew out a big breath. "Well, that's something I wanted to talk to you about. Callie's supposed to spend the next week with you, but Del's got a gig Friday night that she doesn't want to miss. I was hoping you'd spend the weekend at the lodge and then come back here with Callie on Sunday." His bright smile, and earnest eyes almost had me agreeing immediately.

But I resisted.

"I don't know," I told him, searching for any excuse. I didn't really have a reason to decline his offer, but it was almost a reflex at this point. I was so used to being alone, I made up any excuse isolate myself.

"Do you have plans?" Abraham asked, his voice a shade darker than it'd been a moment ago.

"Well, no, not plans. But I usually try to get work done on the weekends…" I trailed off.

"Is it something you could bring with you?" he pushed.

I stayed quiet a minute as I debated with myself. Why was I trying to get out of this? I enjoyed his company, and I enjoyed spending time with (most of) his sisters. I'd gotten along with (most of) his pack and wanted to learn more about them. What did I have to lose by saying yes?

I thought about that poor woman who'd lost her life in the woods instead of me. Hadn't I *just* promised to live *my* life since hers had been cut short?

"Del would be really happy if you came to her show," Abraham added sweetly.

"Okay, I'll spend the weekend out there with you guys."

His answering smile was brilliant. "Okay great, I'll pick you both up tomorrow." He stood and placed his mug on the table as if he was getting ready to leave.

"Wait, you're leaving right now to drive to Asheville, only to drive back here tomorrow night?"

He shrugged his shoulders. "I thought about getting a hotel room for the night."

I scoffed and shook my head. "That's ridiculous. Why don't you stay here? We don't have another bedroom, but you can take my bed, and I'll sleep on the couch."

He was shaking his head before I'd finished my sentence. "No way am I kicking you out of your own bed. Not gonna happen."

I took a look at his tall frame, and then a dubious glance at my couch and back again. "I don't think you're fitting on this couch, Abraham."

Evey piped up. "You've got a king size bed in your room, don't you? Why don't you and Abraham share?" she asked innocuously.

I spun around and crossed my arms. "Evelyn McCoy, have you lost your damn mind?"

Her jaw dropped, eyes blinking slowly before she turned to her brother. "Did she just channel mom, or what?"

I turned to find Abraham with the same wide-eyed look, but he was grinning from ear to ear. "Just like mom," he confirmed.

I huffed impatiently. "I'm not sharing a bed with Abraham. That is off the table."

"She's right, Evey. That would be inappropriate," he chided.

"But I bet you could both use it," she muttered under her breath.

I gasped, but before I could let loose with some choice words for my roommate, Abraham interrupted. "I'll just sleep in my car."

"That's crazy Abey." She sighed in irritation. "You take the guest room, and I'll sleep on the couch." Abraham opened his mouth to argue, but little Evey shot him a fierce glare, and he held up his hands in surrender.

"Are you sure, Evey?" I asked, feeling bad about my lack of accommodations. She nodded once. "All right, if that's settled, I'm going to bed. Evey, could you show him around for me? And Abraham, if you need anything, just ask."

They both made sounds of agreement, and I waved goodnight to them before retreating to my room. If this is what it was like growing up with siblings, maybe it was better off I was an only child.

Chapter 20

I was running through the woods again; the scene becoming painfully familiar. Avoiding roots and rocks, I sprinted as fast as I could, weaving in and out of the thick tree trunks.

The creature's hot breath puffed against my skin, and I knew it would only be moments before it overtook me. With a determined growl, I pushed myself harder, feeling the space between me and my pursuer grow. But it was short lived.

Huge paws landed on my shoulder blades, and I fell face first onto the damp earth. As soon as I hit the ground, the animal's weight left my back. I rolled over to face my attacker, and found that same small, light gray, brown-eyed wolf.

I called this wolf "small", but only compared to the other werewolves I'd seen in these woods. This one was still bigger than me, and I bet it'd be fair to assume it was stronger too.

"What do you want?" I asked.

The wolf's eyes blazed bright for a moment before returning to its normal brown color. It cocked its head to the side and continued to stare at me.

"What do you want from me?" I tried again.

I wasn't really expecting the wolf to answer, but it was clearly sentient.

"Just leave me alone!" I screamed. My palms and knees stung from the fall I'd taken. I didn't know where I was, and I was becoming increasingly cold, wet, and *sick* of running.

I rose to my feet and straightened my sore back. With a steely determination, and arms akimbo, I stared the wolf down as best I could in the nearly pitch-black forest.

"I've just about had enough. I don't know what you want, but if it's a midnight snack, you're gonna have a fight on your hands."

We stood there, both assessing the other for an immeasurable amount of time. Finally, the wolf dipped its head, give a little yip, and trotted off into the darkness. I was almost shocked speechless.

Almost.

"Hey! Where the hell are you going?" I followed it for a few moments, but the darkness grew with each step, and soon I couldn't even see my hand in front of my face. "What were you chasing me for? What do you want?"

A loud knocking, and the sound of my voice coming from far away stopped me in my tracks. "Hello?" I called.

"Elizabeth!"

"Abraham?"

All at once, I opened my eyes, and sat up in my bed, confused and still breathing hard from my race through the woods.

If it was just a dream why am I out of breath?

"El?" Abraham's voice called once more, and I shook my head to clear it.

"Yes! Come in!" I called without thinking.

The door creaked open, and in walked Abraham, naked from the waist up, hair disheveled, wearing a pair of plaid pajama bottoms that hung off his hips.

My mouth went dry, and I might even have gasped a little.

"Are you okay?" he asked, real concern lacing his words.

"Huh?" I asked, wrenching my gaze from his bare chest.

Even in the dark, I could see his bright smile flash across his shadowed face. "I heard you yelling. Did you have another nightmare?"

I nodded sullenly but didn't trust myself to speak yet.

Abraham took a seat at the foot of my bed. "You wanna talk about it?"

I shrugged and finally had to close my eyes to get myself to stop staring at him. "I don't know. This one wasn't as scary as the last one."

"Tell me about it."

So, I did. I recounted all I could remember about the dream, but it was fading fast.

"And you said you didn't recognize the wolf?"

"No. Evey has different coloring, and you're way bigger."

His smile gleamed. "I am pretty big, aren't I?"

A reluctant laugh shot out of my mouth.

His smile widened. "Got you to smile."

"You always do," I answered automatically. Immediate regret swamped me, and I winced.

Too much.

Too soon.

Abraham cleared his throat and mercifully changed the subject. "Do you think you can get back to sleep? There's still a few hours left before you need to be up for work."

I shrugged. "I dunno'. It's hard for me to sleep after a nightmare."

He rose from the bed. "Here, lay down." He pulled the covers back far enough for me to scoot beneath them. "If you lay on your side, I'll rub your back until you fall asleep?"

I tensed. "Rub my back?"

Could I survive that?

He pulled the covers up to my chin and took a seat next to me on the bed. "It's what my mom always did for us when we had bad dreams. Now, roll over."

I did as he asked, and turned on my side, facing away from him. Maybe not having to look at him would help me get through having his hands on me.

Cold air rushed against my back as Abraham pulled down a corner of the blanket. Next, I felt his large, warm hand land between my shoulder blades. He paused there for so long I almost turned over to ask him what was wrong. Then, his hand was moving, rubbing small circles along my spine.

My heart raced with the contact, and it felt like every part of my body was hard-wired to where he touched. Even through my thin t-shirt, I could feel the small jolts of electricity jumping from his skin to mine.

I needed to take my mind off this situation, or I would lose it and do something I'd regret. Like pulling him into this bed next to me and forgetting about all my no-men rules.

But would I regret it?

I ignored that doubtful voice in my head. "Did I wake you up?" I asked instead, hoping that if I could get my mind out of the gutter, I'd be able to relax and fall back asleep like he'd suggested.

"I'm a light sleeper."

I winced. "Sorry."

His hand gave me a little shake. "Don't be. I'm glad I could be here for you."

But why?

Why was he always there for me?

How was he able to anticipate what I'd need, or how I'd feel about things?

How did he know me so well after having met me less than a week ago?

Was he looking for a relationship? Or simply fulfilling his alpha responsibilities?

All those questions and more swirled inside my head, but I kept them to myself. I was afraid if I said them aloud, I'd have to face the answers to them. I'd have to admit what that churning feeling I get in my stomach whenever Abraham's around is. Admit that I get giddy anytime I receive a text from him, and that when I saw him standing outside my work yesterday, it had easily been the best part of my week.

"Hey, try to relax," Abraham chided. "You're all tense. You're not gettin' back to sleep like that."

He was right.

I needed to chill the hell out. This late at night/early in the morning was no time for heartfelt revelations or deep questions.

I closed my eyes and sighed. This back rub really was relaxing. My shoulders relaxed, and my muscles slowly unclenched.

"There ya' go. Just focus on taking deep breaths, and you'll be asleep in no time." His deep voice was quiet and soothing as his large hand ran from my neck to lower back and shoulder to shoulder.

Just as he'd predicted, minutes later I was falling into the blissful darkness of sleep feeling safe and content. Two things I'd never really thought about, but now I wondered how I'd gone so long without.

I felt the weight next to me leave, and the blankets loosen around my prone body. In that gray space between wakefulness and sleep, gentle fingers tucked a lock of hair behind my ear. Moments later warm lips pressed against my temple, and a soft sigh blew across my face.

"Goodnight, my sweet Elizabeth."

An odd flutter deep in my belly was the last thing I knew before I lost the fight to stay awake and drifted off into blissful darkness.

I woke up late the next morning and had to scramble to get ready. I'd hoped I could sneak into the kitchen for a quick bite and avoid an awkward confrontation with Abraham, but I wasn't that lucky. And, my apartment wasn't that big.

When I exited my bedroom, he was leaving the guest room, already dressed and showered.

"Morning," I muttered.

"How did you sleep?" he asked softly, stepping closer, bringing with him that clean, manly scent that drove me crazy.

I retreated, back pressed against my bedroom door. "Like a baby," I squeaked. He stopped a few inches away, and I looked down at our feet. Taking a deep breath, I said, "Thanks for coming in last night." I squeezed my eyes closed. "And, for helping me get back to sleep."

Why couldn't he be a late sleeper?

He leaned closer and tucked a stray lock of hair behind my ear. I fought off a shiver as his calloused finger skimmed along the edge of my jaw. "Anytime." His deep voice reverberated through my chest, making my heart pound faster.

I took a deep breath and braved a peek up at him. He was so close, dark blue eyes so deep, they were bottomless. My breath caught in my lungs as his face drifted closer.

"Elizabeth! If you're not up you're gonna be late," Evey called from the kitchen.

We broke apart, and I took a deep breath of the suddenly plentiful air. Thank god for Evey.

"She's right," I said to my feet. "I need to get going, I'm running late."

I didn't give him a chance to respond, maneuvering past him and into the kitchen. I don't know where he went after that, but I scarfed down a couple waffles, and left for work.

Despite my best efforts, thoughts of Abraham occupied most of my morning. I blamed it on lack of sleep. But what straight, red-blooded woman could forget something like Abraham McCoy shirtless in their room in the middle of the night? Not this one that's for sure.

I was busy all morning, and after lunch, had a meeting with a potential client. Now that I was a senior associate, I was able to have more choice about who I represented. Not that it mattered lately, anyway. The job I'd bled, sweat, and cried over was less important by the day. I still loved law, but I was feeling unfulfilled. Restless.

The walls of my office felt more like a cell, and I found myself counting down the minutes until I could leave. A week ago, I wouldn't have even looked at a clock until the sun went down. Only knowing it was time to leave when the cleaning crew showed up after hours.

"Ms. Montgomery?"

The voice snapped me out of my musings, and I looked up to find the client, a middle-aged man with too much gel in his light-colored hair looking at me.

Damn, I must have missed something.

I cleared my throat, straightened my spine, and slapped the fake smile on my face. "Sorry, could you repeat that?"

"I asked if YOU'D GONE OVER THE DOCUMENTS I SENT YOU YESTERDAY."

Why was he screaming?

I fell backward in my chair.

"MS. MONTGOMERY? IS EVERYTHING ALL RIGHT?"

His voice sounded amplified, like he had a microphone on stage, and I was standing next to the subwoofer.

"Why are you yelling?" I whispered, hands over my ears.

His thick brows drew together over confused eyes. "I'M NOT YELLING, ARE YOU FEELING ALL RIGHT?"

He was still screaming. Or at least that's how it sounded. With my hands still plastered to my ears, I clumsily climbed to my feet.

"MS. MONTGOMERY, WHERE ARE YOU GOING?"

I was halfway to the door already. "Sorry, I'm not feeling well. I'll have to catch up with you later." With that, I yanked the door open, and sprinted down the hall to the elevators.

Thankfully, the hallway was vacant, and I felt safe enough to expose my ears again.

What the hell is happening to me?

I frantically pressed the elevator call button and sighed in relief when the doors opened. The reprieve was short lived, however.

"RYAN, I TOLD YOU, LOGAN'S LITTLE LEAGUE TEAM IS IN THE PLAYOFFS, AND THE FINAL GAME IS THIS FRIDAY. YOU PROMISED YOU'D BE THERE AND YOU BETTER MAKE IT."

I clapped my hands over my ears again, eliciting a nasty look from the woman on the phone. Ignoring her, I pressed the button for my floor, and tried to stand as far away from her as possible.

"I DON'T CARE ABOUT WHAT YOUR LITTLE GIRLFRIEND HAS PLANNED FOR THIS WEEKEND. HE'S YOUR SON, AND YOU NEED TO BE AT THAT GAME. I HAVE CLIENTS I NEED TO SEE ALL DAY ON FRIDAY AND CAN'T BE THERE."

I found that stuffing my fingers in my ears drowned out the sound better than just covering them, and that's how I rode to my floor. When the elevator doors finally opened, I got out as fast as I'd gotten in.

Unfortunately, this floor wasn't as quiet as the last.

"AFTERNOON MONTGOMERY," John Walsh called from across the hall.

I gave him a weak smile and hurried away. Luckily, I didn't run into any other chatty colleagues before I made it to my office. Once there, I shut and locked the door, sagging against it in relief.

What the hell is happening? Was this some sort of werewolf-y thing?

Slowly, the quiet of my office slipped away, and in its place, multiple voices and conversations filled the air. One on top of the other until it sounded like I was in a room full of people.

I ran to my desk and grabbed my cell phone. Without thinking, I called the first person that came to mind.

"Hello?" His voice blared through the speaker, and I winced, pulling the phone away from my face and setting it on the desk.

"Abraham?" I whispered.

"Elizabeth? What's the matter?"

"It's so loud."

Banging and slamming doors could be heard clearly through the line.

"I'm putting my shoes on now, and I'll be right there." His voice was softer, and I silently thanked him for that. "Where are you?"

"My office. Fourth floor, number twelve."

"I'll be there in ten."

"But it's more than fifteen minutes away," I argued.

"I'll be there in ten," he promised. "Do you want me to stay on the phone with you?"

"No, you're too loud."

His laugh barked through the phone, and I glared at it.

"Sorry, sorry," he responded quietly although I could still hear the smile in his voice. "I'll be there soon. Just stay put."

Chapter 21

Like he'd promised, just over ten minutes later, there was a knock on my door.

"Elizabeth?" Abraham's voice whispered from the hallway. I could tell it was a whisper, but it still sounded like he was in the room with me speaking conversationally.

"Come in."

Abraham McCoy stepped in my office looking larger than life. He had on a plain white t-shirt that stretched across his broad chest, a worn-in pair of jeans, and boots on his feet. He couldn't look less like he belonged in this office if he'd tried. And I was captivated.

"El?" he asked softly.

My eyes snapped up to meet his. Seeing the gentle concern in his gaze reminded me of why he was here. "Why is everything so loud?" I whispered.

He sighed and crossed the room to envelope me in his arms. A week ago, being hugged would have sent me into a panic, but his embrace was nothing but comforting. Well, and maybe a little exciting, but I didn't have time to entertain those thoughts right now. It had been hard enough to keep my mind off our midnight rendezvous, I didn't need to add more fuel to the slow burning fire in my core.

"You're becoming a werewolf, El. This is one of those changes I told you about."

I pulled away to look him in the eyes. "So, this is how things sound to you all the time?" He nodded. "Then why the hell is Evey always screaming if your hearing is so great?"

His head tipped back with a loud laugh, and I pulled away to slap my hands over my ears again. I shot him a glare that he responded to with a huge grin. It was almost as if he knew I couldn't stay irritated at him when he flashed me that gorgeous smile of his.

Damn man.

"I'm sorry," he said softly, the contrition obvious in his voice. If I hadn't already forgiven him, his apology would have forced me to. "Evey's always been… exuberant." It was my turn to laugh at his description of his bubbly younger sister. "After a while, you'll acclimate to your new hearing, and things won't be as loud anymore."

"How long?" I asked desperately.

He shook his head sadly. "There's no way to know."

My shoulders slumped.

How long could I go on like this before I went crazy?

Even now, I could hear full conversations from what must have been rooms away. The voices and sounds were piling up in my head, like a mountain of sand threatening to drown me.

Abraham's calloused fingers grasped my chin. "It shouldn't be too long though, and in the meantime, I can help a little." I furrowed my brows in confusion as he picked up the phone on my desk and fiddled with the settings. The dial tone went from blaring, to a more manageable sound in small increments. "Can I see your phone?"

I handed over my cell and watched him adjust the sound settings there too. When finished, he passed it back, and held out two little tan-colored cylindrical pieces of foam. When I looked at him questioningly, he answered, "Earplugs." I took them and stuffed them in my ears. Immediately the conversations from down the hall quieted, and I smiled with a sigh of relief.

"Thank you so much." I looked up to find Abraham's eyes on me, his expression gentle, and kind, and something else. I looked away before I could take a guess as to what it was.

"It's what I'm here for." Amazingly, the volume wasn't earsplitting, but instead sounded like it used to before my hearing went crazy. "The ear plugs won't drown out everything, but they'll help reduce the volume until you can acclimate to your new hearing."

"I wouldn't have even thought to get ear plugs. Actually, I couldn't think at all. The noise was too much, I couldn't hear my own thoughts. I'm sorry I bothered you, I just didn't know what else to do, or who else to call. I suppose I could have tried Evey–"

"Elizabeth," Abraham interrupted, placing his large hands on my shoulders. "I wouldn't have wanted you to call anyone else. I'm here to help you. I always will be, no matter what it is."

His denim blue eyes burned with sincerity, and I lost myself in them. "I–"

A loud knock interrupted us, followed by the door opening. I was equal parts disappointed and relieved.

What was I going to say? How could I have responded to that?

"Montgomery, I'm taking you out this Saturday, and I'm not taking 'no' for an answer," Ben's nasal voice preceded him. When he saw Abraham there with his hands on my shoulders, his expression instantly changed. Where before there'd been a slimy look that I think he thought was charming, now there was one full of suspicion, and distrust.

"Ben, usually when one knocks on a door, they wait for an invitation to enter," I told him sternly, stepping away from Abraham. His hands fell to his sides, expression torn between looking at me with hurt, and at Ben with irritation.

"Well I didn't know you had *company*. Didn't realize it was visiting hour. Don't you have more important things to do now that you're a *senior associate*?"

A low growl came from behind me that I might not have been able to hear yesterday, but today was crystal clear. I gritted my teeth and clenched my fists. "Ben. It doesn't matter if I was alone or had twenty people in here. Do not come into my office again without an invitation. Got it?"

Ben stiffened, eyes flashing with anger, but he nodded. "Of course. I was just stopping by to ask you to go to dinner with me this weekend."

"El," Abraham growled behind me. I could feel the anger radiating off him.

My colleague clenched his fists and squinted his eyes. "Who's this? A new boyfriend of yours?"

"No," I answered.

"Yes," Abraham grunted.

I turned to glare at him, but his eyes were still trained on Ben. I gave him a hard poke in the chest that probably hurt my finger more than it hurt him, but it got his attention. His angry eyes turned to me, and I raised my brows expectantly. He got the hint and relaxed the tiniest bit. I sighed. Clearly that's the best we would do with Ben here.

"He's not my boyfriend, and I can't go out with you this weekend. I have plans."

"With him?" Ben asked belligerently.

"No–"

"Yes," Abraham interrupted, placing a claim-staking hand on my back. I wanted to shrug him off since this caveman routine was working my nerves, but I had a funny feeling he was right at the end of his rope, and that small rejection would be the last of his control.

"It doesn't matter what I'm doing," I glared at the both of them, "I won't be in town."

"Maybe next time," Ben answered with a smug smile.

Abraham growled, and I jumped into action. "Thanks for stopping by Ben," I said as I opened my office door, and ushered him through. "See you on Monday," I placed my hand on his back to push him through the doorway faster. Abraham's low growl increased in pitch with the contact, and I rolled my eyes.

When the office door closed, I spun to face the angry werewolf. "What the hell was that?"

Abraham's eyes were still on the door, hands clenched in such tight fists his knuckles were turning white. When he failed to respond, I yelled, "Abraham!"

He finally snapped out of it, and his blue eyes found mine. There was still a hint of anger there, but it was quickly fading to remorse. "Sorry," he said, his voice still a deep growl. I fought off a shiver and tried to convince myself that his gravelly voice didn't do crazy things to my insides.

"What was that all about?" I tried again.

He shook his head. "I don't like him."

"You just met him. You don't know him."

"I don't need to know him, I saw the way he looked at you, and I don't like it."

I scoffed. "How is it any of your business how someone looks at me?"

Abraham's eyes flashed dangerously as he closed the distance between us. His large hands gripped my hips and dragged me toward him. "You're mine."

I gasped and opened my mouth to protest, but he cut me off. "You're a part of my pack, and mine to look after," he amended. That was slightly better, but I wasn't thrilled with his possessive tone.

Or was I?

"It's my job to make sure you're taken care of and safe, and that man," he spat with a glare at the closed office door, "is not safe. I don't want you anywhere near him."

I rolled my eyes. "I work with him, Abraham. What am I supposed to do?"

"Quit your job and come live at the lodge with me?" he asked with a million-dollar smile.

I rolled my eyes again, but a small smile slipped out. "Not going to happen, McCoy." I pulled away from him, and my body mourned the loss of his heat.

"I'll make you a deal," he proposed.

I raised an eyebrow. "Okay, let's hear it."

He took a step closer, and his clean scent engulfed my senses. "How about you make me a happy man and take the rest of the afternoon off? We can get packed and on the road to Asheville before rush hour."

My initial instinct was to argue. I *was* a lawyer after all. Arguing was what I did best. But I swallowed my first reaction and really thought about it. Would it be such a bad thing to take an afternoon off? I knew with the increased hearing thing, the situation with Ben, and having spent so much time this close to the man in front of me, that I'd be next to useless for the rest of the day.

"Let me check my calendar," I conceded. "If I don't have anything else important scheduled for the rest of the day, I'll leave early with you."

His answering smile was brilliant and made my heart miss a beat. "That's my girl."

I rolled my eyes. "Not your girl, McCoy," I told him as I walked around the desk to my computer.

"Not yet," he answered softly.

I spun to face him. "What was that?"

Did he really want me to be his girl?

Did I want to be his girl?

My rules about not dating were becoming harder and harder to follow.

With chagrin, he raised a hand to scratch the back of his head. "I'm going to have to be more careful now you've got werewolf hearing, huh?"

I shook my head exasperatedly. "I guess you will." With a few clicks, I had my calendar loaded, and took a quick look at the rest of my afternoon. "Looks like you're getting your way. I'm free the rest of the afternoon."

He clapped his hands together. "Sounds great. Let's get you packed up and out of here before Ben comes back, and I need to break his legs."

I laughed until I saw Abraham was dead serious. I'd need to keep those two separate because I did *not* want to clean blood out of my new office's carpet. "All right, Don Corleone, let's get you out of here before you get yourself arrested. Didn't your mother ever teach you not to assault a lawyer? Not a good idea if you want to keep your butt out of jail."

He scoffed. "Please. If *Ben* and I had an altercation, I can assure you he wouldn't be pressing charges."

I stuffed my laptop in its bag and arranged some papers on my desk with a shake of my head. "I don't think you know Ben that well then."

"I don't think you know me that well then," he countered.

I looked up and met his serious gaze. "I guess you're right." Then without thinking I added, "What are we going to do about that?"

I winced internally.

Was I really flirting with him?

Did I even know how to flirt?

Was I doing it right?

With my eyes still glued to the unimportant papers in my hands, I heard Abraham move closer until he had both hands planted on the desk. "Well this weekend is a good start." I nodded my head. "And, you could dance with me tonight," he added.

"Dance?" My eyes met his.

"Dance," he confirmed. "We're going to Del's gig tonight. I was hoping you'd grant me a dance with the prettiest lady there."

I rolled my eyes but felt my cheeks heat. "We're not even there yet. How do you know I'll be the prettiest one?" I couldn't help asking.

Abraham leaned down until he was eye-level with me. "Because, you're the prettiest woman I've ever seen." His eyes bore into mine for an immeasurable moment before he straightened up and smiled. "Don't see that changin' in one night at a dive bar," he added with a wink.

I shook my head, but a big smile stretched across my face.

Damn, he was good.

"So, what do ya' say?" he prodded.

Jeez, was there really a choice here?

"I'll dance with you," I told him softly.

He leaned down again and cupped a hand around his ear. "I'm sorry, what was that?"

I smiled, "I said I'd dance with you."

"Sorry, El, you're gonna have to speak up, it's real loud in here."

With a laugh I smacked his arm. "I said I'd dance with you, you impossible man."

His smile practically stretched from ear to ear. "That's my girl."

"I'm not your girl," I reminded him again, though the words were feeling emptier of conviction the more I said them.

Chapter 22

Thankfully, we got out of the building without Abraham assaulting Ben or any other colleagues of mine. I didn't know if he'd been telling the truth about breaking Ben's legs, but something deep inside told me not to underestimate him. If he felt I was in danger, I knew he'd have no problem taking care of the situation.

But was Ben really dangerous? Sure, he was annoying. And full of himself. And aggravatingly persistent. But did that mean I should fear him? I wasn't convinced.

Abraham's hand on my arm stopped both my feet and my racing thoughts. He nodded over my shoulder. "That's your car isn't it?"

I turned to find my little gray sedan and looked back at him confused. "How did you know where I parked?"

Had he followed me this morning?

Was that weird, or flattering?

Gah, this man was messing with my head!

He shrugged. "I followed your scent."

My eyes widened, mouth falling open in what I'm sure was a really attractive impression of a fish. "Followed my scent?" I yelled, wincing at the volume of my voice.

He pulled me closer. "Keep it down," he reminded me. I nodded and tried to compose myself. "Yes, I followed your scent. You know how your hearing just increased a lot from what it used to be? Well, imagine how your other senses will develop in the coming weeks. Following your scent was easy. I know it so well now."

My brain raced at his words. I hadn't really given much thought to how I would change. To be honest, I hadn't thought much about the whole werewolf thing at all. Nothing had been different besides the dreams. I'd almost let myself forget I'd soon be turning into a creature of legends. I'd experienced the exaggeration of one of my senses, and had another, what, four to go?

How much different would I be at the end of all this?

Would I still be me?

"Hey." Abraham grasped both my arms. "What's goin' on in that pretty head of yours?"

I smiled reluctantly. "There you go flattering me again."

He smiled back. "It's easy to do with you. There's so much material." He winked before his face turned serious again. "But really, what are you thinkin' about? You've got a look on your face."

"A look?"

He nodded. "The kind you get when you're analyzing things too deeply and getting yourself worked up."

My mouth fell open in surprise. "How do you know that?"

He took a step closer until there was barely an inch between us. "I watch you," he said with a shrug. "Now, answer my question. What are you thinking about that's got that look on your face?"

I sighed and shook my head. This man had me spinning.

"I'm just thinking about all the changes I'll be going through. Until now, I hadn't thought much about how I'd be changing. I guess I'm worried about how uncertain my future is."

He wrapped one of his big hands around the back of my neck and tilted my head up to his. "Your future isn't uncertain." I opened my mouth to respond, but he interrupted. "Your eyesight will get better, your sense of smell will heighten, you'll get a lot stronger, and then you'll shift into a werewolf on the next full moon. Simple."

I scoffed. "Oh yeah, simple."

He squeezed my neck gently. "And, even though your body is changing, *you* won't change. You'll still be the Elizabeth you've always been." I nodded and tried to digest his words. "And, the other thing that won't change," he continued softly, "is I'll always be right there next to you."

"Why?" I whispered.

His rough thumb rubbed the side of my neck in slow circles. "Because you're..." He paused. "Part of my pack. I'm in charge of making sure you're always taken care of, and I'll never let you down. You'll always be safe as long as you're with me."

"And, if I'm not with you?"

He craned his neck until our faces were only inches apart. "Then I'll come to you." His sweet breath blew across my face, and I closed my eyes. The tension between us was like a rubber band pulled too tight. Any second it would snap, and I didn't know where that would leave us. But in this moment, I was absolutely willing to find out.

He moved a fraction of an inch closer before squealing tires on the parking garage cement interrupted us. My eyes opened, and I took a quick step away with an uncomfortable chuckle.

I awkwardly tucked a lock of hair behind my ear and met his eyes. "Thanks again for coming here. I guess I'll see you back at my place?"

Abraham's expression was still dead serious, and his eyes blazed with sincerity. "I'll follow you." His voice was deep and husky.

I suppressed a shiver and hurried over to my car. Once inside, I felt my insides unclench, and my heart slow. "That man is going to ruin me." Deep inside, I knew truer words had never been spoken.

His big black pickup truck followed me from the office to my apartment, and I had to admit I felt a sense of security knowing he was close by. Before I left the car, I slipped the earplugs out thinking I wouldn't have to worry about loud noises in my apartment.

I was wrong.

As soon as I opened my front door, Evey was yelling, and even from the other room, it was too loud.

"ABEY? WAS SHE OKAY? I WISH YOU'D LET ME GO WITH YOU. I CARE ABOUT HER TOO, YA' KNOW."

I slapped my hands over my ears and moaned as my eardrums rang with Evey's shrill voice.

"Where are your earplugs?" Abraham asked quietly behind me.

I dug them out of my pocket and stuffed them back in my ears with a sigh.

"Abey? I said is she okay–" Evey stopped short when she came into view and saw us both standing in the doorway. "Hey girl, what are you doin' here?" She reached out and pulled me into a big hug. Without thinking, I wrapped them around her small frame.

"Your brother got me to leave early. He's pretty convincing when he wants to be."

Evey pulled back with a laugh, and I silently thanked Abraham for the earplugs again. "Don't I know it! One time when we were five, Abey convinced all of us to get in the chicken coop, and then locked us in."

I turned incredulous eyes to the man in question. "Is that so?" I asked with a smile.

"Uh huh. Thankfully mama caught him walkin' away from the coop smilin' like the cat that ate the canary. Nothin' got past our mom. She made him let us out."

"How long were you in there for?" I asked, still eyeing Abraham whose cheeks had turned a suspicious shade of pink.

"Only a few minutes. And, I didn't mind so much. Me, Callie, and Del were havin' fun playin' with the chickens. It was Bea who was spittin' mad. You remember Abey?"

He coughed uncomfortably. "If I remember correctly, she got me back for that."

Even through the earplugs, Evey's answering laugh was hard to handle. "That's right! Didn't she duct tape you to your bed while you were sleepin'?" She almost couldn't finish her sentence she was laughing so hard.

"Oh my god, no she didn't!" I wheezed out between laughs.

Abraham shook his head, his face pinker by the minute. "She sure did. Taught me not to mess with her again."

I took a big breath, and my giggles finally subsided. "Remind me not to get on her bad side."

"Don't worry, she'll remind you herself. She's as mean as a honey badger these days."

"Evey," Abraham scolded half-heartedly. "Don't talk about our sister that way."

"Oh, Abey, you know what I mean. I love the girl to death, but she could start an argument in an empty house. I bet she could use a long night with a good man."

"I don't want to hear it!" Abraham yelled, and we both slapped our hands over our ears. Him because he didn't want to listen to any details about his sister's sex life, and me because his voice made my sensitive ears ring.

"Oh honey, you got your hearing in?" Evey asked, softer than I'd ever heard her speak.

I nodded and carefully withdrew my hands. "In the middle of a meeting. It was a disaster," I bemoaned.

Evey walked over to rub my back in soothing circles. The gesture reminded me of the night before with Abraham, except without the scorching heat he radiated. I took a peek at him as the memories flooded my mind. Thankfully, he was looking down at his phone, and missed the heat in my cheeks.

He locked his cell and looked up, blue eyes meeting mine. His expression instantly softened into a look I was becoming accustomed to. "Think you can be ready to leave in thirty minutes? I don't want us to be late for Del's show tonight."

I nodded and stepped away from Evey's comforting touch. With a grateful smile at her, I retreated to the sanctuary of my bedroom where I collected both myself and my things for the weekend ahead of me.

Forty-five minutes later, we were arguing in the parking lot.

"I don't understand why I can't drive myself," I told the stubborn man in front of me.

"It isn't practical. Why would we take two cars? And besides, you're coming out to Asheville for us, I'm not going to make you keep paying for the gas to drive back and forth."

I rolled my eyes. "I can afford gas money, Abraham."

He sighed and took a step closer. "I know you can," he began, wrapping his large hands around my biceps, "but I'd like to drive all of us. It will make me feel better knowing you're with me and safe. Will you please just let me drive?"

His big blue eyes bore into me like a drill mining for oil. I felt the liquid gold seeping up through the earth as I caved in to his request.

Damn. When was the last time I lost an argument?

"Okay. You can drive," I muttered reluctantly.

Abraham pulled me into a big hug that lasted only a few seconds. My heart hadn't even had time to speed up before he'd pulled away and taken my bag out of my hand.

"I call not sitting in the middle," Evey yelled from close behind. When I tensed at her volume, she said, "Sorry, Elizabeth. I forgot."

I nodded and waved away her apology. I had a feeling I'd need to keep these earplugs in around Evey for a while. Hopefully, sometime soon I'd be able to acclimate to my increased sense and be normal again.

A mirthless chuckle escaped my lips. *Normal.* I'd never be normal again. I might as well kiss that concept goodbye.

Abraham loaded our bags into the back of the cab and took his seat behind the wheel. I soon realized why Evey'd so exuberantly called 'not sitting in the middle'.

"I really have to squish in between you?" I whined.

Evey giggled and pushed me toward the truck. "Yup. And, it's a long drive, so you might as well suck it up now."

I groaned, and climbed into the big truck, sliding along the cream-colored seat until I was only a few inches from Abraham. Evey climbed in behind me. "You need to scootch over more," she complained.

I took a dubious look at the few remaining inches and sighed. There was just no helping it. I slid over until my leg hit his, my shoulder grazing his bicep. Evey took her seat next to me before reaching over to fiddle with the radio.

"We ready?" Abraham asked, and I could feel his deep voice vibrate through all the places my body touched his.

God, this was going to be a long ride.

"Ready," both Evey and I answered.

Abraham fired up the massive vehicle, and we were on our way. Evey and I spent the first hour or so chatting like we normally did about everything and nothing at the same time. It constantly surprised me how much I had in common with someone I'd just met who'd lived such a different life than me.

Once in a while I'd take a peek at Abraham out of the corner of my eye, and every time, I'd catch him smiling out the front window. Finally, I had to ask, "What are you smiling about over there?"

His eyes widened. "I didn't realize I was," he confessed.

"You've been smiling since we left Raleigh."

He shot me an incredulous look. "Have you been watching me, Ms. Montgomery?"

I averted my gaze as my face heated painfully. "No. I'm just observant."

Evey giggled from beside me, and I shot her a fierce glare which only made her laugh harder. A reluctant smile spread across my face.

"What's Del's show going to be like?" I changed the subject.

Abraham answered first. "Like any other underground show in a dive bar. When you've seen one, you've seen them all. We just go to support Del."

"I've never been to a show before. I don't even think I've technically been in a dive bar either."

"Never?!" Evey screeched.

I winced and shrunk away from her bringing me closer to the man who made my insides quake. He stuck a finger in one of his ears and wiggled it around. "Jeez Ev, that one even hurt my ears."

"Sorry, sorry! I just can't believe Elizabeth's never been to a show or a dive bar! Do you know what you're wearin'?"

I looked down at the jeans and t-shirt I had on. "Um. This?"

Evey gasped scandalously. "Oh, no you aren't. We'll find you something to wear." She eyed me up and down. "I bet you're a bit closer to Callie's size than mine. I'm sure she's got *somethin'* decent in her closet we can borrow."

"Do I have to?" I whined.

"Yes," Evey answered, and I dropped the conversation there. I'd learned enough about Evelyn McCoy in this past week to know I wouldn't get anywhere when she was like this.

Instead, I sighed and relaxed back in the soft leather seat. Abraham took his right arm off the wheel and draped it across the back of the bench. It was then I realized I was still plastered to his side and straightened up as best I could in the cramped space.

Evey let out a small giggle at my discomfort, and I shot her another glare. I had a feeling this was going to be a long weekend.

Chapter 23

As soon as we pulled up to the lodge, Evey grabbed my wrist, and dragged me from the truck.

"I'll bring your bags to your room, El," Abraham called after us.

Evey gasped. "We can call you 'El' now? That's fantastic! We're big on nicknames as you can tell, and that full name of yours is a mouthful."

"Well–" I began when Evey interrupted.

"Oh, I see," she said, with a sly look in my direction. "That must be Abey's special name for you. I get it."

"No, that's not–"

"Oh no, that's fine. I think I like the sound of Ellie better anyway, and it rhymes with Evey," she proclaimed with a victorious smile. "What do ya' think?"

What *did* I think? I'd never really had a nickname before. My formal parents would rather cut their tongues out than call me by anything other than my full name. Even my gran called me 'Elizabeth', or the occasional term of endearment. But no one in my life had ever given me a real nickname. I guess that was about to change.

"It might take some getting used to," I warned her.

"Then I'll just have to use it more often!" The woman's excitement could not be dampened, and I felt my face stretch into a smile. "Come on, Ellie, let's go find Callie, and get you something sexy to wear tonight."

"Not too sexy," I told her.

She just laughed dragging me through the house, and up the stairs to the third floor. Instead of turning toward the hall that led to mine and Abraham's rooms, she turned down another I'd never been down before. We walked past a few closed doors until Evey stopped in front of one and knocked.

"Come in," Callie's soft voice called.

We stepped into Callista's room, and I took a minute to look around. Her space was a lot less ornate than the other rooms I'd visited in the lodge, but it fit her. The furniture was all re-purposed, and of varying styles, but seemed to fit together. The large king size bed was dressed in shades of brown, and the floors were hardwood.

Callie sat at a large vintage desk against one wall, typing furiously on a small silver laptop. "Just give me one second."

"Take your time," Evey called as she continued to drag me across the room, and over to a set of double doors. Evey pulled them both open to reveal an enormous walk-in closet. I stood there gaping at the space that could have fit my master bedroom in it while Evey made a beeline for a row of dresses.

"No dresses, Evey," I called to her.

She spun around and placed a hand on her cocked hip. "What the heck do you mean 'no dresses'?! Of course, you're wearin' a dress. We all are. Suck it up," she advised before returning to her search.

I sighed loudly. "Fine. Just nothing too short."

She waved my request away as she pulled a few garments from their hangers and draped them across her arm. I shook my head and went to see what Callie was up to.

The curly-haired woman was still typing away at her laptop, but now a big grin spread across her face. She clicked the last few keys with a flourish and flopped back in her chair.

"You look happy," I commented.

Callie turned toward me, and her smile grew. "I am. I just finished a big proposal I've been working on for weeks. Now I need to proofread and send it off. It's a load off my shoulders to be honest."

I sat on a nearby settee. "What kind of proposal?"

She was on her laptop again, clicking the mouse with her brows furrowed, and her lip between her teeth. "This one is to get funding for a program to protect the Blue Ridge Parkway."

"What's happening to it?"

"Businesses are trying to buy up the land lining the parkway which would not only affect the ecosystem but take away from the beauty of the highway. We're trying to get the government to lift restrictions on land preservation in that area."

"Wow, that's incredible."

Callie's cheeks turned a soft shade of pink as she shrugged her narrow shoulders. "It's not one of our more vital interests, but it still needs a voice."

"What *is* one of the more vital interests?"

She perked up, a fire igniting her pale blue eyes. "There are the bees, and the monarch butterflies, and the state parks, and–"

"All right, Smokey the Bear, we get it," Evey interrupted, eliciting a glare from her sister. "Tell Ellie about your tree-huggin' missions another time. I need her to try on a few things."

Callie rolled her eyes. "It's not about tree-hugging Evelyn, it's about conservation. It's about food production, and–"

"Oh, I know all about it, big sister. And you'll have all week to tell Ellie, but right now, I need to get this girl dressed so *I* can get dressed so *we* can leave so Del doesn't kill us when we're late."

Callie took a glance at the time on her laptop and hopped out of her seat. "Why didn't you tell me it was this late!" she hollered as she ran across the room to her ransacked closet.

"I was tryin', but you just wanted to talk about bees!" Evey yelled back. "Ugh, sisters," she complained good-naturedly. She shoved a big pile of fabric in my arms and turned me toward a nearby door. "The bathroom's over there. Go try on what I picked out. Come out after every outfit so I can help you pick."

I rolled my eyes. "I'm perfectly capable of picking out my own clothes, Evey."

The bubbly brunette took a skeptical look at my jeans and t-shirt. "Sure, if you're cleanin' the house."

I opened my mouth to argue, but she held out a hand to stop me. "Quit arguin' cause' you won't win this one. I picked out some things I think you'll like so please, just go try 'em on."

I huffed. "Did you even ask Callie if I could borrow something of hers?"

"She didn't, but you're more than welcome to anything I have!" Callie called from the depths of her closet.

Out of excuses, I locked myself in the bathroom, and sorted out the clothes Evey had picked out. A few things immediately went into the 'discard' pile. Finally, I pulled on a long strapless shirt that flowed past my waist nicely. I took a look in the mirror and thought it might be cute with a belt.

I left the bathroom to show Evey the first thing I'd tried on. As soon as she saw me, her eyes clouded with confusion. "Why are you wearin' your jeans with that?"

"Um. Why would I take my pants off to wear this shirt?"

Evey fell backward on Callie's bed, clutching her stomach as she laughed long and hard at my expense. I huffed and crossed my arms over my chest. "What's so funny?"

"That's a dress, Ellie, not a shirt," she gasped out between laughs.

I gasped, and looked down at the long shirt–no, *short* dress I had on. "No, Evey. In fact, *hell* no. I'm not wearin' this as a dress. You've lost your mind."

Evey sat back up and wiped a tear from her eye. "Ah, I like havin' you around. You're always good for a laugh." At my glare, another chuckle burst from her lips. "Okay fine, I guess that's a little short on you. Go try something else on. And I'll give you a hint: they're all dresses."

My eyes widened. "*All* of them?"

Evey nodded seriously, her pink lips still twitching, fighting off laughter.

I retreated to the bathroom, and sorted through the clothes once more, adding a few more items to the 'discard' pile. Finally, I found an off-white knee-length shirt dress that I thought might look cute. I slipped it on and pulled my jeans off before exiting the bathroom once again.

This time Callie was standing there too, having changed into a cute dress that had tan ruching on top, and blue floral pattern on the bottom with a thick brown belt cinching the waist. "You look great, Callie," I told her earnestly.

She shook her head. "*You* look great!" She turned to Evey, "You found that in my closet?" Evey nodded her eyes still raking my form. "Huh, I don't even remember buying that."

Evey's eyes lit up, and she jumped to her feet. "What size shoe are you, Ellie?"

"Eight, why?"

She didn't answer and instead sprinted from the room. I watched her disappear wondering how long it would take for me to get used to the super speed of werewolves. And, more importantly, when I'd start moving that fast.

Evey came running back in the room with a pair of brown leather cowboy boots with teal filigree stitched along the sides. "Here," she thrust them into my arms, "Try these on."

I toed off my sneakers and shoved my feet in the tall shoes. They fit like a glove. Evey clapped her hands. "All you need is a statement necklace, and you're perfect. Well, besides hair and makeup, of course."

I fingered the thick plait in my hair and shook my head. "I can do my own hair and makeup." Evey opened her mouth to protest, but I shot her a look that made her drop it.

"Fine, fine. But at least let me go find you a necklace. I'll be right back, Del has the best accessories."

Before I could agree, the small woman was gone again. I turned to Callie. "Do I really look all right?"

She nodded. "You look amazing. Abey's not going to know what to do with himself."

My cheeks heated. "I'm not getting dressed up for him," I muttered.

Callie wrapped a thin arm around my shoulders. "Of course, you aren't." Then quieter, "But it can't hurt, right?"

I couldn't help the small smile that spread across my face but did my best to not let Callie see it. His sisters didn't need to know how obsessed I'd become with their brother.

Evey flew back in with a chunky necklace made of teal and gold beads that were bunched together in the shape of flowers. I lifted the braid off my neck and stooped down so Evey could fasten the necklace. When she was done, she patted me on the back, and I turned to her and Callie.

Both women were smiling from ear to ear. "You're perfect!" Evey exclaimed. "Now, go up to your room, and get your hair and makeup done while I get ready. Abey said we're leavin' in twenty."

I turned to Callie before I left. "Thanks for letting me borrow this dress," I said, pinching a corner of the soft fabric between two fingers.

The willowy woman waved me off with a genuine smile. "Please, that dress would have never looked like *that* on me. You should keep it."

"No way. I'm not keeping your dress."

She shook her head, tight curls bouncing from side to side. "It looks better on you than it ever could on me. I want you to have it."

I sighed. "At least let me give you some money for it."

Her curls were still bouncing around her face as she turned down my offer. "No. I don't even remember buying that dress. How could I charge you for it?"

I sighed again. "Okay fine, then I'm taking you to dinner while you're at my place this week."

Callie smiled, her eyes lighting up. "That sounds good to me. Do I get to pick the restaurant?"

I laughed. "Of course. I'll see you in a bit," I told her, and retreated to my end of the floor.

Thankfully, I didn't run into Abraham in the hall. As silly as it sounds, I was hoping he wouldn't get a look at me until I finished getting ready. Although I knew I needed to keep my 'no men' rule in place, I still wanted to impress him. He'd seen me at my worst, broken, bleeding, and filthy, and now I wanted him to see me at my best.

I don't normally wear a ton of makeup, but I whipped out some foundation and blush for the occasion, even adding shimmery eyeshadow to my lids. I finished with black mascara and a rose-pink lipstick, impressed by the reflection staring back at me.

I unraveled my braid, trying to decide what to do with my hair. My thick blonde locks fell around my face in loose waves that looked pretty good. I bent over, flipping my hair upside down, and gave it a little shake before standing back up. Now my hair straddled the line between styled and mussed. I spritzed a bit of hairspray, and then some perfume, and I was ready to go.

A knock came, and I called for them to come in, assuming it was Evey come to tell me it was time to go. Instead, Abraham entered, instantly making my heart race, and my mouth go dry.

He was wearing a fitted, button-down plaid shirt of dark blues and greens that matched his eyes. He'd changed out of his old scuffed pair of jeans into a darker, more formal pair. I smiled when I saw he still had his work boots on.

"El," he breathed, and I met his gaze, the denim blue color almost electric. "You look amazing."

I smiled and hoped the foundation would cover the blush I could feel burning a path across my cheeks. "Thanks," I told him shyly, eyes on the ground.

I watched his tan boots walk across the floor until they were inches from my own. He grasped my chin, lifting my face until it was level with his. "So beautiful," he whispered reverently.

I wanted to look away, but I was a small fly in his spider's web. There was no getting out unless he released me. His rough hand slid along my jaw, and around the back of my neck where he buried his fingers in my thick hair.

My chest rose and fell in time with his, our bodies only inches apart. I licked my lips, his eyes tracing the movement. With a small cough to clear my throat, I choked out, "You look nice too."

His eyes softened, the lines around them crinkling with his warm smile. He leaned in closer until his lips were a breath away from mine. "I was hoping you'd think so." I swallowed nervously. His proximity making me dizzy. "Breathe," he whispered, his warm breath rushing across my open lips.

I took a breath, and he chuckled, making one of his soft lips brush against mine. I sucked in a deep breath at the contact and closed my eyes.

Evey chose that moment to barge into my room.

"Are you ready? Del's gonna kill us if we're late–" She stopped short, and I stepped out of Abraham's gravitational pull. "Am I interruptin' somethin'?" she asked with a Cheshire grin.

I stalked across the room toward the door. "Nope. Had something in my eye. Let's go."

Chapter 24

Thankfully, Abraham had cleared out his cab, so I didn't have to squeeze in the middle again. I was still given shotgun, however.

"You can have the front, Evey," I offered.

She shook her head with a mischievous smile. "Oh no, that's fine. I need to talk to Callie, anyway. You take the front seat."

And, so here I was, once again standing outside his truck, wondering how I would get in while maintaining my dignity.

"I've got you," Abraham said from close behind. His large hands wrapped around my waist, almost overlapping in the middle, and I grabbed his wrists.

"No, really, that's not necessary," I insisted.

He leaned over until his mouth was next to my ear. "If I don't help you in this truck, how do you think you're getting in it? You gonna jump?" His voice held a note of amusement I didn't appreciate.

I huffed. "No, I'm not going to jump."

"Then let me help you."

"I don't need help," I answered instinctively.

He sighed, ruffling my hair, his minty breath making my heart race. "It's just me, El. You can let me in. You can let me help."

I froze.

Could I let him in?

Could I let him help?

Was I brave enough to let down my walls? Would I be strong enough to withstand the fallout when things went south with him? Because they *would* go south. They always did.

"Let's go! We're gonna be late," Evey called from the cab of the truck.

I sighed and loosened my grip on his wrists. "Okay, you can help me up."

His hands tightened on my waist. "It'd be my pleasure." His deep voice rumbled through the small space between us.

Without warning, he lifted me several feet in the air with ease and sat me on the passenger seat. Abraham's heated eyes landed on my bare thighs, and I pulled the dress down as far as it would go. He shook his head and shut my door before climbing in on his side.

As Abraham drove down their long driveway, I realized we were missing a sibling. "Does Bea not go to Del's shows?"

Abraham shook his head. "We all go. She and Del are already there."

Great. Something else to look forward to tonight.

"How far away is this place?"

"Not too far, maybe twenty minutes at most."

I nodded, and fell silent, watching shadows of thick trees fly past the dark windows.

"Are you excited?" he asked me a while later.

"I don't know," I confessed. "A little nervous I guess. I'm not used to going to places like this. I don't know what to expect or if I'll fit in or anything."

He took a long glance at me out of the corner of his eye and shook his head. "You have nothing to be nervous about. You look beautiful."

My cheeks heated, and I looked out the window again. "You said that already," I reminded him.

"And I'll probably say it again tonight."

I shook my head but couldn't get the smile off my face.

A few minutes later we pulled up to a dark building with bright red letters proclaiming it was a "BAR". When we walked up to the front door, we had to pass through a large gray cloud of cigarette smoke produced by a group of loud men of varying ages and sizes.

Abraham's gentle hand on the small of my back led me through the group and into the dark confines of the building. A long bar top ran along the far wall manned by three bartenders in crop tops and cut off jean shorts. To the right was the stage where another artist stood playing a keyboard and singing what sounded like a country song. Small tables ringed a large open space where people were dancing and swaying to the live music.

Abraham led me toward a table near the dance floor. To my dismay, Beatrice was already there with a scowl on her pretty face.

"Thought you were gonna miss her opening number," Beatrice called when we were within earshot.

Abraham shook his head, and took a seat, leaning back and extending an arm to rest along the back of my seat. "Nope. We made it."

"Well, maybe if you weren't coming all the way from Raleigh, you could have been here earlier."

I shrunk a few inches in my seat.

"Would it have mattered? Evey was out there anyway. And besides, we're not late so I don't know why we're discussing this."

"Evey shouldn't have been out there either."

Did she not see me sitting right here?

"Elizabeth needed her there." Abraham said between gritted teeth.

"*Elizabeth* should have just stayed out here and not inconvenienced everyone."

"Excuse me–" I began, already fed up with her shit, but Evey cut me off.

"No one's inconvenienced Bea. I had a ton of fun getting to know our new pack member"

"She's not pack yet," Beatrice ground out.

Abraham cut in. "I'm over this conversation. No one was inconvenienced, no one was late, so drop it."

Beatrice crossed her arms over her chest and flopped back in her chair.

Awkward.

Del chose that exact moment to take the stage, thankfully ending the discussion.

"Hello everybody!" she yelled into the microphone, and I sent another silent thank you to Abraham for the earplugs. Things were really loud with them in, but I'm sure they'd be earsplitting without them.

"How're y'all doin' tonight?" Del asked, eliciting a round of cheers and whistles from the crowd, including our table. Del's pale pink dress fluttered with her movements, the material sparkling in the stage lights. "My name's Del, and I'm gonna sing y'all a few songs," she said, strumming a few strings on her acoustic guitar. "Some of 'em y'all know and love, and a few of them I wrote, and I *hope* you'll love." Another round of cheers erupted, and Del fell silent.

As soon as the noise died down, Del began tapping on the body of her guitar, the rhythm familiar. The beat got louder and louder until she started singing. After a few words, I realized it was a song I knew; "We Are Young" by Fun. She tapped out the notes of the song until she got to the chorus and began to play the guitar. Her voice was beautiful, hitting every cord, doing the song justice while putting her own spin on it.

I swayed in my seat, foot tapping to the beat and sang along with her. When the song was over, she transitioned to another recognizable one. Her acoustic rendition of OutKast's "Hey Ya" was unlike anything I'd ever heard, and now I was openly dancing in my chair.

Evey noticed and held out a hand. "Let's go dance!" she called, and although this was out of my comfort zone, I took her hand, and let her lead me to the middle of the dance floor.

At first, I only swayed back and forth awkwardly, moving my hips in time to the music. Soon though, I had my hands in the air, jumping around and matching Evey move for move. We laughed and sang along with Del, clapping our hands in time to the beat, and gave her an uproarious round of applause when she finished.

Her next song was also upbeat, but I didn't recognize the words and assumed it must be one of her originals. She'd sung the last couple of songs beautifully, but I could tell her heart was really into her own music. As I danced, I watched how her presence lit up the dark room and shone out across the space. She was magnificent.

"Are y'all havin' a good time?" she asked the crowd who answered with screams and whistles. She smiled, a dimple appearing on her right cheek. "I had a special request tonight, and it's gonna slow things down a bit. So, if you got a honey here, bring 'em out on the dance floor, and show 'em a good time!"

The crowd yelled again, a few of them, including Evey and I, vacating the dance floor to make way for the couples. On our way back to the table, Abraham intercepted us.

His massive frame commanded any space he was in, and people swerved to avoid him. Men and women alike gave him a double take as they passed. I greeted him with a smile he returned instantly. "You think I could cash in on that dance with the prettiest lady here?"

I bit my lip as it curved up in a smile. Abraham took my hand and led me back to the dance floor. He spun me until I faced him, grasping my hips, and bringing me closer. Once we were only inches apart, he started swaying to unheard music.

"Why are we dancing if the music hasn't started yet?" I asked.

He leaned down to whisper in my ear. "I already know what song she's gonna sing, so I thought I'd get a head start, and make this dance last as long as possible."

My face heated, and I was thankful for the dark room. "Were you the one who requested it?"

He only nodded as Del strummed the first few chords of the next song. As promised, it was slow, and Abraham was already moving us to the beat. When Del opened her mouth and sang the first few words, I recognized Rihanna's "Love On The Brain".

With Abraham's hands on my hips, my arms hung loose at my sides. I'd never danced with a man before, and I was feeling out of place, and confused about what was expected of me.

His large hands slid up from my hips to my shoulders, and down my arms until he held both of my hands. He settled them on his shoulders before grasping my hips again, pulling me closer.

For the whole first verse, I stared at his broad chest. The third button down on his shirt to be exact. We swayed back and forth as we felt each other out and found our rhythm together.

When I finally braved a look at him, he was already staring at me, his blue, blue eyes bright in the dim room.

We swayed to the beat, our eyes locked in place, silent confessions passing between us. Words and thoughts, I was too afraid to admit, let alone speak. His face inched closer to mine, and I stood transfixed.

A deer in headlights.

Completely at his mercy.

His face lowered until it was only a fraction of an inch away from mine. I could feel his warm breath. His bottom lip grazed mine, the soft warmth shooting bolts of electricity through my veins.

Del sang of desire and yearning as Abraham rocked our hips to the beat. I could relate entirely.

I was captivated.

Consumed.

Drowning in him.

Then with a smile, Abraham grabbed one of my hands and spun me around, so my back was to him.

I laughed in surprise. His chest pressed against my shoulder blades, his hips aligned with mine. We swayed again, but this time more purposefully than before. The song played on, Del sang her heart out, and I tried to control my racing pulse.

Abraham held one of my hands while the other gripped my hip, tugging me closer. Until there was nothing between us.

No space.

No pretense.

No subtext.

Just our bodies, and the silent words they spoke for us.

He leaned over, caging me in further, and rested his chin on my shoulder. His stubbled cheek pressing against mine, the gentle scrape of his facial hair igniting an inferno inside me.

"Elizabeth," he whispered in my ear. I tilted my head, hair falling away from my face and down my back. He leaned closer and ran the tip of his nose along the length of my neck from shoulder to ear. I shivered with sweet anticipation. "Will you go somewhere with me tomorrow?"

I waited until I had my breathing under control before answering. "Did you have somewhere in mind?" My voice was breathy, and so unlike my own. I met his electric eyes. They were so close.

We were so close.

Not just to each other, but to *something*.

Something big.

Important.

Life-altering.

Abraham spun me back around. All pretenses gone, he pressed the small of my back until my entire body was plastered against his. His hand wrapped around the back of my neck, fingers tangling in my hair.

"There's somewhere I want to take you. Something I want to show you. Will you go with me?" His eyes were sincere, hopeful, and a little cautious. As if he didn't dare to hope I'd say yes.

And, for a split second, I considered turning him down. For just a fraction of a moment, I remembered who I used to be. The lawyer who had no friends, and no life. The single woman who lived alone with her cat and cared only for the next case that fell on her desk.

But I wasn't that woman anymore.

In the past week, I'd changed.

Shifted.

He'd changed me. His *family* had changed me. After that split second of indecision, I remembered that woman who'd died instead of me, and the promise I'd made her.

I reached up and placed my hand on the side of his face. His eyes closed for a moment, his broad chest rising and falling with a stuttering breath.

It floored me.

Ruined me.

That I had such an effect on this strong man. That my touch could make him react like that, shook me. From the core of my being, I was changed.

Abraham's eyes were now open, and staring at me, the hopeful light dimming by the second. I gave him a big smile and stood on my tiptoes, so I could whisper in his ear. His scent filled my senses, and I inhaled. Reveling in him for a second before I gave him my answer.

"Yes. I'd love to."

Chapter 25

After I promised to go out with Abraham tomorrow, he'd wrapped me in his arms, and that was how we finished our first dance together.

"You want something to drink?" he asked over the noise, his arms still wound around me.

"Please," I answered, begrudgingly pulling from his embrace.

"What can I get you?"

I frowned as I looked around. This didn't seem like a wine-drinking kind of place, and I was unfamiliar with beer and liquor. "Just get me what you're having."

He grabbed my hand and placed a gentle kiss against my knuckles. His warm lips sent a bolt of lightning straight through me. "If you wanna go sit at the table, I'll come find you there."

I nodded in a daze, and turned toward our table, reluctantly releasing his hand. When I got there, I saw Peyton had shown up with both Clyde and Calvin. I sighed but forged ahead. Four sets of eyes greeted me, and not all of them were friendly.

"Hey, Elizabeth. I didn't realize you were here," Calvin greeted.

"*I* didn't know *you* were here," I told him.

He leaned back and slung an arm across the back of Peyton's seat. "Yeah, me, Clyde, and Peyton got here a few songs late. Don't tell Del though," he said with a wink.

I smiled. "Your secret's safe with me." Then I turned toward the others. "It's nice to see you two," I nodded toward Peyton first, then Clyde. The former lifted a dark brow in greeting, and the latter only nodded.

Well, this is fun.

I tucked a lock of hair behind my ear, and looked around the room, hoping to see Abraham on his way over.

"Are you wearing earplugs?" Peyton's voice was shrill.

I covered my exposed ear. "Um. Yeah. Abraham gave them to me. My hearing came in."

Peyton and Beatrice laughed, and I smiled along with them, not understanding the joke.

"That's so pathetic," Peyton spat out.

My smile fell from my face. "Is it?" I asked, half embarrassed and half irritated.

"You look ridiculous," Peyton continued. "What would possess you to wear those out in public?" She continued laughing in her high-pitched tone.

My anger sparked as I clenched my hands in my lap. It'd been *years* since I'd had to deal with a 'mean girl', but my memory was great. I opened my mouth to let her have it, but Calvin spoke up.

"Lay off her, P. You were what? Thirteen when you went through all these changes? You weren't out in bars and if you were, you'd have needed earplugs too."

"Well then, maybe she shouldn't be here," Peyton told him, her dark eyes flashing with hatred in my direction.

"Maybe that's not up to you," I suggested.

Her eyes narrowed, and Beatrice sat forward in her chair. Peyton opened her mouth to respond, but Abraham showed up, putting an end to the conversation.

"Sorry it took so long, the line was crazy," he said as he handed me a brown bottle of beer.

I accepted it and took a long sip without even looking at the label, my eyes still fixed on Peyton. To my delight, she looked even angrier since Abraham showed up with my drink.

"Abey, you wanna dance?" she asked, turning her laser focus onto him.

Out of the corner of my eye I watched him shake his head and take a swig of beer. "Nah' I'm good. I'm gonna rest for a few. El here wore me out," he said with a laugh as he settled his arm along the back of my chair.

I couldn't help the satisfied smirk that slid across my face. "If I'm not mistaken, it was *you* who asked *me* to dance," I told him from behind my bottle.

I'd never been a big beer drinker, but this was tasty and refreshing, and exactly what I needed right now. Abraham chuckled, his fingers playing with the ends of my hair.

"Is that how you remember it?" he asked with a grin.

"That's how it happened."

Peyton stood and held out her hand to Calvin. "Let's go Cal, dance with me."

I watched Calvin take a long glance at me before doing as he was told, and leading Peyton onto the dance floor.

"You don't need to treat her that way," Bea's angry voice came from across the table.

"Treat her what way?" Abraham asked before taking another sip of his beer.

"Like shit. You know she likes you. Why wouldn't you dance with her?"

I felt my entire body stiffen and Abraham's hand freeze in my hair. My pulse pounded in my ears as I swear I saw red.

Abraham was mine.

I froze, that thought bringing me up short.

Because he wasn't mine.

What was I thinking?

He's not mine.

I have no hold on him.

He can do whatever he wants.

I repeated those words over and over in my head, but the repetition wasn't making them any more true.

Abraham sighed and slid his hand from my back to the top of my shoulder where he squeezed. "Bea, you know I don't have feelings for her like that. I never have. If I'd danced with her, it would only give her the wrong idea."

"But you'll dance with *her*?" Beatrice spat, nodding her head in my direction.

Abraham's hand tightened on my shoulder, and he sat up straighter. "Beatrice, who I do or don't dance with is none of your concern. You need to mind your own business and stop trying to set me up with your friend. It's not gonna happen." His voice had gotten deeper and more serious.

I leaned into Abraham's side to distract him from the argument he was having. Beatrice was being a bitch, but she was still his family. And I was learning how important family was.

When his head whipped around, I knew I'd succeeded. "You wanna go back out?" I asked with a nod toward the dance floor.

Abraham faced me, his lip turned up at the corner in an irresistible smirk. His blue eyes were bright like a clear afternoon sky. "Are you askin' me to dance?"

I downed the rest of my beer and thunked it on the table. "I think I am."

His eyes stayed locked on mine as he finished his own drink. "Only a fool would turn down the opportunity to dance with the most beautiful woman in this bar."

A scoff from Beatrice floated across the table, but we both ignored her. I rolled my eyes and stood with my hand held out for him. "Well then let's go. We'll see if you can keep up."

Abraham's smile was brilliant as he grabbed my hand and pulled me against him. "Challenge accepted," he whispered in my ear.

We found Evey and Callie out on the dance floor and the four of us danced through the next few songs. Abraham was never far from my side and would occasionally grab my hand and twirl me around. We laughed, and sang, and jumped, and wiggled until Del stopped singing and set her guitar down.

"That's all I got for you tonight! Thanks for havin' me!" she called before exiting the stage to loud cheers, and whistles from the crowd. The noise had become too much for me, and I had to cover my ears to cope with the piercing sounds. I'd developed a headache over the course of the night and knew I had my newly enhanced hearing to blame.

Abraham noticed my distress and pulled me into him. With one ear pressed against his chest, and his hand on top of mine holding the other, I made it through Del's applause.

"You doin' all right?" Abraham whispered in my ear. "I probably shouldn't have brought you here tonight. It's too soon after you got your hearing." I looked up and saw his anxious eyes staring back at me.

I shook my head. "You couldn't have missed your sister's show."

"Your wellbeing is more important."

I shook my head again, but he ignored me, and turned to Evey. "Are you ready to go, or did you want to stay a while?"

Evey shrugged. "I'm ready to go if you are."

"How about you, Callie?"

She nodded too. "I've had a long week, I'm ready for bed."

Abraham nodded and ushered us back to the table. Del was there when we arrived, and Abraham stepped away from my side to wrap his arms around his sister.

"Del, you did amazing. I don't think I've ever heard you sound better."

Her cheeks darkened as she accepted hugs from Callie and Evey. "Thanks, Abey. It was a good show." She turned to me and held her arms out. I still wasn't as comfortable with displays of affection and *hugging* as they were, but I was getting better. "How'd you like the show, Elizabeth?"

"You were incredible!" I gushed as I embraced her.

"This was the first time Ellie's been to something like this," Evey added.

Del's eyes widened, but before she could speak, Peyton cut in.

"Never been to a live show before? What, have you been living under a rock?" she laughed.

"No, I was busy becoming a successful attorney, actually."

My response had Del and Evey laughing. Peyton's dark eyes flashed dangerously. Abraham took that opportunity to speak up.

"Del we're headin' out. Did you want a ride back, or are you gonna hang for a bit?"

Del shook her head. "I'm too wired to go home now. I'll catch a ride later with one of these losers," she jerked a thumb over her shoulder at Clyde and Calvin, the latter taking mock-offense to her description of him.

"Abey, I'm tired, and they're not leaving for a while. Do you think you could give me a ride home?" Peyton asked with a honey-sweet voice that made my teeth grind.

"Sure, we got room. You ready now?"

She nodded and wrapped a skinny pale arm around his bicep. "Yup. Let's get out of here." She took off toward the front door, dragging Abraham, and leaving us to follow in her wake.

Abraham glanced over his shoulder at me, and I smiled through my clenched jaw as I stalked after them.

He's not mine.

I have no hold on him.

He can do whatever he wants.

I repeated the words over and over as I wove through the crowded bar. Evey caught up and slung her arm around my waist.

"You know he likes *you*, right?"

"I don't know what you're talking about," I spat and then winced, instantly remorseful for the tone I was using with my new friend. She didn't deserve my anger. The harpy up ahead however, did.

"I know you know what I'm talkin' about Elizabeth Montgomery, so don't play dumb with me." Her sharp words cut through the red haze I was in, and I turned to face her. "Peyton's always had a thing for him, ever since we were younger, but he's always turned her down. You don't need to worry about her. She's just jealous cause' she sees the way he looks at you."

My face heated, and I didn't trust myself to respond.

"You don't need to admit it now, but I know you like him too. It's written all over that pretty little face of yours. You need to stop bein' so hard-headed and let him in. I promise he's a good guy. The best. He's never once let us down, and I know he won't let you down either." I was stunned silent. "You don't have to decide today, but just think about what I said," she requested.

The best I could muster after that declaration of hers was a simple nod, but it seemed to satisfy her.

"Good to hear," she giggled. "Now, what did you think about your first dive bar and show?" At that point Callie came up on my other side, linking arms with me, and joining our conversation.

We laughed as we recounted our night, all the while I snuck glances ahead of us at Peyton and Abraham's backs. I wondered what kind of sickly sweet things she was saying to him, and whether they'd make me want to punch her.

I decided that was likely.

"I can't believe Abey requested Del sing that song," Callie confided, her light blue eyes wide. "He's never done anything like that before."

I shrugged, feigning nonchalance. "Oh, yeah?" I asked as offhanded as I could.

Callie nodded seriously. "Never. He's danced with tons of girls at shows like this and never requested a special song for them."

I gritted my teeth until they felt like they might crack. "Oh, yeah?" I repeated, although this time a little harsher.

"It's different with Ellie, Cal, can't you see that?"

Callie nodded again. "It's totally different," she agreed.

"What's different?" Abraham asked. We'd arrived at his truck by now, Peyton still hanging from his arm.

"Nothing!" the three of us chimed together, which produced a fit of giggles from us, and a sigh from him.

"Great, another woman in my life to gang up against me," Abraham complained with a sparkle in his eye and a smile on his face. He clearly wasn't bothered by our camaraderie.

"I'd never gang up on you, Abey," Peyton purred.

I rolled my eyes and fought to stop the beer I'd had from making a repeat appearance.

"Thanks Peyton," he said as he walked over to the driver's side, ruffling her hair like a kid as he passed.

She frowned at the sisterly affection which made my night just a little brighter. Until she opened her mouth again.

"I call shotgun," she yelled, causing the headache I'd been developing to blossom further.

I shot a furious look at the skinny brunette while I climbed into the cramped backseat between Callie and Evey. I could already tell this was going to be a long ride back to the lodge.

Chapter 26

Peyton spent the whole twenty-minute ride back to the lodge talking Abraham's ear off. I spent it seething in the back. So, I was beyond relieved when we finally pulled onto his long driveway, and up to the lodge.

When we stopped, I slid across the backseat, and stepped onto the gravel drive as fast as I could. To my surprise, Abraham approached me immediately, using one hand to wrap around the back of my neck, fingers tangling in my thick hair.

"Hey," he said simply.

I smiled. "Hey."

"You hungry?"

My stomach took that opportunity to rumble. He must have heard because he smiled and directed me toward the massive house in front of us.

"I could eat!" Peyton piped up, coming around the other side of the truck to stand in our way.

I watched Abraham's face to see how he'd handle this. If he invited her to eat with us, I was going to bed early, empty stomach or not. But instead, he frowned.

"Don't you and Paul have enough food? If not, I can gather whatever you want from the pantry."

Peyton's dark eyes dimmed. "No, we've got plenty of food," she admitted.

Abraham smiled and patted her on the shoulder as he ushered me toward the door. "Great, then have a good night, Peyton," he called as he left her seething in the driveway.

I held my tongue but couldn't wipe the grin off my face.

We got to the kitchen, and Abraham pulled out a stool for me at the large island in the middle of the kitchen. He opened the refrigerator door and stuck his head inside.

"Uh..." he began. I arched an eyebrow and waited for him to finish. He straightened up, holding a couple bags of deli meat. "Sandwiches?" he asked hopefully.

"That sounds perfect."

He smiled his million-dollar smile, and I swear I saw stars. How could this man be so beautiful, so kind, so gentle, and funny all at the same time? There had to be something I was missing. Some bad habit, or terrible skeleton in his closet. He couldn't be this perfect.

"We got ham, turkey, or roast beef," he interrupted my musings.

"Okay."

His surprised eyes met mine. "Okay?"

"Yeah. I'll have it all. Load it up."

He smiled wide. "That's my girl. An everything sandwich coming right up."

I rolled my eyes but smiled back. "Not your girl, McCoy."

"Not yet," he responded.

I scoffed but didn't deny it. Because if I had, it might have been a lie.

"How about some lettuce and tomato?" he asked.

"And mayo and mustard," I added.

He nodded and went back to hunt down the extra ingredients. "Where can I find a cutting board and knife?" I asked.

"Um."

I laughed. "That's right. Your culinary expertise is a recent development. I'll find them myself."

"I was just thinking Ms. Smartypants. Now I remember the cutting boards are in the cabinet next to the sink, and the knives are in the drawer below that." My eyebrows rose in surprise, and he rolled his eyes. "I'm not completely useless in the kitchen."

I helped to slice up the tomato while he put our sandwiches together. We worked together in companionable silence, and it was nice and oddly familiar.

He placed the plates in front of two stools and returned to the fridge for a couple bottles of water. He pulled out a barstool for me and then took the seat next to mine.

Once I'd taken a few bites and a gulp of water, I turned to Abraham, and asked something that'd been on my mind for hours. "So, where are you taking me tomorrow?"

"It's a surprise."

"I don't like surprises."

"Why does that not surprise me?" He smiled behind his sandwich.

"Can I at least get a hint?" I asked sweetly, placing a hand on his thigh.

He froze in his seat, and turned wide eyes in my direction, first at my hand, and hen my eyes. His throat bobbed with a harsh swallow, and he took a long sip of water before answering. "Are you trying to use your womanly wiles to get me to spill my secrets?"

My head fell back with a loud bark of laughter. "My 'womanly wiles'?" He nodded. "I wasn't aware I had any 'wiles'."

He smirked. "Believe me, you've got wiles in spades."

"Well is it working?"

He shook his head slowly as he finished chewing. "You have no idea."

I waited for a few moments before I persisted. "Well?"

He assessed me for a few long seconds before scratching his stubbled cheek. "Okay, I'll give you a hint." I clapped my hands, my smile wide and expectant. "I'd do just about anything to make you smile that way," he muttered. I had no time to respond to that because he kept speaking. "It's somewhere you've never been before."

I waited for more, but when it was clear he was done, I frowned. "Well, that wasn't very helpful. How am I supposed to guess where we're going with *that*?"

He laughed as he cleared our empty plates. "That's the point, El. You're not supposed to guess."

I sighed dramatically which made him laugh again. "Okay fine. Can you tell me *when* at least?"

He rinsed the plates and placed them in the dishwasher. "I've cleared my afternoon, so I thought we could leave around one? Have lunch there?"

I smiled. "My day's wide open."

His expression turned serious, and he slowly walked around the island until he was right in front of me. "You know, the last time you were in my house, you didn't do much smiling."

I gulped. He was so close, his scent overwhelming my senses. "I didn't have much to smile about then."

He took a step closer, nudging my knees apart to make room for his hips. "And, now?"

I was trapped in his gaze. "Now it's different."

He scanned my face. "You're different."

I could only nod.

He leaned in close until his lips brushed against my ear. "I like seeing you happy. I want to keep making you happy."

My eyes fell closed as a shuddering breath left my lungs. His warm lips traveled from the shell of my ear to my cheek where he pressed a slow, tender kiss that was far too brief.

He leaned back, and fire burned in his bright blue eyes. "You ready for bed?" he asked gruffly.

My mouth went dry, my eyes wide as I read between the lines.

Was he asking me to sleep with him?! We haven't even kissed yet!

My heart picked up to an almost painful pace as my palms sweat. Mind racing, I tried to remember the last time I shaved, but couldn't.

I'm not ready!

Abraham watched my reaction with shrewd eyes. Suddenly, his expression cleared, and his head tipped back with a hearty laugh. He wrapped an arm around my waist and pulled me from the stool. Still laughing, he placed a kiss on top of my head, arm still wrapped around me as he lead us out of the kitchen.

"What I meant was 'are you ready for your own bed'."

My face heated painfully as I prayed for a sinkhole or flash flood to take me away.

How could I have been so stupid and presumptuous?

He leaned down until his lips were against the side of my face. "Don't get me wrong, El. I'd love to wake up next to you tomorrow morning, but the time isn't right. And, I'm not that kinda guy."

I regained enough of my composure to ask, "What kind of guy are you?"

We'd made it up the first flight of stairs already, and Abraham didn't miss a beat before responding. "The kinda guy who takes a beautiful woman on a few dates and makes her some kind of promise for the future before he makes love to her."

The burning in my face had subsided slightly until now. I'm sure I resembled an overripe tomato at this point.

Part of me was a little disappointed I wouldn't be spending the night wrapped in Abraham's arms. The other was immensely relieved. I *wasn't* ready. Not even close. Thankfully Abraham's hormones weren't overriding his common sense like mine seemed to be.

We made it to the third-floor landing, and Abraham led me to the bedroom that had become mine. With embarrassment still burning my cheeks, I kept my gaze averted. His calloused fingers grasped my chin and tilted my face until I met his eyes.

"That all right with you?" he asked, his expression soft, but with a bit of cockiness.

I straightened and pulled my chin out of his fingers. "We'll see."

He smirked, a twinkle of mirth in his denim blue eyes. "That's my girl," he said before placing a chaste kiss on my forehead.

"I'm not your girl, McCoy," I reminded him, trying to hide the smile on my lips.

He ignored me. "Night, El. I'll come get you for breakfast."

I nodded and retreated behind my borrowed bedroom door.

Who would have thought a midnight snack could be so sexually charged?

The next morning, I was dressed and ready for Abraham when I heard a knock at the door. I bounded over, and whipped it open, only to find Evey there instead of the man I couldn't stop thinking about. The disappointment must have shown on my face, because Evey laughed, and pushed her way inside.

"Expectin' someone else?" she asked with a knowing look.

My face heated. "Um. Well. No. Uh. Kind of?"

She laughed again. "I won't take it personally." I smiled gratefully. "Abey sent me to get you for breakfast. He said he had somethin' come up and couldn't make it."

My face fell along with my heart. I'd really been looking forward to that... *outing* later.

I would not call it a date.

Evey laughed again and linked her thin arm through mine. "Don't worry, he said he'd still make it to your date later this afternoon."

"It's not a date."

She shot me a sideways look. "Well then, why were you so glum about a second ago?"

I floundered for a response, and she laughed again, her wind-chime voice ringing through my ears, and reminding me to replace the plugs I'd taken out last night. I scooped them off the nightstand and returned to Evey's side. "I'm just excited to go to this special place of his. I'm curious."

"Uh-huh. Keep tryin' to convince yourself of that, honey."

I ignored her and changed the subject. We chatted about the night before at the bar and the cute guy Evey'd danced with as we walked down to breakfast. When we got to the kitchen, it was full of sunlight, boisterous laughter, and muscled men. If there wasn't one in particular I couldn't stop thinking about, this room full of man meat might have tempted me. But I was having lunch with the sexiest of them all.

As I stood there observing the activity in the kitchen, it was hard not to let my mind drift to more sinister thoughts. Was one of these men the killer we were looking for? Could one of them be plotting their next attack even now? There was just no way to know, and I had a bad feeling he was hiding in plain sight.

Evey grabbed us two plates, and we filled them to the brim before grabbing mugs full of steaming coffee. We found a couple seats down by Ms. Elsie, and I was glad. The elderly woman had spunk, and I'd immediately liked her, but hadn't had any time to get to know her better.

"Hey there, Elizabeth, it's nice to see you here again, sweetheart. Looks like the leg healed up nicely," Ms. Elsie commented as Evey and I took our seats.

"Yes, ma'am it did. Hasn't bothered me in a while." I tucked into my eggs as Ms. Elsie prattled on.

"I can't even count for you the amount of broken bones I've seen from these young wolves in my time. It's a good thing Doc Kyle joined this pack when he did. We had a tough time explainin' ourselves at the local hospital when we were there so often."

"How long ago did he join?" I asked around a mouthful of bacon, using my hand to shield my poor manners.

Ms. Elsie looked up to the ceiling, squinting her eyes in thought. "Oh, it's been at least five years now, hasn't it Evelyn?"

Evey nodded, her own mouth full of food. "Gotta' be at least."

"Yeah, Kyle was a great addition to this pack. And that mate of his is just an angel. She gave me this hush puppy recipe that is so good, it gives my mamaw's a run for its money. And that woman could cook, I'll tell you."

"You're a great cook Ms. Elsie. Did you learn from your mamaw?"

Ms. Elsie nodded. "Sure did. I was stuck to that woman's hip from the time I could walk."

Evey swallowed and spoke up. "Ms. Elsie, did you hear Abey's been cookin' for Ellie here?" she asked with a giggle.

Ms. Elsie's eyes went wide. "Our Abraham? Cookin'?" Evey nodded with a wide grin and mischief in her blue eyes. Ms. Elsie shook her head. "Has it tasted all right, dear?" she asked me, her voice full of real concern.

I laughed loudly. "It's mostly been easy stuff like sandwiches. Don't worry about me."

"Speakin' of sandwiches, have you heard about the special ones Abraham used to make when he was just a pup?" Ms. Elsie asked, eliciting a loud hoot of laughter from Evey. I shook my head with a smile, eager for the story. "Well, they were real simple, see, as they only had two ingredients: bread and syrup."

My mouth fell open. "You've got to be kidding me!"

Ms. Elsie shook her head. "I'm tellin' you the truth. He'd make himself syrup sandwiches every afternoon. He was too short to reach the counter, so he'd slap the bread right on the floor, and stand there with the syrup, and just drip it all over the place."

Evey was howling with laughter, and I was having trouble not joining her. "He thought he was such a culinary genius," Evey wheezed, wiping a tear from her eye.

"I've never heard of anyone making a syrup sandwich. It couldn't have tasted very good."

"Oh, they're delicious, you should try one sometime," Abraham's voice came from behind, startling me. He snagged a piece of bacon off my plate and took the seat next to mine. My heart stuttered a few beats and took off running at his unexpected arrival.

"I think I'll pass," I answered drily.

"You been givin' away all my secrets, Ms. Elsie?" Abraham asked in mock seriousness, smiling wide at the older lady.

"Oh, just the one, honey. And, it's not much of a secret. It's almost like pack knowledge at this point, and if our Elizabeth here's gonna be a part of us, she needs to know these kinds of things," Ms. Elsie reasoned.

"Yeah, I'm hopin' we can get her to stick around for a bit," Abraham answered, eyes locked on mine, their blue depths drowning me. "I'm finishing up some work but should be ready to leave soon. That good with you?"

I nodded. "I've cleared my schedule for you today," I reminded him with a smile.

He nodded, and took my hand, grazing his lips across my knuckles. "I'm a lucky man."

I raised a brow at him. "Don't forget it."

His smile turned sincere. "Never," he promised.

With that, he left the table, and the room dimmed without his light in it.

Chapter 27

It was a couple hours later when Abraham found Evey and I in the theater room. We were just finishing up a romantic comedy, and Abraham took the seat next to me to wait it out. I'd been engrossed in the movie, but my attention was now split between the screen, and the man beside me who gently played with the ends of my hair.

When the credits filled the screen, Evey turned the lights back on. "You two have fun on your date," she called over her shoulder as she left the room.

"It's not a date!" I hollered after her. She'd been teasing me all day about my outing with Abraham.

"It's not?" he asked.

I turned to him, torn. *Was it a date?* He hadn't specified, and I hadn't wanted to assume.

Did I want it to be a date?

This was all so confusing.

"Well, you never said it was," I diverted the heat onto him.

He squinted, gaze raking my face, seeing things I wasn't sure I wanted him to see. Not yet.

"Hmm. I suppose I didn't, did I?" He kept looking at me. Looking through me. "Let me remedy that." He turned to face me, took both my hands in his, and looked deep in my eyes. "Elizabeth, will you go on a date with me this afternoon?"

I smiled and rolled my eyes. "I believe I've already agreed to that."

He smiled back. "Apparently it wasn't a date you agreed to, and I want to make sure all the cards are on the table. I plan on taking you on a date today, Ms. Montgomery. Would that be all right with you?" His blue eyes swirled with sincerity, and a tiny twinkle of humor.

My insides were in knots. This was happening so fast. I'd only met him a week ago, and we were already going on a date? What happened to my "no men" rule? All the walls I'd carefully constructed around myself. All the plans I'd made that did *not* include a man like Abraham in them.

I looked deep in Abraham's sky-blue eyes, waiting with endless patience, but just a touch of insecurity.

And I knew.

There was nothing I wanted more than to spend the afternoon with this man.

I nodded, and his answering smile was so brilliant I had to blink to clear my vision.

He hopped up from his seat and held out a hand. "Well let's get goin' then."

I took his proffered hand and rose from my seat. Before he could lead me away, I asked, "Is what I'm wearing all right?" Not knowing where we were going, I'd thrown on a pair of jeans and a long sleeve t-shirt. Also, I got dressed under the assumption that this wasn't a date. Now, I wish I'd worn something nicer.

Abraham took a moment to take me in, his gaze roaming my form slowly. I shivered as I felt his eyes like a caress against my skin, goosebumps breaking out across my arms. Finally, he reached out to tuck a strand of thick blonde hair behind my ear. "You look beautiful."

I rolled my eyes. "You're going to give me a big head."

He reached out with both hands and used his fingertips to probe my scalp. I frowned in confusion.

What the hell was he doing?

"Nope. Your head is still perfectly sized. No worries, I can probably tell you how beautiful you are another hundred times or so before we have to start worrying about it."

I tilted my head back and laughed. His hands slid through my hair. "You're ridiculous."

"No, I'm honest. Now let's go." He held out a bent arm that I wrapped my hand around. "You don't want to keep your date waiting."

I rolled my eyes again but couldn't wipe the stupid smile off my face.

Abraham led me up to the main floor, and out the side door to where the vehicles were kept. He stopped in front of his dark blue ATV and handed me a helmet.

"I still have to wear this?"

He nodded. "You're still fragile. Be happy I'm not wrapping you in bubble wrap until your first full moon."

I laughed, but it dried up in my throat when I caught his serious expression. He hitched a leg over the leather seat and patted the space behind him. I hopped on and soon found myself entirely too close to him. My chest grazed his back, and I tried to create as much space between us as I could.

He reached around to grab my hands, wrapping them around his waist before turning the engine over. "You need to hold on," he reminded me.

Easier said than done.

My hands clasped in tight fists to avoid the temptation to explore his body. If he noticed, he didn't let on. Abraham eased the 4-wheeler into motion, and soon we were speeding down his driveway before turning off into the forest.

"How much longer?" I asked a while later over the roar of the engine.

Abraham turned his head to the side, so I could hear him. "Just another ten minutes or so. Are you doing all right?"

"I'm fine. I just didn't realize we were going so far away."

The corner of his lip turned up. "I can go faster if you'd like."

A jolt of excitement ran through me. "Really?"

He nodded, and the quad jolted forward. I laughed as the trees whipped by in a blur. The increased speed forced me to hold Abraham's waist tighter, or risk falling off. A small tremble ran through his body, and I smiled to myself. At least I wasn't the only one affected.

Even with the helmet on, my hair flew with the speed we were going. A week ago I would have worried Abraham might hit something going this fast, but now I knew he'd never let anything happen to me. I could absolutely trust him with my safety. It was my heart I still worried about.

A little while later, we pulled up to a large lake surrounded by pines at the foot of the Blue Ridge mountains. Abraham cut the engine, and I slid my helmet off, attempting to take in everything I was seeing all at once.

Clear blue water gently lapped at the pebble strewn beach, mountain peaks reflected in its calm surface. To the left of us was a large haphazard pile of boulders that jutted up against a rock wall. A small waterfall ran off the boulders, and into the large lake, disturbing only a small portion of its surface.

"What do you think?" Abraham asked behind me.

I turned to him. "It's incredible, Abraham. I've never seen anything so beautiful." I turned again to stare at the picture-perfect scene before me.

"I know what you mean." His voice was deep, and serious, and so close. He ran a hand down my arm to my hand where he twisted his fingers with mine. "There's more."

I glanced at our entwined hands as he led me away from the shore and over to the rock wall. He let go of my hand and began climbing up the pile of rocks. Soon he was several feet high. "Come on," he called, "The rest is up here."

I eyed the boulders warily. "I don't think I can."

He jumped down, landing in front of me. "I'll help you," he promised. And, for once, I didn't argue.

I nodded and walked over to where he'd begun his ascent. Abraham pointed out the hand and foot holds he'd used and stood behind me as I hoisted myself up the first boulder. Once on top, he scrambled up, and showed me how to get up the next rock. We continued like that until we'd made it all the way up.

The last boulder had a relatively flat surface, and spread along the top was a blanket, held down on all four corners by small mason jars filled with pale pink peonies. I gasped at the site, taking in the basket nearby, and the table settings already laid out in anticipation of our arrival.

I turned to Abraham, my eyes damp and my heart full. No one had *ever* done *anything* like this for me before. The time and preparation he must have put into this floored me. *He* floored me. And, as I stood there, desperately willing my eyes to dry and seeing the hope and uncertainty in his, I felt one of my walls crack, the bricks and mortar crumbling, threatening to fall.

"Do you like it?" he asked, his voice cautious, his eyes so blue, and that cracked wall collapsed leaving nothing but a pile of disintegrating rubble in its wake. I reached up, and wrapped my arms around his neck, my wet eyes dampening his t-shirt.

"I love it," I assured him, my voice wobbly, full of emotion. His arms encircled my waist, pulling me closer as he buried his face in the crook of my neck. He breathed deeply, and something wild in me settled a bit.

When I gathered myself, I pulled away, and smiled. "It's incredible, Abraham. Thank you so much."

His answering smile rivaled the bright sun in the clear sky. "I'm glad you like it. Now, come sit down and eat."

I did as he asked, sitting cross-legged on the soft blanket as he started pulling out food. I looked like he'd grabbed two of everything from the kitchen. When he had everything laid out, we dug in. I practically inhaled my first sandwich before I looked past the picnic Abraham had set up for us.

From this height, I could see the whole lake and the small stream of water that snaked around the rock we sat on. The air was cool, but the sun was warm as I dug into my second sandwich, popping a piece of cheese or fruit in my mouth between bites.

With the quiet forest surrounding us, I took a chance and slipped the earplugs out and into my pocket. Now I could hear the trickle of water as it bubbled over rocks, and twigs on its way to the edge, and the herd of deer lapping at the lake on the far shore. A soft flapping sound had me searching the sky for its owner. A bald eagle flew past us and dove toward the ground surrounding the lake. I couldn't see from here if he'd caught what he'd been hunting, but he flew away shortly after.

The soft wind blew tendrils of hair around my head, and I tipped my face up to the midday sun, letting it warm me. *This* was the serenity and peace I'd come out here for last weekend. *This* was the Asheville I'd been dying to decompress in. I sighed in contentment as I finished my third sandwich.

"Full?" Abraham asked, a touch of humor in his voice.

I groaned. "I don't think I'll ever eat again. Did you make all this?"

He shook his head. "Ms. Elsie helped me. When she heard I was taking you on a date, she insisted."

"Does everyone know we went on a date today?"

Abraham chuckled and nodded. "Welcome to pack life."

Pack life.

This would be my life from now on. These people my family. The idea was still so strange, and I wondered if I measured up. Did they want me in their family? Was I worthy of this pack? It seemed like just getting attacked near their land was my ticket in, but did I deserve it?

"So," Abraham's voice pulled me out of my disparaging thoughts. "Tell me more about you."

"What do you want to know?" I asked cautiously.

He shrugged. "Everything."

I rolled my eyes. "Well, there's really not much to know. I'm pretty boring."

"I disagree with that. And there's a ton I don't know. Like, why did you become a lawyer?"

"My dad's a lawyer, and I'm an only child. It was always the plan for me to follow in his footsteps."

"What about your mother? You didn't want to follow her path?"

I laughed humorlessly. "I'd need a gallon-of-wine-a-day habit, and a love for plastic surgery."

"Oh?" He seemed confused, so I elaborated.

"My mom's a trophy wife. Pretty and useless. She drinks, she shops, and she organizes charity events that make her look good, but she doesn't really care about. That's not me."

"No, it's not," he agreed. "So, did you *want* to become a lawyer, or did you do it for your parents?"

Good question.

"At first, I went to law school to satisfy them, and since they were paying, it was important to make them happy. But as I learned more about law and our government, I began to enjoy it."

"Why criminal law?"

"My father, again."

"He's a criminal lawyer too?"

I nodded. "One of the best in the state."

"Is that what you really want to do though?"

I shrugged. "I don't know. I haven't really thought about it."

He frowned. "You haven't thought about what you want to do with your life? You've never stopped and thought about what would make you happy? What you'd enjoy?"

"I enjoy criminal law." Even I could tell I wasn't entirely telling the truth. So, I amended my statement. "Most of the time."

He nodded. "You can do anything, Elizabeth. You're so incredibly smart, and dedicated, nothing would be out of reach for you." He watched me closely. "Do me a favor. Right now, off the top of your head, tell me the first thing that comes to mind when you think about what you'd really like to do for the rest of your life."

You.

My face heated, and I averted my gaze.

Keep it together, Montgomery. He wasn't asking for your dirty thoughts, you perv.

I cleared my throat and gave him the *second* thing that came to mind. "I'd like to open a private practice."

He nodded. "That's great. Would you still do criminal law?"

I shrugged. "It's all I know." He nodded again still studying me. "What about you? Is construction your dream?"

He smiled. "It is, actually. My dad was a contractor, and he'd take me out on jobs all summer long while school was out. I love it."

Could I honestly say I loved my job?

I thought about that for a long minute, and still couldn't answer honestly. What would it be like to really *love* what I do, and not just be good at it?

Because that's what I liked best about being a criminal lawyer, the satisfaction of knowing I was one of the best in my firm. But to *love* my work– that was something I'd never worried about. Nothing I considered until recently.

Like so many other things in my life, this man, this pack of wolves was changing me. And, I was just trying to keep up.

Chapter 28

"What about your childhood?" Abraham asked. "What were you like as a kid?"

I smiled ruefully. "Wild."

He laughed. "I can't imagine that."

"It's true. Especially in my early teen years. I was a terror. Drinking, smoking, guys–"

Abraham growled deep in his throat. "What *guys*?"

I laughed and slapped his hard chest. "Down boy, that was a long time ago." He huffed, still unhappy, but at least he didn't look ready to hunt down all my ex-boyfriends and make them dog food. Or wolf food.

"So, what happened? The Elizabeth sitting here is nothing like that. What changed?"

I gulped and looked away. This was *not* something I wanted to talk about. Not something I wanted him to know. If he did, there's no way he'd keep looking at me with those soft eyes I was coming to love. "I got in trouble."

"What kind of trouble?" he pressed.

I sighed. "Big trouble. With the law. Thankfully, I was a minor so the record's sealed. After that, my parents sent me to boarding school out here, and that's where I straightened my life out."

"You went to boarding school?"

I nodded. "Most of high school. It was awful, but I'm thankful for it. Who knows where I'd be now if it weren't for that?"

He shook his head. "You still would have figured it out, eventually. You're too smart for that."

I chuckled darkly. "Where were you, and your vote of confidence back then?"

His eyes turned serious. "Just waiting to find you."

My gaze locked on his, trapped in their blue depths. His eyes left mine to glance at my lips, and then back again, my insides clenching almost painfully. Delicious anticipation zipped through my veins as we inched closer. Like magnets, we were being pulled together, the space between us dwindling fast.

And, I panicked.

"So!" I said, straightening, and leaning away from him. "How did you find this place?"

Abraham smiled. "I told you, I know this area, and these mountains like the back of my hand. I found this place years ago and somehow kept it a secret from my nosey sisters." He smiled indulgently. "This is where I come to get away from it all. From being the alpha, and the head of our family, and all the responsibility that comes with it. When things get too hectic, I escape out here to sit on this rock, and just think. Or rather, I work on not thinking. This is a great place to clear your mind."

I looked out over the edge and nodded in agreement. This *was* an amazing place to get your head straight. I could imagine escaping out here with a book, and spending hours on this boulder, losing myself in a great story, or taking a nap beneath the warm sun.

"Wanna know what else I do out here?" he asked, rising to his feet.

He pulled me up next to him. "What?"

He grinned mischievously. "Do you trust me?"

"Yes," I answered immediately, and the shock was obvious in his clear eyes. His smile got wider as he led me to the edge of the rock. He kicked off his boots and pulled his t-shirt over his head.

My mouth went dry, and my heart raced, sounding like a tribal drumbeat to my sensitive ears. Heat infused my face as I realized he must have heard it as clearly as I did.

"You might want to take off your shoes, so they don't get wet."

"*Wet?*"

He nodded toward the lake. "We're goin' in."

I backed up. "Hell no. Abraham McCoy, have you lost your mind? I'm not going in that lake."

"You're right we're not *going* in the lake, we're *jumping* in the lake."

I backed up further. "You're nuts."

"You said you trusted me," he reminded.

I shook my head, hair flying around my face. This was crazy. *He* was crazy.

"Come on, El. I won't let anything happen to you."

I know.

I sighed deeply, tipping my face to the sky as I toed off my sneakers. "I can't believe I'm letting you talk me into this," I told the puffy white clouds.

"You'll love it," he promised.

I didn't believe him.

He walked over, and grabbed my hand, leading me to the edge. I peeked over the side and took a quick step back. "It's so far."

His strong arm wrapped around my shoulders, tugging me against his warm, bare chest. It was a damn shame I was so terrified. A moment like this with a half-naked Abraham should be treasured.

"It's not that far, I promise. It'll be fun."

I shook my head and closed my eyes.

Trust.

I needed to trust him. He'd given me no reason not to, and every reason to.

With a sigh, I opened my eyes, and met his gaze. I nodded once, and his face lit up with a brilliant smile. "Do you want to jump or run?" he asked.

I eyed the edge again, a shiver of fear running down my spine.

He snapped his fingers. "I've got an even better idea. Come here," he opened his arms, and I stepped closer. He wrapped his hands around my waist, and hoisted me up against him, my hips meeting his, and I instinctively wrapped my legs around him.

"What are you doing?" I squeaked. The heat from his bare skin was scorching me through my thin top, and I was getting dizzy. He smelled so good. Like clean man. My senses were on overload. Add that to the adrenaline pumping through my veins from fear, and I was a mess.

His large hands cupped my bottom, hitching me a little higher. One hand stayed cupping me while the other wrapped around my waist. His body dwarfed mine, making me feel feminine and dainty, something I wasn't used to at 5'9".

"We're goin' in together. You ready?"

"No."

"On three." He smiled. "One."

I closed my eyes, breaking his blue-eyed stare, and concentrated on taking deep breaths.

"Two."

My arms slid around his neck, pulling my body closer to his until I could feel his heart beating into my chest. Or was that my heart? The two were synchronized.

"Three!"

He took off running toward the edge, and an involuntary scream left my lips as he ran out of rock. We were free-falling, the cool wind whipping my hair around my face as I clung to Abraham, his arms never loosening from around me.

The seconds stretched into days as everything got quiet, and we fell, fell, fell. And for that immeasurable amount of time, I felt all of my worries fall away as fast as my plummeting body.

I was just a girl, in this strong boy's arms, jumping off a cliff.

I was a kid again, doing something carefree, and a little stupid, just because I could.

Right when I thought my stomach would leap out of my body, and beat me there, we hit the water.

Abraham's arms loosened around me, but his hand found mine. The initial shock of hitting the water had eclipsed the freezing cold temperature of the lake. We broke through the surface simultaneously, him whooping and laughing, me gasping and sputtering.

"That was incredible!" he yelled.

"That was insane," I called back, chuckling as I tread water in the deep lake. My wet clothes were heavy, especially my jeans.

Abraham swam closer, and wrapped his arms around me, pulling me close until our faces were inches apart. "Wasn't that fun?"

My heart was still racing from the jump. Or was that from being so close to him?

"That was fun," I confirmed.

I hadn't done something that careless in a long time. Hadn't made a snap decision, and just *jumped* for years. It seemed like more was changing in me besides my hearing.

"Wanna go again?" His arms wrapped tighter around me.

My body trembled in his arms, my limbs tingling, my toes going numb.

"Are you cold?" he asked, all humor leaving his face, quickly replaced by concern.

He reached out to trace one of his calloused fingers along my bottom lip. "Your lips are turning blue," he noted. I nodded as my body continued to tremble in his arms. "Come on," he spun around and pulled my arms over his shoulders. "Hold on and I'll get us back to shore."

I tightened my knees against his hips, and my arms around his neck. He dove under the surface, and took off toward the beach, swimming faster than I'd ever seen a person swim before. Our bodies sliced through the water as I clung to his back like a knapsack. Within a couple minutes, we'd gotten close enough to walk, and Abraham scooped me into his arms.

When we made it to the ATV, he opened a compartment on the back and pulled out a large white towel. He wrapped it around my shoulders, and used his large hands to rub my arms, the friction warming my cool skin.

He stood there thawing me out for a few minutes, and eventually, I could feel all my fingers and toes again. I must have looked a little better too, because he stopped rubbing, and took a step back.

"I'm gonna grab our shoes, you okay here for a minute?"

I nodded as I willed my insides to stop shaking. He disappeared and was back within a few minutes. Abraham placed our shoes and the picnic blanket on the seat of the ATV and pulled something else out of its storage compartment.

He held out a fresh set of clothes, and I looked around warily. Where the hell was I going to change?

His lips quirked in a smile as he turned around. "Go ahead and change. It's just us out here, I've never come across anyone else."

I *really* didn't want to strip out in the open, but knew I needed to get the wet clothes off if I had any chance of warming up. With a sigh, I peeled my shirt off, letting it fall to the pebbled beach with a loud *plop*.

"I'm sorry, El. That was stupid of me."

I frowned. "Wh–what are you s–sorry for?" I stuttered out between trembling lips.

He sighed, ran a hand through his hair, and scratched the back of his head. "I should have realized how cold the water would be for you. That waterfall comes directly from the mountains."

I yanked his large t-shirt over my head and worked on getting my soaking jeans off my hips. "It's fine Abraham, it's n–not like I've never been c–cold before."

"But I'm supposed to take care of you, not hurt you," he countered.

I slid his sweatpants up my legs and rolled the waistband down a few times until they stayed put. "It's not your j–job to take care of m–me. And besides, it really was a l–lot of fun. I don't regret it."

I reached out, and placed a hand on his shoulder, turning him to face me. His eyes raked my body, a gleam shining in his blue gaze. He grabbed the blanket off the ATV, and wrapped it around my shoulders, dragging me into his warm arms. "It *is* my job," he argued.

His denim gaze drilled straight to my core, hollowing me out, and filling me with everything *Abraham*. I breathed him in, swallowing him down and letting him run through my veins. My eyes closed as I listened to his steady heart beat faster, faster.

"Elizabeth."

His voice was so deep.

So rough.

So unsteady.

I opened my eyes to see he'd moved closer, his face just inches from mine. He took a deep breath, his chest hitching. "I want to kiss you so bad right now," he admitted softly, his eyes anything but.

"Why don't you?" I whispered because anything louder would shatter this moment.

Shatter this fragile thing between us.

"I don't want you to run," he admitted, his voice broken, his words breaking *me*.

"I'm not going anywh–"

His warm mouth found mine and instantly changed everything.

Flashes of what felt like electricity shot through him into me, back and forth, around and around, like a never ending current. Our lips stayed locked, both of us frozen for a long moment before something snapped. Something inside us both fractured.

In the same instant, both our mouths moved against each other, testing, and tasting, teeth, and tongues, and heat all swirling together until we were almost frenzied. His strong hands cupped my bottom once more, my legs enveloping his hips, hands tangling in his thick hair, clutching his face to mine.

I didn't know when he moved, but suddenly my back was digging into something hard, his body pressed against mine. His hard lines digging into my soft curves, our bodies aligned like the planets in the sky, creating a perfect constellation of stars. When his lips left mine, and traveled across my face and down my neck, I gasped for air, my body trembling once again, but this time I wasn't cold at all.

It felt like I was on fire at every point Abraham's body touched mine. I moaned, and struggled for breath, and might have even been embarrassed by the sounds I was making if I hadn't been so enraptured by the man nibbling on my earlobe.

I used his hair to drag his mouth back to mine. He chuckled against my lips, and I swallowed his humor as I clung to him, silently begging for more. One of his hands left my backside and moved to my neck where he held my face with a thumb on my jaw, and his fingers tangled in my wet hair. The other squeezed my backside almost painfully, but not quite.

He moved my face around as he devoured my desire, giving me nothing less in return. We stayed like that, panting and groaning in the quiet forest until our lust had subsided enough for us to catch our breath. He peppered soft, wet kisses around my face, and across my eyelids as my fingers twisted in his hair.

Finally, he lifted his head, and looked at me, my brown eyes meeting his blue gaze. I'd never seen his eyes so clear.

So bright.

So, light.

He smiled shyly, and my heart stuttered, another few bricks tumbling off my highest wall.

"That was even better than I'd imagined."

My smile matched his. "You've imagined this?"

His grin spread. "More times than I care to admit."

And those walls. Those high brick walls that'd been my shelter and protector from everything that could hurt me shuddered. Mortar crumbling, and stones falling. Abraham McCoy was toppling my fortress and I, I'd given up defending the castle, and instead, had opened the front door for him.

Chapter 29

A long time later, I was still pinned between Abraham's hips, and whatever he had us pressed against. Both his hands cupped my face gently, almost as if he were afraid I'd break. Crumble in his grasp. If only he knew it wasn't my body that was crumbling.

He kissed my lips softly; our passion having subsided enough for both of us to savor one another. His lips were delicious, and I tipped my head back, searching for more from him. As much as he was willing to give, which seemed endless.

He used both hands to run a fiery path from my neck, down my arms where he entwined his fingers with mine. Raising our arms until they were above my head, he immediately took advantage of my vulnerable position.

I think by now his lips had met every inch of available skin from my collarbone up. I sighed as his mouth made another circuit around my face, tasting and teasing my lips every time he passed them.

"God, you taste incredible," he murmured against my heated skin, sending extra bolts of electricity straight to my core. That secret place that had been subtly rubbing against his hard abdomen for the past several minutes. I groaned in response, clutching at the hands that still held my own.

He gathered my wrists in one hand, using the other to stroke my side, from my shoulder to my knee. Every time he passed by my hip, he'd stop to cup and squeeze my bottom, pulling me closer. And each time he inched me closer, I hoped for more.

More skin.
More touching.
More friction.
More Abraham.

Unfortunately, reality was seeping back into the haze of lust I'd been lost in. My wet hair had soaked through the thin t-shirt I wore, causing my skin to pebble, sending a shiver down my spine.

Abraham stopped his exploration of my body and pulled back. He eyed me critically for a few seconds before lowering me to the ground. "Shit," he muttered. He retrieved the blanket that had fallen off me at some point and wrapped it tight around my shoulders.

"What's wrong?" I asked, still a little breathless.

He scooped me into his arms and walked us back to the ATV. "I'm an idiot. You're still cold. I should be getting you home, not ravaging you against a pine tree while you freeze."

His eyebrows were drawn, full mouth tight in anger. I reached out a finger to soothe the angry lines across his face. "I liked the ravaging though."

I was rewarded with a small quirk of his lips.

"There will be more ravaging, but first I need to get you home, and warm, before you get sick."

My belly clenched at his words. "Promise?" I asked, my voice soft. Brave, and yet still unsure.

Abraham growled deep in his chest, eyes flashing bright. My bottom hit the 4-wheeler's seat hard before Abraham used one hand to tangle in my hair and pull my head back. His lips were on mine in the next instant, hard and demanding, hot and wet, and I moaned into his mouth.

Tongues dueled, and teeth nipped as we lost all the progress toward sanity we'd just made. My fingers gripped his neck, pulling him down toward me as his free hand wrapped around my waist, pulling me closer.

A few long minutes later, and we had to come up for air. As we both struggled to regain our composure, Abraham used the hand in my hair to tilt my face up.

His eyes were bright and wild, shooting a bolt of desire through my body, and I squeezed my legs together.

"Promise." His voice was deep, and gravelly, and I had to stop myself from dragging his lips to mine again. We wouldn't get anywhere if one of us didn't have some self-restraint.

I couldn't form words at the moment, so I simply nodded, causing his lips to tip up into a grin. He gathered the rest of our stuff while I gathered my senses, and soon he was on the seat in front of me, driving us back toward his lodge.

Unlike last time, I wasn't afraid to get close to him, wrapping my arms tight around his waist, and resting my cheek against his back. He took one hand off the handlebars, and grasped mine, sliding his fingers between my own, and holding it the rest of the way back.

When we got to the lodge, Abraham took the hand he was still holding, and used it to help me off the quad. He brought it to his lips and placed a small kiss against my knuckles. Even after our steamy time back at his lake, he still had the power to make my cheeks warm.

We walked up the stairs in silence, my hand still in his until we made it to my door. Abraham spun me around, pressed me against the wall, and kissed me like it was the first time.

He finally pulled away and placed a gentle kiss on the tip of my nose. "I need to get some work done, and you need to take a hot shower." He eyed the borrowed clothes barely clinging to my frame, his eyes heating. "And as much as I fucking love seeing you in my clothes, you should change into something dry."

The f-bomb falling from his full lips shot a lightning bolt of heat straight to my core.

With a mock-salute, I said, "Yes, sir."

His smile widened, and he pulled me against his chest. "I like it when you do what I say," he growled in my ear, causing goosebumps to break out across my skin.

I wrapped my arms around his neck and stood on my tiptoes, so I could reach his ear. "Oh, yeah?"

His arms tightened around my waist, another growl rumbling deep in his chest. "Yeah."

I nipped his earlobe, following it with a swipe of my tongue, smiling as I felt his body quake almost imperceptibly. "Well, don't get used to it."

He froze for a fraction of a moment before tipping his head back and laughing loudly. I pulled back and watched, enraptured and dazzled by this beautiful man. He placed a kiss on my lips that I think was supposed to be a peck, but quickly turned into something more.

A throat clearing nearby caught my attention first.

"Abey?" A cross voice asked.

I reluctantly pulled from Abraham's arms and peeked over his shoulder.

A very annoyed looking Beatrice stood in front of his office door, arms folded across her chest. Her dark blue eyes narrowed at me before turning their fiery light toward Abraham.

The man in my arms sighed. "Yes, Bea?"

"Don't we have a meeting scheduled now?"

He sighed again, his forehead connecting with mine. "Yep." The word popped out of his mouth. "Go on in, I'll be right there."

The angry woman huffed but did as he asked.

Abraham's lips found mine again, and I let myself get lost for a few moments before pulling away. He had other ideas. As I struggled to drag a breath into my lungs, he continued to place soft kisses on my cheek.

"Don't you need to go?" I gasped as he nibbled on the shell of my ear.

"Mmm hmm," he mumbled, his nose skimming along my throat, and down to the collar of my shirt.

"You probably should then. I don't want her coming back out here."

He sucked on a small patch of my neck and sighed again. "I suppose you're right, but I'd rather stay here and kiss you. Have I told you how delicious you taste?" His tongue made swirling patterns across my collarbone.

"Aah," I gasped. "You might have mentioned it," I breathed. "But really, I don't want Beatrice to hate me any more than she already does."

He stopped his assault on my neck and met my gaze. "Bea doesn't hate you."

I rolled my eyes. "She definitely does."

He shook his head, tucking a lock of wet hair behind my ear. "It's not you she doesn't like, it's change."

I frowned. "What's changed? Don't you get new pack members all the time? Did she throw this kind of fit when Wyatt and Wesley joined?" I asked, hand on my cocked hip.

Why was I getting this special treatment from her?

His eyes shuttered, and he looked away. "Everything's changed, El. You just don't know it yet," he answered cryptically.

Before I could ask what the *hell* that meant, he placed a swift kiss on my forehead, and took a few steps back. "Family dinner at six all right?"

I nodded, thoughts swirling rapidly inside me. He must have noticed my turmoil because he stepped back to place another kiss on my head. "Don't worry, everything's fine. Great in fact." His mouth spread into a brilliant smile I couldn't help but reciprocate. "We'll talk more later. Go get warmed up."

I rolled my eyes. "Yes, master."

"It's 'alpha'," he responded with a cheeky grin.

I scoffed, causing him to laugh as he opened his office door, and disappeared behind it. But I did as he asked, and took a steaming hot shower. Although after that afternoon with Abraham, a cold shower might have been more fitting.

As soon as I finished drying my hair, there was a knock on my door. I skipped over to answer it and found Evey with a wide mischievous grin on her face. I rolled my eyes, but opened the door for her to come in.

"TELL ME EVERYTHING!" she yelled, making me wince. It was then I remembered I'd left my earplugs in my wet jeans. I wondered if they'd made it out of the lake or not. "Sorry, sorry!" Evey whisper yelled.

I wiggled a finger in one of my ringing ears but waved her off. "It's fine. I need to get used to not wearing those things, anyway."

"But seriously, tell me everything!" She commanded and bounced over to sit on my bed.

"Well–"

"WHY THE HELL IS SHE COMING?" A loud voice shouted from across the hall. I didn't mean to, but without the water running or my hairdryer on, it was too easy to hear their conversation.

"You know why," Abraham's voice was low, and serious.

"No, I don't! I don't get what the big deal is about this little human or what's so special about her! You know she won't make it past her first shift anyway, so why are you getting so attached to her?!"

My heart simultaneously sank and raced, Evey's eyes widening in fear. Heat spread across my face. I shouldn't be listening to this conversation. But I couldn't *help* it. I was new to this werewolf hearing thing and didn't know how to turn it off.

"She *will* make it," Abraham responded, voice colder than I'd ever heard it.

"She won't! Bitten wolves never make it! You know that! When's the last time you knew one who did, huh? We all need to stop kidding ourselves. Elizabeth won't be around much longer, and *you* need to accept that!"

A gasp flew from my mouth.

Bitten wolves don't make it past their first shift.

Mine was three weeks away.

I only had three weeks to live.

My eyes sought Evey's, hoping I'd see denial, but all I saw was sad acceptance.

I'm going to die.

"THAT'S ENOUGH, BEATRICE!"

While they fought, my insides twisted, my gut emptying out, my heart stopping completely.

I'm going to die.

The door across the hall opened, and slammed violently, causing both of us to jump. Evey slid off the bed and approached me cautiously.

I couldn't face her, the sympathy in her eyes would break me, and I needed to stay strong right now. Needed to build those walls back up and hide behind them.

"She's wrong, Ellie. You're gonna make it. We all know you are."

I shook my head, hair flying around my face, and obscuring my pain. "Is what she said true?" I whispered. "Do bitten wolves not make it past their first shift?"

"It's different with you, Ellie."

"Answer my question."

"It's not that simple. You're not like the others–"

"I SAID ANSWER MY QUESTION!" My ears rang with my rage, but I didn't care.

Evey shrank away, and part of me felt terrible. But the other part? That part screamed *BETRAYAL*.

"You knew," I said, my voice even and quiet.

"Ellie, listen–"

"You all knew."

"It's not like that, Elizabeth. Hear me out."

"You all let me believe I was just going through a few changes, and everything would be all right." My voice was getting louder, my breaths harsher. "Not a single one of you thought it was important enough to tell me I wouldn't *live* through this change? That this would be my last month alive?!"

Images, and thoughts flashed through my head rapidly.

My future.

My career.

My apartment.

My cat.

My parents, even.

I'd lose it all.

"I thought you were my friend, Evey. I thought I could trust you."

She clasped her hands in front of her, eyes swimming behind tears. "I *am* your friend, Ellie, you *can* trust me. Abey asked us not to tell you, and we all agreed you had so much else to deal with, you didn't need this on top of everything else."

"Abraham told you not to tell me?" I asked, my voice dropping to a pitch I didn't recognize.

This was *his* fault.

She held her hands up in surrender. "He thought he was doin' the right thing for you. And I agreed with him. It's not the same with you. Beatrice is just bein' bitter. We all know you're gonna make it."

Her words fell around me like petals off a withered flower, dead and useless.

I'm going to die.

My breaths were coming harsher, and louder, and I think I was hyperventilating.

I'm going to die.

Evey reached out, and grasped my shoulders, but I shook her off. I didn't want her to touch me. Didn't even want to be in the same room as her.

"I *trusted* you," I told her again, my voice breaking with emotion.

Her sadness slipped out the corner of her sorrowful blue eyes, but I looked away. I couldn't see her pain. Couldn't process it. Couldn't add it to the rest of what I was feeling.

I'm going to die.

That's all that mattered. I had three weeks left to live, and I hadn't done enough living in the time I'd had.

As my lungs fought for oxygen, I stacked the bricks back up in my mind, reinforced them with mortar and painted them black. No one would get through them again. I was an idiot for ever letting them down to begin with.

I *knew* better than to let people in like I have these past couple weeks.

Especially men.

Especially men who looked like Abraham.

Especially men like Abraham who were clearly looking for one thing only. Weren't they all? Didn't they all just think about their own satisfaction, casualties be damned?

Well that was all over.

I would never allow these walls to come down for another person. Never again open a window, or door, or make a special exception for anyone again.

And with a humorless laugh, I realized I only had to keep that promise to myself for another three weeks. After that, none of this would matter.

Chapter 30

"I'll leave you alone, then," Evey murmured from near the door.

I'd spent the last five minutes ignoring her and packing my things. I was *not* staying here. Not with these people who'd all looked me in the eye and lied. Well, I suppose they hadn't *outright* lied. But a lie by omission was still a lie. Intricacies like that were what I'd built my career on.

I continued to ignore her, and finally she sighed, and retreated from the room. My nose stung with unshed tears, but I held them at bay. I really thought I'd found a friend in Evey. Someone I could confide in and be myself with. Someone I could *trust*.

But that clearly wasn't the case.

"SHE WHAT?!"

I cringed as Abraham's voice bellowed from across the hall. The crash of his chair hitting the floor preceded the slam of his door, and the abrupt opening of mine.

"Elizabeth, what the hell is going on?" he demanded, his voice too loud, too harsh.

I ignored him too.

Instead, I continued to pack my clothes, and double check the drawers for any stray belonging of mine. I would *not* be coming back here. If I was going to die on the next full moon, I might as well do it in the comfort of my own home.

"Elizabeth," his voice was softer, and held a note of desperation.

But I continued to ignore him.

I walked into the en suite bathroom and collected my toiletries. When I came back out, I found Abraham unpacking my suitcase.

With a growl I stalked over and poked him in the back. "What the hell do you think you're doing?"

"Oh, so you *can* talk?" he muttered as he continued to pull things from my bag.

I stormed around the other side of the bed and began tossing my clothes back in. "Of course, I can talk, you jackass, I just don't want to talk to *you*."

He released a large breath and ran a hand down his face. "Elizabeth, let me explain."

"You had a whole week to explain this to me Abraham, and you chose not to."

He sighed again. "Please, El, just hear me out."

I finally met his sorrowful eyes and straightened my spine. I couldn't let him wear me down. *He'd* done this, not me. "Tell me something, Abraham: did you know bitten wolves don't make it past their first shift?"

His throat bobbed, jaw pulsing. "Yes."

I tossed my toiletries in my suitcase and slammed it closed. "That's all I need to know."

Abraham pulled my suitcase to his side of the bed, and out of my reach. "That's *not* all you need to know. That's not even the half of it. If you'll just give me a minute to explain–"

"No!" I stomped over to his side and ripped my bag out of his hands. Zipping the suitcase closed in record time, I slammed it onto the floor, and faced him, my eyes narrowed. "You had every opportunity to tell me the truth, and you chose not to. Why, Abraham? So, you could take advantage of a walking dead girl? So, you could get your way with me while I was still alive and kicking?"

His eyes widened in horror. "No! That's not it at all." He growled again and rubbed both hands down his face. "Is that what I've done? Have I taken advantage of you? Made you do things you didn't want to do? Pushed you too far?"

No. He hadn't.

But still.

"No. I haven't. I've been nothing but patient with you. Because I... I *like* you, El. I like you a lot. And, I never wanted you to regret anything that happened between us. I wanted it to be at your pace. Everything I've done has been for you."

"You lied to me *for* me? That's a new one," I scoffed.

"Of course, it was for you!" he yelled, making me wince in pain. His shoulders drooped in resignation. His next words were softer. "All of it was for you, El. And, I was going to tell you, I just thought you should have some time to get used to the idea of becoming a werewolf before having to deal with anything else."

"But I'm not going to *be* a werewolf, Abraham! I won't *live* that long! And, what gave you the idea that it was your job to decide what I could, and couldn't handle?"

"It's always my job! Everything is my job! Everything is *my* responsibility! It's up to *me* to protect every single member of this pack, and that includes *you!*"

I opened my mouth to scream at him some more but realized this wasn't getting us anywhere. The damage was done. He'd betrayed my trust. Lied to me. And, there was no coming back from that. Not for me, and not for him.

This was over.

I straightened my spine and extended the handle of my suitcase. "Well I'm not your problem anymore."

His fiery blue eyes dimmed, broad shoulders falling even further. "Don't leave, El, please."

"My name's 'Elizabeth'."

He winced like I'd struck him.

My nose burned again, and I knew I was seconds from tears. I needed to go. *Now.*

I turned around, and rolled my suitcase toward the door, grabbing my purse along the way. Wasn't sure how I was leaving this place without my car, but hell, I'd walk to town, and pay a cab to drive me back to Raleigh if that's what it took.

"Please. Don't leave me." His voice was low and soft, almost begging, and I swear, a piece of my heart broke clean off. A large, alpha shaped piece I knew I'd never get back.

I'd never be the same after this, and a part of me liked that I'd only have to live with the gaping hole for another three weeks. After that, I'd be free of the agony I was feeling right now.

Free of this pack.

Free of this pain.

Free of this man.

A single tear slipped from my eye, but I halted the rest. "Tell me something," I asked, my back to him. I took a deep breath. "Is there anything else you're keeping from me?"

His silence said it all.

I waited longer than any self-respecting woman should, but I didn't *want* to walk away. I didn't *want* there to be something else he was lying about. Didn't want to *have* to leave.

But I did.

"Goodbye, Abraham," I told him quietly before walking through the door and closing it behind me.

Closing it on him.

On us.

Evey and Callie were leaning against the opposite wall looking the saddest I'd ever seen them. I gave them both a simple nod and went to walk past them when Callie pushed off the wall and stood in front of me.

"Where are you going?"

"Home."

"Can I drive you?"

I eyed her critically. She'd lied to me too. They all had. But at least she hadn't spent a whole week in my house. Talking, and laughing, and eating, and drinking, and bonding, and *lying*.

I nodded once, and she smiled gratefully. Ignoring her, I stalked toward the stairs, ready to just be *gone*.

"Bye, Ellie," Evey called, the sound of her broken voice stabbing me almost as viciously as Abraham's had.

A part of me, a huge, mac-truck-sized part, wanted nothing more than to take the pain out of Evey's voice.

Take the misery out of Abraham's blue, blue eyes.

But I couldn't do that.

They'd betrayed me, and that wasn't something I could just forgive. I had to protect myself. Couldn't fall back into that dark place I'd barely crawled out of last time I'd let someone in, and they'd broken my trust.

I couldn't go back there.

Even for the best friend I'd ever had.

Even for the most incredible man I'd ever met.

I just couldn't.

We made it down to the garage, and Callie pointed me toward a little silver Prius, and I almost laughed.

Of course, Callie would own a Prius.

She opened the hatchback, and I tossed my bag in alongside hers before stomping over to the passenger door. When we were both seated, she took her time checking mirrors, and adjusting her seatbelt before she finally turned the car on, and carefully reversed onto the driveway.

As we drove down the long drive, a gray blur caught my attention out of the corner of my eye. I turned my head to find a large wolf running through the trees alongside the car. It kept pace with us for a few minutes before stopping in place and tilting its massive head back. A long, loud, mournful howl ripped from its throat before the wolf turned the other way and sprinted off.

I knew it was Abraham.

I'd know him in human or wolf form. There was an undeniable connection. A fine, but indestructible thread that ran between us.

I'd have to spend the time I had left severing that.

I didn't want to feel the pain in my chest that I knew wasn't just mine. It was his too. I don't know how I could feel his anguish, or how I knew it was his, but I did.

It was so much larger than my own.

Deeper.

Sharper.

Infinite.

I didn't know how I'd manage both our pain, but I had no other choice. He'd broken my trust, and that was something I'd never forgive. He knew I would die, and he'd let me walk around believing I had a future.

And what's worse, he let me believe *we* had a future.

That there was something building and blooming between the two of us. Something beautiful, and rare, and perfect.

But that was a lie.

It was all a lie.

And as Callie headed toward the highway that would take me away from this, away from *him*, the anger that had boiled, and frothed inside me finally made way for the sadness that had been bubbling underneath. With all the eyes off me, the bravado collapsed, and I let the tears I'd been holding in fall. Let out the pain I'd been hiding.

And, I cried.

For hours.

The tears endless as I cried for myself.

For Abraham.

Even for Evey.

Cried because every pack member I'd met knew I wouldn't make it and had still befriended me.

But none of it mattered anymore.

None of it could last.

Because I had three weeks to live, and nothing could change that.

A while later, Callie's gentle hand on my shoulder roused me from a fitful sleep.

"We're here," she said quietly.

I mumbled something back and climbed out of her little car. It was dark by now, but the sight of my apartment had never been more welcome. I was trudging up the sidewalk when I heard Callie clear her throat softly behind me.

When I turned around, I found her standing awkwardly near her still-open trunk, fidgeting with her hands and shuffling from foot to foot. I raised my brows at her.

"Um, well, the thing is, I was supposed to stay with you this week, but after everything that happened, I wasn't sure…" she trailed off, clearly uncomfortable.

I sighed. "Is it really still necessary?"

"What do you mean?"

"I won't live through it, Callie. What's the point?"

Her brows furrowed. "We don't know that," she replied quietly.

I shook my head, my southern manners kicking in. "You can come in if you'd like, but I don't see what help you'll be."

She nodded and grabbed her bag before following me up the stairs. "We don't know anything for sure yet, Elizabeth," she said behind me, but I ignored her.

I just wanted my cat.

And, my bed.

And, maybe a bottle of wine.

Or two.

We made it in the door before Charlie came barreling toward me, crashing into my shins as always. A reluctant smile cracked across my tight face.

I felt like I'd been soaked in dirty dishwater and then laid out to dry. Cracked, and brittle.

I picked up my cat and stalked over to the fridge. A half bottle of white greeted me, and I snagged it, forgoing a glass to drink it straight from the source. After I'd taken a few swigs, and felt the wine swirling through my head, I turned to find Callie still standing by the front door, bag in hand, eyes wide as she surveyed my apartment.

"You can come in," I told her.

She nodded absently. "Your apartment is so… colorful."

One corner of my lips twitched, and that was the closest thing to a smile I could muster at the moment. "I get that a lot."

Her eyes found me, still snuggling with my tabby. "And, you have a cat," she deadpanned.

I nodded and took another gulp of wine. "Sure do. His name's Charlie."

"And, Evey was all right with that?" she asked uncertainly.

"She didn't really have a choice, but yes, they got along just fine."

Callie nodded again. "Well, if Evey can get along with him, I'm sure I can too."

I shrugged. It didn't matter to me whether she liked my cat or not. Not much of anything did except the crisp bottle of wine in my hand that I was quickly coming to the bottom of.

I tipped my head back and took another large swill before using the bottle to point down the hall. "At the end is a spare bedroom. You can put your things in there. It doubles as my office, but I haven't been using it much." I laughed humorlessly. "And, I won't be using it for much longer, so it doesn't really matter, does it?" I put the lip of the bottle back to my mouth and finished the rest.

Callie shook her head and took the empty bottle from my hand. "*This* won't help." She set it on the counter and crossed her arms over her narrow chest.

"It can't hurt at this point can it?" I narrowed my eyes and went back to the refrigerator for the unopened bottle. I twisted the cap off, and took a big gulp, glaring at Callie who just sighed.

"I'm going to go put my stuff away, and then you and I are going to have a talk."

I took another big sip, my head swimming. "About what? What could possibly matter at this point?"

She sighed again and turned away. "I'm going to tell you a few things Abey should have told you a while ago." She walked past me, rolling her suitcase behind her. "And, trust me, it matters."

I scoffed. "What could possibly matter, Callie?! I'm going to die in three weeks."

She stopped in her tracks, and spun to face me, her pale blue eyes sterner than I'd ever seen them. "There's a chance you might live, Elizabeth. I thought that might interest you." She turned on her heel, angrily swiping the curtain of beads out of her way as she went.

I might live?

A big part of me didn't dare to hope. But that tiny indestructible, and eternal optimist deep inside wouldn't let me give up.

Not completely.

Not yet.

If there was even the slightest chance I might make it, I would take it. Take it and run.

Because Elizabeth Montgomery was above all else, a fighter.

Chapter 31

When Callie returned, I was already sitting on my bright pink couch, cat in one hand, bottle of wine in the other. She'd given me a sliver of hope, but that didn't mean I was giving up the alcohol.

Not yet, at least.

She walked gracefully through the living room, bringing with her the delicate scent of roses, and took a seat next to me. She gave a reproachful glance at my bottle of wine, and I gripped it tighter. I'd wrestle her for it if I had to.

She shook her head. "First, you need to understand that Abey didn't keep this from you out of selfishness." I rolled my eyes and took a large sip of wine. "He's not like that. You haven't known him very long, but I've known him all my life. Those things you accused him of are so far from the truth."

My gut twisted uncomfortably, but I stayed silent. "He'd never keep something from you to benefit himself," she continued. "It was only to protect you. We all knew how hard it must have been finding out werewolves were real, and that you were about to become one. Add onto that all the changes your body is going through, and we agreed it would be best to save this information for later."

I sat up straighter. "When were you all planning to tell me? The night before my shift?" I scoffed.

Callie shrugged. "Possibly."

"That's great. The eleventh hour is a great time to tell a person they're going to die."

"What good would it have done to tell you sooner?" She waved a hand at my wine, and I clutched it tighter again, taking a spiteful sip while she watched. "Look at you, drinking just to cope. How are your next three weeks going to be, knowing you might not live through the shift? What good has it done you knowing this?"

"But it wasn't your decision!" I exploded, causing Callie to wince, and lean back. "I should have been told upfront, not have to hear *Beatrice* bragging about it to Abraham–"

"She wasn't bragging, Elizabeth. She would never do something like that."

I waved away her defense of her sister's character. I didn't want to hear it. Not now.

"It doesn't matter. I shouldn't have had to find out like that. He should have told me. *Evey* should have told me," I added, my stupid nose burning with unshed tears again.

Callie leaned over and placed a hand on my arm. "She was ordered not to. We all were. She couldn't have told you even if she wanted to." Callie leaned back, pulling a sequined throw pillow onto her lap, and tucking a leg beneath her. "When an alpha gives a direct order, you don't disobey it. That's what he did. He ordered the whole pack to keep this from you. So, don't blame any of them, they had no choice."

My chest loosened the slightest bit.

Evey hadn't betrayed me.

My friend hadn't lied to me.

As the load lifted, my stomach twisted with guilt. I'd treated her *terribly*. Accused her of lying when she'd had no choice. What kind of friend did that make me?

My nose burned worse.

"She knows, El. She knows you didn't know. She'll forgive you, don't worry." My watery eyes met her sympathetic ones. "We all love you. We'd forgive you anything. You're pack now. Family."

I sniffed back the emotion threatening to escape me. Instead, I took another big gulp of wine despite her disappointed scrutiny.

"But what about Abraham? Why did he order you all to keep it a secret from me? Why didn't he want me to know? Why did he *lie* to me?" I whined.

"I told you. He thought he was doing the right thing. He didn't want to upset you. He'd do anything to make you happy, you have to know that."

If I were being honest, I'd had an inkling that was the case. But I wasn't in the mood to be honest. I took another large sip of wine, the bottle now half-empty.

"He should have told me," I muttered stubbornly.

Callie nodded. "I agree. Once the shock of becoming a werewolf wore off, he *should* have told you. You were bound to find out one way or another, and it would have been much better coming straight from him, and not from an overheard conversation." She eyed me critically, and I shrunk in my seat.

"I didn't mean to eavesdrop," I whined again. "I'm still getting used to these things." I tapped my ear.

She nodded and waved my words away. "I know, I know." She sighed. "I wish that stubborn man had listened to us and told you sooner." She shook her head. "He just couldn't make himself upset you…" she trailed off, and my stomach twisted tighter.

Have I made a huge mistake?

The stubborn streak in me shook her head violently, and I drank some more wine instead.

"You said I might live?" I asked pathetically. I was afraid to hope, but Callie had planted the seed, and despite my best efforts, it had not only grown roots, but also sprouted.

She nodded seriously. "Some bitten wolves make it. There haven't been many in recent years, but it happens."

I swallowed harshly. "What are my odds?"

"The odds are about twenty-five percent in your favor."

My hope deflated once more. "That's not very good odds," I muttered, taking another long sip of wine.

"*Your* odds are considerably better than that."

I perked up. "Why's that?" My words were beginning to slur.

She bit her lips and averted her gaze. I frowned, confused until it dawned on me. "You're not allowed to tell me that either, are you?"

She shook her head sadly.

"Is that the other thing Abraham isn't telling me?"

She paused for a short moment before nodding, brown curls bouncing around her small face.

I growled and drank some more wine.

"This is bullshit," I said, taking both Callie, and myself by surprise.

I never cursed, but if I was going to start, this was a great time.

"Why don't bitten wolves make it through their first shift?" I asked.

"It didn't always used to be that way. Years ago, the odds were better, but it seems as though the magic is disintegrating, and making it that much harder to transfer to humans."

I sat up quickly. "Magic?"

Callie nodded. "Didn't Abey tell you where werewolves come from?"

I squinted at the wall above her head, trying to get my wine-soaked brain to think straight. With a snap of my fingers, I grinned. "He mentioned magic once. And, witches I think. Or, was it psychics? I'm not really sure…"

Callie sighed dramatically. "I bet a little less wine would jog your memory."

"Leave my wine alone."

She sighed again. "Would you like to hear our origin story? Or, will you not remember it in the morning?"

I frowned at her. "I'll remember it. I'm not–" a hiccup interrupted my sentence and completely discredited me, "drunk." Another hiccup, and a sigh from Callie. "Please, I want to know."

She nodded. "Well it was a long long time ago, back near what we now call Germany. There was a poor shepherd who wanted nothing more than to live a simple life with his wife, a woman he'd loved since childhood. She was the most beautiful woman in their village, and before long, she caught the eye of one of the most revered warriors. This man was a hero in their village and soon took the shepherd's wife as his own."

"That's terrible! Who just takes someone's wife?" I asked, swallowing another mouthful of wine.

"Back then, warriors were aristocracy. They could pretty much have whatever they wanted as long as there was no one to stop them. As for the shepherd, all he could do was watch helplessly as the warrior took his distraught bride from him. Mad with grief, the shepherd sought the most powerful person he knew of; an old witch that lived in the surrounding forest.

"He begged for her intervention. 'Witch, I promise you all the gold I have, and more, if you would get my wife back for me.'

"The witch replied, 'Shepherd, no one can retrieve your wife, but you.'

"The man knew he was no match for the warrior. So, he begged the witch, 'Please, I'll do anything.'

"The witch thought it through and made the shepherd an offer. 'I can make you strong enough to kill the warrior.'

"The shepherd's eyes blazed with the fire of revenge as he paced the old wooden floor. 'Yes, Witch. Make me strong. And stealthy! And cunning!' He turned to the witch and smiled a smile which held no happiness. 'And deadly,' he added.

"The witch nodded and stood. 'I must warn you, Shepherd, all magic comes with a price. Are you willing to pay it? Whatever it is?'

"The man nodded vigorously, 'I will do anything,' he vowed.

"The witch closed her eyes and began to sway back and forth. She reached her arms out, palms held flat, and chanted softly under her breath. He started to feel a tingling sensation all over his skin from head to toe. His eyes widened as he watched thick gray strands of fur shoot out of his skin."

I gasped. "*She* made him a werewolf?"

Callie nodded. "He opened his mouth to yell to the witch, but as his nose, and mouth elongated, his voice caught in his throat. Bones cracked, and shifted, muscles bunched, and reformed. His skin tingled and stretched until he stood on all fours a couple heads shorter than the witch.

"'There. I've made you into the fiercest hunter in the world; the wolf. No man can contend with your strength and speed. You'll be unstoppable.'

"The shepherd-turned-wolf examined his new body before spearing the witch with a glare and cocking his head to the side.

"'Oh, you can turn back into a man anytime you like. Just imagine who you used to be, and so you shall appear.'

"The wolf closed his eyes, and moments later, the shepherd stood once again, although this time he was bare. The witch chortled as the man tried to cover as much of himself as he could.

"'So, that's it? I can go now?' the shepherd asked.

"'Yes, you may go, but remember my warning: all magic comes with a price. I hope you're prepared to pay whatever it costs.'

"The shepherd nodded at the witch and transformed back into the wolf before bounding out of her cottage. He sprinted to the warrior's house and broke through the front door. He was shocked to find the warrior in bed with his wife. Rage consumed him as he leapt for the warrior and sunk his teeth into the man's thigh. The warrior fought back admirably but was no match for the enraged wolf. Fury blinded him as the shepherd struck over, and over again.

"Only the sound of a high-pitched scream was enough to pierce the bloodthirsty haze clouding his mind. He turned to find his beautiful bride cradling her arm, a bright red bite mark marring her light brown skin. The wolf tipped his head back as a howl of anguish ripped through him. In moments, the shepherd stood where the wolf once was."

I gasped again. "Oh, no. He bit her?"

Callie nodded. "He picked his wife up and ran home. Her wound was treated, and only days later, completely healed. The shepherd was so happy to have his wife back, and well, that he forgot all about the price he still owed for the magic of the wolf.

"It wasn't until the next full moon that the shepherd learned what that price was, for as soon as the last rays of light disappeared, his body forcefully transformed back into the wolf. He tried, and tried, but could not get his body to shift into that of a man again. He panicked when he heard that same high-pitched scream he'd heard from his wife weeks ago.

"She was shifting, wasn't she?" I asked, my voice low, and scared, as if I were living through this tale myself.

Callie nodded again, her face solemn, eyes wide. "When he got back to their cottage, he found his wife writhing on the floor, somewhere in the middle of the transformation from woman to wolf. Brown fur covered her arms and legs, legs that were bent at odd angles, and uneven. Her screams turned to howls, and back into screams as the wolf stood there, helpless once again.

"As the sun rose the next morning, the wolf involuntarily shifted back into the form of a man, and his wife took her last breath."

"Oh no," I whispered again.

This was what awaited me.

This was *my* future.

"The shepherd's grief overwhelmed him, and his body once again shifted without his consent. The wolf took one last look at his beautiful, dead wife before he ran out of the cottage, and into the village.

"There he savagely attacked anyone he came upon until he made it into the woods. The shepherd was never seen again."

"Never? What happened to him? What happened to the villagers?" I asked.

"Half of the villagers who were bitten died just like the woman, halfway between the shift. The other half became as the shepherd; half man, half wolf. They later found that the wolf magic passed down to their children. As times changed, so did the magic. It transformed over the millennia to make the wolves bigger, and stronger as well as allow mental communication while in their wolf forms. The price they pay for the wolf magic has always remained the same. Every full moon, they must become the wolf again until daybreak. Like I told you earlier, the magic has deteriorated over time. It's not as strong as it once was. Now, instead of half of all bitten wolves living through the shift, it's closer to a quarter of them."

I sat there quietly digesting the story as I finished the last of my wine. Placing the empty bottle on the table, I sat back on the couch, and ran my hands through my hair.

"Is that a true story?" I asked.

Callie shrugged. "No one knows for sure. I've done a lot of research, and as far as I can tell it's true."

My wine-filled brain struggled to make the connections because something wasn't adding up. "But wait, how do you know how the shepherd became a wolf if he was never seen again?"

Callie smiled. "It's hypothesized that he reemerged at some point and told his story without revealing his identity. There are even some who believe he's still out there somewhere."

"Alive?!" She only nodded "How is that possible? He'd be thousands of years old."

"He holds the origin of the wolf magic. There's no telling how strong that is, considering how strong it still is thousands of years later. A force like that could very well keep a person alive for a sustained period of time. Look at how fast we heal, now imagine that our magic is many, many times over diluted, and really, anything's possible."

I sat there stunned silent, which was a really uncommon thing for me. The shepherd's sad story played over, and over in my head. What he must have felt to ask the witch for something so costly. How anguished he must have been after causing the death of his wife. And, all he'd wanted was her. In the end, she was the first thing he lost.

Knowing what I do of heartbreak, even as infinitesimal as mine is compared to his, I hoped he wasn't still alive. I could barely stand the idea of living these next three weeks without Abraham, I couldn't imagine a thousand lifetimes without him.

Callie stood abruptly and snagged my empty wine bottle off the table. She eyed it before shooting me a reproachful glare. "Have you got this out of your system?"

"I drank everything I had in the house, is that the same thing?"

She shook her head exasperatedly, but a small smile curved her pink lips. "No, it's not. And it's late, you should get to bed. I have a feeling things will look better in the morning."

Chapter 32

Callie was wrong.

Things did not look better in the morning. Because, instead of just a broken heart, I was also nursing a killer hangover.

"Turn the lights off!" I yelled, wincing at the sound of my voice. I pulled the covers over my head and curled into the fetal position.

"I can't turn off the sun, Elizabeth," Callie responded dryly.

My moan was muffled beneath the blankets. "Then close the blinds."

Callie tsked and took a seat beside me. "No. It's time to get up. I've made us breakfast, and we need to eat and get on the road soon."

"Why are you doing this to me?" I whined.

Callie pulled the covers back until she could see my face. I squinted at her through blurry eyes. "Because, I refuse to allow you to mope around the apartment all day. While I'm out here, I'm going to test some water samples in the area, and you're coming with me."

I sat up a little. "What water samples? What are you testing for?"

"We'll be visiting some lakes, and rivers in Chatham, Lee, and Moore counties. Thousands of acres have been leased to fracking companies, and I'm part of a coalition that helps monitors the fresh water near these sites to make sure they haven't been contaminated. If they have, we'll try to get lawmakers involved, but at the very least we can warn the people who might be affected by the contaminated water."

"Fracking?"

She nodded seriously. "It's a controversial new way that companies are using to extract oil. They claim it's safe, but there have been repeated instances of groundwater contamination near fracking sites."

"What happens if the water is contaminated?"

"There have been sensory, respiratory, and neurological damage reported in cases where fracking contaminated water has been ingested. It can also cause nausea, vomiting, and disrupt both fetal, and childhood development. That's just what we know of, but there are still studies being done. There's also air pollution, soil contamination, and potential earthquakes that can occur because of fracking."

Callie's eyes were lit with a fire I hadn't seen from her before. It was clear this meant a lot. I flipped the covers off my sluggish body and crawled out of bed. "Give me ten," I croaked.

She patted my shoulder and left the room. I used the time to take the hottest shower I could stand, braid my hair, and throw on the first clothes I found.

While I worked on making myself appear human, I also tried to divide up everything that took place yesterday, and file it in its appropriate place.

First, Abraham, and I had taken our relationship to a new level. We'd been dancing around this inferno between us and finally taken the plunge. It was magical, and amazing. More than I could have ever hoped for.

Which brought me to my next point. This sexy man I couldn't get my mind off had lied to me. Kept important information from me. And, Callie could say he did it for the right reasons all she wants, but I also see how he benefited from my ignorance, and I can't pretend I don't.

Would I have been up for a date if I'd known I would die in three weeks?

No.

Would I have been hanging out and getting to know the pack if I'd known how little time I had left?

No.

Would I have spent one of my last weekends, in a dive bar dancing, and singing like I had no other care in the world?

No, I would not.

So whichever way you slice it, Abraham lying to me had given him an advantage, and I couldn't forget that.

And, finally, the worst of all, I'd learned I would die. That these changes I'd been going through were all leading up to a shift I wouldn't live through. I'd die horribly, half woman, and half wolf just like the shepherd's wife.

My whole body quaked at the notion. How long would it take for me to die? Would it hurt? Was there someone that would put me out of my misery? Perhaps the doctor would euthanize me before I had to suffer through malformed limbs and half-shifted bones?

That idea brought me up short, and I stopped to stare at myself in the vanity mirror.

Had I really just considered assisted suicide?

Did I want to die?

Did I want to just give up?

My spine straightened, eyes flashing with the fight I'd learned to harness a long time ago.

The answer was *NO*.

I didn't want to die.

I wouldn't give up.

If Callie says there's a chance I can make it, then I'll take that chance. I'll do whatever I have to, whatever I can to live through this because, as I've had to remind myself in the past, Elizabeth Montgomery was a *fighter*. And, if I was going to die, I'd do it kicking, and screaming until the very end.

With newfound determination, I finally made it to the kitchen, and found Callie sitting at the table with a couple plates of eggs, bacon, tomato, and an entire pot of black coffee.

I made a beeline for the caffeine and filled a mug to the brim before burning my mouth on its hot contents. She slid a glass of water in front of me. "This might help too. Why don't you drink it while the coffee cools down? I don't have time to take you to the hospital with third degree burns in your mouth today."

I reluctantly set the coffee down and chugged the glass of water. Surprisingly, I felt a lot better after that. I filled my plate with as much food as it would hold and dug in while Callie split her time between looking at her phone and eating.

I'd been avoiding my cell. Too afraid there'd be a message or call from Abraham. And, even more terrified there wouldn't be. My chest tightened thinking about him, and I tried to rub the soreness out of it.

He'd betrayed me.

Lied.

I can't forgive that.

And, yet I couldn't stop thinking of the afternoon we'd spent together. How could that have just been yesterday? Not even twenty-four hours had passed since he'd talked me into jumping into that freezing cold lake with him. Since he'd warmed me with his big hands as I stood shivering. Since he'd admitted in that scared broken voice so unlike his own, that he wanted to kiss me.

Wanted *me*.

My legs clenched under the table as my mind unwillingly ran through the time I'd spent pressed against him. Legs around his waist, arms around his neck, mouth, and body, and heart, and soul, open to him. Like I'd never been for anyone else in my life.

And, I'd felt his body respond to mine. His heart beat for me. His soul ache for mine. Felt it all as if it'd been inside me the whole time. It had felt like I'd lived as one half of a whole my entire life, and I'd finally found my corresponding piece.

And, it was all over.

All of it.

Done.

Because I couldn't trust a man who would lie to me. Couldn't open my heart again to a man who used me. Couldn't allow myself to fall for someone who I couldn't rely on to catch me.

Callie's words had planted the seeds of doubt in my brain last night, but I blamed the wine for my willingness to believe her. Of course, she would say nice things about her *brother*. They all believed Abraham hung the moon. And, I had too for a little while. But that illusion was shattered the moment I found out about his deceit. There was no coming back from that.

"Are you done?" Callie asked from across the table.

I set my fork down and sealed up the last wall surrounding my poor abused heart. "Yep. Completely done."

It was dark by the time we made it back to my apartment. I helped Callie lug in the water samples before collapsing on the couch. We'd visited several nearby counties, testing as many freshwater sources as we could. And, I was beat.

Callie, with her endless energy stored her samples in the fridge before rummaging through my cabinets, and pantry. "You barely have any food here," she called.

I pulled my sore body upright. "That's because Evey's not around."

At the mention of my friend's name, a sharp pain shot through my chest. I really needed to call her and apologize.

Callie came into the living room, thin arms akimbo. "You mean to tell me you only have food in this house when my sister is here?"

I shrunk a little. These women made me feel like the worst kind of homemaker. "I order out a lot," I explained.

She sighed and took a seat next to me. "Well, it looks like we'll be having takeout tonight. I'll try to get to the store tomorrow while you're at work, but I can't make any promises."

I pulled my phone out, surreptitiously glanced at the notification bar, and sunk a little lower in my chair when I saw I had no missed messages or calls. Shaking off my disappointment, I pulled up my Postmates app, and scrolled through our options. "What are you so busy with tomorrow?"

"Visiting a few local beekeepers."

"Beekeepers?"

She nodded. "I like to visit those working on the front line before working on proposals. It gives me more motivation, and material."

I shook my head in wonder. "You're really into this environmental stuff, huh?"

She rolled her pale blue eyes. "It's not 'environmental *stuff*', it's the environment. It's our planet. We only get one, and if we don't take care of it, we don't get a new one."

"I didn't even know about most of the stuff you talked about before today."

"That's the biggest problem. If people don't know about these issues, they can't care about them. We need to educate the population and get them interested in things like banning bee-killing insecticides. We're up against huge agricultural companies that fill politicians' pockets and get them to turn the other way when bills or proposals cross their desks. But the politicians are there to work for the *people* not corporations. It's their constituents they'll have to answer to come election time. But like I said, it all begins with education."

I shook my head again. "You're pretty amazing, Callista McCoy. Anyone ever tell you that?"

Her pale cheeks reddened, and she looked away. "I'm nothing special. Just trying to do my part."

"You're doing more than your part, Callie. I'd say you're doing a few people's parts at least." That gave me an idea. "In fact, if you ever need legal advice, let me know. I'd love to help if I can."

She smiled gratefully. "That's sounds great, I'll take you up on that sometime." Callie leaned over to see my phone screen. "How about Italian?" I pulled up a menu, choosing my dish before passing the phone to her. When she finished, I placed the order, and sat staring at my phone.

After a few minutes, Callie spoke up. "He's giving you time."

My head jerked in her direction. "What?"

She nodded toward my silent phone. "Abey. He's giving you space. I suspect he won't be able to hold out much longer before he contacts you though."

I scoffed and tossed my phone onto the glittery silver coffee table. "It doesn't matter if he does. I have nothing to say to him."

"Uh huh. And, what about Evey? You have anything you'd like to say to her?"

My stomach twisted uncomfortably. She was right. I really did need to call her.

"Why don't you give her a call while we wait for dinner to get here? I have some work to do, anyway."

Callie was like my own personal Jiminy Cricket, there on my shoulder to be the voice of reason when I needed to hear it most. I released a large sigh, and hauled my sorry butt off the couch, retreating to my bedroom to make the phone call.

It only rang twice before she answered.

"Ellie?!" I winced and pulled the phone from my ear. I'd gotten a lot more used to my enhanced hearing, but I was still pretty sensitive. "I'm so glad you called. I was gonna call you, but Abey told me to leave you be–" She stopped short like she'd said something she shouldn't have. "I'm so sorry, Ellie. You have no idea how sorry I am. I didn't wanna keep that from you, but I agreed it was best you didn't hear it right away. But as soon as you were more acceptin' of the idea of becomin' a werewolf, I think he shoulda told you. It killed me to keep that from you. I'm so so sorry, and I'd understand if you didn't forgive me, but I'd really appreciate it if you did. I–"

"Evey!" I had to yell to be heard over her rambling. She fell quiet, and I heard a telltale sniffle through the phone that twisted my stomach into a knot a sailor would be proud of. "I actually called to apologize to *you*."

"Me?" she whimpered.

"Yeah." I scratched my head and began pacing my room. "Callie told me *he'd* ordered you not to tell me. I understand now that it wasn't your fault. That you didn't purposely lie to me, and I wanted to apologize for the way I treated you yesterday. You've been a great friend and didn't deserve it. Will you forgive me?"

A watery laugh came through her end. "Of course, I forgive you! There's nothin' to forgive, Ellie. It was us that kept this from you. That wasn't fair, and you had every right to be angry."

I blew out a big breath. "Maybe. But I could have stayed to hear you out first. I'm sorry I didn't."

She was quiet so long, I thought we got disconnected. Then, "What about Abey? You think you shoulda' heard him out too?"

I sucked in a lungful of air. "It's different with him," I whispered.

"He only did it to protect you, Ellie. He'd never do anything to hurt you. He's been so upset since you left. I've never seen him like this before," she confided.

My chest felt hollow. Like all the organs, muscles, and tissue that used to occupy that space had disappeared. I gasped around the gaping hole, using my free hand to cover my chest. "He should have told me," I said. The only words I could muster between the alpha-sized hole in my chest, and the burning in my nose that meant I was moments away from tears.

I'd gone the whole day without shedding a single one, and I was not about to break my streak now. Thankfully, there was a knock on my apartment door. Our food had arrived along with a great excuse to end this conversation.

"Listen, Evey, our dinner's here, I have to run."

"Back to Postmates, Ellie?" Her tone was disapproving.

"We have no groceries in the house. We used them all last week, and I wasn't exactly in the mood for a trip to Kroger's yesterday when I got home." That sobered the mood up quickly.

"Yeah, I can understand that," she responded sadly. "Well, enjoy your dinner! I'll text you tomorrow!"

I smiled at the phone. Nothing could keep Evey down for long. "Okay, talk to you then."

I finished the phone call with my heart just a touch lighter. Making up with Evey had been weighing on me all day, and I was glad we were on good terms again. Now, if only I could get over her brother, I'd be doing much better. But my stubborn heart still beat for that man, and I knew deep down that wouldn't be changing anytime soon.

Chapter 33

My heavy head rested on my palm as I tried my best to pay attention. I was in hour two of a three-hour meeting on this big new case I'd been assigned.

And, I was struggling.

A large yawn fell from my lips, but thankfully didn't catch anyone's attention. I'd had very little sleep last night between the newest wolf dream, and that damn broken heart of mine that ached, and throbbed continually, barely giving me a moment of peace.

This dream about the wolf hadn't been like the others. Not at all. Instead of running from the wolf, I'd met her in a clearing. I'm not sure how I knew it was a *her*, but I did, without a doubt. The brown-eyed wolf had approached me in a dark meadow, making several laps around me before coming to a stop a few feet away.

She was so massive, her head reached my chest as she sat, and stared, her intelligent dark eyes watching me. I knew she was looking for something but didn't know what. And, again, I didn't know how I knew that, but I did.

I'd even tried to talk to her, ask her what she wanted, who she was, and what we were doing here, but of course there'd been no answer. She'd simply cocked her head to the side, and let out a single bark before turning around, and sprinting away in the direction she'd come.

I'd done my best to follow her, but the darkness had gotten thicker, and thicker the further I walked, until the view was the same whether my eyes were open or shut. My voice had rung out, and echoed back as I called after the wolf, but she never returned.

I woke shortly after that with Abraham's name on my lips. It was the first dream I'd had without him there to comfort me. I'd clutched my blankets as tears streamed down my face, wetting my pillow, and adding to my misery.

I didn't *want* to cry over him.

Didn't want to think about him.

Didn't want to miss him.

Didn't want to feel the urge to call him and tell him I didn't mean it. That I'd jumped to conclusions, and that I would hear him out. Give him another chance.

Didn't want any of that.

Because, he'd *lied.*

So, as I'd lain there with the tears falling steadily, I'd made a decision. I didn't want to be sad anymore.

Or hurt.

Those were two emotions I couldn't control.

Couldn't master.

Couldn't bear.

Instead, I got angry. Anger was a much easier emotion to harness, and I had years of experience at it. So, while the hours ticked by, and the sun rose, I fortified my poor broken heart, filling in the cracks with fury, and coating it in rage.

I wouldn't allow this to break me. For *him* to break me. I'd come back from worse, and I'd get over this too. Besides, I probably only had another three weeks left. Surely, I'd be strong enough to hold onto this anger until then.

I did my best to stifle the dozenth yawn I'd had in the past thirty minutes, but the glare from my boss told me I wasn't fooling anyone.

"Montgomery are we boring you?"

I sat up straighter in my chair. "No sir, of course not. I just need another cup of coffee, and I'll be good to go."

He waved me away. "Then go on and come back ready to tackle this new case. It's an important one, and I need one of our brightest senior associates firing on all cylinders."

I stood and nodded. "Yes, sir, I'll be right back."

Hurrying as fast as I dared in my three-inch heels, I made it to the break room, and popped a single serve cup in the coffee maker. While it hissed, and gurgled, I slipped my phone from my pocket, and checked for any missed calls or messages.

Not from *him,* just in general.

I was a busy career woman. Any number of people could need to get in touch with me during the day.

Keep telling yourself that, Montgomery.

I ignored my pessimism and typed the pass code into my phone. A little number one sat on the corner of the message icon, and I clicked on it eagerly.

My heart hit the soles of my shoes, my hands clamming up as my battered heart picked up its pace.

It was from *him*.

With shaking hands, I clicked on the message.

"Well, well, well," a nasal voice came from the front of the room.

I jumped, and turned, tucking my phone back in my pocket.

"Hiding out in the break room when you should be working? Tsk tsk. Is that behavior fitting a prestigious *senior* associate?"

I rolled my eyes and turned to my steaming mug of coffee. I'd had *far* too little sleep to deal with Ben today. "It's none of your business how I spend my day. You don't sign my paychecks."

His overpowering cologne preceded him. "What crawled up your ass, Montgomery?"

I shook my head, and closed my eyes, praying for patience. All I wanted to do was check the phone burning a hole in my pocket. And, get away from Ben.

"Nothing. I'm just sick of you questioning me, and my promotion. It's not up to you, so you need to mind your own business," I answered, my back still to him as I doctored my coffee. I heard him move away from me toward the cabinet of mugs and slipped my phone out.

"I'm not questioning you. I was happy you got the promotion. I just want to make sure you don't slip and upset management. I'd hate to see you lose that pretty new office."

I rolled my eyes and ignored him. The new message was glaring at me as I debated whether I wanted to check it now. If I did, I'd feel like I was letting myself down. Showing weakness when I'd just decided I'd be nothing but strong from here on out.

On the other hand, if I left it to later, it would nag at me all day. I'd be useless in that meeting, counting the minutes until I could escape to my office, and read it.

"Hey, a few of us are going to happy hour on Thursday. You should come."

I closed my eyes and took a deep breath. This needed to end now. I couldn't have this stupid little text hanging over my head all day. I'd veered away from sadness, and into anger's lane, and an angry woman would check her texts, if only to scoff at his message.

That's what I'd do. I'd check it just so I could prove to myself it meant nothing. That *he* meant nothing.

"We're hitting that new jazz place downtown. They've got a few good drink specials."

I opened my eyes and clicked on the message before I could change my mind.

Sexiest Man Alive: We need to talk.

I frowned.

That's it?

All that indecision. All that waffling, and debating, and torture I'd just endured for a lousy four words?

And, who the hell was he to tell me what we had to do? I'd said everything I needed to say. He'd lied, and in fact was *still* keeping something from me. In my opinion, nothing more needed to be said.

"So, what do you say?"

I turned to Ben. I think he'd been talking this whole time, but I hadn't heard a word he'd said. "What was that?"

"Drinks. This Thursday. A few of us are going downtown. You in?" His words were clipped, like he was explaining himself to an idiot.

And, maybe he was.

Because his invitation didn't sound half bad.

"How many people are going?"

Ben perked up, like a terrier that'd been shown a ball. "Oh, just some of the guys. You'll like them. Will you come?"

I glanced at my messages one last time, and decided Abraham, and his stupid four-word message could go screw. "Yeah. I'm in."

The rest of the day passed by uneventfully with no further reprimands from my boss, and more importantly, no more texts from *him*.

I was driving home, tapping out the beat to the newest Taylor Swift song when I felt my nose start to run. I grabbed a napkin from my center console to wipe it and gasped when it came back bright red.

I couldn't remember the last time I'd had a nose bleed. It must have been years. And, it was so odd, I'm not sick, my allergies weren't acting up, and I hadn't even touched my nose.

The ride back to my apartment was awkward as I tried to tilt my head back far enough, so I could get the bleeding to stop while still watching the road. Walking up to my apartment with my head tilted back, and a bloody tissue against my nose was not my finest hour, but I was beyond caring.

"Hey, what happened?" Callie called as Charlie came barreling into my legs, stretching up to be lifted into my arms.

"I don't know, it just started bleeding on my way home," I muttered nasally, pinching the bridge of my nose.

Callie rose from the couch and ordered me to lie down. "I'll get you a clean tissue." I switched out the bloody napkin for the soft tissue from Callie and gave it a few minutes before checking my nose's progress.

Thankfully, the bleeding had stopped. But something was off. I sniffed the air a few times and frowned. "Why does it smell like blood in here?"

Callie frowned. "Uh, because you just had a bloody nose?"

I shook my head. "No, it's not my blood. It's someone else's blood. Were you bleeding today?"

Her eyes widened, and she nodded. "I had a pretty bad paper cut today, but that was hours ago."

I sniffed again. "In the guest room, right?"

She nodded again, her eyes clearing, and a small smile tilting her lips. "You just got your sense of smell in."

"Could this explain the bloody nose?" Callie nodded again as I rose from the couch, sniffing the air as I went.

Callie's flowery scent was stronger than ever, like a dozen roses sat blooming in my living room. Next, I smelled Charlie, his scent amplified with a hint of his kitty litter thrown in.

Speaking of kitty litter.

"Oh, his litter box needs to be cleaned, huh?" I asked.

Callie laughed. "I was going to mention it if you didn't do it today."

I walked around the house, taking in all the new scents both good, and bad, and decided my place needed a deep cleaning. Nose wrinkled, I turned to Callie. "How can you stand all the different smells in here?"

She laughed lightly. "Just like everything else, you get used to it. Congratulations. You're one step closer to becoming a werewolf."

With that sobering thought, I went to my bedroom to change. I'd been kind of excited to get a new wolfy sense, but after hearing Callie equate it to me being closer to my shift, that excitement vanished.

Because, one step closer to shifting, meant one step closer to possibly dying. And, I wasn't ready for that. Wasn't ready for the possible repercussions of that shift.

After dinner, I retreated to my room, and spent the rest of the night staring at my ceiling and pretending I hadn't received another two texts from *him*. I'd ignored them both, but it was becoming increasingly difficult. So, I used the hours of tossing and turning to further strengthen my heart. Encase it in stone so thick, not even Abraham's sweet pleas could slither through.

The next few days passed similarly, and before I knew it, it was Thursday. All week I'd felt worse, and worse.

Maybe I was getting sick.

Or, the sleepless nights were catching up to me.

It was getting harder to get out of bed in the morning, harder to concentrate at work. My body ached, and I had no energy. If I hadn't been celibate for so long, I might worry I was pregnant.

Callie's worried eyes followed me around the house as I rushed to get ready. I'd finally fallen into a fitful sleep in the early hours of the morning and slept through my alarm. She hadn't commented, but I knew she'd witnessed my physical decline over the week and I figured it was only a matter of time before she forced some health nut juice cleanse on me.

To make matters worse, Abraham's texts had become increasingly frequent, and pleading. I'd ignored them all.

I'd even had Callie on my case.

"Why are you torturing him?" she'd asked abruptly over dinner the night before.

I frowned. "Torturing who?" I played dumb.

Her arched brow told me it wasn't working. "Abraham. I know he's been texting you. Why are you ignoring him?"

I took that opportunity to study my half-finished plate, hiding my carrots under a pile of mashed potatoes, my appetite suddenly gone. "I have nothing to say to him."

She sighed, her tone irritated. Something I wasn't used to hearing from mild-mannered Callie. "Did you stop to think that *he* might have a few things he'd like to say to *you*?"

I shook my head. "He had over a week to tell me, and he didn't." I shot her a glare. "And, he's *still* keeping something from me. I gave him the opportunity to come clean, and he didn't take it. Why should I give him another chance? Just because he feels like talking now?" I scoffed.

She shook her head, blue eyes sad. "You weren't ready. You still aren't."

I slammed my fork on the table. "Who are you to decide what I'm ready for? Who is *he* to make that choice? I'm a grown woman, I don't need him, or you, or anyone else making decisions for me."

With that I'd stalked off to my bedroom where I spent the rest of the night. I'd felt awful for yelling at Callie that way, but I was tired of the secrets. Tired of the lies, and the subterfuge. I wanted complete honesty, and transparency in my life from here on out, and anyone who couldn't abide by that could get the hell out.

Thinking about the fight with my soft-spoken friend had me angry all over again. My new favorite emotion. I was ready for today to be over. And, maybe apologize to Callie. Maybe.

I shook those thoughts off and turned back to my computer in an attempt to get some work done when I was interrupted.

"Knock, knock," a voice called from my open doorway.

I turned to find Ben standing there with a slimy grin on his pale face. "What is it, Ben? I'm just getting ready to leave."

He frowned. "You're still coming out right?"

It was my turn to frown. "Out?"

His head shook back, and forth as he let himself into my office. "You said you'd come out, and have a few drinks with us tonight, remember?"

I'd forgotten all about that.

And now, the last thing I wanted to do was to go make small talk with a bunch of pretentious lawyers.

"Ben, today's not a good day," I turned to finish putting my desk to rights.

"If you're having a bad day, isn't that the perfect excuse to have a drink?"

He had a point as much as it pained me to admit. To be honest, a glass of wine didn't sound half bad right about now.

And, the longer I spent out of the house meant the longer I could avoid Callie. And, my empty bedroom. And, the sleepless night that awaited me. And, maybe a drink would help cure whatever had been wrong with me all week.

Yeah, alcohol wasn't known for its cures, but I was desperate.

I sighed. "You know what? You're right."

He clapped his hands, smile growing. "Great, I'll drive."

Hell no.

"That's fine, I'd rather take my car. I'll follow you there."

Chapter 34

Missing Abraham was like developing hypothermia, I decided.

First, it's painful. Sharp pains, dull aches, you name it. Your whole body hurts from the inside out. It hurts so bad, you feel like you'll never *not* be in pain. The agony becoming a sick friend. Something that keeps you company in your loneliest of times, like as you toss, and turn all night long, seeking even a few minutes of reprieve from the misery.

After living with that pain for too long, you eventually become numb. You don't feel sad, you can't feel happy. You feel nothing. You feel like you *are* nothing. It takes all you have just to get through the day.

Breaking your responsibilities into small tasks helps.

Crawl out of bed.

Brush teeth.

Put on clothes.

Pretend to eat.

Drive to work.

Sit at desk.

Go to meeting.

All of it done in a state of auto-drive. None of the day's events sinking in or mattering because nothing *can* matter without him. The sun can't shine. The birds can't chirp. You're left in a gray wasteland of nothingness.

As I sat uncomfortably close to Ben in a circular booth at the jazz bar he'd insisted on, I decided if I was numb to everything, I might as well have a second glass of wine.

And, maybe a third. Probably a fourth. Who was counting? Who cared?

"... so, I turn to the jury, and said 'Ladies and gentlemen, if it's not on the tape, it couldn't have been rape'."

His constant chattering broke through the haze that constantly surrounded me. "Tell me you're kidding," I deadpanned.

He shook his head, smile stretching across his pale face. "Nope. They ate it up. Came back with a not guilty decision in less than an hour."

The wine soured in my stomach. "You got a rapist off?"

He nodded proudly. "Sure did." With a sigh, he leaned back, and stretched an arm across the booth behind me. "It's only a matter of time until I'm up on the senior's floor with you."

I downed half of my third glass of wine in one gulp. "Are the other guys getting here soon?"

He eyed me with irritation. "Why, are you not having a good time with just me?"

No.

I shook my head, and finished my glass, signaling to the waiter for another. I'd need copious amounts of alcohol to deal with Ben alone. "It's not that. I just thought you said there were more people coming."

He shook his head and checked his phone. "They should be here soon. Hey, you wanna hear about the drug trafficking case I won last month?"

I shrugged, and off he went. It seemed he needed very little input from me. My phone vibrated, and I pulled it out to see I'd received another text from Abraham. The fifth today.

Sexiest Man Alive: Where are you?

I ignored it. Like all the others. The contents of my fourth glass of wine were dwindling fast as I stuffed my phone back in my pocket.

I should have changed his name in my phone a while ago, but I couldn't make myself do it. It reminded me of a happier time, when things were still new, and easy, and fun.

And, although the words sliced through me every time I read them, I counted them as penance. The atonement I had to make for enjoying that beautiful afternoon with someone who was indeed the sexiest man alive. At least in my world.

My phone vibrated again, but I ignored it as I drank the last of my wine. My head was spinning, my movements slower, and less precise.

And, I didn't care.

The waiter brought over another glass of chardonnay, and I took a large swallow as soon as the glass hit the table.

"So, what do you think?" Ben asked, almost startling me. I'd forgotten he was even there. Now that he'd regained my attention, I wondered how that could have happened.

His cheap cologne, which had always been overbearing, was almost nauseating with my new sense of smell. The nasal self-important tone he spoke with grated on my nerves and curled my stomach. He repulsed me, and I realized I'd spent the last hour and a half with only him.

"Are those guys ever getting here?" I asked again.

Ben's eyes flashed with anger. "They can't make it. Something came up."

I finished my glass of wine and set it forcefully on the table. "When was this?"

He leaned back again, watching me with shrewd eyes. "A little while ago. I thought you were having fun with me. What do we need anyone else for?"

I shook my head and slid across the booth. He grabbed my upper arm, hindering my exit. "Hey, where are you going?"

I glared at his hand until he removed it. "I need to get home."

"What, are you mad the other guys aren't coming? Is there someone in particular you were hoping would come? Someone you're seeing at the office?"

I shook my head incredulously. "I'm not seeing anyone." *I've never been so alone.* I slid along the booth some more until I could swing my legs around to stand. But before I did, I turned to him. "There was no one else coming, was there?"

Ben opened, and closed his mouth a few times before sighing loudly, and rolling his eyes. "You wouldn't agree to go out with me otherwise."

I shook my head again, and stood, wobbling in my heels before catching myself on the table. "That's because I don't want to go out with you Ben. Not yesterday, not last week, and certainly not today. And, I don't appreciate being lied to."

I turned to storm off, but he grabbed my wrist. "Why won't you give me a chance? Is there someone else? Is that why you won't go out with me?"

I shook his hand off violently, placing both palms on the table, and leaning in real close. I didn't want him to miss a single word of what I had to say.

"There is no one else, I just don't like you. I don't like the way you act,

I don't like the way you talk, and I don't like the way you think you're better than me because you've got a tiny dick in your pants. I'm never going to go out with you. Get that through your thick head and leave me the hell alone!"

By the end, I was yelling, drawing the attention of the surrounding tables. Thankfully the band was still playing, and had drowned out most of my words, but they'd clearly hit their mark. Ben sat there fuming, thin lips pinched, eyes narrowed, hands clenched into fists on the tabletop. I didn't wait to see if he had a response.

When I made it out into the cool spring night, I found it had started to rain during the couple of hours I'd endured with Ben. Tonight, was turning into a disaster, and all I wanted was my cat, and my bed. I began walking down the street toward my car when I realized everything was blurry, and I was having trouble staying upright in my heels.

I couldn't drive home like this.

Pulling out my phone, and ignoring the two new texts from *him*, I pulled up my Uber app, and ordered a ride. It was there in under five minutes, and I sat quietly in the back as the driver provided me with a blessedly quiet ride back to my apartment.

When I walked through my front door, the first thing I noticed was a smell I didn't recognize. Soap and spearmint. I shrugged it off and stepped out of my heels. "Ugh Callie," I hiccupped. "Ben tricked me into going on a date with him. It was miserable." Hiccup.

Charlie barrelled into my stockinged legs, and I pulled him into my arms, digging my face into his soft fur. He thankfully still smelled the same, although a lot stronger than when I was just a human.

"Hey, Elizabeth," Callie called, her voice soft, with a note of apprehension. I guess she'd been worried when I didn't come right home.

I started to explain why I hadn't called when I saw *him*.

Abraham.

In my apartment.

Watching from the living room with a look that was equal parts wonder, and fury.

My mouth went dry as it hung open uselessly. Heart pounding, and legs shaking I walked closer, trying to make sure my drunk-brain was seeing things right.

He stood gracefully from my pink couch and stalked toward me. When he was only a foot away, I finally regained control of my tongue.

"What the hell are you doing here?"

He winced. "Have you been drinking?"

My mouth fell open again. I sputtered a few times before I could respond. "What the hell does it matter to you? I asked you a question, what the *hell* are you doing here?"

He ignored me again. "Did you drive home?"

I glared at him as he stared me down. We weren't getting anywhere like this, so I gritted my teeth and threw him a bone. "I took an Uber."

He relaxed for a fraction of a second before his shoulders tensed again. "And, you were out with *Ben*?"

I dropped the cat and threw my hands on my hips with a growl. "I believe I asked you a question: What. The. *Hell*. Are you doing here?"

He leaned back, an unhappy smirk on his lips. "Don't like being ignored, Elizabeth?"

I knew that was a jab at me, and the fact that I hadn't answered any of his texts or calls.

"Um. I'm going to bed," Callie called as she practically ran down the hallway toward the guest room.

"Answer my question, Abraham." I gritted out.

He sighed. "I came here to talk to you. And, since you wouldn't answer me," he glared, "I had to come out to do it in person."

I rolled my eyes and brushed past him. "I have nothing to say to you."

His large hand wrapped around my arm, sending jolts of electricity through my body. It stopped me dead in my tracks.

"You've made it painfully obvious that you have nothing to say to me, but I have plenty to say to you, and you're going to hear me out."

I arched a brow.

His eyes softened. "You owe me the chance to explain." When I hesitated, he added, "Please."

It was that last word that did me in.

I shook off his hand although my skin hadn't felt so warm in what felt like years. With a huff, I plopped onto a chair at the table, and folded my arms across my chest.

Abraham seemed at a loss for words, like he hadn't expected me to agree so easily. He ran both hands through his messy hair, and I got my first good look at him. He looked awful.

His normally tan skin was sallow and covered in what looked like at least a few days' worth of stubble. There were dark circles under his eyes that could rival mine, and his hair looked like it hadn't been washed in days.

He was a mess.

"I don't even know where to start," he confessed. "I've imagined this moment so many times, and I still don't know what to say."

I stayed silent. He wasn't getting any help from me.

Finally, he sighed, and took a seat, his massive frame dwarfing the chair. "First, I need to apologize. Again. I never meant for you to find out that way. That was unfair, and I don't blame you for being mad."

"You never meant for me to find out, period," I interjected.

He shook his head, his greasy hair falling across his tired eyes. "That's not true. I was going to tell you."

"When?" I demanded.

His met my eyes then. He looked lost. "I don't know."

I scoffed and pulled my arms tighter across my chest. He was only incriminating himself further.

"But not for the reasons you think," he added quickly. "It wasn't so I could take *advantage* of you," he spat the words like they tasted bad. "Or, so you'd go out with me." He sighed again and ran his hands through his hair once more. "You were just so... happy."

I frowned.

Huh?

"You'd finally accepted that you were becoming a werewolf. You'd started to let us in." His eyes cut to mine. "Started to let *me* in." I shivered under his gaze. "I didn't want to ruin that."

"So, it *was* for selfish reasons."

He growled and rubbed his hands down his face. "No. No!" He sighed. "I'm not explaining this right. I can't *think* clearly when I'm around you." I frowned, and he chuckled humorlessly. "I can think even less clear when you're *not* around, so I guess I'm screwed either way, huh?"

I stared at him questioningly. I was so lost.

Abraham leaned forward, placing both arms on the table, palms up. "The simple truth is, I didn't want to hurt you. Didn't want to do anything that would take the smile off your face. The bounce from your step. Couldn't imagine doing *anything* that would hurt you. Because your pain cuts me." He slammed a hand against his chest, over his heart. "Right here. It *kills* me to see you upset. I kept the truth from you to protect you. And, I'd do it again. I'd make all these mistakes a thousand more times if it meant you'd get an extra few days of peace. Of not worrying that you'll die when the next full moon comes. And, if that's selfish, I'll take it, because your happiness is the most important thing to me."

I sat there speechless as my intoxicated brain tried to understand everything he'd just said. His words sounded good, but could I trust it? Trust him? I just didn't know anymore. Didn't know anything. Nothing made sense, and everything was wrong, and this man sitting across from me was the epicenter of it all.

Just seeing him sitting there across from me was like a splash of ice cold water in the face. A shock to my system. Like someone had yelled "clear", and placed two electrified paddles against my chest, shocking me back to life.

But was it enough?

Could I accept his apology? Could I trust him again? Was it worth going back down that path with him, only to have him disappoint me again? And, what else was he keeping from me? The fact that he was still lying helped solidify my decision.

"I accept your apology." His eyes brightened as he sat a little straighter in his chair. But I wasn't done. "But it doesn't change anything. You lied to me. I don't think I could ever trust you again," I admitted softly.

"So that's it? You're just going to throw this all away?" he asked, motioning between the two of us.

I needed to be strong.

Needed to remember why I was doing this.

He lied.

He betrayed.

I nodded, and watched his shoulders deflate, eyes returning to their lackluster color as his face fell with disappointment.

He scanned my face, searching frantically for something it seemed he couldn't find. Finally, he dropped his gaze, and rose from the chair.

He turned away from me before speaking. "I understand. Thanks for hearing me out," he said softly before he opened my front door, and left, closing it softly behind him.

The click of the door sounded like the last nail in my coffin as I was buried alive. And, the worst part? I wasn't even trying to break out.

Chapter 35

The silence of the apartment was only broken by the ticking of the wall clock. I stood there stunned as a flurry of emotions battered my insides.

Tick.

He's gone. I'd finally run him off for good.

Tick.

If what I wanted was for him to leave why does it feel like my soul left with him?

Tick.

I struggled to breathe as my lungs constricted. Heart thumping wildly, and I gasped for air.

Tick.

My nose burned as tears formed in my eyes, and I took a shaky step forward. It felt like I was being pulled along behind him, like a child towing their red wagon.

Tick.

I could *feel* him. Not physically of course. But inside me. I could feel his disappointment. And anger. And desolation. And it *destroyed* me.

Tick.

I took another step forward. Until I was right in front of the door, my insides warring against what my mind thinks I should want, and what the rest of my body knows I need.

Tick.

I opened the door to find the light rain from earlier had progressed into a classic North Carolina thunderstorm. The wind whipped through the breezeway, blowing my hair around my face as thunder boomed close by. It seemed fitting that outside looked like my insides felt.

I stepped outside, and closed the door behind me, rain water spraying against my face as I tried to figure out what the *hell* I was doing.

I should let him go.

I need him back.

I have to remember that he lied to me.

None of that matters.

I should go back inside and forget him.

Not a single cell in my body could ever forget him.

I took a tentative step forward. Then another. And another. Until I was at the balcony that overlooked the parking lot.

I scanned the cars until I found Abraham's large black truck, the dome light lit as he climbed behind the wheel.

"No," I whispered.

My body made the decision my brain couldn't.

I ran. My bare feet slapped against each stair as I flew down them as fast as I could. The cold water soaked through my stockings, but I barely noticed.

"Abraham!"

I needed to reach him. Couldn't let him leave. Couldn't let this band connecting us be pulled so taut again. I needed to be near him. Needed to be in his arms again. But there was still so much left unsaid, and unclear.

My body ignored my rambling mind as I sprinted toward his car.

"Abraham!" I yelled again over the pounding rain, and whistling wind. A flash of lightning lit up the dark night, and his eyes found mine.

"Abraham." I didn't need to yell anymore, I knew he could hear me.

He slid out of his car and hurried over to me.

"What are you doing? You're soaking wet! You need to get back in the house."

"I can't do this," I started. Eyes closed, I took a deep breath, and began again. "I can't do this again, Abraham. I won't survive it."

He looked at me quizzically. "Do what again?"

"Lose you!" I yelled as another flash of lightning zipped through the clouds, illuminating the confusion in his blue eyes.

"I don't understand," he admitted softly, his hands reached out to grab ahold of me, but stopped short.

"I don't either!" I yelled, throwing my hands in the air. "I need you to explain it to me, because I don't understand any of it. Why I haven't been able to sleep or eat this whole week without you. Why seeing you felt like the first time I'd been able to take a breath in days. Why your eyes look like home." I used both hands to clutch the soaking wet shirt above my heart. "Why it hurts so fucking bad I can't remember what it was like without the pain. Why it feels like I've missed you all my life, and I've only known you a few weeks." I paused, and dropped my arms to my sides, chest heaving as I struggled to catch my breath. "Why, Abraham? Please, tell me why I can't live without you."

His eyes were wide, jaw slack as I watched him trying to make sense of everything I'd just said. He finally reached out, and grasped my arms, pulling me close until our wet bodies collided. "You feel it?" he asked quietly, eyes drilling straight through me.

"I feel *everything*!" I yelled over the thunder. "Tell me why!" I demanded, using a fist to push against his hard chest.

He closed his eyes, and lowered his head until it rested against mine, water droplets from his wet hair slid down my face obscuring the tears that had begun to fall. "It's fate," he whispered.

"I don't understand," I cried.

He shook his head before pulling back to look me in the eye. "It's fate," he repeated. "We were meant for one another. I was born for you, and you for me. We're fated mates."

My mind rebelled against the notion. I didn't believe in fate.

But a deeper, primal part of me perked up at his words.

"I knew it the first time I laid eyes on you, as you lay broken, and bleeding on that forest floor. The second your eyes met mine, I knew who you were. *What* you were. You're my fated mate, El. We're meant to be together. It's why we've felt so sick this week apart. You can feel me, can't you?" he asked, placing one of his large hands on my chest, the other one tangling in the wet hair on the back of my head. "Right here. You can feel me, like I can feel you. You're mine."

His blue eyes were as limitless as the universe. As eternal as the ocean. And, as they stared at me, stared *through* me, I felt the sincerity of his words. Felt the *rightness* of them in my chest. My heart pounded faster as I rapidly made the connections.

"You've been sick too?"

He nodded. "I've never felt this awful in my life. This time without you has been torture," his words cracked, and he closed his eyes. Regaining his composure before continuing. "We were meant to be *together*, El, never apart."

My body swayed toward him as his words struck chord after chord deep inside me. I *knew* they were true. But my stubborn brain struggled against the idea.

"I don't believe in fate," I whispered. "This can't be real."

His eyes flashed as another clap of thunder sounded nearby, and I saw the determination settle on his face. "I'll prove it."

His lips crashed against mine. Unapologetic, and unforgiving. I gasped in surprise, opening myself to him, and he took full advantage. I was shocked frozen for only moments before my body responded to him.

I wrapped my arms around his neck and pulled him as close as I could while my mouth devoured his. Like I'd been starving, and he was a feast. Like I'd been lost in the desert for days, and he was an oasis.

He pulled back far enough to whisper against my lips. "You feel that? You feel me?" I moaned in response, and he chuckled into my mouth. "That's because you're mine." He captured my lips again, and I lost myself to him.

As we kissed, something warm that had been buried deep inside me slowly unfurled. It started low in my belly, but soon spread throughout my body, warming the places that had been left cold by his absence. Filling my empty spaces with him.

In return, I felt little pieces of myself transfer to him. Felt it as all his cold, and lonely places were filled with me. My skin sizzled like a live wire as we touched, and tasted, and drank our fill of each other.

Abraham's large hand reached down to cup my bottom, and he pulled me up against him, lifting me until my legs were wrapped around his waist, my body fitting to his. He spun us around and pressed me against the front of his truck.

When he finally released my lips, I gasped his name between pulling in great lungsful of air. He kissed, and licked, and sucked down my neck, and across my chest only to repeat the process up the other side of my throat. I shivered under his ministrations, gripping his wet hair with both hands, and writhing against his hard body.

"We need to go inside," he breathed against my heated skin. I moaned in response, and he released me for a quick moment before scooping me into his arms and heading for my apartment.

I wrapped my arms around his neck, exploring any skin I could reach with my lips, reveling in the sound of his growls, and moans as I touched upon sensitive places.

He whipped my door open, and then slammed it behind us, his lips finding mine once more. Still in his arms, he walked us down the hall, tangling our entwined bodies in the hanging beads. I laughed against his wet skin as he growled again and yanked the offending beads out of his way.

We made it to the bedroom, but not much further. He set me down on my dresser, hands sliding up my thighs, and bunching my skirt around my hips as he dragged me forward until I was pressed against him. I shivered as his stiff wet jeans pressed into the apex of my thighs.

I felt his lips smile as they met mine, his mouth swallowing my moans. My fingers found the hem of the t-shirt plastered to his hard body, and I yanked it up, breaking contact with his lips for only seconds while I pulled it over his head. Now that I had unfettered access to his hot skin, I ran my greedy hands over every inch I could reach. He shuddered beneath my touch, and that spurred me on further.

His large hands pulled me even closer to him, my butt sitting right on the end of the dresser. He felt so good pressed into me like that, I rotated my hips, trying to get the seam of his jeans to hit just the right spot. His hands clenched tighter before one slipped beneath my thin shirt, skating across my overheated skin.

His nimble fingers flicked my bra strap open, and I moaned again. With one hand clutching my ass, the other skirted around to my front where he cupped my breast in his big hand. He growled deep in his throat as he pinched the hard peak. I gasped, nails digging into his smooth back as my hips gyrated faster against him.

There was a slow burning inferno building in my core. And, as Abraham hefted and tweaked my other breast that fire raged hotter. Brighter.

His hips were pumping against me, the hard evidence of his arousal hitting just the right spot between my legs. I wrapped my thighs tighter around his waist as that fire made its way up my body, through my veins, and to every inch of me.

When it felt like I couldn't take anymore, like I'd combust if this went any further, my body reached an even greater height, before it exploded into a million tiny particles. I clenched my thighs even tighter, digging my nails into his back as I rode out the wave of the most incredible orgasm I'd ever had. His name fell from my lips repeatedly as he licked, and kissed my skin over, and over again.

He kept pumping his hips against mine as my body tried to piece itself back together. Suddenly, he froze in place, his muscles contracting, and he let out a long deep moan that set off another mini explosion in my core. His hand on my ass gripped so tight I knew I'd have bruises, but I didn't care. In fact, I hoped he did leave a mark. I wanted to be branded as his.

The possessive thoughts might have concerned me if I could have thought straight at that point. Abraham's head hid in the crook of my neck, his breathing wild as I tried to control my own. We sat there in the quiet darkness of my room, struggling to catch our breath as the high of our ardor faded.

His soft chuckle danced across my skin. He raised his head to look at me, his cheeks a little pink, and his eyes glassy. "I can't believe I just came in my pants," he commented drily.

"You didn't!" I said, but knew he had. I smelled his arousal as well as I smelled my own. And blood. I sniffed again. "Are you bleeding?"

He shook his head with a satisfied smile. "I think you got a little carried away."

I gasped and slid off the dresser to walk behind him. Sure enough, there were little crescent moon shaped marks dug into the smooth, tan skin of his back. I ran a gentle finger over the marks before leaning close and kissing each one of them. His muscles trembled beneath my lips.

"I'd never tell you to stop putting those luscious lips anywhere on me you'd like," he called over his shoulder, "But you don't have to worry about me. They'll be gone in a few minutes."

My face heated, and I took a step away from him, the gravity of what we had just done finally sinking in. He must have felt the change in me, because he spun around, and pulled my body against his.

"Don't you dare start to over think this, El," he warned.

I shook my head. "It's just that there's so much we haven't discussed."

His eyes roved over my face before he nodded once. "Okay, then let's get changed, and we'll discuss."

"Really?"

He nodded again. "Really. I'll tell you anything you want to know."

"No more secrets?" I asked, my voice half plea, and half demand.

He shook his head. "Never again. You have my word."

I smiled at his declaration.

I could work with that.

"Now I just need to run out to my truck for some dry clothes," he motioned to his rain-soaked ensemble.

I looked down at my stockinged feet. "Actually, I have some of your clothes here." I took a peek at him to see he was staring at me incredulously. "They were from the day you gave me that spare set at the lake. I still have them. I washed them too."

Without waiting for his response, I walked over to my dresser, and pulled his sweatpants and t-shirt out of the bottom drawer. I'd held off on washing them because I wanted them to still smell like him but relented when they reeked more like lake than him.

I held them out to him, and he took them with one hand, pulling me close with the other. He kissed my lips. "Thank you, baby."

I nodded my head shyly, and he left for the bathroom to get changed. I peeled the soaking wet clothes from my body and pulled on a comfortable pair of sweatpants and a tank top before throwing my long hair into a bun on the top of my head.

When he returned to the room, I was sitting on my bed, cross-legged, and ready to get some answers.

Chapter 36

Instead of sitting on the end of the bed, Abraham pulled down the covers, and motioned for me to get in. I slid beneath the blankets, admiring the way Abraham's large frame slipped between the sheets next to me.

He turned on his side, so he was facing my direction, and waited, watching me with soft eyes.

"Hi," I said shyly.

His mouth turned up into a grin. "Hi." He reached out and cupped my face gently. "I missed you," he whispered.

I gulped, my nose stinging with the tears I felt gathering in my eyes. "I missed you too." Those tall black walls I'd built up around my heart were quaking, threatening to tumble with every sweet word that fell from his lips.

He rubbed a thumb beneath my eye. "Don't cry. Please. I can't stand to see you cry."

I sniffed back my tears and gave him a watery smile. Clasping his hand in mine, I pulled them both under the covers, and laid there watching him, disbelieving that he was here. In my room. In my *bed* with me when just a few hours ago, I had promised myself I'd never have anything to do with him again.

Was I making a mistake?

Abraham squeezed my hand. "Don't do that." When he saw my questioning look, he added, "Don't second guess this. Don't second guess *us*. Ask me what you need to ask and let's put this behind us."

I nodded and let out a big sigh. "Were you ever going to tell me?"

"About the dangers of you shifting, or about us being fated mates?"

"Both."

He took a deep breath, his thumb tracing circles against the back of my hand. "I don't know. Honestly, I didn't want you to know about the odds of you surviving the shift. I didn't think it was important."

I sat up a little. "You didn't think that information was *important*?!"

He shook his head. "It's not. Because I know you'll survive the change. You were meant to be a werewolf."

I scoffed. "And what makes you so sure of that? Callie said there's only about a twenty-five percent survival rate for bitten wolves."

"That's because Callie wasn't allowed to tell you the truth." He searched my eyes for a long moment. "You are my mate, El. It's fated. There's no way you won't survive the shift. I know that with everything inside me."

His explanation gave me pause.

Could he be right?

Could I have been fated to become a werewolf?

Did I really have a shot at surviving the shift?

These questions brought another to mind. I narrowed my eyes at him. "How can I be your fated mate when I was born human? What if I'd never taken that vacation? Or, gone for that hike? What if I'd left work late that day, hit traffic, and wasn't in the woods at the same time as the killer? There's a million things that could have changed the outcome of that night."

He shook his head, blue eyes serious. "I don't know. I've actually been asking that question myself since the moment I found you. Callie and I have done some research, and I've even reached out to a few other packs, but haven't found anything. No one's ever heard of a bitten wolf being someone's fated mate."

My body deflated with his words.

Maybe I wasn't his mate.

Maybe this wasn't fate.

Maybe he was wrong.

He raised our joined hands and used them to tilt my chin up. "I know what you're thinking, and you gotta' stop." He rubbed his thumb along my chin, warming my face beneath his touch. "It doesn't matter if it hasn't happened before, because it's happened now. You're mine. Always have been."

I'm his.

Those words warmed the cold dark places that had formed inside my chest during his absence. I belonged somewhere. To some*one*.

"What about the mate thing? When were you planning to tell me about that?" I asked, one brow arched.

"I was hoping you'd figure it out."

I frowned. "How would I have done that?"

He untangled our fingers and placed his hand over my chest. "Because, I know you feel it. You feel me, just like I feel you. That feeling will only get stronger the more your body changes, and the closer you come to your first shift. And, once you shift, there'll be no denying it. You'll feel everything as strongly as I feel it."

That took me back. "You mean this gets stronger?" I placed my hand over his against my chest.

"Much stronger. You'll see."

I sighed. He had an answer for everything. And, I couldn't even be mad, because they all made sense. I tried once more.

"But why wouldn't you just tell me about the fated mates thing? Why would you wait around and hope I'd figure it out on my own?"

It was his turn to arch one of his thick, dark brows. "Would you have believed me? That we were meant to be together? That we're soul mates? How do you think that would have gone?" I tried to act affronted, but he knew better. "I've gotten to know you pretty well Elizabeth Montgomery, and I know for a fact, you wouldn't have believed me for a second. You would have thought it was a line I was using to get in your pants."

My face heated. He was right. There's no way I would have believed him. The only way I probably would have accepted it was to come to the conclusion on my own.

Damn, he did know me.

I let all that information sink in.

He'd known this whole time we were fated mates. Lived with what I was feeling, but tenfold, and never acted on it. He befriended me, got to know me, all the while knowing we were meant to be together. The kind of strength that must have taken blew my mind.

He laughed at the expression on my face and pulled me closer. "I know something else about you too."

I peeked up at his amused expression, blue eyes lit with mirth. "What's that, Mr. Smarty Pants?"

He laughed, placing a gentle kiss on my forehead. "I know you're hungry. You've probably been eating as well as I have all week."

I smiled. "I could eat."

He kissed my head again, and grasped my hand, leading me out of the room. We got to the kitchen where Abraham spun toward me, wrapping his large hands around my hips, and lifting me onto the counter. He took that opportunity to kiss my lips long, and hard. When he pulled away, his breathing was as labored as mine.

"Enough of that or we'll never eat," he said, placing a small kiss on the tip of my nose before turning to the refrigerator, and putting his head inside. After a few minutes, he stood back up, and turned to me. "Eggs?"

I smiled. "Sounds perfect." I hopped off the counter and ducked into the cabinet beneath to grab a large frying pan.

He got the eggs scrambled, and I fried them for us. With my hands busy, Abraham took that opportunity to pull my backside against his hips. His hands gripped me firmly while he peppered tiny kisses along my neck, and bare shoulder.

I shivered and gasped as he found hidden spots of unexpected pleasure up and down my throat. Finally, I set the spatula down, and spun to face him. "Abraham McCoy, if you don't behave yourself, we're never eatin' these eggs."

He smiled mischievously, and pulled my body to his, soft lips finding mine. When he let us up for air, he whispered against my open mouth, "I'm not that hungry anymore." I let him kiss me for another long moment before I pushed him away.

"Well, I *am*. So, behave yourself." I picked the spatula back up and stirred the stuck-on eggs around the pan once more. When the congealed mixture was cooked well enough, I divvied up the half-dozen or so eggs, and we brought them back into my room. We sat on my bed, devouring our evening breakfast, and taking small glances at each other, smiling when we'd catch the other doing the same.

"Can I ask you a question, now?" Abraham asked.

I shrugged. "Sure."

His face fell slightly, brows drawn. "What were you doing out with Ben tonight?"

I shook my head with a roll of my eyes. "He tricked me into going out with him."

Abraham's jaw clenched. "Oh yeah? How's that?"

I looked down at my plate, pushing around the remaining eggs with my fork. "Well, earlier in the week, Ben mentioned he was going out with a few people from work. At first, I was going to tell him no, but then I got your text, and it upset me, so I agreed." I took a quick glance at him to see his expression hadn't changed. If anything, it'd gotten angrier. "Then when we got there, he said we were early, and the others would be coming soon. So, I had some wine." He cleared his throat, and I rolled my eyes. "Okay, I had a lot of wine. I was upset," I turned pleading eyes to him, and his gaze softened. "When I realized he'd lied about the other people coming, I left, and caught an Uber home. That's all."

Abraham sighed, setting his empty plate aside, and clasping his hands together. "I don't like you going out with Ben."

I laughed. "Me neither. I can't stand him."

"I don't trust him."

I frowned. "Why? You barely know him."

"I could smell his desperation. He wants you badly. I'm afraid of what he'll do to get you."

I scooped the rest of my eggs into my mouth and stacked my plate atop Abraham's. "Don't worry, I can handle him."

He smiled. "I have no doubt you can."

A long yawn caught me by surprise, and Abraham stood from the bed, taking the plates with him. "It's late, you should get to sleep."

"Where are you going?" I asked nervously, scared to have him leave my sight.

He nodded to the door. "I'm going to sleep on your couch if that's okay."

I stood from the bed and grabbed his hands. "Stay with me?" He looked at me longingly, but with a touch of apprehension. "Please? I can't bear to be away from you right now."

His eyes softened as a small smile spread across his handsome face. "I know what you mean."

Taking that as a yes, I dragged him over to my bed, and crawled beneath the covers, feeling the mattress depress as he climbed in after me. He wrapped his strong arm around my waist and dragged me toward him until my back hit his hard chest. His scent enveloped me, and I snuggled closer, entwining my fingers with his.

He pressed his face into my damp locks, placing a tender kiss on my head. "Night baby," he said, the words rumbling through his chest, and vibrating through my body. I stifled a shiver as I drifted off into the best sleep I'd had in days.

Waking up in Abraham's arms was an experience I never thought I'd have yet couldn't believe I'd gone twenty-eight years without.

I was laying on his hard chest, his thick arm around me, and my hand resting on his stomach. When the alarm blared out its terrible tune, his arm tightened, pulling me closer. He reached over and turned the alarm off before rolling back around to kiss my forehead.

"Morning," he rumbled, his sleepy voice one of the sexiest things I'd ever heard.

"Morning," I croaked, wincing at how horrible I sounded compared to him. I peered one eye open and saw he was doing the same. A slow, sleepy grin spread across his beautiful face, and I swear, I'd need a new pair underwear after this.

"You're beautiful in the morning," he commented as he twirled the ends of my hair between his fingers.

I ducked my head into his side, hiding what was probably a horrific sight. I'd forgotten to take my makeup off or brush my teeth before bed. I cringed at what he must have had to look at.

"You're the good looking one in the morning, I probably look like a hungover raccoon," I countered.

He breathed a laugh, stroking the hair away from my face. "You're the most beautiful raccoon I've ever seen."

I shook my head with a groan, and he laughed again, placing another kiss against the top of my head. A whiff of bacon wafted through the door, and I perked up. "Smells like Callie's cookin' us breakfast," he said.

"What are your plans for today?" I asked softly, afraid to hear he was leaving. I didn't think I could stand to be away from him again so soon.

He shrugged. "I brought some work with me. I thought I could hang here while you work, and then we could spend the weekend together."

I sprang up next to him, eyes wide, and a huge smile stretching my cheeks. "You're staying here?"

He shrugged. "If you want." His tone was nonchalant, but his eyes were wary. And I knew it was because of what he *wasn't* saying. He'd asked if that's what I wanted, but what he'd meant was if I wanted *him*.

And I did.

For as long as I could.

Maybe forever.

That thought was a sobering one, but it rang with a truth I couldn't deny.

I leaned over, and kissed him right on the mouth, morning breath be damned. "I want. Very much," I assured him.

A slow, sexy grin spread across his face, blue eyes brightening. "Then you've got me for the weekend."

My smile slipped. "What happens after the weekend?"

His smile dimmed too. "If you won't come back with me, Del will be here Sunday night to spend the week with you."

My chest constricted. "I can't leave my career, Abraham."

Right?

He nodded. "I get it. I know how important it is to you. If I can get away from work, I'll come back out here sometime during the week, okay? And then you can spend the weekend at the lodge again. That sound good?"

I nodded weakly. Any time away from Abraham sounded awful, but what choice did I have? His business, and his pack were out in Asheville, and my career was here in Raleigh. We'd just have to learn to make it work for as long as we could and cross that next bridge when we got to it.

Chapter 37

After dodging sly smiles from Callie all breakfast long, I was thankful she was heading home that afternoon, and I'd get the weekend alone with Abraham. After breakfast, he drove me to my car, searing his presence in my mind with a long, slow kiss that had my toes curling, and my heart pounding. When we finally managed to pull ourselves apart, there was a satisfied grin on his handsome face.

"Have a good day, baby," he murmured, his soft lips against my temple sending shivers down my spine.

I smiled up at him. "Thanks, I'll see you tonight."

He nodded, and brought my hand to his mouth, kissing my knuckles. He leaned his massive frame against his black truck and watched with hooded eyes as I climbed into my little gray compact car and drove away.

The further I got from him, the more uncomfortable I felt. It was like a small hole in my chest that slowly expanded the further I got. At the first red light, I pulled down my visor mirror to find I was red faced, and wide eyed. And happier than I'd ever been.

I soothed down a few flyaways and straightened my suit jacket. I was due in court this morning, and I couldn't go in there looking like a love struck hot mess. The air conditioner blasted against my heated face in the hopes it would cool me down before I arrived.

It was around lunchtime when court was dismissed, and I made it to my office for the first time. There was a pile of messages, and emails I needed to return, and I worked at that for the rest of the day. At five o'clock on the dot, I turned off my desktop, and sprinted for the elevators. I was thankful that my day had been so busy. If I'd been able to think about how Abraham was in my house waiting for me, I would have probably clocked out after lunch, screw the consequences.

When I arrived home, Abraham was at my table, staring intently at his laptop screen. The computer illuminated his features, casting harsh shadows across his face. When he saw me walk in, his face cleared, like the sky after a thunderstorm.

He spun in the chair and opened his arms for me. I wasted no time kicking off my heels and running into his open embrace. He smelled like spearmint, and fresh clean man, and I breathed deeply, having missed that scent all day.

"Are you sniffing me?" he asked, a smile in his voice.

My face heated. "Um. Maybe? I got my sense of smell in," I said in my defense.

He pulled back, his eyes light with humor. "I know. Callie told me."

I pulled back, mockingly incredulous. "You were keeping tabs on me?"

He rolled his eyes. "Of course, I was."

I shook my head. "I can't believe Callie was living in my house whilst reporting to the enemy."

He wrapped his hands around my waist and pulled me onto his lap. "The enemy?" I nodded seriously. "I'm not your enemy, baby." He leaned down and pressed his lips against my neck right below my ear. "I can be your best friend, if you let me."

I shivered under his ministrations, my blood heating along with my face. "The positions already filled," I breathed.

He shook his head, pulling a patch of sensitive skin between his lips, and sucking. "And who is it I need to fight to get that position?"

I gasped. "Aah! Um, that'd be your sister, I believe."

He pulled back and looked me in the eye. "Which one?"

"Well, I love them all," at least most of them, "But I'm closest with Evey. She's my best friend."

A slow smile spread across his face. "I like that," he admitted before leaning down to kiss my throat again. "My girl, and my sister, best friends. A guy couldn't get any luckier than that."

"I'm not your girl." My response was pure reflex. I wasn't sure I believed those words anymore.

He shook his head, his dark hair falling forward to tickle my face. "Aren't you?"

I shook and gasped in his arms as he pulled the shirttail out of my skirt and ran his big warm hands against the small of my back. My head fell to the side giving him better access as I struggled to reach the hem of his shirt. He kissed a trail up to my mouth before gifting me with one of his soul shattering kisses.

We sat like that for a while, me on his lap, and him worming his way under my skin, before something small and furry bumped against my ankle. I pulled away from Abraham's lips to find Charlie looking disgruntled and entirely left out.

I slipped off Abraham's lap and picked up my cat. "Oh I'm so sorry, Bubba. Momma forgot all about you." I nuzzled my face into his soft fur while I watched Abraham try to catch his breath out of the corner of my eye. A small satisfied smile crept across my face that I hid behind the cat.

"Never thought I'd be jealous of a cat," he grumped, reaching out a tentative hand to give Charlie a pat on his head. Charlie tolerated his touch for a short moment before he leapt from my arms and headed for his purple flower cat house.

I met Abraham's heated gaze and realized; I wasn't ready for this. Not all of it. Last night had been a spur-of-the-moment thing, but I didn't think I was ready to just jump in bed with him. We needed to slow things down.

"How about I order dinner, and we watch a movie?"

"Sure, but I'm paying."

I rolled my eyes and shook my head. "My card's the one saved in the app, so I'll be paying." He frowned, and I laughed. "Poor alpha not getting his way?"

He nodded petulantly and pulled me back onto his lap. "At least let me hold you while you do it," he muttered.

"That's a compromise I can live with."

I ordered us a couple of subs and took a shower while we waited for the delivery to arrive. When I came out of my bedroom, refreshed and clad in my comfiest pajamas, Abraham already had our food laid out on the coffee table with the on-demand screen pulled up.

I sat next to him and dug into the food as we debated about what we were going to watch. I finally won that battle too, and keeping with my desire to branch out, I chose The Notebook.

"Do I really have to watch this again?"

"Again?"

How many other girls had he watched this with?

Who was I going to have to beat?

Were they in his pack?

Was it *Peyton*?

My blood boiled as a million scenarios flashed through my head, each worse than the one before it.

Abraham's chuckle broke through my murderous haze. "Down girl. I have four sisters, remember?"

My ire slowly subsided. I guess that made sense too. "You saw this with one of them?"

He nodded, a big stupid smile still plastered against his satisfied face. "A couple times."

I huffed unhappily and took a large bite out of my steak bomb sub. Abraham laughed harder and pulled me into his hard chest. He wrapped an arm around my neck and kissed the side of my head. "You're really cute when you're jealous."

I frowned and pulled away from him. "I'm not jealous."

"Uh huh."

I shot a glare his way which only made him laugh harder.

With a roll of my eyes, I hit play and sat back, resting my head on one of his thick biceps. "Whatever let's just watch the movie." He chuckled again and kissed the top of my head. His laughter subdued a lot of my anger, but I wasn't telling him that.

By the end of the movie, I had my legs draped across his lap, and a box of tissues on my stomach, the tears running steadily. Abraham's eyes hadn't left my face in the past few minutes, and I wondered what he saw. A hysterical woman? A silly girl? An emotional wreck?

Because I doubt he saw what I was really feeling or understood the reason behind my tears. It wasn't the sad ending that made me cry. It was the love they shared. A love I had only previously imagined in my wildest dreams. A love that transcended time and even death.

Abraham reached over to collect my sadness with his rough thumb. "Please don't cry," he begged. I did my best to stop the flow of tears, but they continued to fall. He sighed, and pulled me onto his lap, wrapping his big arms around my shoulders, and stroking the hair from my face.

"That'll be us one day, you know? Fated mates can't live without each other. They always pass at the same time or shortly after one another." He kissed my wet cheek, leaving his lips pressed against my skin as he continued to speak. "I never understood why until I met you." He pulled back, his eyes a dark limitless blue. "Now, I get why they die together. I can't imagine surviving even one minute without you."

His sweet words had my tears falling faster, and soon I was sobbing. "I didn't say that to upset you," he spoke hurriedly, stroking my arm with one hand as the other tried its best to catch the endless tears.

"I'm not upset," I whimpered.

Abraham sighed. "Then why are you crying, baby? It's killing me."

I shook my head. "I don't know. It's just so sad. And so beautiful. I never thought I'd find something like that," I nodded at the television.

He sighed again and stood from the couch with me clutched against his chest. Abraham carried me to the bedroom and held my shaking body as I cried out this overload of emotions.

I cried for a long time as Abraham whispered sweet words in my ear and rubbed my back. When my eyes had finally run dry, I lay spent in his arms, halfway between sleep and reality. I felt him roll over and make a move to get out of my bed, and I clutched his hand. "Stay," I pleaded softly.

He sighed softly and pulled me back into his arms. "Always," he promised as I lost the battle with my heavy eyelids and slept.

The next day dawned with no tears or sadness, only blue skies, and the delicious adrenaline rush of a new relationship. After breakfast, we drove into Durham to hit up their amazing farmer's market. We stayed away from any booths that sold things we'd have to cook and instead patronized the craft stands. I picked up a few 'thank you' gifts for his sisters, and we bought some baked goods from a patisserie before we headed back to Raleigh.

I took Abraham to one of my favorite museums in the city, the North

Carolina Museum of Natural History. It ranked at the top primarily because it boasted a butterfly room. We stood in the steamy little habitat as butterflies of all colors flapped and swirled around our heads. More than a few landed on Abraham, and I laughed as this big hulking man tried to keep still so the fragile little butterflies didn't get hurt.

Abraham took me out to dinner, and when the sky turned dark, I had a brilliant idea.

"I want to take you somewhere," I told him as we climbed into his truck. "It's *my* special place I want to share with you."

He smiled broadly. "Then I want to see it."

I directed him onto I-40 and then to 540. We pulled off an exit, and I guided him to a small, dark parking lot.

"This is?" he asked warily.

I laughed and jumped out of the cab. He turned the engine off and followed me around to the back of his truck. I opened the tailgate, and hopped on, patting the spot beside me for him to join. With furrowed brows, he climbed up into the truck bed, and sat quietly, looking around the dark parking lot with confusion clouding his face.

"What are we doing here?" he finally asked.

I heard it coming in the distance and placed a finger against his lips. He kissed it and pulled my hand into his. "It's coming, just wait."

Abraham did as I asked, and a few moments later, the loud roar of the huge airplane drowned out everything else. It flew directly overhead, so close it seemed like we could stand up, and touch it. Just as suddenly as it'd appeared, it was gone, finding a spare runway at Raleigh-Durham International airport, and landing on its tiny wheels. With my improved senses, I could actually hear the tires squealing against the tarmac, smell the jet fuel from the massive aircraft.

I turned to Abraham, his eyes wide, head still tipped back toward the sky. "What do you think?"

He turned to me. "That was amazing!"

I laughed at his joyful response and lay back on the bed of his truck. He pulled a blanket out of the tool box near the cab and laid it down before motioning me over. We laid side by side, hands entwined as plane after plane flew above us. Some coming, and some going, but all of them making us feel so small, and insignificant when compared to their massiveness.

A yawn escaped me, and Abraham sat up, pulling me with him. "I need to get you home to bed." He drove us home as I dozed in the seat next to him, head on his shoulder, and arms wrapped around his bicep.

When we arrived, he scooped me into his arms, and carried me up the stairs. "I can walk, you know," I good-naturedly grumped.

He smiled wide, his white teeth shining in the dark. "I like holding you," he replied with a shrug, making my insides clench almost painfully. How could such sweet things fall from his lips so easily? Would it always be like this?

He carried me in the apartment, and into my room where he left me on the bed to go change. I stripped, and pulled my pajamas on, leaving the door open when I was done. He peeked his head into my room to find me lying in bed with the covers drawn on his side. I patted the mattress, and he smiled, his eyes softening as he climbed in next to me. Just like the past two nights, he pulled me tight against his chest, and kissed me long, and slow before pressing his lips against my forehead.

"Night, baby," he said, his deep voice rumbling through my chest, the vibrations lulling me to sleep.

And as I lay there tucked against his chest, I opened the door to my fortress, leaving it ajar behind me. I snuck up to the top floor, and into a closet full of things I'd rather forget. Up on a shelf behind years' worth of baggage, I found the highest hopes I'd ever had for my future. I took them down and dusted them off because for the first time in a long time, I had use for them.

Chapter 38

Sunday was all gray skies, and constant rain, mirroring the way I felt about him leaving that night. With outside being so uninviting, we stayed in, and watched a few movies. It was a lazy day where we spent more time eating, napping, kissing, and cuddling than anything else.

When Del showed up around dinnertime, carrying several bags of Chinese food, I decided she was my new favorite sister.

"What've you lovebirds been up to all weekend?" she greeted after pulling both Abraham, and I into fierce hugs. She smelled like cinnamon and cloves, slightly spicy, but also sort of sweet. Her scent fit her personality perfectly. "Gettin' up to no good I hope?" She raised her dark brows suggestively, and I laughed, my face heating.

"Mind your business, Del," Abraham told her as he unpacked the bags of food, their smell making my stomach rumble.

Delilah held both hands up in surrender. "Hey, I'm just happy you dummies figured it out. It was painful watchin' y'all dance around the issue."

I shook my head. "Does *everyone* know?" My cheeks felt hotter than before, and I hid them behind a wall of hair.

Del laughed. "Welcome to pack life, girl."

I've heard *that* before.

We dug into our food as Del recounted her weekend for us. Apparently, she'd met some guy at the bar she played at and spent the weekend with him. "I was almost sad to leave him," she said wistfully.

My stomach clenched with guilt. "You didn't have to leave him for me, Del. I'd be fine on my own."

Abraham growled between bites, and Del waved my words off with a flick of her wrist. "No worries, honey. You can't let 'em get too attached anyway, or you'll never get rid of 'em."

I turned to Abraham, one brow arched. "Don't even think about it," he grumbled, and I laughed, leaning over to place a kiss on his cheek. Del's eyes gleamed with happiness.

When we finished our dinner, I cleaned while Abraham and Del caught up on pack business. I directed her to the spare room and pulled Abraham into mine to say my goodbyes.

His eyes were soft, and I'm sure mine were sad as we stood staring at each other. "I don't want you to go," I admitted pitifully.

He tucked a strand of my long blonde hair behind one ear. "I don't want to go." He watched me closely. "You know you can move out there anytime you want. Your place is with the pack." He pulled me closer. "With me."

I shook my head automatically. "My career." I kept my answer short, and succinct because it was becoming less believable as more time passed.

I realized I didn't have the same passion for criminal law I once had. Had I ever felt passionate about it? Maybe it had just been the rush I was addicted to. The feel of victory, the high of being good at something. Had I ever really *enjoyed* any of it?

I leaned my head against his chest and wrapped my arms around his waist. "What are we gonna do, Abraham?"

He remained quiet, pulling me into his arms, and sighing against the top of my head. "We'll figure it out. If I have to move the whole pack out here, I will."

I gasped. "No! You can't do that! You can't uproot all their lives for me."

He shook his head. "I'd do anything for you." The sincerity in his voice made my eyes wet, and I blinked the tears away with a deep breath. He leaned forward and kissed my forehead. "We'll figure it out," he repeated. "Nothin's gonna keep us apart, El. I won't let it."

And I believed him. Believed there was no mountain he wouldn't climb, or ocean he wouldn't cross for me. I knew he'd make it okay, I just didn't know how.

We stood in each other's arms for a long time, our hearts beating in sync, as we swayed to phantom music. A crash, a hiss, and a curse sounded from the living room, and we reluctantly pulled apart. I smiled grimly up at him. "I should probably go find out what happened."

He nodded, wrapping my hand in his firm grip, and walking us out of the bedroom. When we made it to the living room, we found a cursing Del trying to reassemble Charlie's favorite cathouse, the pet in question missing.

"How the hell do you put this damn thing together?" she growled at the furry purple contraption.

I laughed and crossed the room to assist her. I straightened the house and put the pieces back together properly. "What happened?"

Del huffed. "I was just walkin' by, and I barely nudged the stupid thing, and it went topplin' over, sending that little cat of yours runnin'."

I laughed again. "Poor Charlie." My little buddy has had quite a few changes in his little feline life recently. He was probably sick of all of us.

Abraham piped up. "It's a good thing Del wanted to be a singer and not a dancer cause' she's not known for her grace."

She flipped her brother off, and plopped down on the couch, pulling her acoustic guitar onto her lap. "It's not my fault that thing jumped out in the middle of the walkway."

Abraham laughed. "Oh, it jumped out in front of you did it? You sure it wasn't your clumsiness that was the culprit?"

"Oh, shut up, Abey. Don't you have some more smoochin' to do, and a long way to drive. *Away* from me?"

He laughed again and ruffled her pink-streaked hair as he walked past. She growled at him as she fixed her mussed locks and glared at his back. "I'm goin', I'm goin'. You wanna walk me out?" he asked me, grabbing his duffle bag near the door.

I nodded sadly and followed him out to his truck. He held me for a long time while I tried to get myself under control.

I'd probably see him in a few days. He said he'd try to get back out here as soon as he could. I'd survive without him for that long. I was stronger than the weeping, whimpering woman I'd been reduced to. I had Del to keep me company and didn't need a *man* to make me whole.

Those words sounded good, but the large hole in my chest that grew as our time together ticked away begged to differ.

I needed to get myself together. I had a life to live apart from him. Fated mates or not, I couldn't lose myself to him. To this thing between us.

I pulled out of his arms and gave him a wobbly smile. "I'm gonna miss you. Come back to me soon okay?" Abraham nodded, his eyes dark with emotion. "And call me when you get back to the lodge." He nodded again, reaching up a big hand to cup my face.

He leaned down and pressed his warm lips against mine. We stood there, lost in each other for a long time before I found the strength to pull away. I gripped his hand against my face and placed a kiss on his palm. A little shudder ran through his body, and I smiled.

He tucked his face against my neck, breathing deep, and kissing the tender skin there. "I'm gonna miss you too, baby."

With a sigh, he pulled away, and placed one last kiss on my swollen lips before climbing into his truck and firing up the engine. I stood back and waved as he drove off. The red of his taillights faded into the distance as my heart's beat slowed to a crawl. With a sigh, I shook my head, and trudged back into my apartment.

To my surprise, I found Charlie on the couch next to Del who was picking at the strings of her guitar. She looked up as I walked in the room, eyeing me warily. "You gonna be okay?"

I nodded automatically. "I have to be, don't I?"

She gave me a firm, proud nod, and turned back to her guitar. "It's been a while since I've seen a pair of fated mates together. I'd almost forgotten how it is with them. How hard it is for them to be apart."

I sighed, and took a seat next to Charlie, pulling him into my arms. "It wasn't this hard the other times he's left. Why now?"

"Well, it's a few reasons. For starters, you're closer to becomin' a full werewolf so it's hittin' you harder than ever. The other reason is, you've admitted it. That's half the battle. Once you realize you're fated mates, it's almost like a jumpin' off point for the fated mates magic."

I frowned. "Magic?"

She stopped playing to stare at me. "Of course, it's magic. Don't tell me you think you'd find your soulmate out of all the billions of people in this world and believe magic wasn't involved." She snorted and looked down at her guitar again. "It's what connects you two, binds you to each other. What makes it so hard to be apart, and what will take y'all from this earth together. It's all connected. It's magic, plain and simple."

With a gasp, she pulled a little red notebook out of her nearby purse and scribbled across its crisp pages. When she finally looked up, and caught my expression, she explained. "All this talk of magic's got me thinkin' 'bout a new song."

I did my best to stifle a yawn. "You going to be up for a while?"

She nodded, eyes on her guitar again. "Yeah, I'm a night owl. Is it gonna bother you if I stay out here playin'?"

I shook my head. "Nah, I'm a deep sleeper. I'm going to bed though. I'll see you in the morning."

She laughed. "Probably not. I'm not much of a mornin' person."

"When I get home, then."

She nodded absentmindedly. "Night, hun. Have a good day at work tomorrow."

I highly doubted that.

Instead of going right to bed, I took a long hot shower, and methodically dried my hair, hoping I'd receive a call or text from Abraham before I fell asleep. When I'd waited as long as I could, I finally gave in and called him.

"Hey baby, what's goin' on?" he answered on the first ring.

His voice pulled at something deep inside me, and I sighed into the phone. "I need to get to sleep, but I wanted to hear from you first."

"I'm sorry, El, I'm still on the road. Almost there though."

I yawned. "Okay, well still text me when you get home, so I see it when I wake up."

"Okay baby, I will. Get some sleep, and I'll talk to you tomorrow mornin'. Call me on your way to work."

I smiled. I loved the way he called me 'baby'. "Okay, night."

"Sweet dreams," he replied before I disconnected the call, and curled up in my cold empty bed. It was a good thing it was so late, and I was tired. I don't think I could have gotten to sleep otherwise.

The next few days were uneventful. Work was a chore, the only bright point was when I'd get a call, or text from Abraham. He was the best part of my day, every day. Unfortunately, he had a few issues come up with his contracting business and wouldn't be able to make it out to Raleigh all week. That news made the days trudge by even slower.

Thank god for Delilah McCoy. She was the second-best part of my day.

Del was lively, and rambunctious, brightening any room she was in. She kept my apartment full of laughter, and music all week long. I was even able to return the favor and help her out.

"Tell me about the day you stormed out of the lodge," she asked one night over dinner. Takeout of course since neither of us cooked. In fact, when I'd asked her if she was as good a cook as Evey, or even Callie, she'd responded with, "Girl, do I look like the Betty Crocker type?"

I'd had to admit, with her pink streaked hair, multiple ear piercings, and love for ripped black clothing, nothing about her screamed homemaker.

"Why do you want to know about that shitty day?" Del's foul mouth had been rubbing off on me this week.

She popped the top on a can of beer and took a slug before answering. Apparently, although it wouldn't get her drunk, she liked the taste. I still preferred my wine.

"I have too many upbeat songs, I need to diversify my portfolio."

I arched a brow. "So, you want to exploit my unhappiness for the sake of a song?"

She tilted her head from side to side as if she were thinking about it before breaking into a huge smile. "Exactly!"

I laughed and chucked a dumpling at her head. With her lack of hand eye coordination, she had no shot at dodging it. The fried dough smacked against her forehead and slid onto her plate where she picked it up and popped it in her mouth. I laughed harder at her antics.

"So, will you? I need some sad material for some songs."

I chuckled darkly. "Honey, you want sad, I got sad."

"So, you'll help me?"

It was my turn to tilt my head from side to side as I pretended to think over my answer. She tried throwing a dumpling at me, but not only was her aim terrible, I also had better reflexes. I swatted the food out of the air, and it landed on the floor where it was scooped up by Charlie.

"Smart cat," Del commented before turning pleading blue eyes back to me. "Please, Ellie?" she whined.

I decided to put her out of her misery. "Of course, I'll help you Del." And so, we spent the rest of the night, rehashing some of my darkest days. Thankfully, her constant laughter, and great sense of humor stopped me from feeling too sad. Most importantly, Del got some great material out of my misery.

She was still scribbling in her notebook when I slipped off to bed that night, waving a hand, and giving me a halfhearted 'good night' as I left her to it. I retreated to my bedroom to get ready for bed, and my nightly video call with Abraham. It wasn't nearly enough, but it would suffice until I could see him again this weekend.

Chapter 39

I was in the dark meadow again; the wolf staring hard at me from a few feet away. I took a few tentative steps toward her, watching as she surveyed me with shrewd eyes. When I was close enough to reach out and touch her, she let out a low growl, and I quickly retracted my hand. I stayed still as she rose to her feet and walked away. My steps faltered as I tried to figure out if she wanted me to follow her or not.

When she was a few feet away, she turned around, and stared at me, waiting for something. I shrugged and took a few steps forward. She seemed satisfied that I would follow and took off once again for the dark woods that surrounded us.

She made it to the tree line, and disappeared in the dark foliage, leaving me alone in the meadow. "Hey, wait up!" I called, crashing between the branches after her. I could hear the soft thump of her paws hitting the leaf-strewn ground but couldn't see anything. I followed her blindly for a few feet until I could hear nothing, but the total silence of the dead forest.

"Hello?" I called. Over, and over I yelled to the wolf, but she wouldn't return. Finally, a blasting tone blared through the woods, and I had to cover my tender ears. The incessant sound continued until it woke me from my strange repetitive dream, and I realized it was my phone ringing.

I reached over and grabbed it. With only one eye cracked open, I saw *Sexiest Man Alive* displayed across my screen. "Hello?" I croaked into the speaker. "Abraham? What's wrong?"

"I'm wondering that about you. Were you having another one of those dreams?" he asked, his voice heavy with sleep.

I sat up in bed. "Yeah, how'd you know?"

"You were upset. I could feel it."

I closed my eyes. "Aww I'm sorry. Did I wake you up?"

He sighed into the phone. "*It* woke me, but it's not your fault. Are you okay?"

"I am now."

I could hear the smile in his voice. "Wanna tell me about it?"

He always wanted to hear about my bad dreams. I loved that about him.

He listened while I recounted what happened for him. "I wonder why the dreams have changed."

"I've been wondering the same thing. It's like they've progressed. Like the wolf has warmed to me. But that doesn't make any sense, does it?"

I heard him yawn through the phone, and my gut clenched with guilt. "Your guess is as good as mine." It was my turn to yawn next. "Why don't you try to get back to sleep? You've got to work tomorrow, and then a long drive out to see me." I could hear the smile in his voice.

"I can't wait," I confessed.

"Me neither, baby. Try to get some sleep, and I'll talk to you in the morning."

I hung up with Abraham, and to my surprise, was back asleep within minutes.

If only the next day was that easy.

It all started when I slept through my alarm. I hadn't replaced the phone on my nightstand after my call with Abraham, and had rolled over it sometime in the night, drowning the sound of my alarm in a mound of blankets.

When I finally woke up, I had to rush to get ready, and get to court before they dismissed my case. I hit traffic due to an accident, almost getting in one myself as I flew through the downtown streets.

Thankfully, I made it to the courthouse in time for my trial, but only because the case ahead of ours had run long. I did my job to the best of my ability but had a strong feeling the jury wasn't going to side with my client. And, sure enough, after only an hour of deliberation, they came back with a guilty verdict, ruining my months long winning streak.

After that debacle, I got to my car, and found a ticket on my windshield. "Aw, what the hell?" I yelled as I studied the sign I'd parked next to. Apparently, I'd misread it, and the free parking wasn't until after five pm. With a growl I snatched the bright orange envelope out from underneath my wiper blade and shoved it in my glove compartment.

When I finally got into my office, I had a request to meet in Mr. Hildebrandt's office as soon as I came in. I shot a quick text to Abraham before straightening my clothes and steeling myself for the tongue lashing I was about to receive.

Thirty minutes later, I was dismissed from his office with a stern order to get my act together, and not lose another case anytime soon. We both knew losses happened, but also that this one should have been easy. It was apparent that my head wasn't in the game, and that wasn't something he could excuse.

I locked myself in my office after that and called Abraham to complain as I nibbled on the salad I'd ordered for lunch. It wasn't until I was reading through some case files that the next hammer dropped on my crappy day. One second, I was reading, and the next, everything went black. I blinked a few times but remained blinded. Not even the smallest bit of light could penetrate the darkness I was in.

Soon after, my sight was back, but magnified many times over. I blinked again, and again, as I tried to concentrate, and focus my vision. I tried to continue reading the paper I'd been looking at, but instead of the words, all I could see were the little streaks of printer ink, and small pockmarks, and imperfections in the paper that I hadn't been able to see before.

With a glance at my computer monitor, I saw each pixel that made up every inch of the screen but couldn't focus on any one thing in particular. In a panic, I called the first person that came to mind.

"Hey baby, what's wrong?" Of course, he'd know something was up already.

"I can't see," I wailed.

"What do you mean you can't see?" My breathing was coming faster, and more shallow as my eyes rapidly glanced around the room, finding dust motes floating through the air, and more colors in the bright ray of sunshine than I'd ever seen before. "Calm down and talk to me. Tell me what's going on."

I took a deep breath and closed my eyes before I explained everything that had happened in the last couple of minutes. It was much easier to concentrate when I couldn't see anything.

Abraham's deep voice rumbled through the phone, calming my nerves with just its soothing sound. "Calm down, babe, you're fine. You just got your sight is all."

"*This* is what you see all the time?!" I yelled, making myself wince with the volume of my voice.

He laughed. "Just like everything else, you'll get used to it."

My eyes were still closed as I shook my head. "I don't think so, Abraham, not this time. This is one too many for me."

This was not the day for me to gain a new wolfy superpower. After everything else I'd had to deal with, this might just be the straw that broke the camel's back.

"Elizabeth," I sat up, and took notice. He hardly ever used my full name anymore. "You are strong, and capable. *Nothing* is too much for you. Just listen to me, and I can help you."

I let out a lungful of air. "Okay, what do I do?"

"It's simple really, the same way you ignore a dirty windshield or scratched sunglasses, you need to look past the small imperfections to see the bigger picture. You can train your eyes to not notice the small things over time. For a while though, you'll have to concentrate to see past that stuff."

I cracked one eye open, and then the other, struggling to do as Abraham had instructed. I started with my computer screen and found that squinting helped. With my eyes partially closed, all the pixels blended back together to form the images and words on my screen. I sighed with relief.

I could hear the smile in his voice when he spoke next. "Are you okay now? I have to get back into a meeting, but I can stay and talk to you longer if you need me."

Guilt ripped through me as I realized I'd interrupted his day whining about something he's been dealing with practically his whole life. "No, I'm good. Sorry I interrupted."

"El, nothing's more important than you." His words both warmed and calmed me. "I can't wait to see you," he murmured.

I smiled. "Me too. Talk to you later."

We hung up, and I forced myself to practice seeing past all the fine details to the bigger picture. By the end of the day, I was sporting a huge headache, and wanted nothing more than to be wrapped in Abraham's arms.

When I got home, Charlie came barreling at my shins like always, but instead of meowing for me to pick him up, he hissed loudly, and fled to his cathouse. "What the hell is wrong with him?" I asked no one in particular.

Del came out of the back room with her bag in one hand, and guitar slung across her back. She frowned and sniffed the air a few times. "You smell different. Did something happen today?"

Shocked, I told her, "I got my sight."

She nodded. "That's what it is. You smell more like one of us."

My shoulders slumped, and I stepped out of my heels, eager to be changed and on the road. "Do you think that's why Charlie ran away from me?" I called from my bedroom.

"Probably. Don't worry, if he's gotten used to us, he'll get used to you too. He's probably just confused."

But he hadn't acted confused, he'd acted scared. With troubling thoughts about my pet swirling through my head, I changed out of my skirt suit, and into a pair of jeans and a polo shirt. I grabbed my suitcase and pulled the door closed behind me.

"Bye Bubba, that nice lady will be by to feed you. Behave while I'm gone," I called to Charlie as I closed the door behind me.

Several hours later, we finally pulled into the long drive that led to the lodge. I bounced in my seat, eager to see Abraham for the first time in almost a week. When we got to the massive house, he was standing outside waiting for us. As soon as Del brought her cherry red mustang to a full stop, I was out the door, and in Abraham's arms.

He pulled me so tight to his chest, my feet lifted off the ground as he dug his face into the crook of my neck. Breathing deeply, he kissed the patch of skin beneath my ear. "Hi."

I laughed into his broad shoulder. "Hi."

He pulled me back far enough to lean down, and capture my lips with his, kissing me long, and hard as his sister laughed from nearby. "Nice to see you too, Abey."

He took a hand off my waist to wave at her, but then tangled it into the hair on the back of my neck, using it to tilt my head, and deepen the kiss. His mouth moved against mine, strong and forcefully, like he couldn't get close enough, deep enough to satisfy himself.

Soon that turned to more tender motions as he licked and nibbled on my swollen lips. When we'd satiated our immediate appetites for each other, we pulled apart, breathless, but smiling widely.

He looked so different now with my newly enhanced vision. His beautiful blue eyes were the first thing to capture my attention. I realized they weren't a simple blue color, but every shade of blue I could name swirled within their depths. My eyes scanned the rest of his face, cataloguing every crease, freckle, and stubble of hair.

He was gorgeous.

"I'm so happy you're here. That had to have been the longest work week of my life," he said.

"I'm happy to be here too. This has been the worst day I've had in a while."

He frowned, reaching behind me to pull my bag out of the backseat before entwining his fingers with mine, and pulling me toward the lodge. "Tell me about it."

I recounted the series of things that had gone wrong, starting with waking up late, and ending with my cat rejecting me. My nose burned as I talked about Charlie, and Abraham stopped outside my door to pull me into his arms.

"Hey, it's okay, please don't cry, you know what it does to me." I sniffed back my tears, but knew they were just beneath the surface. "Charlie will come around. If he can get along with me, a big bad alpha werewolf, he'll get over the changes you're going through."

A watery laugh escaped me. I slapped his chest and turned to enter the room that was mine while I stayed here. "You're not a 'big bad alpha', you're more like a big puppy dog."

He laughed, following me into the room, and closing the door behind us. "That's just what you think."

I rolled my eyes and unpacked my things as Abraham tried his best to distract me with his wandering hands. It was only a few minutes later when a loud knock sounded at the door before it was wrenched open.

Evey stood there, one hand over her eyes, the other held out in front of her, as she walked into the room blindly. "If you're naked, please stop so I can see my friend."

I laughed loudly at her. "We're not naked, Evey."

She slowly removed her hand from her eyes, and took a look around the room, only meeting my gaze once she was certain there were no naked bodies to find. Next thing I knew, I was wrapped in her strong little arms, the scent of vanilla and brown sugar enveloping me.

A small sniffle escaped her lips as she held me. "I missed you. Never get mad at me like that again."

My heart bottomed out into the soles of my shoes as I hugged her back just as fiercely. I'd spent all this time worrying about my relationship with Abraham that I'd forgotten he wasn't the only one I'd hurt when I stormed out of here two weeks ago. My nose burned again as she rocked us back and forth.

"I'll leave you two alone. I have some things I need to take care of tonight anyway, but I'll see you at dinner?"

I nodded over Evey's shoulder as I comforted my distraught friend. It had taken me a long time, but I'd finally found a family, good friends, and maybe even love. After the day I'd had, having this reminder was exactly what I needed to snap me out of the self-pitying mood I'd been in all day.

Evey finally pulled away, and looked up at me, her blue eyes bright. "Now, tell me everything!"

Chapter 40

The evening flew by as Evey and I spent hours chatting and catching up. When it was dinner time, we met Abraham in the kitchen, and ate with him and the other wolves that lived in the lodge. He didn't stray far from my side, and when we finished, he dragged me away as I sent an apologetic look toward Evey. She just smiled, and winked, waving us on.

When Abraham finally had me alone in my room, his lips found me fast, pressing me against the bedroom door, and sending my pulse racing. He slipped his hands beneath my shirt, stroking the skin on my back before reaching down, and grasping my bottom. Lifting me with ease, I wrapped my legs around his waist, tangling our limbs together in what was becoming a familiar dance.

Hands gripping me firmly from underneath, he spun around, and walked us over to the bed, laying me down on top of the covers. His hungry eyes raked my body, from my heaving chest, to my thighs still wrapped around him.

He leaned over, and kissed me again, one hand supported his weight while the other pulled my shirt up. I stretched my arms above my head allowing him to yank it off. Abraham pulled away again, allowing his sharp eyes to take in the skin he'd uncovered.

Part of me wanted to cover up while the rest loved being under his watchful gaze. But things were unfair as they stood now.

"Shirt," I panted, "off."

With a smile, he obeyed my breathless command, revealing his taut stomach, and toned chest. I moaned low in the back of my throat at the site of his naked torso. He leaned back down to capture my lips with his. Another one of his marauding hands found the button of my jeans and flicked it open before slowly sliding the zipper down its track.

With a tug, he pulled my pants off, and I lay there in only my bra and underwear. He once again pulled away to examine the new skin he'd revealed, his eyes darkening with desire.

"Abe," I panted, my voice needy.

"Yes, baby," he answered, his eyes still locked on my naked skin.

"Kiss me."

He nodded with a smile. "Whatever you want, love." He leaned back down, allowing me to attack his mouth with a ferocity I didn't know I was capable of. While I threaded my fingers through his thick dark hair, he used both his hands to traverse the parts of me his eyes had already taken in.

"You're so beautiful," he whispered against the hollow of my throat. His lips moved further down until they were above the swell of one of my breasts. He kissed, and sucked on the exposed flesh, causing goosebumps to break out across my body. "So, fucking delicious," he grunted.

I was trying to keep myself from combusting. It felt like I'd waited years to be touched by him. To lose myself in the feel of his body pressing mine against the mattress. To enjoy his attention, knowing he'd never do anything to hurt me.

I *trust* him.

And *that* was a powerful aphrodisiac for me.

But I still didn't want to push it too far. Not yet.

"Abraham," I gasped as his teeth pulled the cup of my bra down, exposing a single pebbled nipple that hardened further with the exposure to the cool air in the room. "Abe," I tried again, "No sex. Not yet."

He shook his head slowly, lips sliding across the tip of my breast, sending warmth through my chest. "No baby. I'm not making love to you yet. But there's a whole bunch of things I can do to this body of yours before I do."

His mouth then captured my straining nipple, licking, and sucking the tip as I gasped, my breaths loud, and embarrassing. He used his teeth, eliciting a deep groan from me, a sound I'd never heard myself make before. His eyes met mine, a satisfied smirk stretched across his sinful mouth. "Oh, you like that, do you?"

I nodded frantically, and he chuckled against my chest, his hot breath blowing against the wet nub, causing a whole new slew of sensations I'd never experienced before. He graced my other breast with a similar treatment while I used one hand to clench the blankets beneath me, and the other to grip his hair. Whether I was trying to pull him closer, or push him away, I'm not sure I knew.

When he'd had his fill of my chest, he turned to my stomach, dragging his wet lips down the middle, stopping to bite or suck any patch of skin that caught his attention. When he made it to my white lace underwear, he stopped, and looked up at me, his eyes clear and concerned.

"Is this okay, baby?"

I nodded jerkily. "Uh huh," I squeaked, making him smile. His eyes darkened once more, and he leaned down to suck the sensitive skin above my pelvis. My hips jerked against his face, his chuckle dancing across my skin.

"Are you particularly attached to these panties?" he asked as one thick finger traced along the edge, dipping just beneath the fabric.

My overheated brain couldn't understand what he was staying. Couldn't make sense of his words. "Huh?"

Abraham didn't answer, instead, he jerked the hand that was holding the fabric of my underwear, ripping them in half, letting the tattered edges fall to the sides. He groaned at the site of me spread out before him, and I swear my eyes rolled around to the back of my head.

"Abe," I groaned.

"Yes, baby?" He placed small kisses along the inside of my thighs.

"I... I don't... I can't," I stuttered as my legs shook, both hands clutching the bedspread desperately.

"I know baby, I'm gonna make it better."

His words alone were enough to make me explode.

His rough stubbled grated against my sensitive thighs, and I shivered as the sweet anticipation built deep inside me.

"You know what I've been wondering?" he whispered, his hot breath blowing across my wet folds.

"Uh uh," I stammered.

"I've been wondering if you taste as good on the inside, as you do on the outside."

I moaned long and loud, and he took that opportunity to trace his stiff tongue from the bottom of my slit to the top. My stomach fell through my toes as he lapped at my insides. Soon a finger joined him, and I wasn't sure I'd make it through this.

"Mmm," he moaned into my center. "You taste even better than I thought you would."

I closed my eyes, my legs quaking as the little spark in the pit of my stomach was doused in gasoline and fanned with palm fronds. "Oh, my god."

He chuckled against my core, sending a bolt of liquid electricity through me. With long, strong strokes, he dragged me up a hill I don't think I'd ever been up before. I'd had plenty of orgasms, though most of them self-induced, but this was different. This felt like my whole body would shatter. Once I made it up this hill, I knew I'd have to come down again, and I didn't know if I'd survive it.

Until now he'd only teased the sensitive button of pleasure between my legs, but suddenly, it was his sole focus.

First, he licked, and my toes curled.

Then he nipped at the overheated flesh, and a long guttural moan escaped my lips.

Next, he sucked the little bud between his full lips, pulling at the delicate skin before releasing it.

Finally, he rubbed his stubbled chin against the sensitive nub, causing an equal amount of pain, and pleasure, and that was it for me.

I was done.

Shattered.

Obliterated.

I screamed as my body broke apart, and reformed over and over, the waves of pleasure threatening to drown me. Abraham kept a slow, steady pace as I came back down that hill he'd just thrown me over. My whole body shook as I recovered from the most explosive orgasm I'd ever had in my entire life.

Could you even classify that as an orgasm? Had I even known the definition of that word before I met Abraham?

My brain was trying to be too philosophical for my shattered state, and I don't even think I was making sense. All I knew, was that had been the single most incredible thing I'd ever felt. And, I had this overpowering need to make him feel as good as he'd just made me feel.

"Abe," I croaked, my throat sore.

Had I been screaming?

I wouldn't doubt it.

He wiped his face against the inside of my thigh, the coarse stubble sending another pleasurable shot of electricity through my spent body. "Let me," I said, not able to articulate what I wanted, but I held my arms open, hoping he'd get the idea.

He stood over me, eyes raking my flushed body with a heat that made me quiver.

He could probably make me come just by looking at me.

When he finally met my eyes, he understood what I was asking for, and shook his head, his cheeks reddening adorably. "Ah, there's no need." I frowned, waiting for him to explain. "I came in my pants again." He scratched the back of his head as a grin tipped up one edge of my mouth. "I seem to do that a lot around you."

I couldn't help the laugh that flew from my mouth. I felt giddy. *High.*

He shook his head and crawled up onto the bed next to me. "How was that?" he asked, and somehow his voice sounded uncertain.

What was this man thinking?!

I rolled over to face him. "That was..." I trailed off at a loss for words.

"Good?" he supplied hopefully, and my wide eyes met his.

"Mind blowing," I corrected.

His smile was slow and self-satisfied, and he deserved it. He placed a small kiss against the side of my face before hopping off the bed and disappearing into the bathroom. "Stay," he called over his shoulder, and I did as he asked.

A minute later, he came back with a wet washcloth, smelling like soap and spearmint. He kneeled between my legs again and gently wiped away the evidence of my arousal. When he finished, he tossed the cloth aside, and grabbed my hand pulling me until I was sitting upright facing him.

His soft eyes roved over my face, his hand reaching out to tuck some hair behind my ear. "You're so beautiful," he breathed.

I shook my head, but he grasped it between both hands, and kissed my mouth deeply, his tasting like the spearmint he always smelled like. When he had my breathing uneven and my heart racing again, he pulled back a little, and whispered against my lips, "I'll be right back."

I nodded and leaned forward to give him another sweet kiss. In his absence, I removed the tattered remains of my underwear and my twisted bra, opting instead for a comfy pair of pajama pants, and an old t-shirt.

When he returned, I was under the covers with one side pulled back awaiting him. He slid between the sheets and pulled me into his arms. "Wanna go to our lake tomorrow?"

I turned to face him "*Our* lake?"

He nodded, pressing a kiss into my hair, and breathing deep. "What's mine will always be yours."

His words settled deep in my heart. Quieting a storm that had been raging for years and settling a wildness I hadn't known needed taming. "I'd love to go to our lake." Then I added, "But I'm going to help you pack our lunch, so we don't have to bring one of everything with us again."

He chucked into my hair. "Okay deal. Night baby,"

I snuggled closer, and was soon lost to a restful, blessedly dreamless sleep.

The next morning, we arrived at breakfast hand in hand, causing more than a couple double takes. The most noticeable being Peyton although hers was accompanied by a fierce scowl.

After breakfast, Abraham pulled me into his arms, and kissed me in front of everyone before leaving me with Evey, who insisted on helping me pick out what I'd wear for our "second date".

When we finally made it to our lake later on that afternoon, I got to see it for the first time with my new eyesight. From on top of our rock, I could clearly see the Blue Ridge Mountains and all the pine trees that dotted them. Beneath us, the water was so clear, there were places I could see all the way to the bottom. Fish of all sizes swam in, and out of a multitude of plants and other debris that had found their way to the lakebed. I could spend hours watching the life teeming beneath the surface.

Unfortunately, our trip back to the lodge was not as uneventful as the one out here had been. Halfway back, I smelled something that burnt my nose, and curdled my stomach.

"What *is* that?" I called over the loud engine. Abraham's shoulders tensed as he revved the engine, propelling us faster through the forest.

"That's death," he deadpanned, and my stomach fell. "We need to get back. Now."

Oh no.

My mind made the connections rapidly as my body shook.

He was back.

He was here.

He'd found me again.

Chapter 41

After a few minutes of speeding through the woods, Abraham brought the 4-wheeler to a stop, and hopped off. He put a hand on the small of my back and slid me forward until I was sitting where he had been. Leaning over, he grasped both my hands, and placed them on the handlebars.

"This is what you press to go," he positioned my thumb above a lever on the handle. "Keep it as steady as you can, and I'll be right beside you."

"I don't understand. Where are you going?"

"I need to shift, I can't protect you like this. I'll be running right beside you though. I'll never leave your sight."

Nodding, I took a deep breath. I needed to keep it together. Needed to stay strong. Even though my body was quaking, and my palms were so sweaty they were slipping off the handlebars.

Abraham leaned over and cupped my face between his big hands. "I'm not gonna let anything happen to you. Trust me." His voice was low, and deadly serious, his eyes flat, and determined. I nodded again, and he took a step back.

Without warning, he reached for the hem of his shirt, and whipped it off his body. I watched with fascination all the skin he'd revealed to my hungry gaze. So transfixed, I missed the discarded shirt he sent sailing my way until it struck me, blocking my view. I growled and yanked it off my head as he chuckled deep in his chest.

He shook his head and caught my eye as he unbuttoned his jeans. I bit my lip and ripped my gaze from his incredible body. "Another time, El."

I peeked at him to see he'd shed his jeans and stood only in a pair of boxer briefs. "What's that?" I squeaked, turning my head again.

The crunching of leaves beneath his feet disturbed the quiet of the forest. He placed the rest of his clothes in my lap before leaning close to whisper. "Another time I'd do something about that look you were just giving me, but right now I need to shift, and get us out of here. Raincheck?" His warm breath tickled the shell of my ear, and I stifled a shiver.

"Okay," I whispered.

He placed a soft kiss on my cheek, and suddenly his heat was gone. The sound of breaking, and shifting bones echoed off the trees, even louder than the ATV's engine.

Within a minute or two, the sounds stopped, and I turned to find a blue-eyed wolf standing where Abraham had been. His ears were pointed straight up, teeth bared as his eyes darted around the clearing. He tilted his head back, and howled, long and loud making me cover my sensitive ears.

Being this close to a wolf this big, in these woods, where the killer had just been was like a sick déjà vu. My body trembled harder as I tried to talk myself down.

It's Abraham.

You just saw him shift.

It's not the killer.

You're going to be fine.

Abraham would never let anything happen to you.

I repeated the words over, and over in my head, eyes closed as I tried to regulate my frantic breathing. The crunching of leaves sounded from nearby, and I ripped my eyes open to see Abraham had padded closer. His big wolf eyes were the same myriad of blues I loved, and they settled my racing heart a bit.

The wolf bumped his huge head against my side, and his message was clear. First, there's no reason to be afraid of him, and second, *get moving!*

I pressed the lever, and the quad lurched forward. The jolt knocked my hand off the handle, and I had to reach for it once more. A soft whine from behind increased my sense of urgency, and I tried again. This time, I pressed softer, and the ATV rolled forward. A little harder, and the vehicle picked up speed until I was moving at a decent pace through the trees.

Thankfully, most of the way was marked by a trail, and I simply followed it while Abraham ran close beside me. If I took a wrong turn, he was there to direct me back toward the lodge with little yips, and gentle nudges. It took me a lot longer than it would have taken Abraham, but soon the lodge came into view, and I took my first full breath since we'd smelled the dead body.

Three large wolves met us in the driveway. Two had similar markings, mostly brown with some black mixed in, and light brown eyes. The third was bigger with gray and black fur on his back, and white underneath. His light brown eyes inspected us keenly.

Abraham stepped forward, easily a head or more taller than even the biggest wolf. His eyes assessed them, and I felt a charge of electricity in the air, like being outside before a lightning storm. The three wolves took off into the forest the way we'd come, and Abraham nudged me with his nose, I presumed to get me going again.

When we reached the garages around the side of the lodge, we were met by all four of his sisters. They each sported varying degrees of worry across their beautiful faces. I dismounted the quad, and was immediately enveloped in Evey's arms, her sweet vanilla scent calming my nerves.

"What happened?!" she cried. "We heard there was another body found, and with y'all out there, we all got nervous."

A few loud cracks came from behind me, and Abraham spoke. "We smelled it on our way back. He must have known we were out there and planted it near the trail we took so we'd find it."

Evey released me from her arms, and Callie pulled me into hers. Next, Del had a chance to pull me into her protective embrace, her spicy scent filling my nostrils. I didn't expect any affection from Bea and wasn't disappointed.

"Should we send out more men?" Beatrice asked, and I looked at Abraham.

He stood there, tall, and proud, and as naked as the day he was born. I quickly averted my gaze, face heating uncomfortably. Evey giggled nearby, and I knew it was at my expense.

"Uh, Abraham? Maybe you should put some clothes on?"

"No time. And besides I told you, nudity doesn't bother any of us here. We've all seen it before."

I studied a tuft of grass that peeked through the rocky gravel drive. "Well, I haven't," I muttered.

"You haven't?!" both Evey, and Del screeched at the same time.

I met their eyes, making sure Abraham's naked form wasn't in my peripheral. "Is it any of your business?"

The sisters looked at each other and smiled wide. "We just figured with the weekend y'all spent alone that you'd have gotten to know each other. In the biblical sense that is," Del said with an overdramatized wink.

"Enough," Abraham commanded, and all of us took notice. It felt like I didn't have a choice but to listen and obey him. "Evey, Callie, and Del, I want you to take Elizabeth inside, and not let her out of your sight. Bea, you shift, and come with me to investigate before we call the authorities."

The four women nodded and sprang into action. Inside, the whole house seemed to be on high alert. Men and wolves alike stalked the halls of the lodge, all looking grim, but determined.

"This could take a while," Del spoke up. "Why don't we go to the game room and play some pool. You play, Ellie?"

I shrugged. "I have once or twice, but I'm not very good at it."

Del nodded, her pink-streaked hair bobbing around her face. "Perfect, we'll give you a few lessons then."

They led me to the basement where there was a long room with a couple pool tables, multiple dart boards, a foosball table, a ping pong table, and even a shuffleboard. Del went over the rules of the game while my mind wandered to Abraham, and what he was doing.

I could feel his worry and anger, so I knew he was all right, but wouldn't be at ease until he was back here with me. A few hours passed as the girls tried to distract me with a couple games of pool, and then a subsequent darts lesson.

When it was time for dinner, we made our way to the kitchen, running into a wet-haired and, thankfully, fully clothed Abraham. He rushed to my side, pulling me into his arms, and nuzzling his nose into my neck. "Hi," he breathed against my skin.

I smiled and wrapped my arms around his neck. "Hi."

"We'll meet you guys in the kitchen," Callie said as she ushered her nosey sisters along.

"What happened?"

Abraham sighed before pulling me into a room I'd never been in before. It had a long table that ran down the middle, with desk chairs strewn around its sides, and a blank white board covering one wall. He led me to the table, and sat me on its edge, nudging my knees apart to fit his hips between them.

"We found another victim."

I swallowed harshly. I knew that. Why was it so hard to hear?

"It looks like she'd been dead for a few hours, and only planted near the trail recently," he continued.

"Was it him?" I whispered, afraid to hear the answer.

Abraham nodded. "It's got his M.O. written all over it." I gulped again, my hands shaking where I fisted them on my thighs. "Hey hey hey," he crooned, pulling me against his broad chest, the smell of his soap filling my senses, and calming my nerves. "You're safe. I've got you."

"He planted her there on purpose, didn't he? That was a message for me, wasn't it?" The thought had swirled around, and around in my head since the moment Abraham had confirmed it was a dead body out there. Why else would the killer put her there? Near our path where we'd be sure to find her. "Was he following us? Did you find any more clues about who he is?"

Abraham sighed. "I think there's no more denying the killer is a member of this pack. It all adds up to an inside job." His jaw was so tense, it was ticking, and his eyes solidified into an icy blue. "And, yes, we think there was a reason behind this strategic placement. He usually leaves them where he kills them, but he moved this one where he knew we'd notice it."

"It was for me. He's coming for me."

His eyes darkened. "We don't know that, El. You can't make yourself crazy over this. I'm *not* going to let him anywhere near you. I've bulked up security, and you'll always have one of us with you. As long as you're here with me, nothing is going to happen to you."

I jerked back in surprise. "Stay here?"

"Of course. Now let's go get something to eat, I'm starving."

I placed a hand on his chest before he could walk away. "I'm not staying here, Abraham. We've talked about this before."

His wide eyes met mine. "But things are different now. The killer has changed his style and seems to be looking for your attention at the very least, and worst case, could be after you. There's no way I'm letting you out of my sight until we get him."

I shook my head. "I have a career back in Raleigh, you know this. And what would I do with Charlie? I can't just drop everything and move out here."

"We'll bring him here. I'll do whatever it takes to keep you safe. If that means living with a cat, then so be it."

I shook my head again. "You're not listening to me."

"No, *you're* not listening to *me*. I will not allow you out of my sight. You will stay here until we catch this guy and that's final."

I pushed him back and slid off the table. "The hell it is! You don't get to tell me what I will or won't do."

His smile was grim. "Actually, as your alpha, I do."

I swear I saw red. "If you think for one second, I'm gonna let you push me around with your wolfy hierarchy bullshit, you've got another think coming. I don't answer to anyone, least of all *you*." I brushed past him and headed toward the kitchen.

"Elizabeth be reasonable," he called as he jogged to keep up with me. "I can't protect you out there."

A small shiver ran down my spine, but I ignored it. I was pissed, and I was on a roll. A little apprehension wasn't going to stop me now. "How would the killer know where my apartment is in Raleigh? How would he find me there? If he's a member of this pack, shouldn't I be far away? If you ask me, it might just be safer out there than back here."

Take *that!*

My logic stopped him dead in his tracks as I continued to stomp toward the kitchen. When I got there, I found three pairs of wide blue eyes staring at me. I ignored them, yanked a plate out of the stack, and heaped food onto it. I was hungry damn it, and I wasn't going to let a bossy alpha ruin my appetite.

"She's got a point, Abey," Del called to her brother who'd finally entered the kitchen.

"Mind your damn business, Del," he growled, storming over, and grasping my arm. Even though I could physically feel his fear and fury, he handled me with the same gentleness he always had. "Elizabeth. I refuse to allow you out of my sight. I will not compromise on that."

I continued filling my plate. "Well then I guess you're spending the week in Raleigh."

"The full moon is Thursday."

My stomach plummeted to the ground as that revelation brought me up short.

So soon.

I cleared my throat. "Well then, I guess you'll be in Raleigh with me until Thursday."

He growled deep in his chest, but I ignored him. I knew he wouldn't do anything to me. I shook my arm free and walked around to join the girls at the table.

Callie's eyes were still wide, and disbelieving, but both Evey and Del sported tiny smirks as they looked between me and Abraham.

"I believe you've met your match, Abey," Del said, the smile never leaving her bright red lips.

Abraham growled once more and stormed out of the room. I pretended not to notice and instead dug into my dinner of steak and garlic mashed potatoes.

When Abraham's angry footsteps faded, Evey laughed hard, head tipped back, and one hand on her belly while the other slapped me on the back. "Girl, I knew I loved you."

I turned to her. "What?"

Callie spoke up. "We're not used to seeing anyone outright defy Abey like that."

I frowned. "No?" They all shook their heads simultaneously. "Huh." I took a big bite of steak and chewed thoughtfully. "I guess you'd better get used to it then."

Chapter 42

An hour later, the girls, and I were on the rooftop garden, flipping through their hoard of magazines, and enjoying the beautiful spring evening. We heard Abraham's angry steps, and harsh breathing before we saw him.

"What are you doing up here?" he barked.

Without looking up from her copy of Cosmo, Del replied, "Practicin' for that double dutch tournament comin' up. You wanna turn?"

We all remained silent as Del's words sunk in. It was Evey's bark of laughter that broke the silence first. I hid my smile behind the issue of Vogue I was reading. Abraham growled and stomped over to me.

"I'm not in the mood for your smart-ass attitude, Delilah."

She flipped a page slowly. "And I'm not in the mood for your pissy bullshit. We can't all get what we want, Abey."

He growled again, and Callie hopped up from her seat. "All right you two, cut it out. We're all stressed and taking it out on the wrong people."

"I'm not stressed. I'm just sick of him," Del poked a thumb over her shoulder at Abraham who was still growling low in the back of his throat.

"Del," Callie warned with a glare before turning back to Abraham. "What was it you wanted, Abey?"

"First, I'd like to know why the four of you are sitting out here, in the open, when I told you to keep her protected." He jabbed a finger in my direction.

Del put her magazine down and scanned our surroundings. "Abraham, we're four floors up. What, did you want us to lock her in the basement?" She scoffed. "Be realistic. Nothin's gonna happen to her all the way up here, and you've got your enforcers prowlin' the property. I know she's your mate, but you need to ease up. She's as safe up here as she is anywhere else."

Abraham opened his mouth to argue, but Callie interrupted. "What else did you want?"

He closed his mouth with a snap, dark brows furrowed over flashing blue eyes. He pointed to me again. "Her." He finally looked at me. "Let's go," he grumbled before stomping off.

Did he expect me to just follow him? I don't take orders from anyone.

My shoulders stiffened as my hackles rose, just begging for a fight. Evey placed a hand on my tensed back and spoke softly. "You better go. When he's in a state like this, it's better to just do as he says."

Del scoffed from her seat across from us. "Looks like old Abey's back. I was really startin' to like the new one too," she mused, voice cool, but blue eyes flashing in undisguised anger.

"The old Abraham?" I asked.

The three girls nodded. "He's been much more mellow since he met you," Evey confided.

"Nicer too," Del added.

"Elizabeth!" he bellowed from the bottom of the stairs, and I jumped in surprise.

"Go on, we'll catch up with you later," Evey said, pushing me toward the stairwell.

I slammed my magazine on the table, and stalked off in his direction, ready to give him a piece of my mind. This grouchy alpha bullshit wasn't going to fly with me.

"Go get 'em, girl," Del called, spurring me on.

I got to the bottom of the stairs, but Abraham had already disappeared. His scent was still present though, and I followed it to my room. I walked into a flurry of activity.

Abraham was pulling clothing from my drawers, and throwing them into my empty suitcase, his movements quick and jerky. "Hey!" I called. "What the hell are you doing?"

"Packing."

My blood pressure rose a few degrees. "I see that," I said carefully. "But *why* are you packing my things?"

A sudden thought hit me, and all the anger fled my body as uncertainty crept in.

Was he trying to get rid of me?

Was I too much trouble to deal with?

He stopped suddenly, cocking his head and looking at me. "What are you thinking?"

I swallowed harshly. "Why are you packing my things?"

He ran a hand through his disheveled hair. "We need to leave."

My heart started beating again.

"*We're* leaving?"

He frowned. "Yes, of course." He stared at me harder. "What did you think?"

I averted my gaze, choosing to study the tan carpet beneath my scuffed sneakers. When I didn't answer, he sighed, and walked across the room to pull me into his arms. "What's goin' on in that pretty head of yours?" he asked, voice softer.

I shook my head, not willing to answer.

Not willing to bear my soul.

Not willing to show him how deep my insecurities ran.

If only he knew what had happened the last time I'd walked in to find someone packing my things.

One of his thick calloused fingers tipped my chin until I met his eyes. "Hey, talk to me."

I held his gaze and made a decision.

If I wanted this, wanted *him,* I would have to open up. Let down those walls instead of just opening a door. Let him in.

I took a deep breath and confessed. "I thought maybe you were tryin' to get rid of me."

His eyes widened, mouth falling open. He closed it, and opened it back up a few times, seemingly at a loss for words. Finally, he pulled me into his arms, crushing me against his hard chest until I could feel the beat of his heart thumping in time with mine. "Elizabeth," he started, cleared his throat, and tried again. "Baby, never."

He pulled back until he could see my eyes, his swimming with guilt. "I'm sorry you thought that for even a second." He leaned in closer until the tip of his nose touched mine. "You're *never* getting rid of me, you hear me? *Never.*" He kissed my lips sweetly and pulled back with a humorless laugh. "El, if you only knew…" he trailed off, and cleared his throat with a shake of his head. I watched as his eyes wavered for a few seconds before solidifying with a decision. "In case you haven't figured it out yet, let me make something clear for you. This thing here," he motioned between us, "is forever."

Forever?

That word echoed inside me, growing louder as it ricocheted around my head. It made my heart pound erratically, and I wasn't sure if it was from fear, or something else, but it felt warm. Like hot fudge dripping down the inside of my chest, coating my interior.

I couldn't find the words to reply to his bold statement, so I focused on something else. "If you're not sending me away, then why are you in here packing my things?"

"Sending you away?" he asked incredulously, pulling me close again, and kissing the top of my head. He sighed loudly, his breath ruffling my hair. "I'm sorry, El. I feel like I'm losing control. Like I'm losing my mind."

He pulled away and began pacing. "Having him that close to you again, knowing he was out in those woods with you nearby, that he's a member of my own goddamn pack is killing me." He grabbed the shirt over his abdomen, stretching the fabric between his big hands. "Gutting me. I need to get you away from here. He obviously knows you're here, and we need to move you. You were right, he probably doesn't know where you live in Raleigh, so you'll be safer there. We're leaving as soon as you're packed and taking Wes and Wyatt with us for extra protection."

I frowned. "Do you think that's necessary?"

He stopped pacing to stare at me incredulously. "I'm not taking any chances. I'll never put your life in jeopardy like that again. If I'd have known he'd made you a target, I never would've taken you out to our lake alone. I never would've done something so reckless. I just didn't know…" he trailed off, looking lost.

I couldn't help myself. I could *feel* how upset and out of control he was feeling, and all I wanted to do was make it better. Covering the distance between us in just a few steps, I wrapped my arms around his waist, and held on tight, hoping to transfuse some of my strength, and surety in his abilities into him. "I know, Abraham. I know you'd never let anything happen to me." I pulled back to look at his handsome face drawn and creased with worry. "I trust you."

He smiled, and held me for a few moments before pulling away, and returning to my suitcase. "I wish I was as confident in my abilities as you are, El," he said as he stuffed more clothes into my half-full bag. "Unfortunately, I keep underestimating this guy." He shook his head. "Never again." His words were like a vow. Whether they were for himself or me, I wasn't sure.

"Why Wes and Wyatt? Couldn't one of them be the killer?" I winced at my words, but knew I needed to ask.

Abraham shook his head. "Honestly? I don't know anything. But Wes and Wyatt got here a while after the murders started, so I figured they were the least likely suspects."

I should have known Abraham would have a good reason behind making a decision like that.

I walked over, and placed a hand on his tan arm, halting his poor packing job. "Go get your things together, I've got this."

He smiled at me gratefully and was across the room in the blink of an eye. "We leave in five," he called over his shoulder.

Exactly five minutes later, we were downstairs, saying goodbye to his sisters as Wes and Wyatt loaded their bags into the bed of Abraham's truck.

"I can't believe you're leaving already," Evey complained, her thin, but strong arms tight around my neck, her warm vanilla scent surrounding us. I hugged her just as fiercely, taking a minute to marvel at how far I'd come in less than a month.

"I know, but I'll be back Thursday for the full moon," I reminded her.

Before I met the McCoys, *hugging* was one of my least favorite things to do, and I avoided it like the plague. The old Elizabeth never knew how hard to squeeze someone, or how long it was supposed to last, or where to put my hands. Now, it was like second nature to be close to people. The new Elizabeth loved the affection and warmth she received from every person that embraced her. Especially this family. Somewhere along the line, they'd become my family too.

Well, most of them.

"I still don't understand why *you* need to leave. Can't you just send her with Wyatt and Wesley? They're more than capable of protecting one little human," Beatrice sniped from nearby.

Abraham answered between gritted teeth. "Because, her safety is *my* responsibility. She won't be going anywhere without me."

"Your responsibility is to your *pack*," she argued.

Abraham growled. "My responsibility is, and always will be to my mate first. My family comes second, and my pack comes third. That's the way it is, Beatrice, so get used to it."

Beatrice's eyes flashed dangerously. "You'd put this girl you've just met before your family? Your pack?"

Abraham met her gaze head on. "Every. Time." His words were clipped, and fully enunciated, and crystal clear.

My stomach rolled at the siblings' harsh words to each other. I didn't want to be the cause of their strife. Didn't want anyone to go out of their way for *me*.

Del pulled me into her arms next, her spicy cinnamon scent filling my nostrils. "Don't worry about her, she's just a bitch." Beatrice growled, and stormed off, but Del ignored her. "And, don't let him get away with being an asshole," she advised. I laughed into her shoulder. I really liked this girl. And her filthy mouth. It seemed I'd been picking up a fair amount from her lately, and I wasn't sure if that was a bad thing or not.

Next was Callie, her sweet rose scent preceding her. "Stay safe," she said softly. It sounded like more a request than a demand, and that was so like soft spoken Callie that it made me smile into her frizzy hair.

"I will," I promised.

Abraham was there next, grasping my arm, and pulling me toward his truck. "If you guys need me, you can call any time. You know Bea's in charge while I'm gone."

"Why is Beatrice in charge?" I asked as Abraham started down the long steep drive.

"That's what a beta's for."

"She's your beta?" I asked. How had I never known this? He nodded as his eyes scanned the darkening scenery around us. "Is nepotism common among werewolves?"

A burst of laughter came from one of the fair-haired brothers behind us, and I caught a small smile on Abraham's face. "To be honest? Yes, it is. Family is important to werewolves. But with Bea that's not the case. She won that position fair and square."

"How do you *win* a beta position?"

"You fight."

My eyes widened. "Everybody?"

He shook his head, smile growing. "No, just the ones who want to be beta."

I nodded, as I let that information settle in. "So, it's kind of like letting job applicants arm wrestle for the position they're up for?"

Both brothers laughed loudly.

"Good analogy."

"So how many people did Beatrice beat to win the beta position?"

His smile vanished, hands tightening around the wheel. "I believe there were ten."

"Wow. She must be really good."

"She's excellent. I couldn't have asked for a better beta."

I digested that information as Abraham sped down the highway, leaving Asheville, and hopefully the killer, behind us. Sometime during our trip I must have fallen asleep because I woke up in Abraham's arms as he instructed one of the brothers to unlock my door.

Once inside, he carried me to my room, and placed me gently on my bed. When he tried to pull away, I wrapped my arms tight around his neck, hoping to keep him there with me.

He kissed my forehead, and whispered, "I'm going to get the guys settled, and set up a watch rotation, I'll be back in a few minutes."

I nodded and drifted back to sleep. What felt like hours later, I woke up again, but this time to the feel of Abraham's warm body pressed against mine, his strong arms pulling me against him. I wiggled back until my bottom was snug against his hips, causing him to hiss softly in my ear.

"Keep still, El. You're causing an uprising."

I frowned, and rolled over, one eye cracked open. "Huh?"

He kissed the tip of my nose and shook his head. "Nevermind. Go back to sleep, baby."

I did as he asked, and drifted off, only to be awoken by a scream several hours later.

Chapter 43

Abraham was out of bed, and across the room in seconds, muscles rippling dangerously beneath his tan skin. I took a moment to admire the sight of his long lean back before I scrambled out behind him.

We arrived in the living room to find two snarling wolves, and one petrified cat sitter in the open front doorway. I hurried to her, apologies flying from my mouth.

"Hey, Fiona, sorry! Down boy," I bopped a wolf on the nose as I passed.

Her wide eyes met mine. "Elizabeth? I thought you weren't supposed to be back until Sunday night?" She turned back to the massive wolves taking up most of my living room. "Are they... wolves?" She asked, her hand shaking where it still sat on the doorknob.

I pushed the nearest wolf behind me, shielding them as best I could. "These guys?" I chuckled uncomfortably. "Uh, they're wolf hybrids, actually."

Fiona nodded her head slowly. "I didn't think hybrids got this big."

I shot a frantic look at Abraham who called the wolves to him. "Oh, uh, they're part mastiff, I think. You know how big those dogs get." Another uncomfortable chuckle. "Sorry I didn't call you sooner. We got in late last night, and I didn't get a chance to. I won't need you to come back for the rest of the weekend."

Fiona nodded again, her eyes still watching where the wolves had disappeared to. Hopefully she bought my story, and I didn't have animal control knocking on my door later today.

I grasped the doorknob, the universal sign for "it's time to leave", and Fiona met my eyes. "Oh sure, that's fine. Glad to see Charlie's got company this weekend. I think he's been pretty lonely lately."

My heart clenched at her words, but I kept my fake smile in place. "Me too, Fiona. And, thanks for taking care of him." She nodded, and turned around, shaking her head as she descended the stairs, and I closed my door.

I turned to find Wyatt and Wesley walking out of the spare bedroom, fully human, fully clothed, and with looks of contrition on their faces.

"Sorry, Elizabeth," one of them said, I think it was Wyatt. "We didn't expect anyone to come through your front door." He rubbed the back of his neck, his face pink. "I can't believe we let a human see us as wolves."

I shook my head. "No, you guys, this one's on me. I forgot I had her checking up on Charlie and should have called to cancel."

Abraham stepped forward, still shirtless, and distracting. "You did good explaining the situation, Elizabeth, I don't think she'll cause us any trouble." He turned to his men. "And, you two were on top of the situation immediately. Good work." Wyatt and Wesley both perked up at the compliment. Abraham turned back to me. "Who else has a key to your apartment."

"Just Fiona."

He nodded and grabbed his cell off the table. After a few taps on the screen, he held the phone to his ear. When he caught my quizzical look, he explained, "I'm getting your locks changed today."

I frowned. "Why are you changing my locks?"

"I don't want anyone to have a key to this place but you, and me."

I raised a brow. "Who said you're getting a key to my apartment? And don't you think you should have discussed calling a locksmith with me beforehand?"

He looked confused as he wagged a finger between us. "Isn't that what we're doing right now?" The call stopped ringing on the other end, and someone answered with a polite greeting. "Yes, hello, I need a set of locks changed today."

I threw my hands in the air and stormed back into my bedroom. "Pushy alpha pain in my ass," I grumbled under my breath.

Apparently, I hadn't spoken soft enough, because one of the brothers barked out a laugh before I heard a slapping sound, and a loud "oomph."

I quickly got dressed, and stomped into the kitchen to make me, and my houseguests some breakfast. But after a week with the culinary challenged Del, there was not much besides takeout containers in my fridge. I rummaged around until I came up with a dozen eggs that must be left over from when Callie was here keeping me fed. Next, I ransacked the freezer, and found a bag of sausage patties, and that would have to be enough.

When the egg mixture was cooking on the stove, and the sausages were sizzling beside it, Abraham walked into the kitchen, and wrapped his arms around my waist. He leaned over and pressed his nose into the crook of my neck. "Whatchya cookin', baby?"

Who would have thought I'd be the kind of woman who enjoyed being called something as cliche as "baby"? I had to admit though, every time he called me that in his deep, gritty voice, it made my heart skip a beat, and my stomach clench deliciously.

But I was still irritated at his high-handedness.

"Breakfast."

He slipped his hand beneath my loose t-shirt and skated his thick fingers across my stomach. "You look so sexy when you're cookin'." I scoffed and felt his lips curl against my skin. "In fact, I bet you'd look sexy doin' just about anything." He nipped at my earlobe, and I gasped. "But I think I might be a little biased," he confessed.

I rolled my eyes and used a pair of tongs to flip the sausages. When I didn't answer, he sighed, and turned to lean against the counter next to the stove. "Are you really that mad that I called to have your locks changed?"

"No, that wasn't a bad idea."

"Then, why are you upset?"

I pushed the congealing eggs around the pan. "Because, you did so without consulting me first. This is *my* apartment, not your lodge, or your pack lands. You don't get to make all the decisions by yourself, and just expect me to fall in line. It doesn't work that way. Not with me."

He sat there studying me while I finished cooking the eggs and placed the sausages on a paper towel covered plate. Finally, he took a deep breath, and ran a hand down his tired face. "Okay, I see your point." He let that big breath out and reached for my free hand. "I just want to keep you safe. It's making me a little crazy, because I feel like I'm not doing a good enough job."

I turned all the burners off and turned to face him. "You're doing a great job. You just have to get it through your head that I need to have some input on my life. I won't let you steamroll over me, even for my own safety."

He smiled. "Your independence was one of the first things I liked about you."

I raised a brow. "I would have thought it'd be the first thing that drove you crazy about me."

He laughed and placed a kiss on my forehead. "It's a love-hate relationship."

Can't fault him for his honesty.

Abraham helped me plate our breakfast, and all four of us devoured it within minutes. We needed more food in this house.

Unfortunately, Abraham insisted I couldn't go alone, so all four of us crammed into my little compact car and went grocery shopping together. We walked down each aisle filling my cart with mountains of food while three giant werewolves shadowed every step. I felt ridiculous, and decided next time, I'd rather send one of them out than feel like I was being protected by the supernatural secret service.

Per Abraham's request, we spent the rest of the day indoors where he knew I'd be safe. We watched movies, and played a few card games, but the peace didn't last. The next morning when I was getting ready to leave for work, Abraham informed me I wouldn't be going alone.

"I am not taking a werewolf with me to work. It's not happening."

Fortunately for Abraham, I was running late, and didn't have time to argue with him. After a few minutes of going back and forth, I finally growled, and stomped off into the bathroom.

"Fine! But whoever is coming better be ready to walk out that door in three minutes," I yelled.

I heard Abraham's exhale of relief, and a pang of guilt shot through me. He wasn't trying to be *difficult*, he was just trying to keep me safe. I needed to keep that in mind every time he annoyed the crap out of me.

A couple minutes later, I stormed out of my room, and toward the front door. One of the brothers was already waiting there for me. "Which one are you?" I barked.

"Wyatt, ma'am."

"Great. Let's go, Wyatt."

Before I could get through the doorway, a hand on my wrist stopped, and spun me around. Abraham leaned down, and planted his soft warm lips on mine, kissing me until I'd completely forgotten why I was irritated to begin with.

When he finally pulled away, we were both breathless. "Have a good day, baby."

I smiled and nodded not trusting myself to speak.

Thankfully, only a few people asked about Wyatt's presence in my office that day. I explained that he was an intern, and that seemed to satisfy their curiosity. And, having him there wasn't that bad. He pretty much sat quietly in the corner, either on his phone, or occasionally taking a peek into the hall, or out my window. What he thought he'd find four floors up, I wasn't sure, but I let him do his thing.

A couple days passed in this fashion, and before I knew it, it was Thursday evening, and I was frantically trying to finish up my work before the long weekend I was taking. We'd decided instead of asking for time off, I'd fake sick, and call out tomorrow. Abraham assured me the pack doc would write me a note to explain my absence.

I stifled a yawn, one of many today, as I drove me, and the werewolf bodyguard du jour, Wes, back to my place. I'd had another wolf dream last night and hadn't gotten much sleep after it.

In this dream, I'd met the wolf in the clearing again, but this time, instead of circling me, and then walking off, she'd bumped her large head into my hand, and only walked away when she was sure I was next to her. We entered the dark woods, the moon shining through the tree branches, giving just enough light that I could see where we were going.

We walked side by side for a long while before there was a break in the trees. When we stepped out of the forest, I found the pack lodge looming ahead of us. I woke up after that, still not understanding what these dreams meant, or why I was having them. Abraham's warm arms had helped to settle my nerves, but sleep had still eluded me.

I walked through my front door to find Abraham and Wyatt's bags piled near the front door. "When are we leaving?"

"As soon as you're changed and packed," Abraham answered.

"I'll need to get Charlie's things together too."

Abraham nodded. "Yes, I suppose the cat will have to come too, huh?"

I rolled my eyes. "Well, if you don't want anyone with a key to my apartment, I can't have Fiona come check on him."

Abraham shook his head. "I can't believe I'm allowing a cat inside my home."

About an hour later, with an unhappy Charlie in his traveling crate, we were on our way out to Asheville. Charlie was still being distant, eyeing me with distrust, or maybe it was betrayal. I'd been his people before, and now I was closer to being like the unwelcome houseguests he barely tolerated. But there was little I could do about the changes I was going through. He'd just have to learn to get used to it. Hopefully.

As we drove the almost four hours to the mountains, I found myself turning inward as I finally let myself think about the coming full moon. Even now, I could see it in the daytime sky, full, and round, and just waiting for me.

Would I survive the shift?

Abraham seemed to be pretty confident I would, but was that just wishful thinking? On average, seventy-five percent of bitten wolves didn't survive. Were any of them fated to be mates with other wolves? Did they know they wouldn't survive? Or were they as ignorant as the shepherd's wife?

I fell asleep during the long ride, my busy brain finally allowing me a short reprieve from the worries. The tires crunching against the noisy gravel driveway woke me.

When we pulled around to the garages, we were greeted by all four sisters. Evey pulled me into her arms first before I was passed to Del, and finally Callie.

"Glad to have you back," Beatrice said to Abraham. Wes and Wyatt climbed out of the cab, the latter carrying Charlie's crate. "What the hell is that?" she deadpanned.

"Charlie," Abraham answered simply, walking with me past his sisters.

"What is a 'Charlie'?" she called.

"Charlie's a cat, dummy, can't you smell him?" Evey answered.

"You brought a cat? Here? To a house full of werewolves?" She scoffed. "What next? How much are you going to change for *her*?"

Abraham spun around and stalked back to his sister. He towered over her and lowered his voice to a deadly level. "Beatrice, I understand you're not a fan of change, but now's not the time. You need to shut your mouth, and mind your business, or I'll make you shut it."

Their stare down lasted a few moments, the air alive with electricity, before Beatrice bowed her head, and Abraham nodded. Spinning on his heel, he stalked back over to grasp my arm, and lead me into the lodge.

"We should have left Raleigh earlier. We don't have much time before the sun sets."

We were in his room, and I was looking out the window at the sinking sun, my stomach mirroring its trajectory.

How much time did I have left?

What if I didn't make it?

What if these are my last hours?

What if this is my last time alone with Abraham?

He'd been rummaging through a dresser drawer, but slammed it closed, and spun to face me. "Stop it. I know what you're thinking, because I can feel what you're feeling. You're gonna make it through the shift. You're gonna be fine. I'm gonna make sure of it." He turned back around and dug through his dresser again. He held out a long white t-shirt. "What do you think? This should be long enough, right?"

I frowned. "For what?"

"Usually we all get naked, but I figured you'd want to wear *something* for your first time at least."

My jaw dropped. "You figured right." I took another look at the thin t-shirt. "Is that *all* you're expecting me to wear?"

He nodded. "I guess you could wear panties too if you want." He shrugged. "It won't last long, so it doesn't really matter what you wear."

I swallowed harshly. "How long will it take for me to shift?"

He walked over to sit next to me on the bed, looking at me with serious eyes. "It usually only takes a few minutes."

"But didn't it take the whole night for the shepherd's wife?"

"Who told you that story?"

"I asked Callie while she was staying with me." I looked down. "What if that happens to me?" I asked quietly.

Abraham tipped my chin up. "It won't." The finality in his voice almost had me convinced. Almost.

I took another look out the window, the seconds seeming to slip away faster, and faster as the sun set. "Abraham, I want you to know, if I can't shift–"

"You will," he interrupted forcefully.

I shook my head. "Please, just listen." He nodded, but his face wasn't happy. I took a deep breath, and closed my eyes, searching for the words to explain what I was feeling. To tell him how much he meant to me. What his love had done for me.

Because here, at the eleventh hour, I could admit that I knew he loved me. It was clear in every touch, and every look, everything he did for me, and every time he was right there by my side. He'd chosen me over his pack, over his family, and loyalty like that didn't come easy.

I opened my eyes, and met his blue, blue gaze. *Did I love him?* I wasn't sure yet. But I knew I felt strongly, and I needed to tell him.

"I just want you to know I'm so glad I met you. You, and your family have done more for me in the past month than my entire family has ever done for me in my whole life. And I don't regret a single second of it. Not being attacked in the woods, not being bitten, none of it. Because it all brought me here, with you, and there's nowhere else I'd rather be."

Chapter 44

After my heartfelt proclamation, Abraham had taken the opportunity to explore my mouth, and every inch of skin he could touch. He didn't say a word, but I felt his intentions in every move he made.

He loved me.

And, he was afraid he would lose me.

Those words hung heavy in the air, blaring, and yet silent in the minutes leading up to my first shift. I would either join him, and his pack, or he'd lose me forever. All of that was said, and repeated over, and over as he ravished my mouth, stealing my breath, and solidifying his place deep inside my heart.

Did I love this man?

I wasn't positive it was a yes, but I knew it wasn't a no. And, that was the best I could do at this time. He didn't seem to mind as he peppered kisses across my face, making sure not to miss a single inch.

A thrill of adrenaline shot through my system, and we both froze in place. "It's coming," Abraham panted. "You need to get changed, and we need to get outside with the rest of the pack."

I nodded breathlessly and retreated to his bathroom. When I returned, I found him wearing a low riding pair of black basketball shorts, the waistband just barely hanging onto his trim hips. My mouth went dry as my eyes skated over all the skin he had on display. Damn, this man was perfect.

Abraham growled low. "Save that look for later," he rumbled.

I shook my head. Now was *not* the time to be ogling. I needed to focus. I needed to survive.

"Is there anything I can do to make sure I shift completely?" I asked, desperate to have some small slice of control.

Abraham nodded as he grabbed my hand and pulled me from the room. "You can focus on becoming a wolf. Don't fight the change, encourage it. Welcome it."

I nodded. I could do that, easily. Because I *did* welcome it. If it meant I got to stay with Abraham, and his family, I'd do anything.

"Just a heads up, you're probably about to see a lot more of the pack than you ever thought you would." I frowned, and he elaborated. "We usually just leave our clothes inside. We'll ruin them otherwise, so there's no point."

My face heated uncomfortably. I was beginning to look forward to this werewolf thing, but to be honest, I could do without the nudity. I nodded and gripped his hand tighter as we descended the stairs.

Abraham lead me out onto the back deck where I'd attended the pack barbecue a few weeks ago. The picnic benches were gone, and in their place stood dozens of people. All of them, to my relief, were at least partially clothed.

Evey came running up to us, wearing a loose t-shirt like mine. "Hey, why is everyone dressed? I just got done telling El everyone would be naked."

Evey laughed. "We all figured she might not want to spend her first full moon tryin' not to stare at all of us in our birthday suits. The pack decided to cover up for her."

My nose burned as my eyes watered. "Y'all wore clothes for me?" I was truly touched that they cared enough about my comfort to ruin a pair of clothing.

Evey slung a thin arm around my waist. "Girl, you're pack now. There's not much we wouldn't do for you."

I sniffed back tears, and wrapped my arm around Evey, pulling her close, and tucking my face against hers. "Thanks girl, I really didn't want to have to stare at everybody's feet all night."

Evey laughed loudly. "Yeah, and if you caught sight of any loose salami's Abraham might have thrown a fit."

I snorted at her description of the male genitalia while Abraham rolled his eyes. "My salami is the only one she's allowed to look at." I laughed again and slapped his arm as we made our way to the rest of the pack.

Most of them hurried over to us to embrace me and wish me luck on my first shift. I could see the worry in their eyes, and I tried to put on a brave face, but we all knew what my chances were. Another shot of adrenaline zipped through my veins, and I watched those around me twitch simultaneously.

"Not long now," Abraham warned. He took a seat on the grass and pulled me onto his lap. "We might as well be sitting, since you'll be on all fours soon enough."

The word *hopefully* floated through my head, implied, but unspoken.

The rest of the pack took seats surrounding us as we waited for the sun to disappear, and the magic of the moon to take over.

It started out slow. Like a subtle vibration along my arms, and legs. I rubbed my limbs, but Abraham grabbed my hands to stop me. "Let it happen," he instructed, and I obeyed.

The vibrations got more intense, and soon my whole body was buzzing. Around us, the sound of breaking, and shifting bones filled the twilit night, but my body just continued to vibrate. I felt Abraham's muscles shift beneath me and slid off his lap. Within minutes, his wolf form stood where he once sat, staring at me with those same blue eyes that were only a little more wild than they usually were.

I looked around to see most of the clearing had already shifted with only a few stragglers in the middle of the process. An odd sensation bubbled beneath my skin, and I held my arms out to see the muscles undulating beneath my skin. Next, sharp pains in both my legs had me doubling over in pain.

A soft whine from nearby preceded the nudge of a wet nose, but I couldn't acknowledge whoever it was. My legs were breaking, and I was in more pain than I'd ever been in.

My skin itched, and I scratched at it with fingernails that had become long claws that gouged at the fragile human tissue. Fur sprouted along my body as the pain in my legs slowly subsided.

I looked down to see my bottom half was human again, and I panicked. "Abraham!" He licked the side of my face, and laid down near my prone body, his large blue eyes sad, and scared.

My legs bent, and creaked, bones cracking, and reforming, and I cried out in pain as my body tried to make it through the shifting process again. This time, my upper half followed suit. My fingers shrunk, and then grew into large paws, my arms bending at odd angles, already covered in fur.

Next, I could feel my face transforming. The bones broke and rearranged themselves until my mouth had elongated into a snout. A howl of pain escaped me as my body wavered from human to animal back, and forth as if it couldn't make up its mind.

I lay panting on the ground as the wolves around me whined. Lifting my head, I could see most of them were laying down surrounding me, trying to offer their support the only way they could. I caught Abraham's frightened eyes, and I steeled my resolve.

I needed to make it through this.

For them.

For him.

For me.

Because I wasn't done living. In fact, it felt more like I'd just begun, and I would not give that up.

"El?"

Abraham's voice sounded inside my head.

"Can you hear me?" he asked.

I whined softly.

"You need to focus. I need you to fight. You're so close baby, just concentrate, and soon you'll be with me."

I focused my mind, letting the magic in instead of fighting it like Abraham had suggested. The full moon's power swirled through my body, changing it, shifting it.

Deep down inside, I recognized a presence. A force. Some wild thing that I'd previously ignored, hungering for release. It clawed its way out of the depths of my body, growing, and solidifying until it filled all the empty spaces inside me with its primitive desires.

Slowly but surely, I felt my bones stop moving, my muscles settle into the positions they were supposed to take. When I lifted my tired head, I saw my body had finished shifting into a wolf.

I was ecstatic, but so tired and sore, I didn't think I could move. So, I lay there for a few more minutes as wolf after wolf walked over. Each one that passed would give my sorry body a little nudge with their wet nose or swipe their tongue across my face. I recognized their behavior as support, and I drew from their strength.

There was one wolf who'd yet to move. Abraham's large body was still plastered against my side, his steady heartbeat a homing signal to mine. I followed the brightness of his heart like a lighthouse in the distance. Soon I felt strong enough to roll onto my stomach.

It was slow going, but a few minutes later, I was on all four legs, the pain subsiding rapidly.

There was a cacophony of voices inside my head. Congratulations, and well wishes from the other pack members, but they all swirled around unintelligibly until one stood out above the rest.

"You did it," Abraham's voice whispered inside my head. I turned to find his bright blue eyes tracing my body. *"And, you're so beautiful."*

I perked up at his compliment and felt something moving behind me. I spun around to catch the culprit but came up empty-handed. The sensation was back, and I turned again, but there was nothing there.

A shrill, mocking laughter broke into my mind next. *"Oh my god, she's acting like a stupid puppy."* Even as a wolf, I could identify the obnoxious voice as belonging to Peyton.

"Don't listen to her, Ellie. We've all chased our tails from time to time." I recognized Evey's voice in my head as she came trotting over.

I looked around at the crowd, and realized, I'd probably never be able to tell them apart. Abraham must have felt my confusion because he stepped closer to bump his shoulder against mine. *"It gets easier to identify them after a while. Use your nose."*

I nodded my large wolfy head, and took in the backyard, through my new eyes. My sight as a human had been almost this good, but my senses were undoubtedly enhanced in this form. A gray wolf that smelled like cinnamon and cloves came running over, and I immediately knew it was Del. *"Let's run!"*

That suggestion had my ears perking, and my tail rising straight in the air. I felt strong. And wild. And capable. And fearless. Like I could take on a grizzly, or swim across an ocean, or climb Everest in this form. Nothing felt impossible. I'd never felt better.

"Let's race," I suggested to yips of agreement from the two sisters. A wolf that smelled like roses came trotting over to join our group.

"I'm in," Callie said softly.

"Not too far," Abraham warned. I heard him call for Wes and Wyatt but ignored him.

"Ready? Set..." I shot off into the woods. *"Go!"* I yelled after I was several feet ahead of them.

Abraham laughed and sprinted to catch up to me. *"Cheater,"* he accused good-naturedly. I ignored him, and ran faster, pushing my new body to its limits as I raced in between the trees, and over rocks, whipping through the forest at speeds I'd never dreamt of.

The girls soon caught up, and I struggled to keep pace with them. It was like my body instinctively knew how to move in this new form, but my mind rebelled against using four legs. So, even though I was moving at a good pace, it still felt awkward, and clumsy.

A while later, we reached a small stream, and stopped for a drink. None of us were out of breath, and the adrenaline high from running through the woods still pumped through my veins.

I bent my head to take a drink, and instead, leapt backward with a frightened yip.

"El?" The fur on Abraham's back stood straight up, and he let out a ferocious growl as the other three wolves circled me. Everyone's attention was on the woods surrounding us while mine was still on the water.

"It's me," I whispered, my mind struggling to catch up. To understand.

After Abraham had assessed the area around us and found no immediate threat, he nudged my shoulder with his wet nose. *"What's the matter, El? What did you see?"*

"It's me," I repeated. I shook my head and took a tentative step back toward the stream. Steeling my resolve, I braved another look at the water's reflection, and saw the creature of my nightmares staring back at me.

It was me.

It had always been me.

"El, you're not makin' sense. I need you to focus, and tell me what's goin' on," Abraham pleaded.

I ripped my gaze away from the water, and met his concerned blue eyes, so similar, and so foreign at the same time. They pleaded with me for answers, and I did my best to choke them out.

"The wolf. From my dreams. It's me."

Abraham looked more lost than ever.

I shook my head again. *"The wolf I've been having nightmares and strange dreams about? It's me. It was me all along."*

"You were having nightmares about yourself?" Abraham sounded incredulous, and I couldn't blame him. I barely understood it myself. But I nodded anyway.

"It was my wolf."

He stared at me for a few silent moments before his eyes found Callie. *"Have you ever heard of this before?"*

Her soft voice answered in my head. *"No, but I can do some digging tomorrow."*

Abraham nodded and turned weary eyes back to me. *"Are you okay?"*

Thoughts were still racing around my head as I tried to make the connections, and to think back on all the dreams I'd had in this new light. I realized she'd been testing me at first. Or, I guess I'd been testing myself? Either way, we'd gotten off to a bumpy start, but during the last couple of dreams, I'd stopped fearing the wolf, and started trusting her. And, it'd seemed she trusted me too. We'd come to some sort of understanding.

I didn't fear her anymore. Or myself, I guess.

This was confusing.

But I knew one thing for sure. *"Yeah, I'm okay,"* I promised Abraham.

He smiled a wolfy grin at me and licked my face. Wolf affection would take some getting used to.

We spent a little while near the stream, drinking and exploring before Abraham insisted we get back to the other wolves. *"I'll feel comfortable closer to the lodge,"* he'd explained. *"Until the killer is caught, I don't want you out in the open, unprotected."*

With that sobering thought, we all took off the way we'd come at a more reasonable pace.

But where was the fun in that?

"You're pretty fast," I told Abraham, circling around him as an idea formed in my head.

He bared his mouthful of wolfy teeth for me. *"The fastest."*

I nodded and pretended to think that over before leaping into a dead sprint. *"Then, I guess you don't need a head start!"* I called. I laughed as he cursed and set off after me. Although in this form, laughing sounded more like barking.

I heard his sisters egging me on, and I dug into the soft ground beneath my paws, pushing myself harder, faster, until it felt more like I was flying through the woods than running.

And that's how I spent the rest of the nighttime hours. Racing, and wrestling, and rolling around in the grass, and learning how to be a wolf. It seemed like every pack member had a word of advice for me, and I listened, doing my best to remember it all.

I realized despite the threat of the killer in the woods and Abraham's overprotectiveness, I was happy. Really and truly. These were my people now. I was a part of this large colorful family, this pack, and I'd never been happier.

When the sun finally rose, my body seamlessly shifted back into a woman's, and I lay on the ground panting for a few minutes before Abraham found me. His large naked body was standing over mine, reminding me of my own nudity.

I jumped off the ground, covering my most important bits and pieces while Abraham stood back laughing at me. Looking around frantically, I found a large scrap of someone's shirt, and used it to cover my front, one hand holding it in place while my other tried to shield my backside.

Abraham laughed harder, but finally took pity on me. I kept my eyes safely above his waistline as he stalked over and scooped me into his strong arms. I curled into a ball and prayed no one was paying attention to my exposed behind.

"No one's looking," Abraham answered my unspoken worries.

I took a cautious look around to see the rest of the pack, naked and dirty, laughing, and talking with one another as if they weren't all stark naked. I didn't think I'd ever be that comfortable with my own nudity, but it made me feel better that no one was staring at me.

I relaxed in Abraham's arms as he carried me into the house, and up to his room. "You want a shower now, or when we wake up?" he asked at the bedroom door.

A loud yawn escaped me, and I snuggled closer to him. "I just want you, and a soft bed right now."

He smiled widely. "That I can do."

And, just like so many nights previous, and hopefully so many more to come, I crawled into bed with Abraham close behind. He pulled me against his hard chest, and I could feel the happiness, and contentment deep inside him, echoed in me. "Night baby," he murmured before placing a kiss on my forehead.

I drifted off to sleep in the early hours of the morning after my first shift, with a brighter future than I'd ever had. It had nothing to do with my work, or my position in a company, and everything to do with the family, and the love I'd found out here with a pack of werewolves in the North Carolina mountains.

Dear Reader,

Thank you so much for taking the time to read my novel, *Shift*. Your support means the world to me. I truly hope you enjoyed reading it as much as I enjoyed writing it. I have two more books planned for this series, so if you loved Elizabeth and Abraham, there's a lot more to come!

Acknowledgements

First, and foremost, I'd like to thank my amazing husband, Ryan. You've always been my biggest cheerleader, and my staunchest supporter. I don't know where I'd be without your constant belief in me, and your unwavering loyalty. Thank you. 1-4-3-3-4.

Next, I'd like to thank my critique partner, and first writing friend, Joynell Schultz. Thank you for helping me through another book, and for responding to my endless emails with the patience of a saint. (She's an awesome author too, you should check her out!)

I'd also like to thank my two beta readers, Brianna, and Gari. Your invaluable insight, and support means the world to me. I can't wait to work on future projects with you!

And, finally, I'd love to thank my readers. Thank you for taking a chance on me, a new indie author. Thank you for reading my words and living in the world I created for a little while. Thank you for your support and thank you for taking the time out of your busy lives to review my work.

More from Heather MacKinnon

Southern Werewolves Series
Shift
Howl
Rise

Southern Werewolf Sisters Series
Chasing Callie
Belonging to Bea (Coming 2020)

Love in Providence Series
Send Sunshine
Beyond Beautiful

Standalones
Changed
Trying

About The Author

Heather MacKinnon is a romance author living in North Carolina with her husband, adorable son, and two trouble making dogs. She grew up on Long Island and spent her young adult years in various states in New England. This led to her subsequent addiction to Dunkin' Donuts lattes and her gratuitous use of the word "wicked". After a lifetime of enjoying other people's words, she decided to write down some of her own. You can get up-to-date information about Heather MacKinnon's books at www.heathermackinnonauthor.com.

Find her on:

Facebook.com/HeatherMacKinnonAuthor

Facebook.com/HeatherMacKinnonReaders

Instagram.com/HeatherMacKinnonAuthor

Twitter.com/HMackAuthor